The Big Cinch

The Big Cinch

Kathy L. Brown

MONTAG

First Montag Press E-Book and Paperback Original Edition January 2022

Montag Press ISBN: 978-1-957010-02-1
Design © 2022 Amit Dey

Montag Press Team:

Cover: Renato Pinto
Author Photo: Jon Aikin
Editor: Charlie Franco

A Montag Press Book
www.montagpress.com
Montag Press
777 Morton Street, Unit B
San Francisco CA 94129 USA

Montag Press, the burning book with the hatchet cover, the skewed word mark and the portrayal of the long-suffering fireman mascot are trademarks of Montag Press.

Printed & Digitally Originated in the United States of America
10 9 8 7 6 5 4 3 2 1

Dedication

To my first writing teachers, Aimee Mepham and
Bob Earleywine. You said, "You've really got something
here," and I believed you.

Chapter One

Goodwill

I tapped the Judge's office door, once, then twice more. At his beck and call day and night, I was. "That must be him now," Judge Dolan rumbled through the oak panel. "Come on in, Joye." He was behind his desk, and a swell doll in a smart black dress sat across from him. He gave me a nod and a wink and said, "Mrs. Humphrey, please meet my assistant, Mr. Sean Joye."

The lady stopped rooting through a beaded bag on her lap and looked up. Pale blue eyes behind a short net veil met mine. They gave me the once-over. A high-society doll and not a bad looker at that. She hadn't bobbed her hair yet, like half the women in the city. It was all pinned up, mysterious-like, under her wide-brimmed purple hat. Whatever this job was, it couldn't be all bad.

"Sean, this is Mrs. Taylor Humphrey," said the Judge. "She brings me an interesting problem."

"Mr. Joye," she said, extending a small hand with long, slim fingers. "Please call me Violet."

I didn't think she meant it. I shook her sweaty palm, which smelled of Shalimar and jumpy nerves. "Mrs. Humphrey, an unexpected pleasure. This fine morning is now brighter, indeed."

Her look told me, "Cut the blarney, paddy," but she said, "The old woman in the lobby predicts snow. The ghost from the elevator shaft told her so."

I didn't know which old woman she meant but pretended I did, doubling down on the brogue. It seldom failed me. With American women, anyway. Gents? Not so much. "Pulling your leg was she?"

At that time, I didn't know any better than old granny tales, that ghosts were merely folks carried off to Faerie, come to pay a bit of a visit to our mortal realm. Not that I'd ever seen any of the fae, including ghosts. At least, not in the courthouse lift. Other places perhaps? I'd just as soon not dwell on that.

Violet returned to the bag and fished out a photograph. The Judge took it, gave it a glance, and handed it back to her. "Why don't you explain your problem to Mr. Joye?" He folded his hands across his tweed waistcoat, leaned back in the chair, and smiled. I'd never seen him more pleased with himself. "Of course." She took a deep breath. "This is difficult." I dumped my coat and fedora on the coat rack and pulled up a chair. "It's about my sister, Lillian. Lillian Arwald." She indicated the photograph in her hand and handed it to me.

A pretty young woman—a child, really—in a white, high-collared dress that hung near her ankles, smiled out of the sepia-toned picture while her eyes challenged the world. She looked about sixteen years old. Long blonde hair was pulled back from her face with a fancy comb and hung in loose curls down her back.

"We had a small family squabble, and now Lillian's run off." Violet looked down at her lap. She bit her lip, like she was about to cry or something.

I didn't buy it. Something had spooked her, but it wasn't the need to discuss her sister's indiscretions with a circuit court judge. "Do you think she's in danger?" I leaned in closer. "Sounds like a job for the cops."

"No, no. Nothing like that. Her debut is this weekend at the Piasa Lodge Ball."

"Debut?"

"A party. Where young ladies are presented to society."

I nodded like I understood. I didn't understand. "And it's in a piazza? Somewhere on the Hill, I guess." I tried with difficulty to picture which courtyard in the tidy Italian neighborhood, not far from where I stayed, could hold a fancy society party—in February, to boot.

"No. Piasa. Pie-uh-saw," Violet said as she crossed her arms. "The American Indian mythological figure? The painting on the river bluffs discovered by the first French explorers?" The Judge looked embarrassed at my ignorance. "At least a dozen businesses in St. Louis and even more across the river in Alton are named for it," he said, smiling at her. "And, of course, the premier civic booster organization of the city."

Well, la-de-da. "So, nothing else for her to hide from?"

"She's been a bit wild." Tapped the picture in my hand, Violet said, "That's from a few years ago. Now her hair's cut short. Skirts too."

I liked the twinkle in Lillian's eyes and something about the smile. The girl had a secret or two, just waiting for the right moment to bust loose.

"She's just in a phase," Violet continued. "She's engaged to be married to a respectable attorney."

"Trouble with the boyfriend?"

"Perhaps." But from the look on her face, the boyfriend had nothing to do with it.

"We know—we think we know—where she's staying. We need someone who can go there, talk to her, and get her to see reason."

I glanced at the Judge. He beamed at me. Really. Like a damned gold-plated, overgrown cherub.

"She's hiding in the Mount St. Michael Convent," Violet said. "The administrator—a nun—won't even admit she's there, let alone allow me to see her." Violet was flummoxed. Flummoxed and seething. Someone had told her no.

Now I got it. A prominent Catholic politician like the Judge, who dined with the archbishop on a weekly basis, had the pull to open convent doors. And the Arwalds, whoever they were, would be in the Judge's debt. "Mr. Joye is quite skilled at motivating people. Under my direction," he said. "He'd be happy to help you."

"'Course," I said.

Violet clasped her little bag and stood, a doubtful look on her face. "You seem a bit young for such a responsibility. I'm sorry if that sounds rude—"

I jumped to my feet. "Not at all. And I'm much older than I look." I was twenty-three years old. I extended my right hand. "Until next time."

She was about my height and looked me straight in the eyes. She shook my hand, calmer now, all lady-of-the-manor-in-charge again, then put on her lavender gloves. "I expect to hear from you soon."

"Looking forward to it." I smiled, all charming and suave. Hoped so, anyway.

She looked amused, then glanced at the Judge before she turned her cool blue eyes on me again. "Mr. Joye—" she emphasized the 'Mister,' "bring her home." She then exited stage right, the heavy door's latch clicking after her.

The Judge chuckled, then snickered. I sat down and leaned back against my chair's cool red leather. He took up guffaws, which yielded to belly laughs. I packed a pipe, lit a match, and rolled it across the bowl, drawing the smoke. Outside the window, flags flapped in the breeze in front of the courthouse. I was warm, comfortable, and safe on a dirty, raw January morning in America. Silent Cal Coolidge sat in the White House and robber baron Andrew Mellon had the run of the treasury. The Big Cinch was firmly in charge of everything. America got rich minding its own business while Europe still lay in ruins five years after the armistice.

"What's so funny?" I asked the Judge.

He dried his eyes and blew his nose on a large handkerchief. "Oh, that felt good. A good laugh adds a year to your life. This has been worth a decade."

I nodded. He was in one of his humors, but it did me no harm. He selected a fat Cuban cigar from the humidor on the desk and then clipped and lit it. "Joye, today I continue your education about our fair city. That was Violet Arwald Humphrey. On her mother's side, the De Noailles. Old money. Old, old Protestant money. Which puts them at the top here, in the social order."

"OK. I get that part. It's—what's that word—ironical, her sister with the nuns. Probably the most annoying thing she could think to do. Kids are like that."

"Yes, the irony is delicious. But their father, Joseph Arwald, sent her—he must have, she wouldn't come to me on her own—for help." Then he was off in a fit of giggles again.

"And?"

The Judge often wheeled and dealed with the Big Cinch—the people that own everything, run everything, decide everything. "They've already had one free favor. Taylor Humphrey—" he pointed with the cigar at the door by which Violet had just left us. "Her husband, a professor, I believe, from England, wanted offices here in the courts building."

That struck me as odd. What connection could an Englishman have with the Missouri state court system?

"Now they're gonna pay, right?"

"God, yes. Arwald is stinking rich. Stocks and bonds. His people are East Coast arms dealers. The family's fortune was made in the Civil War." He frowned. "But the Humphreys have had their troubles. Remember last fall? That baby kidnapped and murdered?"

I felt bad for the pretty lady.

"Must have missed that."

I'd arrived in St. Louis in the summer of 1923, fresh from the Irish Civil War, which had followed hard on the heels of our armed struggle against the British. The American gangs' battle to control bootleg liquor's flow was at its height here and I'd fallen in with—let's just say, "the wrong elements." I got nicked doing something stupid and by sheer luck ended up in the Judge's court one fine day. He dismissed the charges and offered me a job, citing my wartime reputation. I wasn't supposed to have much of a wartime reputation; my intelligence work with General Collin's squad was top secret. I'd stuck close to the Judge since then, purely in self-defense.

"You were working for me by then, but maybe out of town."

By "work" he meant anything not quite above board that needed doing and by "out of town" he meant picking up moonshine in the wilds of Southern Illinois.

"Lillian Arwald's my priority today?" I asked. "I'd planned to visit Hannigan about his campaign contribution."

"Is he late again?"

"And he was short last month. You've given him a couple or three second chances."

He considered that. "Pains me to say it, but at this point, he needs to experience the consequences of his bad decisions. But it can wait until tomorrow."

I'd also planned to meet with the Judge's rumrunner. "How's your supply holding up?"

"Fine, fine. Not much entertaining lately. But that shall soon be remedied," he said as he stood, went to the coat rack, and handed me my hat. "The Mound City Piasa Lodge Annual Parade and Ball is Friday. And the 1924 festivities will see this upstart, shanty Irish politician included in their party." He buttoned his suit coat over his wide belly and donned a homburg and topcoat. "Come along, Joye. Lunch at my club. I'll make a man of the city out of you yet."

I tapped the tobacco ash from my pipe into his spittoon. Grabbing my coat, I followed him out the door.

*   *   *

"Good day, Judge Dolan. Mr. Sean." Jinx, the lift operator, was splendid in his sharp-pressed gray wool uniform, the brass buttons polished to a fair-thee-well. "Lobby?"

"Jinx, my good man," said the Judge. He tucked a cigar in the operator's breast pocket. "You are correct, sir. What a marvelous day."

"Thank you, Judge." He raised his eyebrows at me as he secured the gate. I shrugged.

Jinx pulled the lever to begin our descent. We rode the lift to the lobby in silence, the Judge chuckling to himself occasionally. A worried-looking stuffed shirt got on the lift just as we got off. The Judge tipped his hat. "Good afternoon, Mr. Humphrey." So that's Violet's husband, I thought. Humphrey didn't appear to hear and hurried away.

But it seemed nothing could spoil the Judge's good humor, and we crossed the dark cave of a lobby toward the giant black columns that guarded the Twelfth Avenue entrance. The Judge had been in his digs at the brand-spanking-new Civil Courts Building just a few months and he liked it fine. "I'm thinking of giving Humphrey that stone ax." He was talking about an old artifact. Mississippian, I've since learned. That means "prehistoric American Indian." I got schooled on that too.

The construction crew found quite a bit of loot during the grave robbing—I mean digging out—for the courthouse foundation, and lots of the pottery, ornaments, and whatnots ended up among the swells. Apparently, the city fathers needed to not only knock down tenements that housed hundreds of families but also put their civic progress atop burial mounds. St. Louis is famous for the mounds, even though they've mostly been leveled. "Mound City" is part of lots of business names and such around town.

The Judge was so proud of the trophy, I had to pull his leg a bit. "That rock on your desk?"

"Yes, Joye," he sighed. "The ax is made of stone. But Humphrey is an archeologist and might appreciate its significance."

"Didn't he already get his share of the loot?"

The Judge's glare told me I was on thin ice and we separated to push through the revolving door. When I caught up with him outside, he was speaking to a bent old woman wiping soot off the door jamb. "You're telling ghost stories to my visitors, now, Mrs. MacSweeney?"

Just then a couple of lawyer types hopped out of a cab, dashed across Memorial Plaza, and ran up the wooden steps. "Judge Dolan," one said.

"Just the man I need to—" the other started to say.

With that, the three of them huddled up to rig a jury or something.

It would be awhile before I needed to pull the Packard around. I turned up my collar against the damp fog off the river mixed with the coal-soot-laden air.

As I pondered the ways of the well-heeled, I couldn't help but notice the charwoman hadn't polished a knob since we stepped out of the building and, in fact, was staring at me. "Mrs. MacSweeney is it? I'm Sean Joye. Liking the new building, are you?"

She thought a minute, then wiped her hands on her apron and reached toward me to grasp my coat lapels. "You see them, too, don't you?"

I looked around. The Judge was still busy jawboning with the lawyers. "See who?"

She dragged me around the corner of the building to the loading dock off Chestnut, pulled a flask from her apron pocket, and offered me a swig. When I passed on that, she shrugged and took a good pull herself. "You know right well what I mean. Haunts and other vile creatures."

A chill crept up my spine that had nothing to do with the cold and the damp. The fae are a thinned-skin lot and to talk about them directly is just asking for trouble. I'd hoped to leave them, particularly a faerie named Éire, behind me with the life in Ireland I'd abandoned. But I suspected Éire had followed me to St. Louis. And I'd found America has its own sort of faerie spirits who might not take kindly to Mrs. Mac's insults.

"Sure you're not meaning the Good People, now?"

The fae hail from a place called Faerie, the source of magic in our world. I'm told it looks a lot like Ireland. My granny McGuinn taught me to call them the "Good People," if I had to mention them at all. They might appear fair as a spring morning or even wear the face of a long-dead loved one, but I still had the good sense to avoid them and their business as best I could. "I should bring the car around for the Judge."

"I'm a good Christian woman, and I don't want no traffic with the Devil." Mrs. Mac grabbed my hand. "You're one of them charmers. Tell 'em to move along."

She didn't mean she liked my nice manners and dimpled smile. I hadn't heard the term, "charmer," since I was a child at my grandparents' farm near Carrickfergus, and then only whispered behind Granny's back. Sometimes people said cunning folk, faerie doctor, or wise woman. Neighbors sought her out for spells, healings, and hexes in their attempts to use every means at hand to impose their will on the world around them. For that's all magic is, after all.

"I'm nothing of the kind. I've got to be working and you should too." I started to walk away. "Lay off the poteen and the haunts will lay off of you."

"Don't get bold with me, boy. Why do you think I drink it? It's the only way I get any peace."

Still not my problem. "I really have to go now."

"I'm not done with you. I know you can help me."

I escaped just in time to see the Judge's friends take off toward City Hall. He looked around, expecting to see his new Packard Straight-Eight. And to be seen in it, by as many people as possible. "Sorry, I'm not your man on this one," I called back to her. "Best find a priest."

Mrs. Mac spit on the sidewalk and huffed back into the Civil Courts Building.

*   *   *

I was relieved "his club" for lunch was the downtown athletic club and not the Judge's latest hobby horse, the golf course. That was a good hour's drive away in Normandy and fetching him there and back would eat up my entire afternoon. Still, luncheon with the Judge was nothing to be rushed through, what with the meeting and greeting from the time he hit the front door until he took his leave.

The Missouri Athletic Club was about destroyed in a fire ten years ago, but they'd rebuilt it, bigger and better. They do a nice grilled salmon there, and I generally don't turn down a square meal on someone else's tab. The Judge filled me in on the Arwald family gossip, but with all the interruptions, I may have pieced the story together a bit off-center.

The gist of it was the young Arwald ladies were Twentieth Century Girls. The older, Violet, was not so much wild as independent. Educated in England, she got stranded there for the duration of the Great War. The younger, Lillian, bobbed her hair and ran off to the speakeasies at the first opportunity. She drove her family up the wall and cost her father a fortune to keep her out of jail and the newspapers.

As Violet had told us, the present spat was over the Piasa Lodge Ball, part of a whole winter Carnival season of balls, parades, parties, tableaux, musicales—you name it. Lillian was supposed to be presented to society at the debutante ball put on by her father's lodge.

Society debut was probably a big deal for eighteen-year-old girls before the war, but I imagine most of them, like Lillian, had been to a dance or two by now. Anyway, Lillian had been at some special pageantry function that was just too boring to be endured and she'd run off. That was the family's theory anyway. No one had talked to her in days.

*   *   *

After I finally got the Judge stashed back in his office, I headed to the Mount St. Michael Convent on the far north side, practically in the country. I left the city's smog and fumes behind me. The air was clear and sky blue, a lovely mild afternoon in the middle of winter.

In those days, I didn't pay too much attention to the soul of a place. I credited any odd turn I felt as worry over being shot or arrested. I wasn't in any particular danger anymore, but life's patterns become ingrained. I entered by the door marked *Visitors,* into a foyer that smelled safe and dark. A refuge.

The Judge's name got me as far as the mother superior's office where an impossibly young novice indicated I should wait in the hall. I heard church bells ring three o'clock as I sat on a wooden chair shifting my hat from knee to knee and sweating in my wool topcoat. On a table across from me were the remnants of the recent Christmas season, a fancy porcelain Nativity scene.

Mother Superior Mary Gabriel charged through a side door toward her office, a blur of gray with a sheer white veil flying behind her. She unlocked the office as she gave me a curt, "Come in." There she plowed into the piles of papers on her desk as she waved me into a chair.

A nun's age is hard to guess. The best I can do is sort them into too young, about right, and maybe time to retire. Mother Superior seemed about right. She spoke without looking up. "Yes? How can we help the Judge today?" She didn't sound very interested in helping the Judge.

"What a peaceful place you have here, Reverend Mother. Lovely view of the courtyard. And hearing the bells chime—"

She held up one hand, lifting her eyes from her work. "You can be saving the patter—" from her accent, I'd guess she was from County Cork, long ago, "for the locals. What's your point?"

"The Judge has sent me to speak with Miss Lillian Arwald."

"Who?"

"Lillian. Young flapper, eighteen years old or so. Been here a few days."

Mother Mary Gabriel continued to stare.

I felt my throat constrict and my stomach rumble. I glanced at the desk in search of a ruler, the school nun's weapon of choice. "Her family's quite concerned. Worried enough to ask the Judge for help. If I could just have a few words with her, it could resolve some bad blood in the family." I'd mangled my fedora good and proper and endeavored to smooth out the crushed brim.

Mother Mary Gabriel sighed, "I suppose you could talk to her." Standing, she continued, "No bullying. Miss Arwald's under the protection of Our Lord here. And myself."

She led me down corridors and up staircases, across courtyards, and through cloisters until I was entirely lost. I'm sure that was on purpose. She deposited me in a small rose garden, the beds mulched, and shrubs cut back for winter. In the center was a grotto and concrete statue of the Blessed Mother. A bench faced it.

"I'll send her out if she's willing."

I'd no more than paid my respects to Our Lady and sat down when I heard footsteps crunch the gravel path. The girl from the photograph, in a novice's gray dress and a bulky sweater, approached.

I stood and tipped my hat. "Miss Arwald?"

She nodded and looked over at the convent. "You some kinda cop?"

Through a window, I could see a flash of gray and white: Mother Mary Gabriel watching over her lamb. "Not at all. My name is Sean Joye." I pointed to the bench. "Could we sit and talk for a minute?"

Lillian nodded again and perched on the edge of the bench. "I'd kill for a smoke."

I offered her a cigarette.

"No, no. She'll see. Stand in front of me."

I stood so as to block the view from the window, lit a cigarette, and handed it to her.

She accepted it with a shaking hand. Lillian inhaled to her toes and released her breath. Wreathed in smoke, she closed her eyes and communed in bliss.

I waited.

At last, she opened her eyes and handed the cigarette back to me. "You're a good guy, Copper. Kinda cute too. I could fall for the black curls, green eyes combo."

I flushed. She looked like a novice nun in that outfit and they generally aren't all that flirty.

Lillian smiled, satisfied with herself. "My old man send you? Or grandfather?" She set her chin in the pout of a six-year-old. "I'm not going back."

"Your sister wants you to come home."

"Violet?" She seemed puzzled. "She sent you?"

"Whatever row you had with your family, this won't solve anything. It just postpones the problem."

"You don't get it. They don't get it. Their party's a joke. Expecting me to parade around in the Piasa Lodge Court." Lillian waved her hands to emphasize the stupidity of the world. "I'd die, simply die of embarrassment."

I sat next to her and finished the cigarette. She slipped her hand into mine and watched me, making a point to inhale the second-hand smoke.

"That the only reason?" I asked. "Can't you stand one last humdrum party to please the old folks?"

"It's more than that. The whole charade stands for the Big Cinch's power. Over their wives, their daughters, the city." Lillian glanced up at the window again. "Say, you don't have any hooch, do you? You strike me as a party kinda fella."

"Sorry. Don't care for spirits. So, a Roman Catholic nun you're being now?"

She laughed. "Naw, I'm just pulling Father's chain. I read about 'sanctuary.' People hide in a church and the law can't touch 'em. It's all gothic and creepy."

"Your father's not the law, miss."

"Above it, you mean?"

I shrugged. That was my impression. "Look, if you got something to say to him, say it. While you can. The world won't end." I searched the Blessed Mother's face for some hint of guidance, but she took no pity on me. "You're on your own, sucker." A cloud covered the setting sun and the garden turned cold. "The money might end, though. If that matters."

Lillian's worried look made me think it did matter, quite a bit, but she squared her shoulders and pouted. "It's easier to hide." Her face was a tad pale. Maybe the cigarette wasn't a good idea, after all.

"If you don't intend to take the veil, you can't stay here for long. And your interests are elsewhere, right?"

She sighed, "Maybe." Lillian leaned her head against my shoulder.

"You OK, doll?"

"Dizzy spell."

"Not used to the smokes," I said. "And Mother Mary Gabriel's not going to think much of us spooning out here in her garden."

She laughed, turned green, and ran to the nearest flowerbed to vomit in the shrubberies. I handed her a handkerchief. She wiped her eyes and mouth and blew her nose. "Almost supper time. I've gotta go peel potatoes or something." Lillian stood close and looked up at me with eyes I could imagine were adoring. Adoring and calculated. "I'll wash out your hankie and get it back to you."

"Keep it. And you're going to have to guide me outta here."

She smiled and took my hand. "Don't talk inside the building. You'll get me in trouble."

We walked through the garden and chatted about nothing in particular until we entered the convent and took on the restful silence of the place. The bells rang four o'clock. It was almost dark. The fine, spring-like afternoon had turned cold. It was still the dead of winter. We paused at the Mother Superior's office door, closed and locked for the day. Lillian toyed with the Nativity scene while I wrote a note to Mother Mary Gabriel thanking her for her help. "Violet sent him," Lillian murmured under her breath to Baby Jesus.

I waited, hat in hand, and hoped she'd decide to come with me. But if I had learned anything at all in life, it was not to press a mark too hard, too fast. She had to think it was her idea.

"Thanks for the smokes, Copper." Lillian gave me a hug and a peck on the cheek, unexpected but not unwelcome. "When you come back," she winked, "bring some gin." She inclined her head toward a heavy oak door at the end of the hall. "You go out that way." Then she slipped into the shadows for her kitchen duties.

As I made my way toward the door, I noticed Baby Jesus no longer lay in his manger crib.

Chapter Two

Return on Investment

I arrived home a bit later than I expected only to find the charwoman from the Civil Courts Building, Mrs. MacSweeney, awaiting me. "Home" is my brother Padraig's place, the Belfast Bar on Tamm Avenue. She sat at the bar and glowered at anyone who stood close to her. It was a busy night, and Padraig looked none too pleased to have her parked on a stool and not buying a thing. I touched her elbow. "Mrs. MacSweeney."

She let out a yelp and gathered her shawl and pocketbook to her chest. "Oh, 'tis you." She shook her head. "You gave me a turn."

"Shall we sit in a booth, then? Have a bit of quiet?" I steered her to the least popular booth, under the stairs to the second-floor flat where we lived. That booth was hot in the summer, drafty in the winter, and the servers never seemed to notice folks who sat there.

She clung to my arm and was willing enough to be led away from the din at the bar.

"Had your supper yet?"

Mrs. Mac thought about that a good long while and then shook her head.

I left her long enough to step into the kitchen and order some food and then drew a couple of pints of Bevo, an odd yet legal brew, from the tap behind the bar. I gave Padraig the ten dollars I got from the Judge that day. He indicated his pleasure with a nod and a "Fuckin' about time," and skipped his usual chiding that I should get my own place.

I made my way back to my visitor with the drinks and sat across from her in the booth. She looked a bit wild-eyed and took a swig off her hip flask. "Hey, cut that out. Want to get this place shut down?"

"Aye, shut it down, burn it down, and all its haunts with it." Her voice was low and dripped with scorn. "The dead sit with us here and now, evil blood pouring out across this table. And you propose to eat dinner here."

She had such conviction I half expected to see a pool of blood forming under my pint glass. But no, just scarred, water-stained oak. "Put away the whiskey. We'll move if you don't like the booth." I found her an acceptable table near the front door about the time my niece, Maud, showed up with our fish and chips. "Eat your dinner," I told the old lady.

Mrs. Mac didn't pick up her fork. "You mean to tell me you can't see them over there?"

I made myself look back at the booth, just to prove she was wrong. I didn't see any haunts, but I couldn't deny I felt something. Something not right. And now that she'd pointed it out, the haze and smoke of the room seemed to linger there, heavy on the air. Hard death had touched this place and left its mark. Suddenly nervous, I scanned the room, catching a glimpse of the faerie woman, Éire, behind the bar. Since I more than half suspected she'd somehow made her way to America, that gave me a bit of a turn. I had to laugh at myself when I realized it was but a poster, proclaiming the Republic and bedecked with the typical image of Ireland as a beautiful woman, Éire's favorite glamour. "Let's put aside my brother's ghost infestation for the moment. What did you want from me?"

Mrs. Mac's whiskey seemed to take effect and she tucked into her dinner like a starving person. "I'm a God-fearing, Christian woman. I've never been a drinker. I marched with the temperance ladies. I've no truck with the devil or his wiles. But the new courts building is cursed. I've felt it since we moved in. And it's getting worse. The vile things are bolder every day."

"Why don't you find a different job?"

"Aye, that's easy enough to say, you young fool. I'm eighty years old. My knees are bad and I can't half see. I only have the position because of the Judge."

"The Judge got you your job?"

"Oh, I live in his old ward, from back when he was alderman. Just down the street from here."

"So you were a political supporter?"

She snorted. "Far from it. My husband argued with him daily about everything. From the government to the weather to the old country. But when Jamie died last year, the Judge sent a fella around with an envelope and an offer of steady work."

That was the Judge all over. He'd have the whole city in his pocket before he was done.

"But why do you think I can help you with ghosts?"

She considered her words.

I waited, anointing my fish with malt vinegar. We batter the cod here, as Grandmother Joye did. No soggy bread crumbs. Makes all the difference.

"I say 'get thee behind me, Satan.' But I was cursed with a bit of the Sight, I suppose," she said at last. "'Twas worse when I was a girl. But when you came outta the lobby this morning, I could see their mark on you. They've claimed you as one of their own."

One way or the other, the fae are responsible for humans with the Sight—a knack for seeing the unseen and knowing the unknown—and we recognize each other. Perhaps outright, or maybe just an attraction to a kindred spirit. But in those days, I refused to look at many things I could plainly see.

"Do you want pie? I want pie." I half stood and waved at Maud. "Is there apple?"

Mrs. Mac sopped up the grease on her plate with a bit of bread and popped it into her mouth. "No one believes me. I've about been sacked for warning folks."

"What can I do?" I had a thought. "Shall I find you a priest?"

She about choked on her Bevo. "The Church of Rome has no answer here, boy." She looked pleased though, as Maud brought warm pie with cheddar cheese. "No offense. I know it's the way you was raised and you don't know no better."

"None taken." I agreed to coffee at Maud's suggestion and the child poured it for the two of us. "So, not saying you are right or wrong about me and what I might see or feel or know—"

"I want them to leave me alone. To go back to Hell and leave me be. Seeing as you know them, I thought you could tell the haunts that."

I couldn't deny I'd run smack dab into the Veil before. But I didn't need this bother right now. I didn't want it. "I'm sorry," I said. "I just don't see how I can help you."

Her faded blue eyes turned bright with anger. She gripped her fork like a weapon. "'Tis a shame you're marked for damnation."

"Damnation, you say?" Lillian stood by our table. I hadn't noticed her come in. I was slipping. "Copper, I didn't know you were so interesting."

I stood and pulled out a chair for her. "Miss Arwald. I didn't expect to see you again so soon."

She smiled, traced my lapel with a gloved hand, and turned so I could help her with her coat. She was out of the nun garb and all shimmery in a smart cocktail dress and feathered headband.

"Mrs. MacSweeney, meet Miss Lillian Arwald." What could I say about Lillian? "This very afternoon she had a religious vocation." I winked at Lillian and she stuck out her tongue. "Miss Arwald, meet Mrs. Charity MacSweeney. She works at the new Civil Courts Building. I hear your brother-in-law has an office there."

Lillian extended her hand. "Charmed, I'm sure."

Mrs. Mac took her slim hand in both her rough, chapped ones and held on tight. "Tell him to move. The haunts are out for blood. Mark my words, there'll be murder. Bloody murder. That place is the mouth of Hell."

Just then Maud appeared with a coffee pot. "More coffee, ma'am?"

Mrs. Mac released her glare on Lillian and turned to Maud, all sweetness and light. "Yes, dear. Just a drop."

Maud filled our cups and then turned to me. "I need to talk to you when you have a minute." She pretended to just then notice Lillian. "Something for you, miss?" she mumbled.

I couldn't imagine what had gotten into the child. Thirteen years old, by now she'd worked at the pub for ages and knew better than to ignore a customer.

Lillian ordered gin, which we don't serve, then settled for a Coca-Cola.

Mrs. Mac chatted with Lillian, giving me the cold shoulder for a few minutes, and then gathered her belongings and left.

"What an extraordinary old bird," Lillian said after the charwoman banged out the front door. "A particular friend of yours?" She fished a cigarette out of her handbag, fit it into a long holder, and waited for me to light it.

I was pondering Mrs. Mac's ghosts and took a second to notice. "Sorry." I struck a match. "She wants me to find the ghosts in the Civil Courts Building and tell them to leave."

"My, my." Lillian blew a perfect smoke ring. "Is that a service you provide?"

I laughed. "No, it's not."

"Well, if you do, I want to see it," she said as she dug around in her purse again. "I don't know what got into me this afternoon." She slid a wallet across the table. My wallet. "Maybe I wanted an excuse to come and find you."

Lillian was good. Very good. I picked it up and put it in my pocket. "I must be getting old and off my game."

She snorted. "You don't look any older than me. What are you—Nineteen? Twenty?"

"I'll be twenty-four in June. You ready to go home?"

"Yeah. I thought I'd let you take me. Get the credit with Violet, or whatever. I bet there's a fee. We could split it." She snubbed out the cigarette. "Hey, Copper, you got food here? I could eat first, before I face the music."

"Coming right up." I took her order and told the cook. When I came back, she was in a darts match with a couple of old-timers.

Lillian sure didn't need me to entertain her, and my poor niece had a roomful of customers, so I excused myself, ran orders out from the kitchen for a bit, and then helped Maud bus the tables.

"Did she give you anything today?" my niece asked.

"The old lady? Well, the evil eye, and more than once. Or do you mean Lillian? She stole my wallet and brought it back."

"No, silly." Maud stood straight and stretched out her back to the left and right. "Mrs. Judge. Did she send me a magazine?"

"I didn't talk to her today. Sorry." I picked up the tub of dishes. Seeing Maud's sad little face, I sat the tub down again and lifted her chin. "You done with that poem she sent you last week? Ready to school me all about it?"

Her face lit up. "That's what I wanted to talk to you about. Yes, I did read it. But also, Matthew wants to join the group."

"The kid who washes the dishes is interested in Mr. Yeats' thoughts on the Easter Rising?" More like, interested in Miss Maud Joye. I pictured my brother's reaction to our black kitchen helper courting his daughter. Not a pleasant scene. "And you and me are a group?"

Since I'd moved in, Maud had roped me into a sort of Gaeilge study cell that would do the Irish internees at Frongoch prison camp proud. That's generally what us Irish prisoners of war did, back in the day. Teach each other our stolen culture.

"With a third, we'd be a group. And he's not a kid. He's almost sixteen. The Easter Rising means something to him, too. His Da was killed in the East St. Louis riots when he was little."

Maybe I was new to America, but of course I'd heard about the worst race riot in the country's history. Seven years ago, at least a hundred black citizens were murdered by white mobs in a labor dispute just across the river from where we now stood. The government—East St. Louis police and Illinois National Guard—did nothing at all to stop the slaughter. Some say they encouraged it.

Maud's voice dropped. "Not so different than Granddad."

"Fair point," I allowed, as we walked back to the kitchen together. "Of course, I don't mind. And you're the teacher, anyway. Whatever you want."

*   *   *

I brought the Model T, a 1915 touring model, around to the front of the pub. The car belonged to the Judge but I had free use of it. The Judge's secretary had given me the Arwalds' address, a mansion on a private street off Union Boulevard in the Central West End.

Lillian was chatty, happy with her performance at darts. She'd won fifty cents and a pint of Bevo from the old codgers at the bar. As we progressed north on Kingshighway, however, she grew quiet.

"You're taking me to my father's house, aren't you?"

"I guess." I told her the address Violet had provided the Judge.

"No, I don't want to go there. I live at my grandfather's."

"Your sister said—"

"I don't care." She was the pouty schoolgirl again, face stony and arms crossed.

It didn't matter much to me where I took her. "Where do you want to go?"

Lillian gave me an address in Lafayette Square, so I made a couple of turns to get headed south.

We arrived at the front door around eleven o'clock. The house faced the park, just across from a police station. This block of houses always made me think of tall, elegant ladies a bit past their prime, clutching their shawls at the upstart warehouses and factories that crowded in from all sides. She pointed out a house that could've stood a slap of paint around the windows and a lot of yard work. I walked her to the door. Just as she retrieved a key from her handbag, a taxi pulled up to the curb, and the driver assisted an elderly man to the sidewalk. He made for the steps, leaning on two canes. A small portmanteau dangled from his wrist.

"Grandfather." Lillian dashed down the steps to his side. She took the bag, which I could now see was what doctors carry about on house calls.

I followed to help and offered him my arm. "Ah, thank you, young man," he said, grasping my left elbow. "Been a long day." He turned to Lillian, who had taken his other arm. "A longer day for the new mother. A difficult birth."

"I can't wait to hear all about it." She said it as if she meant it.

We hauled him up the steps—there were a lot of them—then she unlocked the door.

"Thank you, thank you," the old man said, and then released his death grip on my arm. "Welcome to my home. My wife is disinclined to come into town from our country place, so I must rough it as a bachelor."

Lillian hung up his hat, muffler, and coat and took the medical bag into an office off the front foyer. Without his coat, I could see he was a twisted old gent. The back brace under his old-fashioned frock coat didn't seem to do a great deal of good. The outline of a right leg brace showed through the fabric of his trousers, and the boot had a built-up sole.

He waved me into the parlor and heaved himself into a rocker. He hung the canes on the edge of a nearby table and pointed to a chair opposite his. I wasted no time to sit, rubbing my numb elbow where he'd clung to me.

"Now, young man. Who are you and why are you bringing my granddaughter home at—" He pulled out a pocket watch and consulted it, then closed it with a snap, "Eleven o'clock at night?"

His eyes were sharp, peering over spectacles perched on the end of his nose. His hair was thick, white, and hung to his shoulders. A tangled, tobacco-yellowed beard covered his jaw. He shifted, obviously uncomfortable.

"Sorry, sir. I'm—"

He pointed at a drinks cart with bottles and glassware near the front bay window. "Would you mind? A bit of brandy. Then add a drop or two of medicine, in the bottle there."

The medicine was labeled *Tincture of Laudanum*. I mixed the drink as instructed and brought it to him. "I'm Sean Joye. Pleased to meet you."

He looked at the glass. "I've never known an Irishman to be so stingy with liquor, boy."

I laughed and returned to the drinks cart and amended the "bit of brandy" to a half snifter.

"Thank you," he said. "I'm Antoine De Noailles. Welcome to my home. Pour yourself a drink. It's perfectly legal and quite pure. I write myself a prescription as needed and the pharmacist sends it over."

"Ah, no thanks, sir. I should be going. Mrs. Humphrey asked me to collect Miss Lillian and drive her home."

At that moment Lillian joined us. She'd kicked off her shoes and walked across the room in her stocking feet to kiss her granddad's fuzzy cheek. "I cleaned out the bag and put all the instruments in Lysol."

"Ah, my little nurse. Thank you, dear. You're such a comfort to me, especially when Esther isn't here. Now, why did you need a ride home? I forget."

Dr. De Noailles had already drained his glass and was holding it out to me for another. He looked relaxed, leaning back in the chair, slowly rocking, his gray eyes soft and unfocused.

"It's not important." Lillian said as she dropped to the floor to unfasten his brace and pull off his boots. I caught her eye, held up the glass, and indicated the drinks cart with a questioning look. She shrugged and nodded.

"I saw that," he said. "I'm a physician, surgeon, and grown man. I've forgotten more about safe and effective medication use than you two know, combined."

I apologized and brought him another drink. He smiled as he accepted it. "My bark is worse than my bite, young man. I thank you for your help."

Lillian covered his legs with a plaid blanket and took my hand to lead me toward the foyer. "He'll sleep now. Poor old dear."

"Should he be delivering babies?"

She smiled. "People think they're lucky if he'll take their case because he's a famous, high-society doctor from an old-money family. Not that there's any money now, old or otherwise."

At the door, she slid her hands under my topcoat and across my chest. "What's this now?" She pulled the Webley I carried when I'm out at night from its shoulder holster and hefted it in both hands. "That baby's got some weight to it."

"Got some kick to it too. Not for little ladies."

"I'm not a little lady." She got huffy and waved the gun in my face. "My fiancé showed me how to shoot his derringer. And isn't the safety on, anyway?"

"Sorry. I just meant it's too heavy for you. The recoil would knock you over. And a revolver like this doesn't have a safety. I just use it to scare people." That was a lie.

"Show me how it works. I've never seen one like it before."

So, I did. For good or ill. Lillian had a mechanic's mind, interested in the revolver as a machine as much as in it as a weapon. She particularly admired the top-break extraction mechanism.

I had to promise to take her out in the country to teach her to fire it before she'd give it back, and then she stood on tiptoes to kiss me good night. She was lovely and warm, as comfortable in my arms as a deep sigh. She tasted malty and minty from Bevo and chewing gum.

"I called Violet," Lillian said. "To let her know I'm home. Since apparently, she cares now." She wound her arms around my neck, pressing my body tight with hers.

I kissed the back of her neck, her short, smoke-scented curls tickling my nose. She sighed and clung to me even closer.

"She—" Lillian's voice caught, and she cleared her throat. "She wants to talk to you tonight."

All my attention was on the fine line of her collarbone.

"Drop by her house, anytime. They stay up late." She held my face between her hands and kissed me again. "Grandfather will be passed out cold for hours. You could stay a while if you want."

"Do you want me to?"

"You can't tell?" she said as she pulled me into the doctor's examination room, a hard, clean, white place where wicked-looking doctoring tools were soaking in a steel pan of Lysol.

Even then, I felt Lillian was playing me in some way, but she needs a friend, I told myself. So, right or wrong—OK, it was wrong—we examined each other for the better part of an hour until the phone rang from deep in the house. She went to answer it, and I pulled myself together and smoked a cigarette.

When she returned, I said, "I should be going to see your people. It's getting late."

Lillian nodded. "That was Violet." She led me out to the hall and found my coat and hat. "Sorry I lifted your wallet. Sometimes I do things. To see if I can, I guess. Or to find out what will happen."

"I understand." I kissed her head, her nose, her mouth. "Bringing it back to me got you out of the convent."

She laughed, "That it did."

*   *   *

I made my way to Washington Terrace. The guard in the massive gatehouse was expecting me and opened the wrought-iron gates. The Arwald pile was about halfway up the block. Two flags hung from the roof line. Emblazed on each, the details hard to see in the moonlight, was the image of a monster, a sort of dragon with antlers and a bearded, human face. "Piasa Lodge Queen, 1914," was embroidered in red script on one. The other, much more faded, said "Mound City Piasa Queen, 1892."

I stood on the threshold, hat in hand. The door opened almost immediately at my knock. Violet answered it herself.

"Good evening," I said. "Morning, I guess it is."

She pulled me in and shut the door. "She's agreed? To the debutante ceremony?"

"Yeah. Lillian thinks it's silly and 'embarrassing'—her words. Your da's going pay dearly in favors and merchandise for quite a while."

"That's fine. That's fine."

I could just glimpse a grand staircase off the entrance foyer. A familiar-looking middle-aged gent descended the stairs, limping slightly. He had a trim, athletic build, and a fresh haircut, graying at the temples in a becoming way. He wore a deep red quilted smoking jacket and good quality black wool trousers, as sharply creased as if he'd just taken them off the ironing board. He approached us with a broad smile. "Thank you for this good news."

The Judge had pointed him out as Taylor Humphrey on the lift earlier in the day. Now I could get a good look at him. He carried himself like a British Army officer and spoke like an Oxford don, at least one from the cinema, the only sort I'd ever encountered. We shook hands like Americans, and I made noncommittal, "it was nothing," sort of noises as I edged toward the door.

"Violet, my dear, why haven't you invited our guest in?"

She blanched, but he rolled on. "Come in, honored guest. Fáilte isteach. I'm Taylor Humphrey, and I know you are Mr. Sean Joye."

About the last thing I expected of him was to talk to me in Irish, though I could barely understand a word he said, with his Munster accent. His government had done its level best to steal our language over the centuries, but I'd never met an Englishman who made any good use of their spoils of war.

"Dia duit, á Seán," he continued. "Let me take your coat. And pardon me practicing Gaeilge on you. I've no outlet in America, at all."

He stripped me of my topcoat as he spoke, and a sleepy-headed young footman appeared out of nowhere and walked off with my coat and hat.

"Ah, you won't get much practice from me, I'm afraid," I said. "My grandparents in the country spoke it and I studied a bit in prison, but I grew up in Belfast speaking the King's English like everyone else."

Humphrey dragged me into a dimly lit library, and Violet followed. The book spines and bronze lamps winked in the moonlight pouring through the high clerestory windows. He put me in a throne of a chair near a cold fireplace and thrust a double brandy in my hand without batting an eye at my mention of prison. Either he didn't hear me or didn't care, perhaps well aware of the throngs of Irish political prisoners in jail at one time or the other since the Republic was declared less than ten years ago.

"Well, we must remedy that," Humphrey said, still keen to teach me my own language. "Form a tutorial. I'm currently reading Merriman's 'The Midnight Court.' In the original Irish, of course. Jolly good fun."

That old poem is a bawdy commentary on men's failure to meet women's needs. Considering how I'd spent my evening entertaining Lillian, I felt safe from Faerie Queen Aoibheall's judgment, for the moment at least.

"My family had property near Tara," Humphrey blathered on. "I spent many a happy summer in my youth, exploring the countryside and talking to the old folks about the old ways." He poured more brandy. "There's interesting lore all over Britain, isn't there, dear?" he turned to Violet and handed her the glass. "New Forest in Hampshire, for example. That's where we met." He stood next to his wife and put his arm around her shoulder. "Violet was some sort of scout leader—"

"The Order of Woodcraft Chivalry," she yawned.

"At this camp-out—"

"Lammas," she corrected with a sigh.

The old harvest festival. I knew it as Lughnasadh. Every summer I spent on my grandparent's farm, I'd kept it. The holiday involved quite a bit of hiking, as I recalled, but a grand picnic.

"But the best minds in folklore and Celtic history were there, so I popped in."

Violet slipped out of his grasp and set down the brandy snifter. "My father is in Cuba, but I know he would thank you, as well. Lillian's too young to understand how these things work. Being the queen of the ball isn't even about her. It's about the family. Our position in society."

I nodded and swirled the brandy around in the glass. "Well, I just wanted to let you know."

"Violet was queen for her debut, weren't you, dear?" Humphrey picked her discarded snifter and toasted toward a portrait hung over the fireplace, barely visible in the shadows. "Like her mother before her."

Violet went to the door. "I think I'll take Lillian's gown over to Grandfather's and stay with her until the party. Just in case she changes her mind and tries to take off again."

"Do you think she might?" Humphrey wondered, seating himself near me on another throne. "I'll miss you, Violet, but perhaps that would be for the best." He showed me lots of small teeth under a clipped little mustache.

I'd had about an earful of their plan to make Lillian do this party. "If she doesn't want to go to the ball, why force her?"

"Oh, my dear chap." He leaned over and patted my knee. "You're a true gentleman. Lillian's knight errant, as it were. Of course, we wouldn't force her. Never, ever." He took the brandy snifter out of my hand. "Thank you again for coming by. Violet will write you a check."

I know when I'm getting the bum's rush and stood to leave. "Thanks for the drink. And that's not necessary. I work for the Judge."

"We'll settle with him, then."

I was sure they would. Knowing the Judge, this little favor was going to cost the Arwalds plenty.

Chapter Three

———∽◇◇◇∽———

Initial Public Offering

I spent the next afternoon, Thursday, with the Judge's tailor, having an off-the-rack suit of evening clothes altered. Not at all how I'd expected to occupy myself that day. But, true to his prediction, that morning a messenger delivered the Judge's invitation to the Friday night Piasa Lodge Ball. I was pleased for the Judge since he wanted to go so bad, but what it had to do with me, I'd no idea. He was quick to inform me that a man of his stature in the community couldn't just show up at an important event without an entourage and his choice of presentable flunkies was pretty limited.

So, there I was on Friday night, leaning over the Civil Courts Building's twelfth-floor mezzanine rail to observe the festivities spread out across the marble-clad floor below me. Before a dais set up in front of the band, a parade of the city fathers presented their daughters to polite society. And on the dais, presiding over the whole shenanigans, stood a masked figure, "Chief Ouatoga."

The lodge picked their bravest member to appear at the party bare-chested and bare-legged in a feathered cloak and a kilt. Around his neck hung a beaded necklace with a good-sized conch shell as a pendant. He wore a wig to provide the long, black hair lacking in the typical city father. I figured he was supposed to be a Native American since they called him "Chief." But his costume was nothing like what I'd seen in Wild West films—no long, feathered war bonnet or leather leggings. I'd didn't quite know what to think of it all.

I grew up in a city where the Protestant Orange Order dressed up in strange garb and paraded about with stranger ritual every July in honor of 1690's Battle of the Boyne, but this show took the biscuit. I didn't think Americans fancied ceremony, though they'd demonstrated their fascination with the English monarchy plenty since they'd gotten rid of Old King George.

The girls were a lot more interesting than the chief. They were all in fancy white dresses and carried big bouquets of white flowers. An emcee announced each young lady and then the orchestra swung into an appropriate tune. Miss Katherine DuBois and her father, Vincent DuBois, for instance, fought the bouncy rhythm of "K-K-K-Katie" to maintain the slow, grave step the show called for. Each deb walked the length of the ballroom on a red carpet, clinging to her father's arm. They made their way to the chief's reviewing stand, curtsied, then moved off to the side, lining up to his left and right.

Sharp, bright smiles were glued to their faces, and I saw more than a few trembling bouquets. But they appeared to be happy, excited young girls, pleased to be at the grown-up party. Probably more pleased when they could ditch the old man and partner up for dancing with their many young admirers.

Lounging against the rail a few feet away from me, a tall drink of water watched the ceremony with a bemused expression. He flipped and caught a coin with impressive sleight-of-hand skills. Like me, he wore evening clothes. Unlike me, his were not off the rack. His tailor must love his work—those broad shoulders would make anything look good.

I nodded toward the chief. "In a dime novel, he'd be the enemy, right?"

"Yet, from the safe distance of our dubious victories, we love to project romantic fantasies." The gent slipped the coin into his pocket and strolled over to offer me a smoke, leaning in to spark a flame with a silver Ronson lighter. For a moment my head swam in a haze of bay rum and naphtha.

"He's supposed to be a Mississippian ruler. What the lodge imagines that to be, anyway," he said as he tapped the ash off his expensive-smelling cigarette into a nearby ashtray.

Mississippian? Like the Judge's stone ax? "The Mississippian tribe?"

He smiled and my heart took a header into my guts.

"It's complicated," he said.

"Aren't most things?" Like his patter, for instance. I didn't totally get it, but it sounded good.

"Mississippians were the indigenous people of this area over a thousand years ago. Possibly the ancestors of the historical tribes from your films and novels. There's a lot of debate on that, I understand, but it makes sense to those for whom it's important."

This conversation was way too smart for me. "Well, don't you learn something new every day?"

"Very true. You know the legend?" He pointed at one of the prominent banners, embroidered with the colorful Piasa image, draping the balcony. "Of the Piasa?"

I shook my head.

"A journalist named Russell collected and published the Illini myth almost a hundred years ago. Piasa means, 'The bird that devours men.' The story goes it fed on humans, especially the young and helpless."

"Hmm," I said, much more interested in his eyes. They were some shade of navy. Or maybe it was just the dim light.

"The Chief, Ouatoga," he said as he pointed at the old gent on the dais, greeting one pretty girl after another. "Organized twenty warriors with poison arrows and placed himself as bait at the mouth of the Piasa's cave. The warriors shot and killed the Piasa when it attacked him. The Piasa fell into the Mississippi River and was never seen again, except in the mural high on the cliffs, commemorating the victory."

Sure that sounded like a crock, but I guess I've heard worse. "You're pulling my leg."

He shrugged his broad shoulders, "Well, that's the tale. Our early explorers, Marquette and Joliet, documented the cliff paintings in their journal."

An awkward moment of silence followed. His eyes met mine but slid away to the spectacle unfolding below us in the candlelit ballroom. The evasion made me wondered what he saw when he looked at me. If it had scared him, somehow. "Oh, I heard something about the cliff paintings the other day." I ground out the cigarette he'd given me in a nearby ashtray. "I'm Sean Joye." I nudged his elbow and pointed. "I'm taking care of the Judge down there."

"Ah, I know him. Been in his court. Running for mayor next cycle? Care to comment?"

I held up both hands in protest, then offered my right hand.

He took it with a firm squeeze and shook it. "I'm Kyffin Bernard."

"A Welshman you are, is it?"

He laughed—solid, honest. Some folks are pleasant enough but then turn out to have an annoying laugh. Not Kyffin. "In a way. My mother's family name. But I'm from St. Louis."

I was supposed to be watching the Judge, not gabbing with displaced Welshmen, but His Honor was safely tucked away—near the service entrance, I noted. Grew up over my family's pub in Belfast, so I know a bad table when I see it.

"Did you see the parade?" Kyffin asked.

"A bit of it." Not satisfied with flipping pancakes for Shrove Tuesday—Mardi Gras, they call it here—St. Louis kicked off Carnival season as soon as Twelfth Night was over. The city was immobilized by parades as all the mystic societies took turns strutting their stuff, each procession more elaborate than the last. The Piasa Lodge parade was the icing on the cake. A good show of illuminated floats—each a tableau of praise to some industry or other, stressing how it benefited the commonwealth. Last but not least, a papier-mâché and floral beast with the face of a man, the horns of a deer, the beard of a tiger, and a fishy tail so long it passed around the body, over the head, and between the legs. Smoke came out of its nose and fire from its mouth as it let loose with blood-curdling roars that set the children both screaming and scrambling for the candy thrown by its attendants.

"Now that float with the dragon makes more sense," I said.

"Exactly. That was the Piasa, namesake of the lodge."

Bands and veterans' units marched as well, and the latest cars transported the city fathers and robber barons, waving more or less pleasantly at the throngs. I don't know if they expected trouble—a streetcar operator strike had been rumored for weeks, but the entire police force seemed to be out as well to walk the route alongside the dignitaries.

A trumpet fanfare signaled us all to wake up, as the emcee announced, "It's my honor to present, the Queen of the Confluence, reigning for the year 1924. Miss Lillian Arwald."

Lillian entered the ballroom on the arm of a solid, middle-aged gent I took to be her father. I wouldn't have recognized her pale, blank face, truly, if I hadn't heard the emcee call her name, but she did look like a queen. Her gown was so white it hurt my eyes. The only bit of color was the mass of red roses in her arms.

They'd somehow made her bobbed hair look like it was a chignon. A few tendrils curled about her temples and sweet nape. Lillian and her father made their way to the dais where they saluted the chief. He left the dais, approached the pair, and old Arwald handed her off. I was struck by how like a wedding it was. Well, a big formal church wedding with a mass, not the simple vows in the rectory most can afford.

Lillian and the chief ascended the dais and turned to the crowd. She knelt on a large cushion and the chief removed a glittery crown from a small pillow a child had carried to his side. Then he placed the crown on her head and helped her up. The crowd applauded. The band struck up a waltz tune as the chief led Lillian to the dance floor. They danced alone for a minute, then other girls and their fathers began to join them. The balcony's lights came on.

"Now the party will really start," Kyffin said. "I guess the time has come for me to rescue my fiancée." He shook my hand. "I've enjoyed our talk."

"Likewise. See you around."

He hesitated a moment, still pressing my hand. "Let me buy you a drink sometime when ceremonial duties don't press so heavily."

I'm not much of a drinker, but I didn't mind his company. "I'd like that."

He made his way toward the lift. "I'll be in touch. Enjoy the party."

As Kyffin entered the lift, a proper dance tune filled the air. A swirl of beaus picked off the young ladies from their fathers. After a few minutes, I noticed, then lost track of, Kyffin's sandy blond head in the crowd. I returned my attention to the chief and Lillian. I was glad to see him back up on the dais where he belonged and Lillian in the arms of a tall, solid young man—none other than my new friend Kyffin. That pleasant conversation would've been a bit more awkward if he'd known about my carnal knowledge of his intended, and I made a note to avoid drinks with him, after all. A further acquaintance would lead to nothing good. Sometimes I wish I'd stuck to that plan, but I'm nothing if not morally weak.

With a sudden wish to be someplace, anyplace, else, I paced the balcony. The Judge caught my eye, motioning me to come to him. Just as I exited the stairwell, I ran into Violet Humphrey. Literally. She was plowing through the partiers toward the promenade, a sort of lounge that opens onto a balcony that overlooks the city.

"Sorry, Violet." I caught her as she stumbled against me. "I mean, Mrs. Humphrey. I didn't see you coming through."

Her face was tight, like something big was going on inside, but in her eyes, that something was ready to tear its way out. "Mr. Joye?"

"Sean. I'm with the Judge. He couldn't settle for just his missus to come along."

She nodded and shrugged. I guided Violet into the mostly deserted lounge and found us a settee in a corner. With her blonde hair pulled up with dozens of sparkly picks and a shimmering purple gown cut low and off the shoulders, she was right regal herself.

"Are you alright, Mrs. Humphrey?" Maybe this was a bigger deal than it appeared to an outsider like me.

She sat, her back to the ballroom, facing the French doors that opened onto the balcony. City lights twinkled in at us through the glass. "Of course, just a bit overcome. Please call me Violet."

"Well, Violet, Lillian looks very pretty," I said. "Big honor, winning the—" Was the selection a contest? Probably a contest of bank accounts. "—queenship."

She snorted. "Do you have a drink on you?" Her expression was as frank and forceful as any Twentieth Century Girl I'd ever met.

"Normally the Judge stashes his flask on me, but it didn't work out so well in this monkey suit. He figured there'd be booze enough here, anyway. Shall I get you some punch?"

Violet leaned back on the chaise lounge. "No. Just stay with me for a minute. It's helpful not to be alone."

Preventing her from being alone was no problem. I was reasonably certain whenever I made my way to the Judge, I'd find him deep in conversation and I'd be forced to wait half an hour to learn whatever task for me he'd dreamed up.

"Do you ever question your decisions?" Violet closed her eyes and rubbed her temples. "Wonder if you're doing the right thing?"

"Sure look. All the time," I said. "Well, I used to. Now, I'm pretty certain I'm always wrong."

She nodded. "Nothing is clear, is it? For someone to win, others must suffer."

"That's usually the way it works. But the losers, they get by somehow. Maybe their turn will come later." That sounded a bit wise. I surprise even myself sometimes.

Violet seemed to think so too. "Thank you," she said. "Running into you was just what I needed." She stood and gathered her bag and her fan.

"Happy to be of service, ma'am. Anytime at all."

She reached over and straightened the carnation in my buttonhole. "I'll remember that."

*   *   *

All the Judge needed was for me to drive Mrs. Judge home because he'd settled in for a night of jawboning with his tablemates. It might be a swank crowd, but most were men of finance, business, or politics, and the Judge had a lot of insight they weren't too stupid to seek out. For his part, he was testing the waters for a mayoral run in 1925. The Arwalds had opened the door by inviting His Honor to the party. A civic-minded fella had even offered him a ride home in his limo.

The Judge's lady, a formidable woman of about forty-five, said her goodbyes. She watched the dancers as we headed toward the cloakroom. They'd brought in Bix Beiderbecke and the Wolverines from Iowa. A dozen young couples cut the rug while Mrs. Judge watched. Her hips swayed, just a tad, in time to the band.

"Are you thinking you'd like a turn about the dance floor before you call it a night?" I asked.

She blushed, then said, "He brings me to these things, then spends the evening with the men."

I didn't need to get betwixt the Judge and his lady, so I had no comment on that observation. "Well, you're here. The best party of the year, the music's grand, and I'm asking you for a dance. Whadda ya say?"

Mrs. Judge laughed, called me a silly young man, but let me lead her to the floor. The band had just struck up the Charleston, the most popular dance that season, but we skipped the new-fangled shenanigans and stuck to a quick foxtrot. For her size, Mrs. Judge was light on her feet and plenty graceful. "Dolan and I used to win dance contests, twenty years ago," she said.

We danced close to Lillian and Kyffin a few times. They were an odd sort of pair. Both were good-looking, yet they didn't at all seem like a couple. And Lillian worried me. Her eyes were hollow, dead, and not a hint of recognition flickered. *What'd they done to her to get her to hop through the hoops this evening?* Kyffin seemed concerned, too. He kept searching her face for something. Occasionally, he'd bend down to whisper in her ear. She gave no indication that she even heard him.

We danced through the Wolverines' version of "Tom Cat Blues," a Jellyroll Morton tune played more or less constantly in all your finer speakeasies that winter. By then Mrs. Judge was a little winded and sent me for her coat, ready to go home. As I stood in line at the coat-check room, a waiter with a small tray approached. He stopped at a respectful distance and offered the tray. "Sir." Centered on it was a cream-colored calling card, engraved in fancy letters, *Doctor Antoine De Noailles*. The right upper corner was bent and *p.r.* was written in a spidery scrawl after the engraved name. Lillian's grandfather. My first thought was that he'd heard me and Lillian in his examination room on Wednesday night. From there my mind leaped to things the Judge had told me about young Antoine De Noailles. How he'd returned home from the American Civil War with a short temper and a duelist's reputation. Losing a war can do that to a man. Winning one, too, for that matter.

I finished my business with the coat-check girl while noting the closest exit and then picked up the card. "Where is he?"

The waiter tried to hide a smirk as he told me, "The De Noailles-Arwald family is at the head table, sir."

"Of course they are."

Mrs. Judge stood near the lifts. She listened to the orchestra, but some of that foot tapping was impatience rather than appreciation.

"Well, I'm with somebody, so tell him to hang on."

The waiter's face froze for a second. "Very good, sir." He turned to go.

I made my way to Mrs. Judge and laid out the situation. "So, I'm for taking you home." I didn't need her to witness the unpleasantness that was about to happen. "I can come back here within the hour."

"Antoine De Noailles?" She linked her arm with mine and pulled me, as nonchalantly as she could manage, toward the head table. "Are you an idiot? Dolan would *not* want you to keep him waiting."

Mrs. Judge and I approached the table where Dr. De Noailles sat alone, watching the dancers with a blank stare. I didn't see any weapons, but there could be a sword in the cane.

"Dr. De Noailles?" Mrs. Judge said. "I'm Pauline Dolan. We met at the history museum when you were so kind as to give a lecture to our ladies' club on the ancient Mississippian mounds."

The doctor turned at the sound of her voice, his face still blank and his eyes somewhere far away. He took a moment to focus on her and then replied, "Ah, yes. I remember the event. And you, Mrs. Dolan. Your husband is one of the circuit court judges, no?" He took her hand and brushed the back with a kiss. "Forgive an old man for not standing. The cold and damp weather has my hip at a disadvantage. Please sit down, the two of you."

Maybe he wouldn't want to discuss grievances in front of Mrs. Judge, her presence perhaps a stroke of luck. I pulled out a chair for her to Dr. De Noailles's left and then sat down myself on his right.

"Mr. Joye," he said as he took my hand. "Thank you again; we're in your debt."

Since I was expecting a challenge to a duel or something, I was puzzled until I realized he was talking about getting Lillian to show up at the party. I probably go to the cinema too much. "It was nothing." I motioned to the dance floor. "She looks swell, doesn't she?"

"Yes, of course," he said, watching the dancers. "A little wan, perhaps. She doesn't take care of her health. But that's an old grandfather's overprotectiveness." He turned to me again, "As I say, we're in your debt." Any vague rheuminess in his eyes vanished, and he gave me a look as sharp as a man of twenty. "And I don't like that. What can I give you?"

"I'm well paid for my work, sir. If you owe anyone, it's the Judge."

"Yes, of course we owe Judge Dolan. But you too. Come around and see me tomorrow."

"Glad to." The old gent seemed friendly enough after all.

He raised his voice, so we both could hear him. "I found the presentation quite inappropriate, not that anyone pays attention to what I think." He then turned to Mrs. Judge, "You're a scholar. Did you find it appropriate, ma'am?"

She hemmed and hawed a bit.

To distract him, I threw in my two cents. "It seemed like a stage thing. Like Wild West films. Or in a penny novel." I'd read one or two, myself. Just to pass the time.

Dr. De Noailles nodded. "An entertainment—" He looked around with barely concealed disgust. "For the sort of people that are here. And it was successful?"

"Oh, I'm sure they were all entertained."

"My great-grandmother practically raised me. She was an Osage. More properly—Wah-zha-zhi—People of the Middle Waters. And of the Isolated Earth Division, to boot. The keepers of the rituals. She became the 'country wife,' as the expression was, to the first De Noailles in America—Vicomte Guy-Luc De Noailles. Escaped the French Revolution but left his lady behind him. He had no legitimate heir. And so—" the doctor grinned, "here I am. But my son-in-law prefers I don't tell this story." He took a sip from the teacup before him. "Thus, I tell it as often as I can." He turned back to Mrs. Judge. "But pardon me, my dear. I humbly beg your forgiveness if I shock you with indelicate matters. I'm a forgetful old man."

She smiled, "No offense taken. And your family started the lodge here, to honor your heritage?"

He thought on that a bit. "In a way. Much cultural conflation, downright adulteration, has occurred over the years. I often wonder what the ancestors would have thought of the ersatz Piasa Lodge. 'Piasa' isn't even a real word."

"You're doing your best to keep some sort of memory alive," Mrs. Judge said. "It's not easy. I believe *The Delineator* has just published an article on the subject."

"I don't generally read that journal, but with your recommendation, I'll make it a point." Still seated, the doctor bowed to her and kissed her hand again. "Thank you for attending the ball. My best to your husband." He turned to an attendant, who'd appeared at his side via some secret signal I'd missed, for assistance to stand. "And now I believe I'll take my leave. The night belongs to the young people."

I stood, helped him get underway, and then escorted Mrs. Judge to the lift.

She wrapped her mink stole around her shoulders and took my arm. "Did you speak to your brother about Maud going to school?" We'd been through this before. She continued to harangue me as we rode down to the lobby and waited for the Packard to be brought around to the Eleventh Street exit. "She's intelligent and sensible. She'd do well. And it's so important for her future."

"Her folks feel they know what's best for her." Without discussing private family business, there was little explanation I could give. "They have definite ideas." Without Maud at home, the entire enterprise would probably go down the pipes. She took care of the little boys and the baby and helped with the pub while the adults were all out scrapping for wages to keep the rent paid and the coal scuttle full. But my brother would certainly kill me if I breathed a word of his problems to my employer's wife.

Mrs. Judge went on in that vein all the way home. "And friends. She'd make friends that would be helpful in the future. It would be no expense. I'd pay all the tuition and books. Everything she might need."

I said "Mmm," and "Uh-hum" a lot and thought about Lillian and Kyffin. And what Grandfather Antoine might be up to.

The Judge had left our Irish neighborhood in Dogtown for the Compton Heights district a few years back. His new house of red brick and green tile roofers was one of the smallest dwellings among Hawthorne Street's swank mansions, but the address was still on Hawthorne and that's what mattered.

After I walked her into the house, she had me wait. "I have the new *Delineator* for Maud," she called over her shoulder as she stepped across the hall into her morning room. "'The Vox de Mulieribus' column is excellent if I do say so myself. A piece on preserving cultural heritage. Apropos of our discussion tonight with Dr. De Noailles."

"Huh?" I said.

"Promise me you'll speak to your brother about Maud."

I told her what would make her happy, parked their Packard in the garage, and collected the Model T to head home.

*   *   *

I was a bit too wound up to sleep right away after I dropped off Mrs. Judge. I let myself into my brother's place through the kitchen, stopped to make a cuppa, and brought it into the bar. The pub wasn't closed yet, with only a few stragglers still hanging about the place. They proceeded to heckle me and my fine clothes. "Ain't you the high-and-mighty?" "What's with the getup?" "Don't be getting notions now."

"Welcome, your fucking lordship, to my humble abode." Padraig tugged his forelock and bowed.

My only ally in the room was the kid sweeping the floor, Matthew Rouse. "You look very nice, Mr. Sean," he said. Matthew came in every afternoon after school to peel potatoes, wash dishes, and generally do anything about the place that needed doing. And to moon about after my niece. I needed to keep an eye on him.

"Ah, here's a fellow who appreciates the finer things in life. Sláinte." I toasted Matthew with my teacup. "To the swells."

About that time an elderly gent entered through the front door, dressed against the cold in a barn coat, muffler, and plaid hunting cap, flaps dangling over his ears. He looked about as shook as I've ever seen a man.

"We close at one," Padraig said, without looking up from polishing the bar. "You'll have to make it fucking quick." For whatever Padraig lacked in creative cursing, he made up for in loyalty to his favorite swearword.

The man looked a bit taken aback at the greeting. "Excuse me." He took off his cap and loosened his coat. "Y'all know a Mr. Sean Joye? Does he live here?"

At that, Padraig shot me a sideways glare.

I could only shrug. I'd never seen the man before in my life.

"Ain't you the butcher from down on Manchester?" asked one of the more perceptive barflies.

The old man looked pleased. "Ike Dalton," he said, shaking hands all around. "Dalton and Sons, Fine Meats and Cheeses. My boys run the shop now." I recognized his drawl from my business trips to Southern Illinois. A special sort of twang, similar yet distinct from the Ozark accent of Missouri's backwoodsmen. A bit more guttural, each phrase coughed up from deeper in the throat. Probably the effects of the coal dust.

"I'm Sean Joye," I admitted. "Let's sit over there," I said, pointing to a table at the far end of the room. "You sure you don't want something to drink? Hot coffee?"

"Much obliged, but no. I'm a mite rushed." He followed me to the table, and we sat across from each other. Ike Dalton was old but had a strong, upright stride and a full head of white hair. "I come about my neighbor—" He paused. "My friend. My lady friend, Charity MacSweeney."

Widow MacSweeney had a beau. That was hard to figure. Every pot has a lid, I guess.

"What about her?" As if I didn't know.

"She's mighty upset about her work. The building where she works."

"I know. She thinks it's haunted."

He nodded. "My oldest boy—the one who went over there, to the war—he says she's a mite 'tached, pure and simple. But I don't know." Mr. Dalton looked at me, defiance in his eyes. "Could be haunts. No need to get all highfalutin." Under his breath, he muttered, "Just 'cause ya been to Parisfrance."

"Why're you here at one o'clock in the morning?"

"Charity worked this evening, but ain't home yet. And when she left for the courts this afternoon, she was powerful riled up."

"There was a big party tonight. She's probably cleaning up from that."

"No." He shook his head and loosened his muffler. "She was just doing the offices, as usual. The party folks got their own crew. Something has happened. Something bad."

"But what am I supposed to do about it?"

"She said you'd understand. That you could help."

"What the fuck's in it for him?" Padraig was standing right at my shoulder. I hadn't heard him approach. People could sneak up on me right and left it seemed. I slipped more into American complacency every day.

"I ain't got no money." Then Mr. Dalton's face lit up. "Soon we'll slaughter the spring lambs back at the farm. We got the best meat in the city. Perhaps a nice leg of lamb?"

"I got a fucking big family," said Padraig. "Make it three."

"One's enough. It will be of a good weight. So tender. I'll throw in some mint jelly my daughter-in-law makes."

They talked over my head as if I weren't even there, which disturbed me almost as much as these crazy old people demanding that I hunt ghosts for them. "Hey, wait a fecking minute," I said.

"One still won't be enough. Two?"

"Done. If he goes right now. I'm afraid she's in trouble."

*   *   *

Out-maneuvered, I saw Mr. Dalton to the door, changed clothes, and headed over to the Civil Courts Building. Given the late hour, I brought my Webley revolver. Heavy and awkward, at least it looked intimidating. I was much more concerned about encountering random drunk gangsters than ghosts. The Rats, the Irish gang that had run things for thirty years, and the Greens, the upstart Italians, had been tearing it up pretty good of late.

Two o'clock found me at Market and Twelfth watching street sweepers clean up parade debris. Music and laughter from post-parade parties spilled out into the night from the saloons and flophouses across from the courthouse on Chestnut. I parked on Eleventh Street—fewer prying eyes could see that side of the building.

The west wind had shoved the smog over the river into Illinois during the course of the evening. The night was clear and I could admire the courthouse in the moonlight. With twelve levels of state courts and offices, it was by far the tallest building in the city.

A Greek-style temple crowned the business floors of the courthouse and housed the law library. And if a Greek temple perched hundreds of feet in the air weren't enough to show those rubes in Chicago, atop the temple was a stepped pyramid—a ziggurat, and atop the ziggurat were two huge winged lions with ladies' faces.

These beasts were supposed to be something called a griffin, and they guarded our east and west flanks. Attacks from the north and south, well, I guess we'd be on our own.

The plaza out front was deserted and the lobby locked up tight. Lights shone through upper floor windows. I counted the rows of windows to eleven. Maybe the party was still going on. *But the party was on the twelfth floor, wasn't it?*

Sticking to the shadows, I walked around to the Chestnut Street side and picked the employee entrance door. I switched on my electric torch, walked down the short flight of steps, and headed to the service hallway. In the distance, I could hear Mrs. Mac's curses. Telling off a haunt, by the sound of it. I followed her voice to the timeclock room and opened the door.

She talked to the far wall. "Stay back, you." Then she took a slug from her flask. "You aren't wanted here."

"Mrs. MacSweeney," I said from the doorway. "A good evening to you."

She jumped a foot in the air and whirled around, brandishing a mop. "Ack—'tis you." She lowered her weapon.

"I take it they're troublesome tonight?" I indicated the wall she'd addressed.

"Well, I heard doors open and close, voices upstairs, but echo-ish."

"A fancy party was going on here tonight."

"Them folks is long gone," she said. "I think I caught sight of the queen once. I thought to come down here to get some peace, but I heard footsteps. And moans and groans, clanking chains."

"A queen?" I came into the room and turned off my torch. "Like with a crown?"

Mrs. Mac hit me with the mop she still clutched. "Eejit. These haunts be Indians, most of 'em, anyway. I say 'queen' because she looks to be in charge. She's dressed all fancy. The others do what she wants."

I'd seen enough American films to know "queen" wasn't the right word. "Shouldn't you call her 'chieftess'?"

"I ain't calling her nothing. If 'chieftess' gets rid of her, then you go right ahead and say that."

"Shall I look through the building with you?" I hoped to find a logical explanation for her haunts and be done with it. Despite her high opinion of me, I had no idea how to get rid of ghosts.

Mrs. Mac and I took the freight lift to the thirteenth floor. "How many are there?" I asked.

"I've never seen more than three or four at once. The queen just started coming 'round. Now it's a wild rummle every night."

We started our search in the library, the uppermost level of the building, apart from the roof. All the doors—offices, reading room, the judges' lounge—were locked. I thought I heard ragtime music, but so faint, I couldn't tell the direction. "Do you hear that?"

"Hear what?" Mrs. Mac said as she threw open a door to reveal an assortment of old magazines, a Christmas wreath, and a couple of broken umbrellas. "Stick to your job, boy."

"Why would Native Americans haunt this building, anyway? It's brand new." As soon as the words left my mouth, I knew the answer. "People tore down their mound to build this place." It was a plot of a book I'd read.

She shrugged. "They should just move along, then."

We took the lift up one level to the library mezzanine and paused in the hall for a moment as our eyes adjusted to the dark. The music was fainter here. It must be coming from the speaks across the street. Suddenly I felt Mrs. Mac grab my arm and pull me back flat against the wall.

"What's that?" she hissed in my ear.

I followed the direction of her gaze past shelves of law books to one of the floor-to-ceiling windows. A figure was silhouetted against the moonlight.

I motioned for Mrs. Mac to stay. I drew the Webley from my shoulder rig and moved toward it as silently as I could, using the shelves as concealment. The figure was shorter than me and seemed pretty damn solid. It held a light, which twinkled and picked its way around the room. The light found the old lady and she screamed just as I tackled my quarry. The person—a flesh-and-blood person, no haunt at all—twisted away with a ripping sound while swinging the electric torch at me. The torch connected solidly to my left temple, leaving me with a headache and a handful of white gauzy fabric as the figure ran down the hall.

Mrs. Mac attacked with a whoop, "Got you now, demon!"

I skidded across the polished marble floor to rescue them from each other. Pulling the combatants apart, I recognized our ghost: Miss Lillian Arwald. "What're you doing here?" I said.

Before she could answer, Mrs. Mac grabbed my elbow and nudged me to look down a corridor to our right. "See? Right there."

I beamed the torchlight among the shelves and saw nothing. But cold air poured down the passage toward us and the air smelled of a lightning storm.

"It's the queen."

A chill hit me right between the shoulder blades. And then I saw her. About fifty feet away stood a woman. She looked solid. Tall, regal, in the prime of life, and with an air of power about her—real authority, more like a priest than a boss. She was dressed in a skirt and a feathered cape, a bit like the outfit I'd seen on "Chief Ouatoga" at the party earlier in the evening. Her breasts were covered by thick layers of seashell necklaces. Her long hair hung down her back and she wore a cap decorated with dangling feathers.

The faint music I'd chalked up to the speakeasies across the street suddenly grew louder. And I heard voices and very human laughter. Whatever the source, she looked pretty angry about it. Then her eyes met mine. She seemed surprised that I could see her, and then angry at me, too.

I raised my arms in surrender. "Whatever mischief's going on, it ain't got nothing to do with us."

Just as I turned my head to ask Mrs. Mac if she'd ever tried to talk to the priestess, the haunt let loose with a stone hatchet. It spun through the air and split open a book on the shelf just behind me.

"Go, go, go," I said, shooing the two women around the corner toward the lift.

"What's with you, Copper?" Lillian said. "What are you running from?"

Just my luck, the lift car was gone. A glance over my shoulder told me the priestess was still hunting us. "Come on." I pulled them to the stairwell and down the steps. Mrs. Mac didn't have to be told twice, but Lillian protested the entire time. We didn't stop running until we were outside. Huddled on the loading dock, Lillian and I leaned on each other and panted.

"They've never attacked me before," Mrs. Mac said. "What a great lummox you are. I believe you've made things worse, not better. Why'd you even come here?" She swigged her hip flask.

Lillian took the flask from her. "I don't mind if I do." She drank a nip and offered it to me.

I shook my head. "You were about to tell me why you're here."

"I—I don't remember." Her blank stare gave way to panic. "I don't know. I think I was dancing, then it's fuzzy, and—" A tear trickled down her cheek.

"Ye brute. Now look what you've done," Mrs. Mac said. "Made the lass cry."

I gave up. "Let's take a break and get some coffee." I wrapped Lillian in my coat and bundled her into the car.

A few minutes later in an all-night diner around the corner, Mrs. Mac sipped some milky tea and fumed. Lillian poured Mrs. Mac's gin and a great deal of sugar in a cup of coffee while we waited for the slinger I insisted she eat.

"So, tonight was different," I said to Mrs. Mac. "I was there. Lillian was there. But what else?"

She slurped and put the cup down. "The queen usually prowls around the basement. Don't even act like she sees me."

Lillian picked at her food at first, then seemed to realize she was hungry and dug in.

"Someone else was there," I said. "Playing that music. Maybe cleaning up after the party. The priestess could've been mad at them. And she took it that we were part of that crew." I turned to Lillian. "Remember anything yet? Were you looking for someone?"

She swallowed a bite of eggs and chili. "Not really." She stopped eating and looked ready to cry again.

Mrs. Mac's gnarled hands reached across the table and took mine. "*Now* you believe me."

"Sure how can I not? A ghost priestess damned near smashed my skull in."

I drove Mrs. Mac to her house and left her under the worried care of Mr. Dalton, and then started for Dr. De Noailles's Lafayette Square home.

"Tonight, I'll go to father's place, I think," Lillian said. She'd dozed a bit, her head resting on my shoulder.

We paused at Washington Terrace's gate while the attendant let us in. A car had just entered the street ahead of us. I watched its red tail lights disappear as it turned into an alley about halfway down the block. Another late-night partygoer, I supposed.

I parked the Model T near the front door, which opened as soon as I stopped the car. When I started to get out, Lillian took my hand. "Don't bother. I can manage." She planted a kiss on my cheek and was gone. I sat there a minute and smoked, looking east toward the city. It was almost dawn. Something felt off. A ghost-infested courts building should have been bothering me. Or Lillian's strange behavior and the Arwald family drama. But no. I thought on Kyffin Bernard. What a jam he was getting himself into with Lillian. What a waste.

I made my way home under hazy gray skies. Birds chirped and splashed in oily puddles as I crept up the stairs to our flat above the pub. Maud slept the honest sleep of the exhausted on the small settee in the main room. I tiptoed around my cot in the nursery, so as to not wake my young nephews, and collected fresh clothes and soap. I took a bird bath under the cold water tap in the pub's jacks, shaved, and changed. It was too late, or too early, to sleep.

The Angelus bells rang at six and I remembered it was a holy day. Candlemas, February 2. And I'd somehow missed St. Brigid's Day with all my swank partying. My long-gone little sister's name day.

I slipped into the back of St. James the Greater Church just as the first mass of the day started. I didn't take communion, of course, but queued up for the blessing.

"Let there be no darkness in the house of your soul," the priest said as he lit a candle and handed it to me.

"Amen."

Chapter Four

Overdrawn Account

The Judge had some chores for me that Saturday morning, which he dismissed when he found out Antoine De Noailles had invited me to pay a call. Eleven o'clock found me on the doorstep of the doctor's Lafayette Square townhouse.

You might wonder why I even bothered with the gruff old man. Although his interest in me didn't hurt my standing with the Judge at all, I had my doubts he still had the juice to help the Judge's political career. Someone like that Kyffin Bernard might be more useful in that regard. The thing is, I had my reasons to visit Antoine De Noailles. No one gets out of Ireland without a head full of fairytales. Some, like me, had heard, seen, or even met the Good People. It's not an experience I wanted to repeat, yet for close to a year I'd been tripping over the uncanny in America. I needed to know more about the spirits of the place. Dr. De Noailles seemed like a person that maybe could help with that.

Annie, the maid, practically a child about Maud's age, left me to cool my heels in the foyer for twenty minutes while she disappeared into the depth of the house. Eventually, she returned to put me in the parlor, where I awaited Dr. De Noailles for another twenty minutes. A pair of oil paintings I hadn't even noticed the previous evening ruled the room. One was a young woman I presumed to be Osage, her hair in neat plaits, the middle part painted red. Her dress seemed to be woven of colorful ribbons. She turned her head to the left, as if to look at the other portrait, a fine-featured, aristocratic man, dressed up like Daniel Boone or some such person. He turned toward her, his gaze that of an adoring spaniel. Crowded below and around the portraits were shelves full to overflowing with mice-chewed books, arrowhead cases, stone figures, and pottery. Curio cabinets crammed with beaded moccasins, small mounted animals, and birds' nests crowded the room's back corners. A layer of dust covered everything, although here and there a clean spot indicated an artifact must have been moved or some trash thrown away. A pottery bowl made in the shape of an animal sat on the mantel: Snakish body, antlers, and a feline face with sharp teeth in a grimacing mouth. Then I heard someone with a limp and the click-clack of canes walking toward the parlor.

"Mr. Joye," Dr. De Noailles said from the doorway. "Good of you to come."

"Thank you for inviting me, sir." I started to help him to a chair, but he waved me toward a seat as he took his own.

"I can manage. Sit, sit. Did anyone offer you anything?" He pulled a tapestry bell pull. "Why are you sitting here in the dark?"

"It seems bright enough."

Annie entered the room and curtsied.

"My dear, we need tea. And perhaps some of those lemon cakes. And open the drapes." They were already open, but she fussed with them before she bobbed off for the tea.

The previous night Dr. De Noailles eyes held sad, resigned pain. Today, I guessed he was back on his medicine. His pupils shone, tiny points of piercing energy.

"You like my She'-ki?" he asked as he pointed to the object on the mantel.

"I took it for a bowl."

He sighed. "Yes, it is a bowl, a Mississippian artifact rescued from grave robbers. I speak of the image. She'-ki is the Great Snake, ruler of the world under the water as well as the night sky. He guards the Milky Way, the path to the afterlife. And is also Chief of all the Underwater Spirits. Such spirits are often incised or painted on rock in deep caves or above pools and streams. The Underwater Spirit of this area is called 'Piasa' by the ignorant locals."

About then Annie showed up with the tea and biscuits, serving them with shaking hands. The doctor didn't seem to notice her terror or perhaps didn't care. I took the cup she offered me.

"Thanks."

She curtsied and picked up the cream pitcher. "Milk?"

"Yes, please." She giggled and poured, and I took a sip as she fled the room. "Don't look much like the Piasa in the parade yesterday."

He scooted to the edge of his seat and leaned forward to say, "Yet obviously referencing an Underwater Spirit, who has many different names—different persona, even—depending on the tribal origin of the lore."

"Persona?"

His brow wrinkled, deep in thought. "In some cultures, the Underwater Spirits, although capricious, can be a friend to man. In others, a more malevolent narrative dominates."

"An evil spirit?"

Dr. De Noailles almost fell out of his chair in his eagerness to lecture me. "Not in your Christian sense. Always a powerful Other-Than-Human Person, due reverence and respect." He waved his cane about to emphasize the point. I was glad to be out of range.

"The concept of Underwater Spirit is ubiquitous among tribes of Eastern America," he said. "But some explain the tragedy of accidental drownings as the work of such a spirit. The young and weak were taken away, their bodies found later, ears, eyes, nose, and mouth caked with mud."

"So why did they paint the Underwater Spirit on the Mississippi River bluffs?"

He slurped tea. "I suspect it was a warning sign. The turbulence at the confluence is frightful, as the Illinois River meets the Mississippi. Obviously, the site of a portal to the underwater realm. While the Underwater Spirits' chief, She'-ki, is a highly revered symbol of life, danger clings to the pantheon, in some cultures, anyway. The image would caution travelers to steer clear and make appropriate offerings." The doctor's eyes twinkled as if he were about to tell me a juicy bit of gossip, and he beckoned me closer. "I hypothesize the Mississippian culture is a primary source of the beliefs."

"You don't say," I said and went to the mantel to look at the bowl again. It wasn't as fancy as the Piasa I'd seen on the parade float yesterday but seemed more real somehow.

"You've been most patient, Mr. Joye. I hope I'm not boring you."

"Not at all, sir. I like to know what's behind things."

"Just as I thought. Now—" he thumped his cane on the floor, "as we discussed, I pay my debts."

"If you could answer some questions, I'd call it square."

"Such as?"

"Do you know anything about—" I drank my tea. "Ghosts?" In for a penny, in for a pound, I blathered on. "The city tore up an old burial mound to build the Civil Courts Building. A stone ax from the site sits on my boss's desk, as we speak. Would that disturb the rest of those dead and buried?"

"Disgusting, irreverent practice," he said, making a face. "Come here, boy. Bring your chair close." Dr. De Noailles shivered. "And the fire needs stoking. Close those drapes." He had a lifetime of ordering servants around, and I had a lifetime of being so ordered. I hopped to it without even a second thought.

At last, we were settled, the touch of manic in his eyes having clouded over. "'Ghosts from a looted Indian burial mound sounds like a tall tale to me." His voice seemed to come from far away. "When I was a child, I heard ghost stories, of course, when I visited the Osage settlement in Kansas."

Maybe shipping city kids to the country cousins is a universal practice. "As did I, at my granny's in County Antrim."

"The Osage, and presumably the Mississippians, believe the soul after death moves along to a place of spirits. 'Ghost stories' are generally about the recently dead who haven't started their afterlife journey for some narratively interesting reason."

"And if I told you haunts in the Civil Courts Building, dress and armed like Mississippians, have attacked people?"

"Assuming those people were reliable witnesses, I'd say something is very wrong. Thousand year-old-ancestor spirits?" Dr. De Noailles shook his head. "Nothing in the traditions or lore describes a passage back to our world."

I pressed the case a bit harder, saying, "They wouldn't want to punish the living?"

"The penalty for such a crime comes from within the culprit himself. To take on such a dreadful taboo—"

A voice from the doorway interrupted him. "I'm home, Grandfather." Lillian looked pale, tired, and as pretty as I'd ever seen her. She crossed the room and kissed his cheek, barely giving me a glance.

I stood. "Good day, Miss Arwald."

"Hey, Copper," she said, as she perched on a footstool and rested her head on the doctor's knee.

It seemed a good moment to leave, though, in truth, I dearly wanted to sit with her by the fire for a bit.

*   *   *

I tried of course to see Lillian again. We'd gone from strangers to lovers in the course of a day. I felt like a heel, but try as I might, I couldn't figure the exact point I'd stepped out of line. I eventually gave up on the examination of conscience and decided to court her properly. Better late than never. She was engaged to be married and by all rights would turn me down, but I had to at least give it a try.

She was a swank lady, used to swank entertainments. After many conversations with Mrs. Judge, I finally settled on an evening of theater and a high-class supper club. Problem was, I didn't have nearly the scratch for that. My only option for quick cash was a one-time, no-strings-attached side job for Dint Colbeck, who ran the Eagan's Rats gang. He wouldn't for much longer, but he did at that moment, anyway. I guess it was a fortnight after the debutante ball, the middle of February, before I rang up Dr. De Noailles's house to ask Lillian to go out on the town with me.

The Irish child-maid, Annie, answered the phone. "Ah, Mr. Joye. Sure look. Ain't she went and gone traveling? 'Tis been a week or more now."

"Is Dr. De Noailles there?"

"So sorry, sir, but we's packing up to go to the Alton house for a bit. The doctor's directing the move. Mr. Arwald's car is here and the chauffeur's taking out the bags now. Is there a message you'd be leaving?"

"No. No message."

So, winter gave way to spring, then summer, then fall. I went on with my life and work. Mrs. Mac's ghosts went quiet and she sobered up. I saw quite a bit of Kyffin Bernard, but we didn't talk about the Arwald sisters all that much.

All that changed the morning Violet showed up on my doorstep.

Chapter Five

———⚬⚬⚬⚬———

Contingent Liability

"It's my sister, Mr. Joye." Violet was in a bad way. "I've just come from the hospital." It was barely six o'clock, Sunday morning, September 28.

I'd only taken the time to put on some trousers before I answered her pounding on the pub door. I pulled the braces up over my undershirt. "Come in, come in."

She proceeded me into the bar's empty public room. I seated her at the nearest table. "What happened?"

"Lillian's in—" She held herself very still as if she'd fall apart with the smallest movement. "I guess you'd call it a coma."

"What?" I reached out to take her hand, but that seemed mighty forward. "You need a drink." Hell, I needed a belt myself. I nipped upstairs for the poteen jug and poured us each a stiff one. Violet downed the drink in one gulp. Then she had another. The shell-shocked look left her eyes only to be replaced by a few tears. "Lillian's been bleeding, extensively. And she has a raging infection. They expect her to die. She was—with child, but is no longer."

"She didn't tell you she was in the family way?"

"My sister's been abroad. I've had only a few letters over the summer. Lillian isn't supposed to be home for another month." She poured herself a third drink. "I'm as surprised as anyone that she's in town."

"I'm sorry for your troubles."

"It's obvious to me she's had a back-alley abortion." Violet took my hand and looked me square in the eyes. "Find this monster for me."

Well, that was a slimy pit, and I didn't want to get in it. "Hospital said that?"

"Can you just accept a thing I tell you without an interrogation?"

"Sure you're knowing lady stuff—and your sister—better than me." I drank my whiskey.

"Will you help me?"

"A lot of blokes would do a better job at this kind of thing than me." That was a lie. Nine-tenths of my time in army intelligence was spent snooping around. "Like the police."

"Out of the question," Violet said.

I didn't see why. I'd bet money her father owned the local force. "There's lots of real private detectives out there, like Pinkerton's. Or Continental Ops."

"We trust your discretion."

Meaning, they thought they could buy me directly, bypassing the Judge. It felt like some sort of trap.

"I'm sorry. I wouldn't be of any help," I said, standing. "Can I take you back to the hospital?"

"No. My driver's outside." She whirled out the door. The only evidence of her visit was two dirty glasses and a sick feeling in my gut.

*   *   *

As the sun rose, I turned on the lights and went to the kitchen, trying to figure what to do. I still lived with my brother's clan in their tiny flat over the bar. Every time I made a move to find my own place, Maud would have a right hissy fit, and I'd drop the idea. That temper sure didn't come from our side of the family.

Given my early start to the day, I progressed from whiskey to tea to coffee and then to more coffee. By the time I parked the Model T near Union Station, I had energy to spare and jitters to walk off. Hoofing the few blocks to the Civil Courts Building seemed a good idea. I knew I'd find the Judge in his office with some task or other for me. It didn't matter that it was Sunday. He'd be sure to hit noon mass at the new cathedral, the better to glad-hand the populace. I suppose I felt guilty about not doing more for Lillian, but I didn't see what I could do that would help the situation one whit.

I strolled up Twelfth Street in the brown autumn haze. At least the factories weren't churning out new smoke on Sunday morning. The ugly bric-a-brac pile that is City Hall loomed across the street. I'd never felt like it approved of me, but it was particularly hostile that morning. A car horn tooted and a sleek yellow Stutz Bearcat, top down, pulled over just ahead of me. It was Kyffin Bernard.

"Need a ride?"

Kyffin had turned out to be an interesting sort of friend, fond of fast cars and faster airplanes. Embarrassed about my fling with Lillian, at first I tried to avoid him, but he was everywhere—the Judge's club, speakeasies, the courts building.

After about six weeks of cat-and-mouse, I finally accepted his invitation to drinks. Ash Wednesday, a good day to come clean. I figured I'd confess the hanky-panky with Lillian, he'd bop me in the jaw, and we'd be done.

Things didn't work out exactly as I'd planned. The quick drink turned into a long, gabby steak dinner—and me supposedly abstaining for the holy day. Not the worst of my sins, by far.

Kyffin found my late-night tryst with Lillian in the doctor's office funny, and it soon became clear the engagement was some sort of business arrangement. The longer we talked, the more I was convinced he was queer as a nine-bob note. Yet no one seemed to know and they wouldn't hear it from me. I'm quite used to holding other people's secrets as close as my own. After that, we often met for dinner, poker, or drinks. And he knew a few good spots out in the wilderness for fly fishing. I was drawn to Kyffin in ways I aimed to avoid. I knew right well the friendship was an occasion of sin for me. I'd promised both my confessor and, more importantly, myself that nothing unnatural was ever going to happen again.

Kyffin was obviously involved with his roommate—a real live-wire named Evan Blake, and I'm no homewrecker. Evan would join us for dinner sometimes. He sold real estate—a friendly, pick-up-the-check kind of guy, until he caught wise that I had no money for Florida property. Kyffin and I would start to talk about our wars and Evan would look bored and get quiet. Eventually, he just stopped coming to dinner.

Kyffin was in France since almost the beginning of the Great War, flying missions with Escadrille Americaine. It sounded a lot cleaner than my own grubby experience, but he assured me he could see the enemy's eyes from a plane's cockpit. Bits of skull didn't spatter him in the face, which sometimes happened to me, but I didn't hold that against him. I didn't hold much against him in those days. But it looked like he'd made important promises to two different people, so I kept my mixed bag of feelings to myself.

Kyffin's car was an eyeful. "New toy?" The Judge's Model T suited me just fine. I prefered to go unnoticed.

"New to me. Hop in."

I took my life in my hands and climbed in the roadster. "I need to check in with the Judge," I said as we pulled out into the light traffic. "Don't get me killed this morning."

"Duly noted." He laughed his good laugh and talked about his car, the third one he'd owned in the few months I'd known him. "It's the '21—the first DH model." He filled the air with chatter about engine heads and the pros and cons of moving the steering column to the left side. But he had to take a breath eventually.

"Violet came to see me about Lillian," I said.

"Yes."

"Want to talk about it?"

"Not really."

That much was obvious. "She'll be OK. They'll patch her right up."

"I was there a few hours ago. Lillian looked—" We were in a warehouse district, the streets vacant. Kyffin gunned the engine and sped down the block. "I've seen dead bodies before."

He drove north in silence, and I did the math in my head, cyphering my stake in the situation. It had been just the one time, so—not possible, right? We were approaching North Broadway, where I'm told the Big Mound once stood, torn down to make the road. "You drove past the Courts Building five minutes ago."

"Oh, yes. Should've mentioned I've been sent to fetch you. By Joseph Arwald."

I'd no idea what Lillian's father would want with me. "He's done raking you over the coals?"

Eyes still fixed on the road, Kyffin said, "I didn't make her pregnant."

I lit a cigarette, took a puff, and handed it to him.

He took a deep drag, stopped at a red light, and looked over at me. "You, on the other hand—"

We'd been pretty much driving around in circles and were now miles from the city center. "Old Man Arwald thinks I'm to blame?" Things could get dicey, right quick. "But Lillian must have got knocked-up over the summer, right?"

The light changed to green. He drove on, laughing, "I doubt Joseph knows the details of her romantic entanglements."

"But he didn't assume it was you?"

"Perhaps she's shared more with her father about our arrangement than I realized."

I'd always given his relationship with Lillian a wide berth. It was more like I forgot she existed when I was with Kyffin. "Arrangement?"

"A lavender marriage was Violet's idea. It will satisfy the meddlers. I'm the most eligible bachelor in town. Literally. The *Post* society page had a vote on it." He snubbed out the cigarette in the built-in ashtray. "Don't misunderstand. It's not that I don't like her enormously. We'll make a satisfactory life together."

I doubted that, very much. An oncoming delivery van honked. "Jesus, Mary, and Joseph, man." *I'm gonna die in a state of mortal sin.* I crossed myself as he maneuvered us out of danger with a flick of the steering wheel. "I was married once," I said. Although I never willingly talk about Norah, he was so blind to the biggest mistake of his life, I had to say something. "She betrayed me in so many ways."

"And?"

"Just because some woman tells you to marry her doesn't mean you have to."

Kyffin squeezed the wheel and sped up. "It's not at all like that." He squealed a right on Washington, back toward the city center. "It's my responsibility to take care of her, don't you think?"

"I guess I feel responsible too," I said. "Maybe that's just the way she affects men."

"But you won't find out who hurt her?" There was no blame in his voice. Just clearing up the facts.

The day was getting warm. I sighed and loosened my tie. And I stuck with the story I'd told Violet. "The Arwalds need a professional person for this job. The police or a private investigator, but someone who knows what he's doing. I said 'no', so they'll get an answer sooner rather than later."

Kyffin had made his way downtown while I talked. He nodded, pulled up to the curb on Chestnut Street in front of the Wainwright Building, and set the brake. "We must agree to always protect Lillian. No matter what."

"I can't argue with that."

The moment was solemn. Kyffin and I were promising each other something. That something was a serious matter, maybe impossible to accomplish, but an oath to try to do it, anyway.

We took the lift to the penthouse. The outer suite was crammed with desks, all empty. The shades were drawn, but the polished marble walls shone, even in the dim light. Kyffin pointed toward oak double doors set into the opposite wall, tall as cathedral portals and carved just as fancy. "Need me to hang around?"

I shrugged. "No. Thanks for the ride."

"Sorry for my role in whatever he's going to do to you," he called as I picked my way around the desks.

"You owe me one, mate," I said over my shoulder as I took a deep breath and knocked.

"Enter." I recognized Taylor Humphrey's voice.

"Shite," I said under my breath as I opened the door. I can't say Violet's husband was my favorite new friend in St. Louis.

Through a cigar smoke haze, I saw a sturdy middle-aged man hunkered behind a massive oak-and-marble desk before a floor-to-ceiling window that framed a view of the Civil Courts Building, police headquarters, the central library, and the city hall. I had seen him at the debutante ball last January. Lillian's father, Joseph Arwald.

It took me a moment to locate Humphrey in a dark corner of the room near a cold fireplace. True to his word, Humphrey had pursued our acquaintance over the summer, and, of course, the Judge encouraged him. In addition to teaching me Irish, he liked to hint around about the magic of ancient ruins and such. He said magic with a flourish—"Magick." And he wanted something from me, that much I could tell.

The fire silhouetted another figure, twisted and hunched. Dr. De Noailles. I'd visited him a few times right after the debutante party. A card inviting me to tea would arrive in the mail or by messenger at random intervals. I might see him twice in a week, then not again for months. I hadn't heard from him since July and had taken to reading through the obits with a bit of dread.

At first, he'd go on and on about lore, generally what he thought the old Mississippians believed. Once spring came, he left that off—because the spirits had awakened and might hear him. In the fine weather, he'd totter through his garden, pointing out medicinal plants and whatnot. It put me in mind of walks with my Granny McGuinn.

I removed my hat, acknowledged Humphrey, and approached the man at the desk. It was a long walk. A family of six could live comfortably in that office. Arwald took my hand like I was offering him a day-old fish and waved me into a chair.

"Coffee?" His voice was that of a man near the end of his rope. A fat Havana cigar burned untouched in an ashtray. The desk was spread with business papers he pretended to read.

"No, thanks," I said.

"I understand my daughter attempted to retain your services, Joye," Arwald said. "While your reluctance to accept a commission from a young woman is understandable, I assure you her request has my full backing. Her husband's as well." He looked up, at last, to show eyes hard as his marble fortress and inclined his head toward Humphrey and Dr. De Noailles. "Our entire family is in agreement."

"The morning is a bit brisk, ain't it, sir?" I called across the room to the doctor while I tried to think of something to say to Arwald. Dr. De Noailles had looked to be dozing but opened his eyes at my voice and waved one of his canes at me.

I turned back to face Joseph Arwald. I wondered if this was his usual deal-making attitude. His eyes held open contempt, like negotiating with the riffraff was a new experience. "I've a job, a good job, and snooping for people other than His Honor isn't generally part of it." I'd turned both Violet and Kyffin down about this job. I sure as hell wasn't going to let Old Man Arwald pressure me into it.

He glanced at Humphrey, who hadn't stirred an inch, then leaned back in his chair. "Perhaps Mrs. Humphrey wasn't clear. Simply trace Miss Arwald's activities last week. Find out where, who—" Arwald's eyes took on a kind of wild glint. He stood and menaced me from across the desk. "Names and addresses of anyone she visited or even spoke to. How and when did she get home? Who saw her? That's what I need. Now."

I'd swear he wanted to grab my lapels and give me a good beating. Frankly, I didn't expect that much spine from him and he went up a notch or two in my esteem. I wouldn't mind having a go, at another time, in another place.

Arwald got a grip on himself and sat back in the chair. "The Judge won't mind. Although I'd appreciate, and pay for, your discretion in that regard."

Humphrey rose from his seat and came over to the desk. "Joseph, I believe our friend merely requires sufficient motivation," he said, voice calm but desperate concern lurking behind his half-smile and bloodshot eyes. "Good of you to come, by the way. It's a difficult day. How can we help you discover the malfeasance behind poor Lillian's injuries?"

"Gents, it's not that I object to extra money," I told Arwald and Humphrey. "Or wouldn't do a favor for folks who would do me one down the road. Or that I don't care about Lillian and want her to have justice or whatever it is you're after. You must see I'm not the best person for this job. I don't have the experience, the connections, or the skills to do it well." Their request was cock-eyed; they must know that. I'd given them a reasonable answer.

"We disagree," Humphrey said as he grasped my arm. "Just name your price."

Arwald rifled through some papers on his desk. "And this property. At 1317 Tamm Avenue. Some sort of public house. I'd hate to report it to the Bureau of Prohibition."

Padraig took a pig-headed kind of pride in being a law-abiding future citizen, never mind that the native-born Americans ignored the Volstead Act every day of their lives. I shook off Humphrey and clenched my fists but stuck them in my coat pockets. "My brother ain't running no speak."

Humphrey stepped between me and Arwald. He shrugged, draped his arm across my shoulders, and led me toward the door.

About then Dr. De Noailles spoke, "I'll walk out with you, Mr. Joye, if you'd be so kind." I helped him to his feet and he steadied himself with his canes.

I put on my hat. "Good day, gentlemen."

Arwald glared. Humphrey smiled and said he'd be in touch. Dr. De Noailles and I crept the length of the room and out the door. The journey across the foyer of desks was painful for both of us—I needed to walk off my rage and he required several stops to sit and rest.

At last, we approached the lift and the operator snapped to attention to conduct us into the car. Dr. De Noailles gripped my arm as the man maneuvered the steel cage to the ground floor.

"I imagine you expect me to further urge you to take on this task for my family," he said as we meandered across the lobby.

"Sir—"

He held up his hand. "I don't know the right thing for you to do. I only ask you to go see her before you decide your role in our little drama."

We'd reached the curb, and I hailed a cab for him. "Can she even have visitors?" I asked as he climbed in the back seat.

Dr. De Noailles acted like he didn't hear me, although I'd learned his bad hearing came and went, depending on whether he wanted to acknowledge what I'd said or not. "I'll give you a lift." He told the driver, "Barnes Hospital." As we rode, he took one of his fancy calling cards from a silver case and wrote a note on the back. He handed it to me. "This should suffice as an introduction to the maternity ward matron. She knows me."

*   *   *

The taxi dropped me at the front door of Barnes Hospital and after a few inquiries, I made my way to the maternity ward. The place buzzed with cheerful people. A few couples, the gents pushing their ladies in wheelchairs, kept watch at a large picture window display of new babies. The folks all pointed and waved and cooed. Nurses in high white collars and caps stiff with starch marched from room to room. They looked pleased with their work. A matron at a desk near the visitor's lounge seemed to be in charge. "Miss Lillian Arwald?" I asked.

"Visiting hours end at eleven." She glanced at the wall clock that dominated the waiting area. "In fifteen minutes. Are you family?" Her expression said she didn't believe that for a minute. Then I could see the moment she pegged me for Lillian's lover, her gaze a mix of accusation and sympathy.

"No." I handed her the card. "I'm a friend of her grandfather."

She snorted. "Dr. De Noailles. The Great Man himself. Well, you have—" She looked at the clock again. "Thirteen minutes. Room 516." She pointed down the hall. "The private room at the end."

"Thanks, ma'am," I said, then turned to go.

"Just a minute there, sir. You don't think I'd give a single man free rein to roam my ward?" the matron said as she got up from the desk and led me down the hall, her white apron floating in the breeze.

We stopped at the open door to Lillian's room. Looking at a watch that hung from her waist, she said, "You have ten minutes. I'll be right here."

"Is she going to die?" I'd seen enough death.

The matron's face softened as she said, "I can't say. She's young. Your visit will surely help her hang on."

Her wrong ideas were getting out of hand. "It's not like that. I barely know her."

She shrugged. "I'll be here. And now you have eight minutes. We start to bring the mothers their babies promptly at eleven and I can't have men on the ward."

I took a deep breath and walked over to the bed. A chair was pulled close and I sat in it. She was still and pale, her short blond curls arranged neatly on the pillow. She was thinner than I remembered, except for the bulge of her belly and no-longer-flat flapper chest. A bottle of blood hung from a stand. Thin tubing wound through the bedclothes and connected to a wicked-looking needle stuck in the large vein of her right arm.

I turned to the matron at the door. "Does she need more blood? I'm sure I have it to spare."

"No, this is the last unit ordered, for now at least," she said as she relaxed a bit and smiled at me. "Talk to her. She can hear you."

I turned back to Lillian. "Hey, doll."

Of course, she didn't move. I took her hand. "Long time, no see. Last time was at your house. With your grandfather. Day after the big party, remember?"

She could have been carved from marble.

"Visiting hours are over," I heard from the doorway, along with happy chatter as people shuffled down the hall toward the lift.

"See you around." On an impulse, I kissed her stone-cold forehead. No, she didn't wake up. This isn't a fairytale.

Chapter Six

Hire=Purchase Agent

My day went from bad to worse after that. The weather turned warm and muggy, for one thing, the air thick with moist soot.

While you'd think a hospital entrance would be flush with cabs, it took me fifteen minutes to flag one down. Then we had a flat tire on the way back to the courthouse. The cabbie had only a vague idea of how to change it and in helping him I got axle grease on my shirt. By then it was well past noon. I knew the Judge would've gone to mass and then home for dinner, most likely steamed that he had to drive his own Packard his own self. I caught up with him at home just as he was getting up from the table. He dressed me down for everything from being so late to the unseasonably warm weather. Then I got treated to a rant on votes for women. Since ladies here in the States had the federal vote for four years already, and the Judge did right well among female voters, I pegged this particular rag to something his wife was lobbying for. Mrs. Judge is smart, a lot smarter than him, but that wasn't the day to point that out.

I didn't think mentioning the Arwald's play for my services would do his mood any good at all. Finally, I set out on the Judge's urgent errands only to get myself lost in the wilds of St. Louis County. Then I ran out of petrol.

Dragging in well past suppertime, my sister-in-law, Eliza, lay into me about moving out. "Ain't we stacked up like cordwood here? The baby's no baby anymore, the boys are getting bigger, and Maud's practically a grown woman."

"Sure look wouldn't you think the extra cash—a lot of extra cash, I might add, is a help?"

Without another word, she took up baby Francis, crying in her skirts, and flounced downstairs.

But the flat was her place and I knew she was right. About the crowding anyway. As I packed my suitcase, Maud came in to fight with me for leaving. She chewed me out good and proper, so I hung my best suit back on the peg and stowed the suitcase under the bed. I could at least wait until heads cooled and I talked to Padraig.

I didn't feel like sitting in the pub, pretending to be sociable, so I stayed upstairs and played checkers with the boys, Gerald and Patrick. I had them tucked in for the night when Eliza came back and put Francis down. She spoke not a word to me. About ten o'clock Maud came upstairs for bed. Her bed being the settee where I was parked, I thought I might as well walk off my dark mood.

The evening was damp and cloudy, which made me a bit homesick. I found myself at the Kingshighway dogleg by the hospital. Kyffin's place was just a few blocks north. I thought of dropping by, but it seemed a bit late to disturb him and Evan.

Lillian was the real reason I was standing on this street corner. Evening visiting hours were long over, of course, and the ward matron had kept Dr. De Noailles's admission card. So I walked in on the coattails of some reporters swarming the emergency room over a gangster hit. Breaking away from the pack, I found a deserted backstairs that I thought might lead me to the maternity ward.

I found the correct floor and peeked through the stairwell door. An ancient matron at the nurses' station nodded over her knitting needles. I took off my shoes, padded past her, and slipped into Lillian's room. The bottle of blood and tubing were gone. She was flushed and sweaty with a white cloth across her forehead.

A clipboard with papers, Lillian's medical chart, hung at the foot of the bed. An admission form was the top sheet of the stack. Next to *Differential Diagnosis* someone had written *Spontaneous abortion vs induced vs live birth.* On the *Complications* line, someone else had written *placenta adherans.* Beyond that, it was a lot of numbers, symbols, and squiggles: The doctors' writing was atrocious. I could make out that a D & C happened, whatever that was. She'd gotten four bottles of blood, it appeared.

I rinsed the cloth out with cool water and put it back on her head. I sat and watched her chest rise and fall, willing her to take each breath.

Then I smoked my pipe and talked. I talked for over two hours, freshening the cool compress every so often. I told her my whole story. Lillian was restless at first, making faces and tossing in the bed. But then she settled down and didn't move a muscle. I confessed every sin of my life I could think of, from the first person I ever fucked to the most recent person I killed. Maybe I aimed to shock her into her senses. Or maybe I was convinced she was going to die that night, thus sworn to silence.

I could feel the gathering shadows. Death was in the room. I stared out the window, the pipe cold in my hand.

Suddenly in need of air, I pushed up the window a bit. The cool scent of rain and burning leaves breezed in, putting me in mind of peat fires and the faerie woman, Éire, who seemed to think I owed her something, all the while insisting she only wanted to help me, to be "thine familiar," as she put it. I heard her laughter in the rustle of sheets as a weak voice croaked, "Is someone there? Water. Please." I turned to see Lillian, confusion in her wide-open blue eyes.

I offered water from the glass at her nightstand. "Just a sip. One." I pulled it away as she tried to take the whole glass and down it. "You'll make yourself sick."

She searched my face and her memory. Eventually, she came up with, "Copper? Brought me home from the convent, right?" She smiled, already up to divilment. "Then I fucked you in Grandfather's office."

"Not the way I remember things, but, yeah."

She thought about me for a minute. "Sean Joye," she said as she looked around. "Where are we?"

"Hospital. Don't you remember anything?"

She flopped back against the pillows. "It's coming back. In bits. I remember a cab. I didn't mean to go to a hospital. I meant to go to Father."

"You were bleeding quite a bit."

"Oh," Lillian said as she picked up the glass to take a sip of water.

"Your family wants to know where you were last night," I said, feeling her head. The fever had broke. "And who you were with. You don't need to protect him."

"Who?" Her confusion didn't seem fake.

Something wasn't fitting. "The opinion around here is you had an abortion that went south. Your family's hot to arrest the doctor."

"That's ridiculous," she said, struggling to get up. "I've got to get out of here. Where are my clothes?"

"Slow down. They just got your bleeding stopped and you topped off."

"And you know so much about medicine."

"A bit." I'd given my share of first aid.

Lillian wrinkled her nose. "Oh, yeah. In prison, when everyone was down with the influenza."

She had heard everything I said. And hadn't died. "Where do you think you're going, anyway, in the middle of the night?"

She threw back the covers, tangling her feet in the hospital gown as she tried to swing her legs out of bed. "I need to see Father." Her eyes were wet as she grabbed my hand and held it to her chest. "Something strange is going on. Has been, since the Piasa Ball. I don't remember stuff."

I eased Lillian back into the bed, straightened out the sheets, and pulled them up to her chin. Then I heard steps in the hallway, stopping every few minutes. "The nurse is coming. I got to leave before they throw me out."

She blinked away a few tears. Squaring her shoulders, she said, "I don't know why I trust you, but I do. Please help me, Sean."

My self-preservation instincts flew out the open window. "Whatever you need."

"Remember Mother Mary Gabriel, at the convent? Tell her I'm OK. And you come see me tomorrow."

"Sure thing, doll. Get some sleep."

*   *   *

I couldn't see Lillian before the morning visiting hours, so I thought I'd go to the convent and deliver her message for Mother Mary Gabriel in person. It didn't make much sense, but I did it anyway.

The day was too warm for September, the clouds piled thick, and the air damp from the early morning rain. Arriving at the convent around eight o'clock, I was told Mother Mary Gabriel was in meditation after mass, but I could wait for her in the public garden. At about half-past eight she showed up.

"Mr. Joye. What does His Honor want now?" She looked the same as my last visit in January, but less irritated with me. Effects of the sacrament, I guess.

I stood and tipped my hat. "Good morning, Sister. The Judge wants nothing. Doesn't even know I'm here."

She indicated I should sit down and took her place on a bench opposite me, late roses cascading around the feet of the Blessed Mother on a pedestal behind her.

"My, that's intriguing. Do I detect some sort of interior life? Are you in search of a spiritual director, perhaps?"

"Probably just what I need, but I'd be a big project for a busy sister such as yourself," I said, standing again, suddenly uncomfortable on the hard seat. "No, I'm still delivering messages. This time, for Lillian Arwald." I thought I saw a second of eagerness on Mother Mary Gabriel's face before she shut it down. "Remember her?"

"Of course. What's the message?" Her voice sounded casual, but her eyes again looked eager for news.

"Lillian wants you to know that she's OK."

Mother Mary Gabriel smiled. "I'm glad to hear she is well."

"I don't guess you've kept up with her in the society columns?"

"You'd be surprised on what I—as administrator, of course—need to be current. Apparently, she's been abroad. Her fiancé consoles himself with mountain climbing, race car driving, and aero plane acrobatics. That about right?"

I played a hunch. "She's not abroad, she's in Barnes Hospital. Her sister says she had an abortion. Lillian's not telling much. Couldn't, until recently."

Mother Mary Gabriel was a cool customer, alright. Didn't bat an eye or say a word.

"Her first thought was to contact you," I went on. "Is she looking to you for advice, then?"

"When you first came to me, Mr. Joye, you were obviously working for the Arwald family. That gave me no reason to trust you then. Or now."

"But today I'm working for Lillian," I said, "and will until she tells me to get lost."

"Quit fidgeting, young man. You make me nervous. Smoke if you need to so badly."

I realized I'd been taking a pack of cigarettes and matches out of my pocket and putting them back in for the past few minutes. I lit a smoke while I thought of what to say to her. "Sister, isn't she trusting only two people at the moment? I think we'd help her best by trusting each other."

She didn't reply, but her face softened, perhaps forgiving me my evil companions, like circuit court judges and high-society stiffs.

"Lillian has gaps in her memory," I said. "She feels like something's going on around her that she's not in on."

"Her instincts are sound. But—"

"But what?" I turned my head to blow the smoke away from her.

"There's no proof, you understand," she sighed. "And I'd hate to be one to spread rumors."

"You're not spreading a rumor by telling me something."

She stood and wagged her finger in my face. "I wouldn't trust Taylor Humphrey to put anyone's welfare ahead of his interests." She looked upset to have even spilled that much.

"Was she here Saturday night, Sister?"

Her eyes narrowed. "Why would you think that? Are you working for him? Or his lodge?"

"No, I'm not with Humphrey. He wants me to be, but I'm not," I said as I turned to leave. Mother Mary Gabriel hadn't answered my question with words, but I had gotten the information I was after.

*   *   *

I arrived at the hospital to find the entire Arwald-De Noailles clan, minus Kyffin Bernard—I guess he wasn't technically in the family yet—in Lillian's room, arguing about where she'd go next. To help matters, the matron was in there, too. She maintained Lillian shouldn't be discharged at all.

Lillian pretended to be asleep. I caught the matron's eye and jerked my head toward the still figure in the bed. She caught my drift and announced, "Let's sort this out in the conference room. Miss Arwald's attending physician will be here shortly." They all trooped out, with Violet lingering behind to whisper, "Find out where she was. It's crucial."

Lillian peeped out from beneath the covers.

"Coast is clear," I said.

"Were you here last night? Or did I dream that?" she said, sitting up. "Go get me my clothes and let's sneak out."

"That's not going to work. You'll have to go home with someone, whether you trust them or not."

She sighed and put the sheet over her head.

"Who are you least suspicious of?"

She dropped the sheet. "I need to talk to Father, alone." Lillian sat up in the bed. "But I guess I trust Grandfather the most. And he said Esther has come from the country house to take care of me."

"Esther?"

"She's a nurse that works with Grandfather. Well, much more than that," she said as she winked. "They are close. Very close." Then she got all solemn. "She practically raised me when my mother died. I think I could trust her not to be in on it. Whatever 'it' is."

I heard voices in the hall and the squeak of a wheelchair being pushed.

"Violet will try to make me come stay with her, but Grandfather will insist on his house," Lillian said. "Come see me there this afternoon to help make a plan."

Things played out just as Lillian predicted. Dr. De Noailles took her side, which would, of course, sway Dr. Attending Physician.

Violet admitted defeat, pretty gracefully, I thought, and shooed me out so she could get her sister dressed and primped for the trip home. I joined Old Man Arwald, Dr. De Noailles, and Humphrey in the waiting room. They stared at each other and the babies in the nursery. Humphrey picked up a tattered copy of the *Post-Dispatch* from a table and thumbed through it.

I expected some pressure to take up the quest of tracing Lillian's movements. Now that I had a pretty good idea she'd at least visited the convent since she got back from Europe, I wondered exactly how to play it. But Arwald only said he hoped if Lillian did share something relevant with me, I would let him know, for her own good.

Humphrey was engrossed in the old news, but interrupted his father-in-law, "Now this is fascinating, Joseph." He turned to the doctor. "Relates to the lodge, Dr. De Noailles." He paused to find the line in the article he wanted to read to them. "Oh, you too, Joye. Are you interested in New World antiquities at all? We always seem to talk about Newgrange." Newgrange is an archeology dig in County Meath he assumed I knew all about. I attract eccentrics and Humphrey was one of the most annoying. But today I considered him from a new perspective—Mother Mary Gabriel's.

"I try to learn stuff."

"Excellent. Good man. This is from a few days ago, the twenty-fourth, 'Now the Terrifying Piasa Bird is Coming Back to Perch on Alton Bluff.'"

"We already knew that," interrupted Arwald. "The Lodge has given a sizable donation so the Boy Scouts could repaint it."

"Here's the interesting part, 'Instead of its having been a man-eating bird-beast, a thing of evil for the tribe of Illini, as the legends say, it was the familiar dragon of the Celestial Empire, placed on the rocks by prehistoric Chinese, the first to explore the Mississippi Valley.'"

That sounded like a crock, but before I showed my ignorance by saying so, Violet approached with the matron beside her, pushing Lillian in a wheelchair. I left them all at the lifts and promised Lillian I'd visit her soon at her grandfather's place.

*   *   *

I went to noon mass at the new cathedral, grabbed some lunch, and then made my way to Lafayette Square to see Lillian. The maid, Annie, parked me on a bench in the foyer. A family meeting seemed to be going on in the parlor. The doctor'd left his medical bag on the bench. One of those tools doctors use to listen to hearts stuck out the top. Even with that, it was still hard to hear them clearly.

Violet said, "Not hopeless—Incubators—Atlantic City."

A door clicked. Dr. De Noailles said, "Show him in." Annie muttered, "Yes, sir," and the door clicked again.

Then Old Man Arwald chimed in, "Bernard—Cabbie."

About then I heard a light tread from the far end of the hall and put the thing back in the bag.

Annie brought me to the parlor, crowded with Arwalds and artifacts. Dr. De Noailles greeted me like it had been months, rather than hours, since he'd seen me. "Good progress, yes? Our girl is on the mend and in her own home."

"Just a matter of keeping things quiet," said Arwald, and gave me a stern look.

I heard someone open a window and turned around to catch the eye of a tall, light-complexioned black woman. Her pose was the same as the portrait on the wall behind her, and the resemblance was remarkable. I just stared, my mouth gaping open like a fish out of water.

"She's been wanting Mr. Sean as soon as he arrives," the woman said. "You?"

Her eyes were remarkable. I fell head first into the deep golden-hazel pools, reflecting every light in the room.

Dr. De Noailles said, "My dear, you're correct. This is Mr. Sean Joye. Lillian's gentleman caller."

I let his bit of match-making stand for the moment, swallowed over the lump in my throat, and bowed or something awkward like that. "Ma'am. Pleased to meet you."

"Mr. Joye, meet my wife, Esther De Noailles. She's also an expert midwife who has assisted my work for years."

I was pretty sure such a marriage wasn't legal in Missouri, but I knew what he meant.

A damp current of air from the open window caressed my face as I took Miss Esther's offered hand, and I plunged into a memory. My eleven-year-old self stood at the foot of the bed where my Da's mother had died just a few days before. The room still smelled like her, a sick old-lady mixture of urine, blood, and lavender, but Eliza had just birthed Maud in that same bed. A basin held bloody rags, afterbirth, and a sharp knife the midwife had used to cut the cord. The smell, the blood, or maybe the baby's wails punched me in the gut. I couldn't breathe and felt quite sick, indeed. Rather than disgrace myself by vomiting in front of everyone, I walked over to the window and opened it. Recovering my senses, I released Miss Esther's hand.

The doctor was still talking. "She's the perfect person to oversee Lillian's recovery."

Her appraisal was frank and I doubted very much if I measured up. "And I raised Miss Lillian since her mother died. She is as my own child." I didn't recognize her accent and her voice was of this place but certainly not this city. Falling water, bubbling springs, and the roar of the rivers' meeting all sounded in her words.

"Yes, yes, Esther," Violet said. "You're an absolute rock. We couldn't get by without you. When you bother to show up." She then turned to me, "Lillian trusts you for some reason." She shrugged. "Clear this up. We simply must know what happened, if there's any way—" Violet, unlike her sister, was a terrible liar. I could see the moment when she remembered the yarn she'd told me about an abortionist. "We need to know who hurt her."

"What she needs is her rest," Miss Esther said. "But I'll take you to her."

I followed her while Arwald and Violet resumed their bickering. She shut the door behind us and turned on me. "No badgering," she said, loud enough to be heard in the next room. "She'll share what she wants to share."

We climbed a flight of stairs and entered a bedroom at the front of the house. Lillian was propped up on a well-cushioned window seat, writing in a notebook. She looked fresh and pink and so much better than even that morning.

"Hey, doll," I said and took a chair near the door.

Lillian looked up and put down her notebook. "No, no, come here," she said, making room for me on the window seat. "I can't shout across the room at you."

Miss Esther smiled. "I'll leave you to visit with your friend. Appears to be what you need, after all this hullabaloo."

I moved to the window seat by Lillian as Miss Esther left us alone. She was way too close, and smelled too good for me to concentrate on the serious situation. "OK. Whisper your secrets." *And let me get out of here.*

"I know I'm being a bore, but do you swear to not tell them anything. Not yet?" She touched my face and made me look at her.

"Whatever you want." Somehow, in the pit of my stomach, I knew she was in this jam because of me. Lillian had known best, to get away from that society debutante ball, and I'd made her go to the party, anyway.

She took a deep breath. "OK. I've a healthy baby girl. She is safe and well-cared for. She was born on Saturday night, just before midnight. She's good sized, I think. They're so little, you know, it's hard to judge."

"And you don't want your family to know this because—?"

"They've acted so strange for months. And the gaps in my memory. I feel like I just walked into something, and no one will tell me what I missed."

"You seemed kind of lost when we found you wandering around the Courts Building."

"I don't remember much of that night. Violet and Taylor were being secretive before that, but—"

"Is that why you ran away?"

"Not really. I knew I was pregnant. Esther could tell."

"Didn't you think of marrying as soon as you knew?"

Lillian shrugged as if rules didn't apply to her. "I had to get away and think."

"Wouldn't the baby's father want to know she's been born?" That seemed a clever way to broach the subject uppermost on my mind.

"Possibly. But I don't know who that is."

I was relieved. But maybe a little disappointed. She moved much closer. There wasn't anything to comfortably do with my arm besides put it around her.

"Maybe you could sleuth that someday," Lillian said as she took my right hand and held it. "But what I want you to do is check out my family. Pretend to take their job, checking on me. Find out who I can trust."

"You think your family would hurt you?" I asked, squeezing her hand.

She rubbed her round belly as a grimace passed over her face.

I started to stand. "I'll get Miss Esther."

She shook her head and pulled me back to the seat. "Just cramps. After the baby, it takes a while for everything to get back to normal." She smiled and said, "I've missed you," as she loosened the knot of my tie.

I stroked her belly, the muscles still hard from the baby, a perfect curve, snug in my palm. "You haven't given me a thought since February."

"Well, I am now," Lillian whispered. She snuggled closer, grabbed my face in her hands, and kissed me like we both were about to face the scaffold in an hour.

*   *   *

Lillian fell asleep in my arms, spooning there on the window seat. I held her, which was nice, until my arms were all pins and needles, then carried her to bed and tucked her in to finish her nap. The room was hot, so I opened all the windows wide. I heard a tap at the door and Miss Esther entered with a stack of stiff, pressed sheets. She sniffed the air, looked me up and down, and frowned. "You conjuring in here?"

Maybe that's what they called it where she was from. "Ah, no. I don't think so."

"So young," she said as she patted my cheek like a granny, searching my face. *Looking for—what?* At last, she said, "Take care to mind your own heart, now." I sat in the window seat, smoked, and admired Miss Esther's grace as she moved through the room. She somehow changed the bed linens without disturbing Lillian and tidied up the room, all in about five minutes.

She opened the door to leave, dirty laundry heaped in her arms. "Say goodbye and go for now. No harm will come to her in my care." I believed her.

Chapter Seven

Limited Partnership

"**D**o you have a telephone I can use?" I asked Miss Esther as we stood in the back hall at the foot of the stairs. A doorbell rang from deep in the house. She twitched at the sudden noise, then frowned. "Yes, Miss Lillian convinced Dr. De Noailles he needs one of those disgusting devices so his patients can trouble him at all hours of the day and night."

Annie popped in from the backstairs to say, "Pardon me, Miss Esther. Ain't a man from the railway done left Miss Lillian's steamer trunk at the kitchen door?"

"Well, take it to her, dear."

"But, ma'am, it'd be as big as me. And William don't come in for the heavy work until next Friday."

"I can get it," I offered. "And do you mind if I make a quick call before I leave?"

"Don't trouble yourself with her luggage," Miss Esther said. "You're a guest in our home."

"I'm glad to help."

"'Tis quite in the way there, in the kitchen."

"Well, if you don't mind," Miss Esther said. "And, of course, telephone anyone you need to speak with. Dr. De Noailles would like to offer you refreshments in the parlor before you leave." Patting my arm, she confided, "The others have all gone."

"That'd be grand." I could sound out Dr. De Noailles, and maybe Miss Esther, without the family horning in. If Lillian could at least trust the people she lived with, it would go a long way to ease her mind.

The leather trunk was, indeed, roomy enough to store a small housemaid in comfort. Colorful stickers marked its journey across Europe—England, France, Spain, Germany—as well as Canada and various cities in the United States. I handed Annie my coat, rolled up my sleeves, and put my back into it as I hefted the steamer on my shoulders with ease. Either I didn't know my own strength or the trunk was practically empty.

Annie was suitably impressed and guided me to Lillian's dressing room, a small chamber attached to her bedroom and entirely given over to her wardrobe. "I'll take care of it from here," she said. "Thank you again, Mr. Joye."

"You're entirely welcome," I said as I fixed my sleeves and reinserted my cuff links. "Don't feel like it has much in it."

"Ah, well," Annie said, "William swore over it mightily, when Miss Lillian went off." She smiled and squeeze my bicep. "You must be quite the strong one."

Extracting my coat from her grasp I said, "Well, I've a phone call to make and the master of the house to see." I beat a retreat and found the phone in an alcove near the jacks and the backstairs. Soon the operator put me through to the Arwald house. The servant who answered wouldn't say if Violet was there, but she picked up the line in short order.

"Mr. Joye? What is it? Is Lillian alright?"

"Oh, yes. Sorry. I didn't mean to scare you."

"Did she tell you what happened Saturday? Where she was?"

"No," I lied. "She complains of memory gaps." Well, that much was true. "She's not quite right—not exactly off her rocker, but not so logical, either." My reflection in a large hallway mirror shot me a reproving look. But Violet said, "Our concern, entirely. How can anyone respect her wishes when they are so likely detrimental to—" she paused, "her health."

I wondered what she'd meant to say. "Anyways, I'd be happy to look into things for you if that would help. I do know a few people. Have some ideas for leads."

The line was silent.

"Hello? Mrs. Humphrey?" There was clicking and static on the line. "You still there?"

"Yes, sorry," she said, sounding rather far away. "That would be most kind of you. Please do that. Of course, we'll reimburse you for your time and expenses."

I felt a little guilty, like I was scamming her out of money, but not bad enough to turn it down. "I appreciate it. Probably won't take much time at all. What do you already know? Friends, favorite hotels, where she would get money, stuff like that."

"Stop by later for a letter of introduction. And I'll look up some names and addresses."

We said our goodbyes and I heard the click of the call ending on her side. Then some fuzz and a second click.

The late afternoon light streamed through the etched glass of the high windows and bounced off the mirror and dusty light fixtures along the hall. I hung up the receiver and went to the parlor to find Dr. De Noailles.

*   *   *

The first time I'd been in this house, last winter, I'd noticed the typical parlor had been converted to Dr. De Noailles's medical practice office. What he and Miss Esther called the "parlor" was a group of chairs and a settee around a fireplace and bay window in the near end of the dining room. There the doctor's piles of birds' nests and mouse-chewed books had grown over the summer. Since I'd last been here in July, he'd hung bunches of herbs near the fireplace to dry and taken up mineral and gem collecting. A large glass-doored curio case, full of sparkling crystals as well as non-descript chunks of rock, now partially blocked a window. How Miss Esther tolerated it all was a mystery to me.

The She'-ki bowl was still in its place of honor above the fireplace. Miss Esther stood at the mantel and stared at the bowl. Dr. De Noailles dozed in a lumpy, stained chair nearby but perceived me first, somehow, and awoke with a start. "Ah, Mr. Joye. Sit, sit," he said as he pointed his cane at a chair.

"Will you have tea?" Miss Esther said. "We normally do about now." She crossed the room to a bell pull. "I'll ring."

"Tisane would be the correct term," said the doctor. "Or a cocktail? We're not entirely behind the times."

"A hot cuppa would be grand, Miss Esther. Thank you."

"Sit, sit," said Dr. De Noailles. "I've heard my wife's assessment of the patient, but what do you see?"

"She's tired and hurting—you know all that, better than me. She's confused," I added. "Maybe the fever would do that? I've seen blokes take a bit to come back from the ague. Fries their brains, it does."

Annie arrived with the tea tray at that moment, placing the tray on the table. We sat in silence while she curtsied at me before starting to fuss with the cups.

"Thank you, Annie. I'll pour. You can go," said Miss Esther.

"Yes, ma'am," the maid giggled and bobbed off.

The lady of the house served me and the doctor, then poured her own cup. I took a sip. It wasn't normal tea.

"Dried elderberries, mostly, a touch of poke, and a bit of clary sage leaf," the doctor said. "Autumn tonic. Very good for you, young man. Keep away the chills and vapors. Help you see clearly, especially that which is hidden."

I drank some more. It didn't taste bad, just different, like a late fall day, deep in the backwoods, sweet and pungent at the same time. Drinking it, the veil between the worlds felt very thin indeed.

"Now, brain damage from fever, you say? Transitory effect, I would hazard, with a young healthy patient," he said as he slurped his tea and eyed an oatmeal biscuit dotted with raisins. "I was expecting more from you. You see things, feel things." He smiled at Miss Esther, who'd watched me drink my tea the entire time. "My wife agrees with me. You've access to the power of the spirits and the ancestors. We can tell that about you."

I'd aimed to question him, not the other way around. I set down the teacup. "I don't get your meaning."

"Yes, you do," he said, munching a biscuit. "I've observed you all summer."

I watched Miss Esther refill my teacup. "Really? All summer?"

"You may pretend to be one of these typical dull-witted clods around here. Whether or not you acknowledge and use your gift, you have it—"

"So, use it for us," I finished his sentence. And felt a darkness enter the room. I told myself it was just the fading light. 'Twas the gloaming time of day, after all.

He laughed and then choked on his biscuit, gasping and turning a nasty shade of purple. Miss Esther leaped to his side and pounded his back. Wet crumbs tumbled into his beard. He stilled, pinked up nicely, and took her hand. She murmured comforting words I couldn't make out and took her seat.

"Maybe I should go," I said, standing.

He glared and motioned me to sit. His eyes said it all: I don't have a lot of time on this earth—don't waste it.

"She had a healthy baby Saturday night." I wasn't sure what compelled me to blurt that out. I sat down again.

He looked unimpressed. "I've cared for pregnant women and attended births for fifty years. Tell me something I don't already know."

"Don't you think there was something odd about her back in February, the night of the big party?"

"If my great-grandchild—" He paused, perhaps distracted by the word "grandchild." "Boy or girl? But, to answer your question, if this child is truly a healthy full-term infant, Lillian would have already been pregnant by then. Maybe the effects of nausea medication would explain her fatigue and demeanor. She's always felt free to help herself to the pharmacy box in the office."

I needed time to think on the idea that she was already knocked up in January. "A girl."

He threw a contented smile at Miss Esther and mouthed, "A little girl." She smiled back at him.

I thought about Lillian's squirrely nature and easy access to drugs. "Maybe she was high—she says she can't remember the night of the ball." I drained my elderberry tea. It was quite tasty.

Miss Esther refilled the cup again before I could stop her. "Keeps up your strength, boy."

I obediently drank more of her brew. "But you asked me about—what my granny called the Sight."

He nodded. "It is a gift. Herbs help me, some, but—"

Thinking of Mrs. Mac, I said, "You should hear how much a gift a friend of mine finds it."

"Burdensome responsibility?"

"To put it mildly. Anyway, I can't shake the feeling that there's something not right about the night of the Piasa Ball. And other things seem off, things I find with my head or even my heart." I set my empty teacup on the tray.

"Analytic thinking versus emotional responses," the doctor said as Miss Esther refilled my cup again. "The scientist and the poet are one, yet they believe they are opposed."

I pretended I hadn't seen her pour me more tea. "But under it all, a dark feeling that raises my hackles like someone's walked across my grave."

"Have you shared these feelings with Lillian?" he asked.

"She's worried about the memory loss," I said as I looked from him to Miss Esther. "And not knowing who to trust."

"Is that also an intuition of yours?"

"No, Lillian came up with that on her own." I couldn't sit still a moment longer and stood. I needed the jacks after all that tea tonic.

"And us?" Dr. De Noailles said.

I shifted back and forth, inching toward the door. "I really should be on my way."

Understanding spread across the doctor's face. "I had an indoor water closet installed last summer, since my patients expect such conveniences."

"I'll show you," Miss Esther said as she stood.

"Don't trouble yourself. I saw it by the telephone."

Blessed relief achieved, I found Miss Esther waiting in the front hall, my hat in her hands.

"Perhaps you are less distracted now and can answer the doctor's last question."

"I will. If you'll tell me how in the world you came to be with him." I immediately regretted the bold question.

She only smiled, her eyes deep golden pools of taking-the-long-view. "He needs me as no one else has in so very long."

That much I could well see. I wondered what Miss Esther needed. But I just nodded, happy I hadn't offended her. "To answer his question, I can't figure any percentage for Dr. De Noailles to be against Lillian. And I think you both love her."

"Quiet your mind," she said. She stood so near I could smell the elderberries on her breath and notice the sweat beads on the frizzy little curls of dark hair along her nape. The hall had heated up, for sure, in the afternoon sunshine.

I did as Miss Esther suggested; easy enough with the tea's effect and her standing so close. I felt like a shade. "You're both on her side."

"We are, of course."

"But the others? I don't understand what she's so afraid of."

As she led me to the front door, she said, "That's for you to discover, I suppose. Come see Lillian tomorrow. Let's get that baby home where she belongs."

*   *   *

I went straight to the Arwald's mansion on Washington Terrace to pick up the leads from Violet. The gatekeeper was expecting me and waved me through to the gray stone castle she called home. The sun had set by the time I arrived and my growling stomach reminded me it was about suppertime. I resolved to make the visit quick and sleuth another day.

An ancient butler told me to wait in the foyer. I stood a good while. Although the place glowered like a fortress from the outside, the inside was light and open. The foyer walls were the faintest shade of pink and covered in slim silver-framed mirrors and leafy countryside paintings. Violet and her father eventually showed up.

"Joye," Arwald said by way of welcome as he picked up a stiff sheet of gray stationery tucked under a mass of fresh flowers on a long table. "Here are the names and addresses you asked about." He handed it to me.

Violet and her father were all dressed up in their own house, he in a dinner jacket, her in a knock-out of a green gown, neckline cut low with some fluffy lavender material draping the bodice. Her eyes were red-rimmed and her face was lined. "Sean Joye. We meet again," she giggled as she stepped toward me and stumbled.

I caught her. "Careful there. The floor is slick."

She tottered on fancy shoes and then steadied herself.

"Always the gentleman." In her evening shoes, she was a bit taller than me and looked down at my face. "Except when you're not."

"Ain't that the truth," I said as I folded the paper and slipped it in my breast pocket. "I'll be going. Give you a call tomorrow."

Just then Humphrey came down the stairs, straightening the cuffs of his dinner jacket. "Joye," he said as he hurried down the remaining stairs and rushed over. Well, as much as a man who took shrapnel to the hip at the Somme could rush. He shook my hand. "Dia diut, á Seán. Well, it's night, not day, but you know what I mean."

He took my elbow and, guiding me further into the house, said, "Have a drink. Have two." Humphrey glanced at the fedora in my hand. "What's this? Carson—" he turned to the butler lurking in the shadows, "take Mr. Joye's hat, please." To me, "Honestly, you can't get good help these days."

"I just dropped by to pick up Lillian's friends' names and addresses," I said. "I'll be going now. Getting to work."

"Nonsense. Come in, come in," Humphrey said as he steered me into the library where a trolley of spirits, ice, vermouth, and crystal barware stood at the ready near the fireplace. He deposited me in one of his thrones and set to work pouring a bit of this and a bit of that into a shaker and agitating it.

Violet and Old Man Arwald followed us in and took seats. They had no choice, I guess, no matter how much they had wanted to hustle me out of the house.

Humphrey ceased his shaking, poured his creation in a fancy glass, and crowned it with a lemon garnish. He then handed it to me. "The latest cocktail from Paris—the Scoff-Law. Droll, yes?" Pulling up a seat near me, he said, "Now, what is your clever plan? Did Lillian say anything else?"

"Well, no," I said, racking my brain for a clever plan I could share as I sipped the drink I didn't want. My actual clever plan was to snoop on him, Violet, and Old Man Arwald. "Tomorrow, I thought I'd talk to Lillian's friends. Check with cabbies." I set the cocktail on a spindly table near the chair. "But I still advise you to call the police."

Old Man Arwald sniffed and poured himself a drink. A triple. Straight. He flung it down his throat then said, "No police."

"Did she write from Europe? No hints of being—" I said as I took another small sip of the sweet, lemony swill, "in a family way?"

"No," Violet said. "She was just being childish and stubborn."

"Now, dear." Humphrey got up and stood behind his wife's chair, his fingers caressing the delicate bones of Violet's collar and neck. "Lillian is our dear sister, young and impetuous. We love that about her, but it can cause an uproar. She will come to her senses soon, but in the meantime we have—" he pointed to me, "Mr. Joye. We just need to discover a key bit of information, just enough for her to realize there's no point in lying, and she'll be right with the program again."

I wondered what program he meant.

He then made himself a Scoff-Law and took a seat. The conversation turned, as it habitually did with Humphrey, to the ancient tourist attractions of Ireland: Tara, Wexford, and the Giant's Causeway. He knew a lot more about those places than I did, I'm ashamed to say. Then on to the mounds at Cahokia, just across the river in Illinois, where he hoped to start a proper archeological dig when he got the funds together. He had artifacts from the destroyed St. Louis mounds and needed more grave loot to tie the sites together.

Humphrey looked at his father-in-law. "I love the American can-do attitude," he said, looking a little glassy-eyed. "But the wanton destruction of the indigenous culture—" he continued as he downed his cocktail. "Remember the photos of the Big Mound I showed you, Joye?"

I vaguely recalled some picture of a huge dirt pile with a donkey, cart, and old-timey gents on top of the remnant of the mound.

Old Man Arwald sputtered, "Get a grip, man. Old, dried-up bones? Broken pots? You're talking about prime real estate. That meaningless mound was in the way of progress."

Humphrey, deflated, slumped in a chair near the liquor trolley and poured himself another glass of gin. He didn't bother with any of the fixings. "Not even a proper archeological survey or excavation. The knowledge, all lost—" he mumbled to himself. Or maybe the gin.

Arwald said nothing. Violet broke the silence with small talk for a few minutes, her husband's fit sobering her up. Only one of them could be on a bender at a time, I guessed. The party pretty much broke up after that. Humphrey continued to drink alone in the corner and barely looked up when I bade him goodbye.

Violet walked me to the front door. "Thank you, again. Check in often. But be discrete. And—" she glanced back toward the open library doors, "you needn't bother Father or Taylor with your information. Please, call me directly."

"You're the boss," I said as I put on my hat. "Mr. Humphrey going to be alright?"

"Taylor's passionate about antiquities." She sighed. "Once he gets the funds together for the survey in Cahokia, he'll be better."

"And this money is coming from. . . ?"

"He can make it happen if anyone can."

Chapter Eight

Capital

I shoveled in a quick supper at my favorite greasy spoon, then spent the rest of Monday night making a few visits for the Judge. The evening yielded a collection of fat envelopes and a jar of spiced apples. If the Judge was smart, he wouldn't eat them.

I was up bright and early Tuesday morning, intent on a visit to Kyffin's roommate, Evan Blake, at his midtown real estate office on Grand Avenue. Evan wasn't my favorite person in the world, but he'd lived in St. Louis his whole life and was as gossipy as an old woman. I hoped for the lowdown on the Arwalds. So, at nine o'clock I was pulling over to the curb across from the Rialto Theater just as Evan alighted from a streetcar, a couple of morning papers tucked under his arm. A bit pudgy perhaps, he was a dandy fella in a bowler and crisp wool suit with a white carnation buttonhole.

I got out of the car. The morning was bright and cool but starting to warm up. A brisk southern breeze kept the brown haze from the factory smokestacks moving along. He caught sight of me, stopped, and stared. I normally don't have such an effect on people, unless they owe the Judge money. "Blake." I approached. "Sean Joye. Remember me?"

"Of course I do," Evan said, then commenced his salesman act, shaking my hand as he slapped me on the back—hard. "It's been a while. Dare I hope you're ready for the investment opportunity of a lifetime?"

"Not today, I'm afraid. I'm doing a little research and I couldn't think of anyone who knows the city half as well as you."

He lifted one eyebrow. "Research for the Judge?" I didn't correct him. "I'll try my best to help."

"Thanks. I'm trying to untangle some threads."

"Let's not talk on the street corner," he suggested as he led me toward a row of green-awning storefronts and through a glass door stenciled "Blake and Son, Realtors." A poster-sized advert of blue skies and bathing beauties in the window recommended "Sunny Florida Beachfront Property! Hollywood By-The-Sea!" The rest of the wide plate-glass window was covered with photos of homes for rent or sale. "Come in."

A young lady typist looked up from her work. "Good morning, Mr. Blake. Nice to have you back. You've had a few calls," she said, handing him several pink slips of paper, "and Mr. Blake wants to see you."

"Thanks, Sheila. Tell Dad I'm with a customer." He winked at me. "This way, Sean," he said, pointing toward the back of the suite. "We can talk in my office."

We passed a large office to the right, where a sixty-year-old version of Evan shouted into a candlestick phone. He waved and nodded approvingly at us as we made our way to a much smaller office. Evan closed the door behind us. "Coffee? Something stronger?"

I knew he meant hooch, but his expression said "arsenic?" "No, thanks." I paused, gathering my thoughts before asking, "My questions are about the Arwalds and Dr. De Noailles. Kyffin is in their inner circle, but—"

He laughed then said, "But what's the real scoop? Kyffin wouldn't tell you, would he? He'd die for those girls. Loyal to the end." He slapped the newspapers on his desk and hung up his umbrella and hat on a rack in the corner. "Usually."

So, he'd had some sort of tiff with Kyffin. I pushed the Arwald gossip angle. "But is that loyalty earned?"

Evan buzzed a squawk box on his desk. "Sharon, could we get some coffee in here? Thanks, honey," he said, then took my hat. "Trustworthy? Certainly not. Arwald's legacy was established from arms sales during the Civil War. To the Union and the Rebs both, people say. Joseph Arwald came to St. Louis to marry Dr. Antoine De Noailles's only daughter, Susan, and stayed to start a branch of his family's stock brokerage. In on the Big Cinch, for sure. Quick rise to power through ruthless business practices."

"Such as?"

As Evan flopped my hat on the rack, he said over his shoulder, "For example, he crushes unionization whenever it's tried."

I thought of Dr. De Noailles and what his daughter must be like. "What does the missus think of that?"

He sat behind his desk and started looking through his mail. "Susan Arwald died young when Lillian was a baby," he explained and then looked up at me, still standing in the middle of his office. He hadn't invited me to sit as of yet. "Kyffin, of course, never spills any interesting details."

About then Sheila-Sharon entered with the coffee and sat the tray on a small table in the corner of the office.

"That'll be all, Suzie," Blake said as he moved to a settee and indicated I should sit beside him.

"Thanks," I said to her. "I'm Sean Joye. And you are—?"

"You're welcome, Mr. Joye. Just doing my job." She started toward the door, then turned back. "I'm Sonja."

"Pleased to meet you, Sonja."

She dropped her brittle workplace mask and smiled for real as she left us. "And what does Dr. De Noailles think of Joseph Arwald?" I asked, joining Evan on the tiny sofa's overstuffed upholstery.

He poured coffee for the two of us and handed me a cup as he said, "Ah, the good doctor. A much more interesting character. Old Creole family, here almost from the foundation of the city. The first De Noailles, Guy-Luc, took an Osage wife. His lady back in France may or may not have already been guillotined."

He plunked four sugar cubes in his coffee and a generous amount of cream. "Slaveholders, in a small way. The good doctor is a Confederate veteran."

"I thought this was a Union state."

"It was both," he said, shrugging. "I don't understand the details. Kyffin will bore you with that sometime if you ask. Back to De Noailles—all the money in land. The family fell on hard times, I gather. Their power now is their name, connections, and influence. But, that's changing, I'd say. Nowadays, cash talks."

"The doctor seems close to Lillian."

"Well, I couldn't speak to that," he replied as he sipped his coffee milk and lounged back into the settee cushions. He smirked, "She's got you under her spell, too."

I shifted, hot and trapped in the deep upholstery.

"Lillian generates the really interesting gossip in the family, although Violet had her moments. I bet you could tell me a few things."

The invitation to dish the dirt hung in the air between us. I sipped the black coffee.

The moment passed and Evan said, "Where was I? Ah, yes, De Noailles facilitated Arwald's quick rise. Got him on the right boards and into the proper clubs." He sat down the cup. "One thing I'll grant the old doctor—He's never made public statements against the unions."

"He's not political, you mean."

"Well, that's not totally accurate," he corrected himself as he lit a cigarette. "He's certainly concerned about the displacement of American Indian tribes in general, the Osage, the major local tribe a hundred years ago, in particular. He writes letters to the editor about it."

"Which editor?"

"All of them," Evan shrugged. "Currently, he's convinced there's a conspiracy to murder the Osage in Oklahoma. Steal their oil wells."

This town had at least six daily papers, not counting the German ones. That's a lot of letter writing. I set down the coffee cup and got out my pipe. "Do you mind?"

"Not at all," he said. "A relaxing smell." He leaned in to take a whiff of the open tobacco pouch. "Much nicer than these coffin nails."

"The pipe was my father's," I said as I filled the bowl with tobacco and lit it. He was a hair too close for comfort, but I didn't want to break the mood. I dropped my voice to say, "I sense that Dr. De Noailles is a very private man—"

"But what do I know of his common-law wife?" Evan interrupted. "I've never met either of them. I do know that they've been together forever." Our eyes locked. "I'm for leaving people alone. What business is it of the government—or the nosey parkers—who's sleeping with whom?"

I leaned in a tad closer. "It wouldn't be possible, would it, for them to legally marry?"

He shook his head, then said, "Even if it weren't for the anti-miscegenation laws—" his voice dropped to a whisper, "they say she's some sort of cousin to him."

Evan smiled at the little bomb he'd just dropped, then settled into the cushions. He draped his arm across the back of the settee and watched me smoke. "That's a nice blend. What is it?"

"Nothing special. Prince Albert." Some business between us hung in the air along with the tobacco.

"Kyffin often came home smelling like that."

I suddenly felt guilty, though Evan had no reason for concern. Maybe *I* had been carrying a torch for Kyffin, but he was as loyal as the day is long. "We have a drink occasionally, 'round town," I said as I finished my coffee. "That's all."

"I'm sure it is," Evan said as he stood. He dropped his cigarette to the floor and ground it under his heel.

I tapped the pipe's ashes into my empty coffee cup and looked up at him. "I've heard an Arwald grandchild died recently."

He nodded. "National news. Hell, world news."

"I missed the details."

"You'll find plenty in the papers. One-year-old boy, Violet and Taylor Humphrey's child, was kidnapped from the De Noailles home in Alton and later found drowned. That was last year—fall of '23."

In 1923 I'd just found my way to St. Louis and been coerced into the Judge's employ. In a free moment, I might scan a newspaper for information scraps about the tumult that was the Irish Free State and the sham of self-government the Six Counties—what the English and the Orangemen call "Northern Ireland"—had become. A high-society family tragedy was about the last thing I'd have read.

Evan fetched my fedora. "I can't help but like you, Sean Joye, despite myself. Will you let me give you some advice?" he said as he handed me my hat. "That sheba is bad news."

I can take a hint. I wrapped the pipe in my handkerchief and stowed it in my pocket. "You mean Lillian Arwald?"

He opened the door, saying, "You know it, too. She'll drag you down and never shed a real tear over your demise."

*   *   *

I brushed aside Evan's warning about Lillian as some variety of sour grapes. But as we'd talked, I realized Violet and Humphrey's loss explained a lot about their behavior. Violet clearly wanted me to find Lillian's baby.

Nancy Radeburg, Lillian's best friend, was the girl most likely to be in on Lillian's secrets.

I headed south on Grand toward Compton Heights. It was a swank neighborhood built just as the century turned. A place of wide lawns, mansions in all the popular styles, and pleasantly curved streets. A few of the double lots had been recently divided and more modest, yet still quite swank, houses tucked in between. The Judge and his missus had built just such a home on Hawthorne last year. I drove past it and turned a few corners to find Nancy Radeburg's place, the grandest beer-baronial pile of bricks on the grandest street in the subdivision.

The maid didn't leave me long in the foyer. She led me out to a terraced garden off the back of the house. Nancy, a serious-looking redhead with green eyes behind cute little spectacles, was reading a book. Not a head-turner, but pretty. Her old man was one of the local beer barons—Adolphus Radeburg. A *Relax with a Radeburg* sign still hung in Padraig's place. They didn't brew beer anymore, of course. They'd turned the brewery over to the production of ice cream, cheese, and a cereal beverage: Louie Malt Tonic. Not nearly as good as Bevo, in my opinion. I'd heard Radeburg had diversified into petrol and railroads long before the Volstead Act passed.

Nancy pointed to a wrought-iron chair as she took off the glasses and folded them away in a pocket. "Violet asked me to talk with you, Mr. Joye. I confess I don't understand why. I've already told them everything I heard from Lillian while she was in Europe and what she said on Friday." Glancing at a watch pinned to her blouse, she said, "And I don't think Father would approve of a stranger here." She looked a bit scared.

I went into the song-and-dance. "Mrs. Humphrey just has some questions about the hospital's account of Lillian's illness. Since you were probably the closest person to her—"

"She has a fiancé," Nancy said, holding the fact up like a shield. "Tea, Mr. Joye? Or a late breakfast? I'll go tell Cook." She bolted into the house before I could reply.

I waited alone in the garden, watching leaves fall in the park across the street. The red ones were from a tree called sweet gum, which dropped treacherous pods all over the sidewalk, year-round. I knew that much. The fancy water tower in the park and me kept an eye on each other. The sun moved higher in the sky and warmed things up nicely. More time went by.

Nancy brought out the tea tray herself. Now people like her, one thing they are not, is outright rude. Such as leaving a guest alone for the better part of an hour. What version of the truth had she come up with in the kitchen, watching water boil?

"So, was she already in labor Friday?" I said, sipping what was undoubtedly the best cuppa I'd had in a Yank house in the last six months.

Nancy stared at me, opening and closing her mouth before blurting, "Why, uh, why would you say that?"

"Was she?"

"No. Yes. Why would you say that? I don't know about such things. Father doesn't approve of me talking about—you know—things like that. Perhaps you should talk to Father. That would be best."

I set down the teacup and let the silence build. I turned my face away from her in my best father-confessor pose. All I needed was the purple stole.

Finally, Nancy spoke, "You already know—I told them—Lillian was here on Friday. In the family way. She'd have these little pains but said they didn't mean anything."

"What did she want from you?"

"Money, mostly. As if I've much allowance at all. I tried to get her to at least lie down and put her feet up. Although Father—" she managed to look afraid, ashamed, and angry at the same time, "wouldn't have let her stay. Luckily, Lillian had a place to go but wouldn't tell me where."

"Did she say why she couldn't tell you where she was going?"

"She didn't want to bring me trouble. She was very worried, I could tell, but vague." Nancy looked a little weepy and gulped her tea. "I'm so sad that she didn't feel she could turn to Kyffin. That's the worst, to be in such a jam, alone."

"Lillian said she couldn't tell him?"

Nancy nodded. "She couldn't trust anyone but me. 'They might all be in on it,' she said."

I helped myself to more tea. And a very nice shortbread biscuit dabbed with strawberry jam.

"What can you tell me about the debutante ball last winter? It was your debut, too, right?"

She looked surprised, then said, "I don't see any connection."

I smiled as charmingly as I could. "Can you tell me everything that you saw, start to finish?"

She shrugged and leaned back in her chair. "We were all to be there by half-past six, at the latest. Lillian came in about a quarter to seven." Nancy laughed and said, "This is silly. You seem like a policeman."

"Please go on. Was she alone?"

"No, her sister, Violet, brought her in."

"How did Lillian look to you?"

"Tired and—" Nancy stared across the street at the water tower, "maybe sick?"

"Why do you say that?"

Nancy stood and paced the flagstones. "She was quiet. I thought to myself, 'her big night, and she's got a cold or something coming on.'"

"Then what happened?"

Nancy, now on the far edge of the paved area, turned back toward me. She smiled, bright and fake, holding up her hands to frame her face. "The photographer took lots of pictures."

I laughed and said, miming a notebook and pen in my hand, "Miss Radeburg, Miss Radeburg—how do you feel about this great event? Any comment for our readers?"

Nancy tilted her nose and patted her chignon in a perfect impression of a film star. She pitched her voice low and with a thick and convincing German accent, said, "Darling readers. Enjoy film. Ja?" She blushed and then continued in her normal voice, "We practiced walking and curtseying." She demonstrated, treading the patio—step, pause, step, pause, step. "Then our fathers showed up to escort us, and we had to practice walking and curtseying with them."

"Doesn't sound fun," I said, putting away my imaginary notebook. I couldn't picture Lillian playing along with any of that.

"Well, it was rather awful, in some ways. We had to stay in the court en banc room. The chaperones wouldn't let us sit down or we'd wrinkle our dresses. And we couldn't risk a stain, so we couldn't eat or drink anything." Nancy pulled her chair closer to me and sat down. "But it *was* fun," she said. "All my friends looked so pretty. We passed the time redoing each other's hair and rouge." She looked at me, appraisingly, then whispered, "A few girls snuck in cigarettes. The chaperones kept sniffing around, trying to find them," she laughed.

What a sweet girl. "Nothing harder?"

Nancy looked shocked. Shocked and dismayed. "Like a flask? I heard there was one but didn't see it."

"What was Lillian doing all this time?"

"She sat in a corner alone, unless someone came over to her. Violet stayed with her until their father arrived." Nancy looked at her watch.

"Lillian didn't chase down the cigarettes? Or the flask?"

"No, not at all."

That, I couldn't picture. Lillian was as fun-loving as any of them, always up for a bit of craic. "What happened next?"

"Well, about half-past seven we had to line up, just to wait around some more. At last, the debut began. Lillian was last, of course, because she was queen."

"Notice anything strange when she walked in?"

"She was already strange," Nancy said as she closed her eyes and wrinkled her brow, thinking hard. "She didn't curtsey. It's funny, I'd forgotten that. Her father had to nudge her."

"Then the dance."

"Yes, she danced with the Chief alone for a little while, then everyone else had a dance with their father."

"At last the party could start." I ate the last biscuit.

Nancy nodded and said, "We filled out our cards and danced. We had supper about ten o'clock."

"Any change in Lillian at the meal?"

"Not really. Kyffin kept trying to get her to eat something, but she just pushed the food around the plate."

"What happened next?"

"More dancing," Nancy said as she looked thoughtful. "You know, I don't remember seeing her after we got up from the table about eleven o'clock. The men went off to smoke or whatever it is they do, and we all powdered our noses and made our way back to the ballroom."

"Did you see her in the powder room?"

"I don't think I did."

We sat quietly for a moment, drinking tea. "Tragedy about Mr. and Mrs. Humphrey," I said.

"Oh, yes. So sad. So wicked."

"Child was kidnapped, I heard?"

"Yes, that's right," she said. "At first, they thought he'd just wandered off, which is scary enough—all those cliffs and bluffs along the river over there at Dr. De Noailles's country house. The sheriff formed a search party, but the next day, the ransom note arrived." She looked flushed and weepy. "I can't imagine." Obviously, she could imagine, and had, frequently.

"Please don't distress yourself," I said, handing her my handkerchief. "Violet seems strong."

Nancy dabbed her eyes. "Oh, yes. She held the family together. Mr. Humphrey took to his bed and wasn't seen for weeks. And with their mother dying so similarly, I would think—"

"What?" All I'd heard about Violet and Lillian's mother's death was "young."

"Well, not as similar as all that." I waited while she talked in circles. "Susan Arwald wasn't kidnapped, but she did drown at the Alton property. In the same little creek. Father thought it strange. Tragic, but strange."

"And a murder, like the little boy?"

"No, no. An accident," she said. "If you go to the library, you could see all the newspaper stories. I tried not to read them, but—" she wiped another tear, "the coroner called it an accident." Nancy's green eyes froze me to the spot. "Case closed. Except for two little girls without a mother. But what does the tragedy have to do with Lillian's baby?"

I felt like I'd worn out my welcome. And all the biscuits and tea were gone. I stood. "That's what I'm trying to find out. Thank you for your help, Miss Radeburg."

Nancy stood as well, saying, "Oh, do you have to go?" She gave me my handkerchief back, a bit damp but none the worse for wear. "I've never invited a gentleman to luncheon before. I'm not sure what father would say." She had that beaten-dog look on her face again. She knew exactly what father would say, if it was me that appeared at his table, anyway.

"Kind of you to offer, but I'll be going. You've been very patient with a most unpleasant conversation. So, unless I could interest you in a turn about the park on this fine day—"

Nancy blushed. "Why, that would be lovely, Mr. Joye. If we only talk about pleasant things."

I offered her my arm. I can be pleasant when I set my mind to it. And the Judge could wait another hour. He was most likely still in court if I remembered his schedule right. "Miss Radeburg, it's a deal."

*　　*　　*

When I arrived at the Judge's office, he had just recessed his court for lunch. He flung his robe at his secretary as he rattled off his food order to her and looked expectantly at me since I was supposed to be the one to go over to the Courtesy Diner and fetch it.

"Give the fry cook a minute," I said. "I've a few things to talk to you about."

"Do you now? You must be a busy man. Haven't seen you in days."

The Judge had last seen me Sunday afternoon. "Yeah, about that—"

"I spent last evening at a scientific lecture with Mrs. Dolan," he said as he glared at me. "Could've been you there, instead of me."

"Sorry to miss it." I grinned at the thought. One of his favorite gags was to send me to boring events with his missus. "What was it about?"

"Oh, dinosaurs. Flying dinosaurs. That crazy rock painting that used to be on the cliffs over in Alton. The Piasa Bird? Was actually the—" The Judge shuffled papers on his desk and came up with a folded program. "Pterodactyl." He read further. "Or Ramphorhyncus. Actually, Professor Whelpley pretty much discounted that species. Pterodactyl it is. The old Indians saw them and painted the beast on the cliffs."

"You seem to have got a lot out of the lecture."

"It was bullshit. And a waste of a perfectly good poker night."

"I'm sure your lady showed her appreciation."

He smiled, straightened the knot of his tie, and looked away.

"Anyway, I'm up to my eyeballs in the Arwalds again." I gave him a brief rundown and then said, "So, Lillian Arwald has me investigating Violet and Taylor Humphrey, her father, Dr. De Noailles and his mistress, and possibly the whole Piasa Lodge organization. Maybe Kyffin Bernard, if he turns out to be dirty." I doubted that one very much. "Violet Humphrey thinks I'm tracing Lillian's movements over the past few days, specifically where she spent Friday and Saturday. Violet's story is they're looking for an abortionist, but it's a lot more likely they're looking for a baby."

The Judge sat down, his expression a mix of happiness, concern, and how-do-I-play-this-hand puzzlement. "First. Stay close to the family. Do whatever they want. Take all the time you need and don't worry about me." He punched a button on his intercom and said, "Doris, honey. Run over to the diner and pick up my lunch, would ya', doll? Thanks." He punched it again. "Oh, and call O'Riley in. I might have some errands for him over the next few days."

The box squawked and squealed.

"What was that, honey? Sean? He's going on special assignment for a while." He winked at me and turned the intercom off. "Next. Make sure Taylor Humphrey and Joseph Arwald know *I'm* letting you help. Deal with them directly."

I started to protest. The Judge held up a hand to stop me. "The ladies may be more pleasant company and easier to get around," he said, "but I need Arwald to know I'm doing him a favor here."

"But Violet runs the show, as far as I can tell."

"Not the whole show. Not the big show. You can't imagine—" he said as he shook his head. "Anyway, they're important to my mayoral run next year. Third thing. Keep me informed. Call me a couple of times a day, at home if you need to."

"Suppose you're at a science lecture?" I said, grinning as I settled into my usual red leather chair across from his desk.

"I won't be at a science lecture. Anything else you need?"

"Last winter you mentioned a kidnapping."

He stood and paced the room. "Lord, that mess. I heard part of the case, sent it to Illinois. I don't see how it's connected."

"I don't either, but I don't know enough."

"Well, briefly—" The Judge looked out his window at the plaza below. "The Humphrey's one-year-old was reported missing from the De Noailles country estate in Alton. Everyone called in: sheriff, search parties, dogs, the works. The next day, the ransom demand shows up. Two men were arrested at the money drop in St. Louis. That's how I got involved. What a bollocks."

"In what way?"

"In every way. Idiots just walked up to the drop site, expecting the money to be there. The two of them. No evidence of a third party, so who guarded the kid?"

I lit a cigarette and said, "Maybe he was already dead."

"Maybe. The autopsy was inconclusive. He'd been in the water too long." Lowering his voice, the Judge said, "I doubted the defendants had any part in the disappearance or death. When questioned separately, they couldn't present a consistent story about how they knew where the kid would be, how they snatched him, where they held him, why no one saw them—nothing."

"Where are they now?"

"Menard. Illinois maximum-security pen in Chester." The Judge took his spectacles from a case on his desk and cleaned them with his handkerchief. "Pending execution."

What a bollocks, indeed. I remembered well the six months in 1921 I'd spent in Crumlin Road Gaol, awaiting the King's pleasure to be hanged. "So, there's a real kidnapper still out there?"

"Or the kid fell in the creek and drowned," the Judge said, putting on his glasses and opening the top file in a stack on the corner of his desk. "And those idiots, out for the fast buck, got in way more trouble than they expected."

"Could I see that autopsy report? And the cops' records, too?"

"That's easy enough. But you'll have to go over to Madison County, where the crime happened."

I had a few other items of business for him, and then his sandwich arrived right about the time the phone rang. The intercom squawked, but apparently he understood the message and replied, "Put him through."

The phone jingled on the Judge's desk and he pointed at it. "It's for you," he said.

I held the receiver to my ear.

"Sean?" It was Kyffin. "Do me a favor. Can you drive Lillian someplace?"

Chapter Nine

Hostile Takeover

As I drove to the De Noailles house in Lafayette Square, I hoped Lillian had decided to bring the baby home. She was right about the danger she and the child faced, but she had Kyffin to help her. And maybe she'd come to trust her grandfather again, somehow, and I had no grounds to argue with that.

Lillian was sitting on the front steps when I arrived. Pale, with dark circles under her eyes, she hadn't bothered with make-up.

"I take it we're bringing the baby home," I said as we walked to the Model T in the late afternoon heat. With the morning breeze long gone, the city lay in a blanket of humid smog.

"Yes, yes. And we have to hurry. I wish Kyffin would've taken me a half-hour ago."

"Why didn't he?" I wondered as I held open the car door for her.

"Oh, some urgent errand for Grandfather."

"So, why the sudden change of heart?" I asked as soon as we'd got in the car.

She checked the rearview mirror, then waved me forward, shouting, "Drive."

"Isn't the baby better off wherever it is you've stashed her?" Mount St. Michael Convent, but Lillian had never told me that.

"I miss her." She slumped in her seat. "And it's not fair to the—babysitters," she explained, looking around again. "I think we'll be safe if we can get to the house in Alton."

How was the place where Violet's little boy was kidnapped and drowned safe? But I didn't challenge her. "How're you holding up?"

"I didn't get much sleep," she said as she reached over and touched my hand on the steering wheel. I looked at her, and she smiled. "Well, some, yesterday afternoon—thanks to you. But last night I was up and down."

I just drove and listened to her worry.

"I must have slept, because I had nightmares that I couldn't move. Or maybe not dreams, maybe I really was paralyzed. That's a thing that happens, isn't it?"

"There's drugs that will do that. Called a Mickey Finn," I explained as I waited for more, but she looked out the window.

"Where might I be going, anyway?" I said. We were well along the route to Mount St. Michael Convent, but she didn't need to know I'd been poking around in *her* business.

"Violet, Taylor, and Father—even Grandfather and Esther—think you're snooping on me. I've played along and pretended to be mad about it. It's confusing."

"Yes." Keeping lies straight is a challenge.

Lillian took in a deep breath and announced, "Mother Mary Gabriel has my baby."

I nodded and glanced at her.

My reaction clearly not up to muster, she went on, "Right after she was born, I had a dream—a horrible, vivid dream—that someone was about to kidnap my baby. It was so real." Lillian sobbed a little and whimpered, "I ran away to distract—whoever." With a sigh I handed her another handkerchief I knew I'd never see again. She blew her nose, then continued, "You've probably heard all about what happened to my nephew last year."

"No details until this morning," I said.

"What a lovely little world you must live in, not subjected to other people's dreadful tragedies night and day."

I could think of no response fit for her privileged ears, so I continued toward the convent.

Lillian cut the drama and said, "Grandfather's always been my best friend and we had a heart-to-heart this morning. He's on my side, don't you think?"

"That's my gut instinct, but I'd like more concrete proof."

"Well, he wants you to visit us tomorrow in Alton. You must've acted too interested in his prehistoric stuff."

"I *am* interested."

She ran a finger up my neck and whispered in my ear, "Oh, and Kyffin insists on marrying me right away."

"What?" I guess I shouldn't have been surprised.

She laughed. "It's ridiculous, but he's quite old-fashioned. He thinks society will scorn me, so we must marry before anyone knows about the baby." Lillian might be a Twentieth Century Girl and think rules didn't apply to her, but a baby out of wedlock would cause a lot of talk and worse troubles, like shunning for the whole family. Physical attacks weren't out of the question, not so long ago, not so far away. Lillian should have married Kyffin—or someone, anyone—months ago.

She took a compact out of her bag and powdered her nose. "And it would please Father."

We were almost out of the city, the traffic growing much lighter as I approached Fairgrounds Park. "Fathers like to see their daughters settled in life," I said.

"Maybe," Lillian replied as she snapped close the compact and put it away. "Anyway, you're Kyffin's friend, and I thought you'd like to know."

"I'd like to think I'm friend to both of you."

"Yes, indeed." She'd cranked herself into rare flirtatious form, resting her right hand on my knee while the left worked its way across the back of my neck. "Don't think that I don't appreciate it. You're certainly invited—" she said as she snuggled closer to my neck. "To the honeymoon."

I turned a corner and glanced up the street to the convent gates. I couldn't believe my eyes. I slammed the brakes, and Lillian went flying back to her proper side of the car.

"What'd you do that for?" she said. "Can't take a joke?"

"Look," I said as I pointed out the windscreen.

*   *   *

The closed gates barred the way to a gray Rolls Royce limo. Violet and Humphrey stood next to the car, bickering with an elderly gatekeeper, by the looks of it. And charging through the pedestrian entrance to the side of the gate was Mother Mary Gabriel. She extracted a shotgun from a canvas case as she marched along, hoisted the weapon to her shoulder, and leveled it at Humphrey.

"Stop them!" Lillian clawed at the steering wheel. "They're going to take her."

I wrestled back the wheel and punched the fuel pedal, screeching up the street. "I'm more worried about Mother Mary Gabriel stopping them forever."

Our car squealing to a stop distracted the sister for a moment, and Humphrey took that opportunity to make a play for the gun. You would think he could easily take on a middle-aged nun, but she wasn't giving up the shotgun without a fight.

"Stop it!" Lillian jumped out of our car and flung herself on Humphrey, pulling on his coat sleeve. "Leave her alone."

"Dear Lillian," Humphrey said as he looked over his shoulder at her, continuing to tug on Mother Mary Gabriel's shotgun. "We were only—"

"Going against my expressed wishes," Lillian finished, clawing at Humphrey's hands on the gun.

I approached Violet, who watch the whole scene with gape-mouthed amazement. "You'd better snap out of it," I whispered in her ear, "and end this before someone gets hurt."

Violet nodded and turned to Lillian. "Darling," she said to her sister. "You've been ill. We only wanted to help."

Lillian lifted her eyes from Humphrey and saw me standing by Violet. "Well, I'm fine now," she spit the words at us. "I don't need any help."

"Of course," Humphrey said, finally releasing the shotgun. He inclined his head to Mother Mary Gabriel, murmuring, "Pardon me, my good lady." Only then did Lillian release him. Humphrey turned to her and took her hands, saying, "Please, let us be a family again. You and the baby will be so much more comfortable in our home."

"No. Kyffin and I will be married in a few days. I'll have a new life with my husband and child."

The color drained from Violet and Humphrey's faces. Their shock was strange, since marrying as soon as possible was the most logical thing in the world for an unwed mother to do.

"Sister, can we do without the gun now?" I asked Mother Mary Gabriel. "And maybe take this discussion inside?" The street corner was a pretty public place for a Roman Catholic nun to be holding off a couple of high-society swells at gunpoint.

"Yes, of course." Mother Mary Gabriel lowered the shotgun. "Miss Arwald is welcome inside." She stared long and hard at

Humphrey. "Take your wife and go." If looks could kill, he'd already be on ice and laid out for his wake. He turned away from the nun. "If you ever want to visit our church for prayer—" Mother Mary Gabriel said to Violet, "without the accusations and threats, please come again. The public worship hours are posted."

She wouldn't open the gate until Violet and Humphrey piled back in their limo and headed off toward the city.

I drove Lillian up to the convent. "I can wait out here," I said as I opened the car door for her and took her hand to help her out. Lillian just sat in the car and stared at the clipped hedge, its little leaves bright red now, frost-touched. Then she snapped out of it, pleading, "Come in with me, Copper. And I'm sorry I got mad at you. I thought for a second you'd told Violet where the baby is."

"I didn't. But your sister's not dumb. You did hide here before."

Lillian lowered her head and slunk out of the car.

*   *   *

A novice greeted us in the hallway outside Mother Mary Gabriel's office and showed us to a windowless parlor where the nun waited. I couldn't hear what Mother Mary Gabriel said to the novice, but the girl looked crestfallen, and then nodded and slipped out through a rear door into what, judging from the exterior layout, would be the convent proper.

"Glad to see you sisters aren't shy about defending yourselves," I said, indicating the shotgun on the fireplace mantel.

Mother Mary Gabriel glared and I shut up quick. She clucked over Lillian, guiding her to the only comfortable-looking chair in the room. With a flick of her wrist, she indicated I should sit on a beat-up mahogany number with deep red upholstered cushions and crocheted doilies to protect the arms and headrest. From what, I don't know. It was already a pretty moth-eaten affair.

"I trust you are here for your daughter," Mother Mary Gabriel said with a smile, standing over Lillian.

"Yes. I'm going to my grandfather's country home for a while, and then I'll be married in a few days."

"Good. Very good indeed," said the nun. "Let's have the wedding right here, and the baptism the same day."

Lillian open and shut her mouth a few times, speechless for once.

I shifted in my chair, decided against putting my oar in, and then hopped to my feet as the novice came in with a white bundle.

She placed the child in Lillian's arms. "Hi, there," she beamed. "Miss me?"

"I can guarantee she did," said Mother Mary Gabriel.

I stepped up to get a look at this object of contention. Very small and pink, just like Lillian had said. A fine fuzz of blonde hair. Other than that, she looked nothing like Kyffin, but I didn't think that would matter much. She squeaked and rooted around at Lillian's dress front.

"Would you fetch Sister Agatha?" Mother Mary Gabriel asked the novice. To us, she said, "The infirmarian was a hospital nurse for many years until she came to us for a contemplative life."

Lillian and I both blinked at her, puzzled-like. At least I was. The nun sighed and said, "We've been giving the baby boiled, thinned milk with Karo syrup in a bottle. But she smells you now, and mother's milk is best. Sister Agatha will help you learn to nurse her."

Lillian nodded, still with nothing to say.

Eventually, the elderly sister shuffled in, and we left them to it. Mother Mary Gabriel took me into the church. Frankincense and lemon wax hit me square in the nose and made me wish for a moment I was back home at St. Paul's, serving mass.

At the nave's altar rail, three sisters knelt before the Blessed Sacrament, taking their turn in the perpetual adoration conducted by the order.

Sister and I slid into a back pew near a side altar dedicated to St. Michael. My name saint, although I'd always been called, "Sean," so as not to be confused with my father.

"Let us offer prayer for the safety of the young mother and child," she whispered as she swung down the kneeler built into the pew's underside and knelt, laying a firm hand on my shoulder so that I couldn't help but do the same. I tried to pray, but nothing came to mind.

The church was a fortress: Massive stone walls, turrets, and arches hunkered low to the ground, with narrow slits for windows at ground level and stained glass at the clerestory. The images on the glass—actually, throughout the church—were symbols, not Bible stories like you usually see. I recognized a few of the squiggles: the Greek letters, alpha and omega, for instance. One window was marked with an eye, another a hand. The style was weird, but I could at least recognize them. Other images had a math-ish look to them. I only got as far as algebra in school, but a teacher had shown me a geometry book once. Still others were maybe runes from some language I'd never seen before, set down in a flowing script.

Mother Mary Gabriel prayed in silence for a few minutes, then gazed at the Lord in the form of the Blessed Host displayed in a golden monstrance. She looked at me, and then back at our Lord. At last, she sat back in the pew, so I did, too.

"What's on your mind?" I whispered.

"I can't help but fear for Lillian and her child. Dark forces gather around them."

"The world is a dark place. Could you be more specific?"

The nun didn't answer right away, but eventually said, "I sense your interest, but I can't gauge your devotion to protecting the girl and her baby."

"I've been devoted to a cause since I was seventeen."

"Let me guess. Typical idealistic Fenian youth, fighting over government and politics. As if the English were the only source of evil in our lives."

"I'd go up against them over Orangemen any day." I thought of the loyalists in Ulster who'd set fire, and worst, to the Catholic sections of Belfast in the pogrom of 1920.

Mother Mary Gabriel grabbed my shoulders and looked me square in the face. "Don't be distracted by trivial details. Look around you. Demons walk the earth, ensnaring and corrupting the weak-willed. And they want that child."

She'd said it with such utter conviction I believed her for half a second. Glad to be sitting, I stammered, "What—?"

"Guard her well. As will I, but I can only do so much from here."

The nun stood, kicked the kneeler back into place with a loud thump, and marched out of the pew, almost forgetting to genuflect toward the main altar. She exited the nave and I followed her out to the chapel porch. Granite vaulted over each of the doors as if to lean in and listen.

I grabbed her by the elbow, and spun her around to ask, "Does this danger have something to do with the little boy who died last year? Violet and Humphrey's kid?"

"That tragedy—" Mother Mary Gabriel looked thoughtful. "Might be part of the evil that concerns me." Contemplating the masonry, she whispered, "And what of the mother?" Her fingers traced the engraved filigree of the arch hunkered over the door. "Perhaps an intertwining branch." She squared her shoulders and turned back to face me. "I've followed a pattern. It led me here to St. Louis."

"And?"

She didn't answer and led me away from the building as the full afternoon sun broke through the clouds and sparkled off the granite steps. I followed her into the Stations of the Cross, fourteen images from Christ's passion story, posted for devotional visits and placed along a gravel path that meandered through a copse marking the property line. "For some years," she said, when we were well away from the church, "I've found evidence of maleficium—dark magic if you will."

That may have been about the last thing I expected Mother Mary Gabriel to say. "How? Why?"

"The how is not important. A sorcerer leaves his path of devastation through time and space. Why? The evil men do has a source, a root. We dig that root out, wherever we may find it."

Her words made me feel adrift in waters way over my head. I'm not a strong swimmer. I was at the sun's mercy with my hat left inside, and my shoes were covered in white dust from the limestone path. I tried to ferret out whatever her point might be while I wiped off my shoes with my handkerchief. "By, 'sorcerer,' you mean Taylor Humphrey?"

She strode along the path away from me, crushing the limestone beneath her heels. "I've followed the trail of a dark magical cult throughout Europe and the United States. A path of stains— rips, even—in reality." The nun stopped and turned around, waiting for me to catch up. "The evil grows larger, more insidious, and scars more souls as time goes by. Someone on this plane calls the power of darkness. And it answers. Or perhaps the influence is the other way around." She poked me in the chest with her index finger, as she said, "I've been close to the power's physical manifestation more than once. And always at property owned or rented by a group controlled by Taylor Humphrey." Mother Mary Gabriel spit on the ground at his name.

I was shocked. I'd never seen a nun spit.

Her voice dropped, "I can smell the evil on him. In London, a young prostitute named Anna Medvedikova and her newborn disappeared. The girl was fished out of the Thames and the baby, Martin, never located."

I felt sweat trickle down my back, the September air moist and heavy as a summer's day. A bit shook and aiming to hide it, I said, "I bet that happens in every city in the world, and not infrequently."

"Yes, but Taylor Humphrey visited her often. Brought food, clothes, and things for the baby. He paid her rent."

"How would you know that?"

We stood, faced-off, before the Eleventh Station: Jesus is Nailed to the Cross. She bit her lower lip, close to tears, and said, "She told me so, the time we met." She looked at the carved image of our suffering Lord and talked to Him, "I couldn't convince her of the danger. I tried. I did."

She turned back to me, her voice now a frozen calm, and said, "And Lillian has shared the same fears."

I needed to be able to trust Mother Mary Gabriel. "What kind of sister are you, anyway?"

"I might equally ask what kind of man are you?"

We glared at each other. The rustle of wings filled the air, as birds roosted for the night in the trees all around us. I caved first. "I'm a sinner. You name a commandment, I've broken it. On purpose. Killed people, enemies of Ireland, generally, but still I killed them. Been—let's just say promiscuous. Maybe I honored my parents." I looked at Jesus' face and had to confess, "But no. Getting my Da murdered instead of me wasn't intentional, but it happened all the same. And my Ma; she's a hard woman to love." Maybe I was looking for someone, anyone, to forgive me. I'd poured all this out to an unconscious Lillian just a few days ago.

"I discern a spiritual power," she said as she touched my head to bless me. "God hasn't given up on you."

"Spiritual? Well, if you count the Good People's visits and now the haunts, and—" I looked at the sky and said, "Oh, it's spirit-filled, alright."

It was easy to see I hadn't impressed her much with my wickedness, even at the talk of faeries, ghosts, and assassinations. "And her?" Mother Mary Gabriel nodded toward the convent, where Lillian learned to be a mother even as we spoke.

"I did a simple errand to look good at my job. I took Lillian from this safe place with you, and she landed in a world of hurt. If I can fix it, that's what I aim to do." I was tired of spilling my guts. "But what about you, sister?"

She folded her hands into her sleeves and strolled on toward the Twelfth Station: Jesus Dies on the Cross. "Let's just say I have other obligations besides running this convent. My order does more than pray about the evil at work in the world. I know no motive and have no proof, but I know that Taylor Humphrey is behind Anna's death in London, her missing baby, and the shadow of dark magic I've discovered. He is the devil incarnate. Perhaps that is motive enough."

We left the copse and walked toward the convent entrance. Bees buzzed in the late roses that bloomed along the circular drive in front of the church.

"Your penance is to discover his interest in Lillian's baby," Mother Mary Gabriel said as she stopped and bent over to pull a few weeds that had dared sprout among the rosebushes. "That may yield motive and proof for Anna and Martin's murders. As well as others."

As I gave her a hand up, the weeds disappeared into a sleeve of her habit. "Or, you could kill him, if you must—" she held out her hand to shake mine, "and I'll do anything I can to help."

Chapter Ten

—◆◆◆—

Market Research

I planned to start work for Mother Mary Gabriel and Lillian bright and early Wednesday by checking old newspapers for the baby kidnapping story before going to read police reports in Madison County, the scene of the crime. Maybe the kidnapping wasn't relevant to Lillian and Mother Mary Gabriel's suspicions of Humphrey, but I just didn't know. Evan had recommended a visit to the *Post-Dispatch* office, but Nancy had said the library had newspapers from all over the country.

I finished my coffee in the pub kitchen as I looked over the morning paper. The day was overcast, yet rain seemed unlikely, and it was already as warm as midsummer. I can't say I relished being stuck indoors all day, reading. Matthew came in the back door and said, "'Morning, Mr. Sean." He looked around the kitchen as if he hoped to see someone other than me.

"Fine day, isn't it?" I said. "Going to be warm, I think." He generally came in at night, to a sink full of dishes from the whole day. "Why are you at work so early?"

"I left my Irish notebook last night and wanted to study a bit today." He adjusted his wire-rimmed glasses. "Miss Maud around?"

Maud had been schooling the two of us once a week or so. Lately, she was quite fond of Lady Gregory's Celtic mythology tales. "She's getting her brothers dressed."

Whatever was between him and my niece would end in tears. Padraig was already glowering in the kid's general direction and had asked me to warn him off, warning folks off their wrong-headed choices being a particular skill of mine. I'd only made noncommittal noises about things blowing over on their own.

Matthew was always helpful and polite to the whole family, me particularly—obviously aimed at getting on Maud's good side since she paid a lot more attention to my opinions than her folks. I've been a kid with an all-consuming crush myself and know how these things go. But it gave me an idea.

"Want another job? Or do you have school?"

He apparently accepted any and all jobs offered to him and would be happy to help me look through newspaper records. I then had another thought. "Didn't I hear you started life over the river there in Illinois?"

"Yes, sir. When I was little. Until—" Matthew studied his shoes. "Those bad riots in East St. Louis."

Not quite seven years ago, the industrial burg just across the river, East St. Louis, Illinois, had erupted in an all-out race war over jobs. The Big Cinch had recruited thousands of southern black men to head north for good factory jobs. They didn't bother to mention those good jobs were as scabs to break the back of the trade unions.

"I need to find a place out in the country, near Alton," I told him. "Know the area?"

"I could try to give you directions," he said, looking a little doubtful. "But that was a long time ago when I was a little kid. Maybe my Ma—"

"I have directions, but if you might recognize landmarks, it would help." The trees and dirt roads of the American wilderness all looked the same to me.

"Oh, I could do that. Glad to."

Me and Matthew dashed out to be at the central library when it opened. The periodical room was a palace of marble, gilded wood, and light, the whole place a monument to Mr. Andrew Carnegie's generosity. Or guilt over how he'd made his fortune.

The kidnapping was a recent event and of huge interest to everyone. I could tell the librarian hoped for more of a research challenge, but he set us up on a work table and promised to be right back as he went to retrieve the stored newspapers from the archives.

We waited. And waited. Matthew read the morning papers. The day was already warm, but the reading room was cool, with a little hazy light filtering down on us through the high windows. We waited some more. I walked around the building and smoked a cigarette. I returned to find Matthew still waiting. He'd moved on to the Chicago dailies. At last, the librarian approached with a couple of long, wide boxes. "I don't understand it," he said setting them down on the table. "And I apologize. Some of the volumes are—" He shook his head. "Not missing. They have to be somewhere."

"Just not where they belong?"

"Exactly. So, you can start with these, and I'll keep looking." He squared his shoulders and marched back to the archives. "There's gonna be hell to pay, pardon my French. This is simply not acceptable."

I opened one of the boxes, the *Evening Star*, to the smell of ink and decaying paper. I believe it had the smallest circulation of the half dozen or so St. Louis dailies. I'd never actually read it. Matthew took the other, the *Alton Telegraph*. He pulled a Big Chief tablet from a satchel.

"Lend me a piece of paper, will you?" I said.

"Of course, Mr. Sean," he said, handing me a couple of sheets. He then produced a handful of sharp pencils from the bag. "Need one?"

I had a slightly leaky pen, which librarians frown on for some reason, so I borrowed a pencil, and we dove in.

The child disappeared on Friday, September 21, 1923, but I didn't see anything at all about it in the Saturday edition. "I got nothing on Saturday."

Matthew indicated the page in front of him. "Well, here's a paragraph in the *Telegraph's* police blotter column. 'Boy wandered away from home into the woods on Friday. Deputies searched for lost child. Tracking dogs to be brought in.' Doesn't identify the family."

The Arwalds could keep quite a lot out of the papers. At least at first. "OK, here we go." I'd found a story. By Sunday the paper had a full spread: A photo of the Alton house and grounds, the Arwald and De Noailles houses in St. Louis, and file photos of Violet and Humphrey's wedding. They ran a picture of a small child that I later learned was Lillian, so the picture must have been stolen or purchased by an enterprising reporter.

"Oh, look at this," Matthew said as he picked up the next newspaper in the stack and tapped the front page. "Monday. A reward."

I saw the same news in the *Evening Star*. A $30,000 reward was offered for information leading to the return of the baby. It included a photo of a smiling, blond toddler. For the next three days, having nothing new to report didn't stop the papers from running stories. They printed new pictures of the Madison County sheriff's deputies with the search dogs and blurry shots of people getting in and out of cars in unremarkable driveways.

We worked steadily for about an hour. Well, Matthew worked steadily. I went out to smoke. To the jacks. To make phone calls. Really, anything I could think of besides sitting in a chair. The kid looked up as I returned from my third trip to the water fountain, swallowed hard, and straightened his bowtie. "Don't mean to intrude, but—this is hard for you, isn't it?"

"Maybe," I said as I checked my watch. "Librarian ever come back?"

"He came by to apologize some more and threatened to fire the clerk."

"Let's pack it in. We gotta get over to the Sheriff's office."

Flipping over the last *Alton Daily Telegraph* in the stack to put it away, I noticed an advert for plows. It featured a drawing of a prosperous-looking gent, riding some sort of farm machinery pulled by a team of familiar dragon-type animals. Below it appeared, "Piasa Bird Plows. By Hapgood Plow Co., Alton, Ill."

The engraving blurred as my eyes began to burn and my head hurt. I sat down and closed my eyes, listening to the echo of footsteps on the marble floor, the drone of Matthew's voice, and the traffic outside. Matthew was taken with the engraving, which was a hoot, I won't deny.

"That's some picture," he said. "Oh, I've heard this story before." He began to read the little piece that accompanied the advert. "The Legend of the Piasa Bird," he said as he cleared his throat. "Wish Maudie could see this."

I opened one eye to give him as hard and stern a stare down as I could manage, and he returned to the story. "Long years ago, the Illini were terrified at the appearance on the inaccessible bluffs of an immense and hideous animal, half-bird, half-beast, which they called 'Piasa.' The bird swooped down and carried off the people, one by one, to its den in the rocks." He paused.

"Go on."

"But Chief Ouatoga had a plan to save the tribe, an ambush, but it needed a human sacrifice. The braves repaired to their secret place as directed by their leader, near where the victim was to stand. Judge then their astonishment, when dressed in his proudest robes, Ouatoga held up his young son as the victim. Just as the Piasa's awful talons grazed the child's head, twenty-five bow strings twanged, and twenty-five sharp arrows sped as were never bolts shot before, piercing the monster's breast," he said as he closed the paper. "And they painted the Piasa, up on the rocks there, to remember the battle. So, the story goes." Matthew packed away the newspaper in the box and replaced the lid. "Wouldn't you think they'd paint the Chief's picture?"

"Now the story I heard—" I started to say as I picked up my hat. I needed to get some lunch. "Is that the Piasa is an Underwater Spirit that lives in the river along there. The painting warned folks that the spirit makes the waters real dangerous."

"That makes sense," Matthew said. We gathered our notes, went back to the car, and headed north then east over the McKinley Bridge into Illinois.

*   *   *

I chalked up my headache to hunger and started to look for a place to eat as soon as I got clear of the bridge. The countryside brimmed with signs of autumn. Bright red and orange bushes lined the road and haybales awaited gathering from the fields on either side. We rattled past a farmhouse or two with pumpkins, green tomatoes, and dried Indian corn set up for sale on wooden crates.

The first town we came to was Venice. The streets flooded up to the porches every time it rained hard. A dog lay in the middle of the road and refused to move, so I pulled over to the curb near a little cafe, the Cedar Street Diner. I guess that meant we were on Cedar Street. The place looked busy enough to be good, and the dog had recommended it.

An old Model TT truck with "Madison County Sheriff" painted on the door was parked right in front. That gave me pause. I generally carry a gun when I'm out and about in the backwoods and today was no exception. But I didn't need it in a restaurant, and I sure didn't need to have it on me if I ended up rousted by the county bulls, which happened with a good frequency. I shoved the Webley in the glove box and got out of the car.

Matthew didn't budge from the passenger seat, saying, "Uh, Mr. Sean. I'm wondering if they serve my kind here."

I hadn't thought of that. The rules for getting by in Ireland are intricate, but we've got nothing on the Yanks. "What makes you say that?"

"Just a feeling," he said. "I'll wait while you get something."

I opened the passenger side door. "That's fecking shite." The day was hot, the road dust stuck in my throat, and we'd earned a break. "You're with me, so it'll be fine."

"I don't want no trouble."

"Me neither," I said, looking the diner over again, carefully. "I don't see no sign."

Pity was written all over his face. Pity at my stupidity. "Supposed you was back in Ireland? Facing—What did Maudie call them? The Orange Order? What would you do?"

A good question. When I was near his age the Orange Order burned down the Belfast shipyards to expel the Catholic workers. "I threw a lot of bricks, back in the day. Got beat up regularly."

"So, you're brain damaged or something?" he said, smiling.

"Something. Sure look this is Illinois, after all. We're not really in the South."

His eyes said, "You poor deluded fool," but he straightened his tie and crawled out of the car. He joined me to walk toward the cafe.

As I opened the door, a tiny bell rang. I tipped my hat to the congregation of overall-wearing farmers. "Good day, neighbors," I said, affecting the local accent.

The patrons sat in stone-cold silence.

The place was busy, clean, and bright. Blue-checkered curtains hung over the windows. A few blue Naugahyde-and-Formica booths and a counter with stools provided the seating. I spotted a couple of places at the counter and grabbed them.

The waitress danced menus, coffee refills, and food plates up and down the counter, a blur of efficiency. We locked eyes and she smiled. Then she looked to my right, at Matthew, and frowned. She shook her head and jerked it toward the door.

I pretended not to see and turned to the fella next to me. His uniform said he worked for Pevely Dairy.

"Say, sport, you done with that there menu?" I twanged at him.

"Oh, yeah. Sure, buddy," he said, handed it over, and then really looked at us. "Your friend's in the wrong place. Best to mosey." His eyes slid over to a large man in one of the booths, who shoveled in a platter of food while he read the newspaper.

"He's just a kid," I said to the dairy man. "In my employ."

He shrugged, gave me an "it's-your-funeral" sort of look, and accepted pie from the waitress.

"We'll have Coca-Colas to start," I said, as she turned her back to me and walked away.

Matthew whispered, "We need to go, right now."

But I was mad. It takes a bit to rile me up, but we were there. "Ah, miss." I raised my voice. "We're ready to order."

She worked her way back up the counter and at last stood in front of me, arms crossed. "I'm going to say this once. Leave," she said as she pointed to a hand-lettered sign on the wall. *We Reserve the Right to Seat our Customers.*

I changed tactics and tried the brogue, "What? You don't like the Irish are you saying now?"

The waitress sighed, tired and annoyed, maybe, that I'd interrupted her dance of efficiency. "I warned you." She turned to the man in the booth and called out, "Charlie. Would you show these travelers to the door?"

Charlie lifted his head from his meatloaf and potatoes and looked at her and then us.

I stood, left her a dollar tip out of spite, and put on my hat. "Let's run," I said to Matthew.

He was already up, his thin shoulders squared, and eyes raised to look at the man who advanced toward us.

As wide as he was tall and with about twelve inches on me, Charlie was a breathtaking ox of a man.

"Told you so," Matthew whispered.

"We're just leaving, buddy," I said to the giant.

"Damn right you are." He grabbed me by the shoulder and shoved me toward the door.

"No call for that, sir," said Matthew. His tone was calm and soothing, but he looked all the world like he meant to punch the big man.

I managed to catch the kid's eyes and shake my head as Charlie pushed me out the door. Fortunately, Matthew wised up in time. He shoved his fists in his pockets and followed us out. I stumbled, tripped on the warped wooden boardwalk, and fell, tearing a hole in my trousers at the knee.

"I'd move along, if I was you, paddy. And take your boy with you," he said wiping his hands on the dinner napkin still tucked into his shirt collar and left us.

Matthew dusted me off and handed me my hat, which had fallen to the ground in the scuffle.

"Well, that was fun," I said.

"Some fun," he replied as he hurried across the street and walked around to the passenger door.

"Thank you," I limped after him. "You really could've got hurt back there." I gave the engine a couple of cranks and it coughed to a start. "That stunt was stupid, even for me."

He shrugged and said, "You gotta pick your battles."

I got back in the car and eased out on the road. The dog had abandoned us.

"So, what do you usually do for food?" I asked Matthew. "Out traveling?"

"Me? I usually don't go nowhere," he laughed. "Generally, my folks plan ahead. Pack a lunch. And my aunt clips advice articles and saves travel pamphlets for my uncle."

"Well, I didn't plan on this, so sing out if you see a joint that looks lucky."

He was quiet for a few blocks. We came to a railroad crossing just as a freight train whistled its approach. I stopped.

"Out with it," I said. "You've something more to chide me with." The train rumbled past.

Matthew watched it for a minute then said, "Look, Mr. Sean, it's not the same for you and me."

"I know."

"Don't think you do. Maybe crackers and Klansmen hate Catholics, too, but you're a white man in America. You can change your clothes, change your voice even, lie a bit if you need to, and get by, at least for a while. Dressing up and talking proper don't help me much at all."

I nodded. "You're right. I was wrong." I rattled the Model T across the now-clear tracks. "I could have got you nicked, or worse, just trying to make a point."

"I got nothing against making points, but I can't afford to be stupid."

"Well, I'm sorry."

Matthew continued to look out the window for signs of accessible food. Eventually he said, "So, you wouldn't mind putting in a good word for me with Maudie?"

He had me in a tight spot, alright. "Maud seems to know her mind, without me sticking my oar in."

"Yeah, but she admires you a lot."

Pulling up to a stop sign, I turned to him. "Don't you think she'll catch on you'd put me up to it?"

He looked innocent enough, but said, "People generally don't even know you're playing them."

A wagonload of pumpkins cleared the intersection, and I rattled the Model T past the stop sign. As we left Venice's business district, Matthew spotted a couple of black schoolchildren walking down the street. For the moment, at least, he dropped his scheme for me to play the matchmaker. "Let's ask them kids about lunch," he said, so I pulled over. He leaned out the window for a quick conversation, and then fished a couple of pennies for the kids out of his satchel. He pointed ahead. "Go up one more block, to the church on the corner, then right."

I obeyed and soon we were seated at an outdoor picnic table, chowing down on bar-b-que pork steaks, cold lemonade, and apple pie. The lunch was well worth the wait. And the old couple who provided food from the backdoor of their home had no problem serving the Irish, for which I was grateful.

*   *   *

Well-fed, we reviewed the case as we drove to Edwardsville. The Wednesday papers screamed in banner headlines that the child had been found dead. On Thursday they screamed equally loud that two local truck-patch farmers had been charged with the crime.

The news on the first of October was devoted to the funeral and the case against the suspects. Then the hysteria all went away, as suddenly as it started. A brief trial in January of 1924, a guilty plea, and a death sentence. The next news about the Arwalds was Lillian's antics on the society page followed by the Piasa Lodge Ball and Parade, when the family entered my life.

The sheriff's office was in the rear of the county courthouse in Edwardsville, a grand hunk of gray granite that took up most of the block. The car park was deserted but for a few police vehicles. I pointed out bars on the second-story windows to Matthew. "Jail up there." He nodded and straightened his bow tie.

We were only a few minutes late and a sour-faced deputy ushered us into a vacant office. I say "vacant," but in it were stored all manner of unwanted things. It held a desk covered in boxes, a maze of file cabinets, and an unusually large number of hunting trophies, all the animal heads covered in a thick coat of dust.

The deputy left us to cool our heels quite a while. Apparently, the Judge's influence only went so far. Matthew soon had his nose in a book he'd brought while I snooped through their old files on the off chance I'd find the death record on Susan Arwald. Violet and Lillian's mother had also drowned at roughly the same location as the toddler.

Although the room was a mess, the filing system was not. I crawled through the file cabinets and located the 1906 drawer. There she was, right at the front. I wiped off the desk with my sleeve and had just opened the file when I heard footsteps approach. I shoved it in Matthew's satchel and looked up.

The deputy entered. "Here's what we have. The sheriff said to give you an hour with the files."

"Thanks," I said. "But it might take—"

"An hour. He should be in soon if you want to ask him for more time."

"If you could let me know when he gets here, I'd appreciate it."

He snorted, but positively, I thought, and left us.

I opened a window to catch a breeze and looked out on the fine day. The morning clouds were long gone. The sky was clear and the temperature hot. Adjacent to the courthouse, a dry cornfield awaited the combine. 'Twas a good day for reaping. I wondered idly about the farmer's priorities.

I gave Matthew the thinnest file, the initial missing person report and search for the lost child. I kept the other, the kidnapping and murder investigations. At first glance, anyway, mine looked complete: A thick section of witness statements, a long, detailed complaint, photographs of the crime scene, and also onionskin carbon copies of the St. Louis arrest file.

I started with the autopsy report, to get it over with. Matthew was in his own little world, scribbling notes.

"This is interesting if you're not the squeamish sort," I said.

He lay down his pencil and looked up. "I am not."

"The legal time of death is set down as 7:15 a.m., September 26, 1923. Declared by Dr. Antoine De Noailles. He stated that at dawn, he went out for a walk. While checking the ripeness of his persimmons, he found the boy near a creek about a quarter of a mile from the house."

"Didn't they already search the creek?"

I flipped some pages and skimmed the report. "Yes, several times. The family on Friday, the deputies again Friday night, Saturday with dogs. Sunday the ransom note arrived in St. Louis, and they stopped the search." The child was in the water for a while, which made guessing the time of actual death just that, a guess. I continued, "Stomach contents—Really?"

Matthew pushed his glasses up on his nose. "Go on."

"He had a little bit of wild berries or something like that in his stomach. Water in the lungs. And mud caked in his mouth, eyes, and ears. Rigor mortis was mostly gone, whatever that is. But he was underwater for a while. Best guess for the time of death, Monday night."

"After the kidnappers' were arrested," Matthew said.

The doorknob rattled, and we both looked up. Filling the frame was Charlie, the ox from Venice. He'd put on a sheriff's uniform and badge, which made him look even bigger.

"Your highfalutin Missourah judge gotta understand—" he started to say, then he laid eyes on me and stopped. "You—You—You—"

"Yes, it's me," I stood and closed the files. "Just about to go."

Matthew jumped to his feet and said, "'Afternoon, Sheriff," as he slapped his cap back on his head so he could tip it.

Sheriff Charlie charged into the room leaving the door wide open. I was out from behind the desk in a flash, grabbed Matthew by the arm, and he grabbed his bag. We dashed toward the door.

"Thanks for your help," I called behind me as we sprinted toward the exit.

"Hey, what about the files?" asked the deputy at the front desk.

"On the desk," I said as I ran past him. I didn't mention the Susan Arwald case file I'd stuffed in Matthew's satchel.

*   *   *

Matthew read the report to me as we drove to Alton. Susan Arwald had gone out in a midnight rain storm for some unclear reason and been found near the creek bank in the morning, soaked in water and smothered in mud. She wasn't in the stream, but her lungs were full of water.

"Strange," I said. "How'd she get out of the water?"

"Well, creeks rise and fall, you know," he said. "Pretty fast."

"They do." I'd gotten completely cut off by flooded roads a few times in the past on runs to the Judge's moonshiner.

As I drove past miles and miles of brown fields and yellow trees, I thought about what I'd learned. Besides to steer clear of the law in Madison County, Illinois. Money don't protect you from tragedy. And two drownings at the same place, in the same family, struck me as too much coincidence.

Matthew let me think in peace, looking out the window and occasionally consulting the written directions Lillian had given me.

"So, you grew up around here?" I asked.

"In East St. Louis, but I have a grandma and cousins in Alton. Where we're going—I think I used to play right around there."

"Small world."

"Seems the Lord put me in your path," he said as he pointed to a dirt road as I blew past it. "I think that was it."

I guess I expected a fancier entrance to the De Noailles property, but the drive looked like any other country roads, a packed dirt trace crowded by red-leaved shrubs.

I backed up to turn into the drive. A gate stopped us about fifty yards in, just around a bend in the road. Matthew got out and unlatched it while I pulled through.

Chapter Eleven

Intangible Assets

The car chugged up the steep grade. Weeds as high as the car's running boards threatened to take back the road and trees hung low over the driveway scraping the Model T's roof as I picked my way among the ruts. At last, we broke through the canopy and were on a bald knob. I drove along a cliff that overlooked the river. A house, perched on the highest point, was up ahead.

The house was nice, but no mansion. Covered in white clapboard, the place was built into a small hill. The front of the house crouched low and the roof peaked out, just a bit, at the shady front lawn. I parked in the circular drive, and me and Matthew climbed the flagstone path, past labeled plant beds, to the front door.

Lillian met us, her face pale and with dark circles under her eyes. The baby yelled from somewhere in the depth of the house. Lillian gave me a hug and a peck on the cheek. "I've never been so glad to see someone," she said as she dragged me through the small vestibule into a sunny parlor. French doors directly across from the entrance were wide open, framing a view of the river.

"Hard day?"

"After a very long night," she said, turning to Matthew and extending her hand. "I'm Lillian Arwald."

"Where's my manners?" I said. "Miss Arwald, meet Matthew Rouse. Works for my brother but grew up around here. He offered to help me find your place."

"Well, thank you for getting Sean here in one piece," she said to him, then smiled at me. "Didn't know you were afraid of the country."

"Afraid is a strong word. 'Confused' might be more accurate. Matthew, meet our employer, Miss Arwald."

He released the hand he'd been shaking all this while and murmured, "Ma'am."

Wherever the baby was in the house, she quieted down and Lillian sighed in relief. About then Miss Esther came into the room to announce, "She's asleep." Noticing the torn-out knee of my trousers she said, "Mr. Joye, what've you done to your britches?"

"Oh, nothing. Fell over a crack in the sidewalk, like the eejit I am."

She tsk-tsked at me, dragged me down a hall, up a short flight of stairs, and into a window-lined turret room snuggled like a leafy nest in the trees. She demanded my trousers. I started to protest but saw I had no play at all and handed them over. "Won't take any time to mend," Miss Esther informed me as she took a seat. Although the room was bright, she adjusted a work lamp, and then threaded a needle.

I stood around in my pants and felt about as awkward as can be. As I watched her work, I couldn't help but admire the smooth curve of her cheeks, the firm jut of her jaw, the way the light glowed amber in her downcast eyes. *Wasn't she fine, then? Old enough to be my mother. But what of that?* My embarrassment at not wearing trousers was replaced by a different sort of embarrassment altogether. I paced the sewing room to look out the window. "You wouldn't be having something else I could wear while you do that mending?"

She laughed at me as I heard scissors snip. I turned around to see Miss Esther look up from her work. Her eyes picked up the light from the trees that filled the windows. Gold-green-yellow-orange. "All done," she said as she offered the trousers, the mending hardly visible.

"Thanks," I replied as I took them from her. "I can't even tell where the hole was."

Miss Esther blushed a bit. *So pretty.* "Nonsense. I didn't have quite the right color." A frizzy little curl fell across her face. I reached over to push it back behind her ear. At the touch, I was transported to a still space apart from time but of all time, if that makes any sense at all. Just her and me, wrapped in quiet. I might well be dead—my heart stopped, my breathing ceased—and I didn't care a whit. Miss Esther patted my cheek and whispered, "We should get back."

I felt frozen to the spot.

"Put on your britches."

I released my breath, and the spell was broken. *What had gotten into me?*

She put away her scissors, needle, and thread while I dressed. We rejoined Lillian and Matthew in the parlor. She lounged on a fainting couch and he was sorting through a pile of gramophone recordings. "Something quiet and soothing," Lillian was saying.

"Debussy?" Matthew asked.

"Perfect."

He placed the record on the Victrola's spindle and set the needle in the groove. The music was, indeed, quiet and soothing.

Miss Esther closed in on Matthew. "You, young man, need a sandwich."

"But ma'am, I've just had lunch." But she'd already offered him her arm, and he had no choice but to escort her to the pantry.

Lillian opened her eyes. "Let's sit outside. Esther prescribes more sunshine for me."

"Is your grandfather here?" I asked as we walked out through a sun porch to a flagstone veranda overlooking the river. I could still hear the phonograph music, even outside.

"Yes," she said as she glanced at her wristwatch. "He's just had his medicine and is asleep. He has a lot of pain, you know. He'll be up later and at his best to talk to you."

We sat on curvy wrought-iron furniture, well-padded, of course, and I watched barges chug by, far below us on the river, while we listened to Debussy. With more than a little regret, I got back to business. "Do you remember anything about the party?" I said. "Still feel like that was a key event?"

Lillian sighed and looked at me sideways. "Sometimes I feel on the verge of remembering, in the early hours of the morning."

"Having a dream?"

"No. I don't think so. At least I don't remember any dreams. But I can't move when I awake, and I feel—dread—a presence, hovering. It's hard to describe. Then it's gone. It's like grabbing at spiderwebs."

"Mother Mary Gabriel seems pretty firm against your brother-in-law. And maybe the lodge."

Lillian got up and whacked at her chaise lounge cushions, then sat down again and leaned back.

"Does Humphrey come here much?"

An upstream tugboat tooted at a fellow riverman headed downstream.

"When he first came to St. Louis, you'd think he wanted to marry Grandfather rather than Violet, the way he'd hang around and chat about prehistoric Mississippian people. We've a mound here and other things—rock paintings. A cave. Couldn't get enough of it."

"Maybe he was trying to impress the family." Nor did it strike me as the evil scheme of a sorcerer, as Mother Mary Gabriel liked to call him. "And his field *is* antiquities."

The angle of the sunlight had changed and Lillian squinted. "God, my boobs hurt." She got up to pace the flagstones and asked, "Got a smoke?" I could help her out with that, at least. She took a deep drag on the cigarette I lit for her and then handed it back to me. "How's the investigation going?"

"For you or Violet?" *Or Mother Mary Gabriel. I sure had enough clients.* "Violet must think it's over. Baby located."

Lillian nodded and said, "I just don't trust my sister."

I shrugged. "I wonder how losing her own child has affected Violet in all this."

She got up and went in a rear door and came back about ten minutes later with glasses, ice, and lemonade. She poured me a glass. "I could have been nicer to Violet."

"Maybe her panic over you was reliving her baby's disappearance," I offered, taking a sip of my drink. It was stronger than lemonade.

Lillian fixed herself a glass of lemony booze and said, "I didn't think about that."

"Was Humphrey just supporting her yesterday at the convent?" I said, setting the not lemonade down on a glass table. "Maybe he has some angle of his own?"

"I don't know. But—" She knocked back half her drink in one gulp. "I don't want him around my baby. Hell, *I* don't want to be around him." She knelt beside my chair, took both my hands in hers, and looked up in my face, all scared and panicky. "You won't abandon us to him, will you?"

Lillian's fingers were cool and wet from holding the drink. "Of course not," I said.

She got up and draped her arms around my shoulders to give me a hug.

"And you're getting married," I said, patting her hand. "What could Humphrey possibly do to you with Kyffin around?"

She guffawed in my ear then said, "Kyffin? He's a dear, but so boring. And Violet's always owned him."

"So, Violet and Kyffin are—in love?" I was pretty certain he loved Evan Blake, not that it was any of my business. I unwrapped her arms and she wandered across the veranda, back to her lemonade pitcher.

"No, not like that. More like—" Lillian pondered the sky. "Best friends. They don't remember not knowing each other. He's happy to do what she says. I imagine the parents hoped something would come of it, but he prefers men."

"And Violet suggested you marry him?"

"Yes, she did. A lavender marriage," she said as she poured the rest of the spiked lemonade into her glass. "It's not like Kyffin has any real money, but the idea pleases Father. A fat wedding present check will help with my cash flow."

What a gold digger. I stood, suddenly sick of her. "You don't have to entertain me."

Lillian yawned. "You're a real sport, Copper. I should sleep while the baby sleeps. Grandfather will want to talk to you though if you don't mind waiting for him."

"I'll just enjoy the view."

She went inside, leaving me alone. For more than six months I'd thought of her as a cute little sheba, mostly harmless, and always up for a bit of craic. In the story in my head, she was the victim. That she would use someone as swell as Kyffin without a bit of remorse, well, it made me look at Lillian in a new light. A not-so-flattering light.

*   *   *

This was as good a time as any to match the locations on the property to the stories I'd just read in the newspapers and police reports. I walked around and acted like I admired the flowers and vegetables. I glanced back at the house a few times, but no one seemed to notice me, at least that I could see.

I ducked into the woods at a likely clearing and prayed I didn't get lost or walk off a cliff, two distinct possibilities. The creek where they'd eventually found the little boy's body sounded like the same place they'd found Lillian and Violet's mother, Susan Arwald, seventeen years earlier. I needed to see that spot.

I located a dry creek bed where a large black snake sunned itself on a bed of round stones. I gave it a wide berth, only to see a couple of more small snakes, their pattern and color blending well with the fallen leaves, a few yards away.

I focused again on the job. This snake haven was swollen with rain a year ago. I imagined the rushing waters and followed them to a point about a quarter-mile from the house. There, a willow, its roots exposed by the stream's flow, had caught the child's body. According to the autopsy, he'd been in the water for some time. His face, especially the eyes, mouth, and ears, was full of mud.

The fact that searchers had already covered this area on the day he went missing could be evidence that the kidnapping story was legit. But I supposed he could have been wandering around somewhere else and circled back. Or they just missed the body the first three times through the area.

A bit of water pooled in low spots, here and there, and I soon found the source, a deep pool fed by a spring bubbling out of a rock crevice. Not far away, I spotted a cabin—more of a shack, about to fall in on itself and almost swallowed by vines and holly bushes by the door. While it looked uninhabited, that didn't mean it was, and poking around was an excellent way to get myself shot. I reached for my Webley and realized I'd left it in the car.

"Hey, anybody home?" I yelled as I inched forward. "Don't want no trouble."

The only reply was a rustling, tinkling sound as a few yellow leaves floated to the ground. I looked up to see the trees were hung full of glass bottles, shining green and yellow in the afternoon sunshine. And I felt like I was being watched, not by a human intelligence, but more like the woods itself. That happens to me sometimes and nothing good ever comes of it.

I crept toward the shack, but stomped my feet and kicked up leaves, aiming to scare off the snakes I imagined lurked under every fallen leaf. Time passed, but I didn't seem to make any progress. My mind would float off to God knows where, and when I found myself again, I stood under the same tree with the same green and yellow bottles rattling overhead.

Although I was still doing my level best to ignore the fae and the sinking feeling that Éire had managed to follow me to America, I was pretty damn sure I'd walked into a protective ward. Now I know what to call that particular magic. Then, it was just some sort of fae foolishness to me. By sheer willpower, I managed to shuffle through the twigs and leaves to a stream about a yard across that flowed directly off the spring and was full of clear water. And snakes. I jumped back about as far as I'd struggled forward, then peeked over at the stream again. Swimming snakes. Crawling snakes. Snakes creeping out of the water, then diving in again. Snakes having a fine old fecking time.

I crossed at a different point, where no snakes swam. But I'd walked no more than few steps until I saw a large snake on the path to the shack. It hissed at me and reared up on its tail in warning.

By this point in the proceedings, I'd gone from scared to irritated. City slicker that I am, even I knew this was strange snake behavior. At last, I caught wise to the glamour—a fae illusion.

But not being a total fool, I armed myself with a dead tree branch cudgel and approached, my mind clear and focused on the job—*get into that shack*. The snake danced about, bobbing and striking at me, but just as I got within whopping distance, it was gone.

I turned and addressed the woods, "Éire, this has got to stop."

No reply.

"I don't owe you nothing. And I don't want nothing from you."

No reply.

"I'm going inside. I need to see what's here."

The tree bottles tinkled in laughter.

I reached the cabin with only a vague sense of dread and whispers in my head to turn back. A couple of black hens and a rooster scratched about in the dirt around a fire circle. The charred wood and ashes were cold and looked to have been rained on. The poultry fussed at me as I peeked in the window. Light through holes in the roof illuminated the room a bit. The back part was dark, but it seemed much more spacious than it looked from outside. As I mounted the single step to the entrance, my foot brushed away a line of red chalky dust spread across the stoop.

Though the day was near ninety degrees by that point in the afternoon, I shivered in a blast of cold air as I opened the packing-crate-salvage door and went inside. In my distraction, I almost tripped over a broom laid across the threshold. Hackles raised, I looked around the dim room.

Animal skulls and rusty tools hung on the walls, with dry snake skins and bundles of herbs tucked amongst the rafters. Water plunked into a bucket from a hole in the roof.

Candle stubs—many, many candle stubs—adhered to a craggy stone back wall. The shack fronted a small cave that added a good twenty square feet of space. At the rear of the cave was a nest of blanket-covered straw. The pallet had an abandoned feel about it, but I noticed a pair of dungarees, like American farmers wear to work outdoors, rolled up for a pillow.

A workbench was strewn with a mortar and pestle, jars of dried plants, and tin cans full of keys and nails. Heaps of bits and bobs—like doorknobs, a baby shoe, and a Bible—cluttered some shelves. I peeked in a leather pouch to see it was full of small animal bones.

A rough plank was stacked on cinder blocks in front of the shack's only window. Having served mass at least once a day for five years, I know an altar when I see it. A white handkerchief lay spread across the altar. Five Mason-jar candleholders were arranged in a cross shape. Dried plant bits were mixed in with the melted candle wax of the center jar. Under it lay a photograph of a serious-looking young black man in a military uniform, a sharpshooter's rifle hefted to his shoulder.

I was pondering the altar when a voice from the doorway made me jump.

"Watch out for snakes. They don't sleep yet." Miss Esther stood backlit in the doorway, the fading daylight creeping in around her.

"Good advice," I replied, my heart racing. Perhaps from thinking about snakes, but maybe the sound of her voice. "You startled me. I'm usually a bit more aware."

She smiled. "Dr. De Noailles is awake and feeling strong. He hoped to talk to you."

"Good. Glad to hear it." I tried to drum up a story of what I was doing in the shack. "I kinda wandered away, following that creek. And found this—"

She strolled over to the shelf and, picking up the baby shoe said, "You'd call it a shrine, I suspect."

"A place to pray?" I said.

"You can pray here if you like." Miss Esther took scissors from her pocket, clipped off some of the dried herbs hanging from the rafters, and put them in a jar. "It's one of many places of power on this land."

"Well, I'm sorry I intruded," I said as I followed her outside. She pointed to the cabin wall, where folded slips of paper were tucked into gaps in the wood.

I looked at her, questioning.

"Petitions. Others come here to pray, too. Not so bold as you, perhaps. But they come."

I nodded and we walked past a blur of plants and grass and trees. A scent filled my heart—tangy, metallic, with spice and musk and decay. I couldn't tell if it was the woods or Miss Esther.

The attraction I'd felt back at the house was still there. No, attraction's not the right word. More like passion. Or worship. The physical desire I'd felt was the most understandable and least important part. With what seemed like a simple kindness she'd forged a bond between us. Or extracted a promise.

Miss Esther seemed to feel no need to fill the air with idle chatter, but I, of course, blathered on about this and that to cover my awkward affections.

At last, she said, "My daughter, Lillian, tells me much."

"It's nice you raised her after her Ma died."

"It was a hard time for me, as well. Caring for her was a comfort." She glanced at me sideways. "Lillian finds you very attractive, you know."

"That's flattering. But she's getting married in a few days."

She stopped and took my hands then said, "And yet she uses you as her own."

I was in a tight and uncomfortable spot. "And what do you call this tree?" I asked as I pointed to the branches above our heads. "Beautiful red leaves."

"Sexual intercourse is not a service required of you, just because she asks."

A blush burned my face, and I gulped, "What makes you say that?"

Miss Esther held my face between her smooth warm hands and fixed those deep golden eyes on me. "You need to hear it."

Maybe I did, at that.

*   *   *

Miss Esther and me strolled along the creek back to the house in silence. I ran through a quick examination of conscience, which was becoming a daily event. Mother Mary Gabriel would be proud. *Did I always do whatever was expected of me, wrong or right, whether I wanted to or not?*

Dr. De Noailles sat on the veranda, reading a letter. As we approached, he pointed to a seat. "Ah, there you are. You've visited Lillian?"

"Yes." I was still pretty sore at her. "We spoke."

"Please, sit. Sit. Have some tea."

I sat and poured myself a cuppa.

He waved the letter at me and explained, "Just reading this note from my cousin in Oklahoma on the Osage Reservation." He shook his head. "Bad business. You've heard, of course."

I thought I'd heard something about the Osage Reservation. Oil wells, maybe? "About what?"

Dr. De Noailles flung the letter down. "Someone's murdering members of the tribe for their oil money." He pointed at the letter and said to Miss Esther, "You should read this, too, my dear. Something must be done. I'll write my senators again."

She put it in her apron pocket, murmuring, "I will. After supper. Enjoy your talk."

As I watched her walk across the veranda, I smelled acrid smoke, the odor particularly rank, worse than the Judge's cigars, even. I turned to see Dr. De Noailles inhaling from a hand-rolled cigarette. He held the smoke in his lungs for a good ten seconds before a slow exhale. He offered it to me, and I shook my head. I needed all my wits about me. "You're own special blend?" I asked.

The doctor chuckled and said, "I've cultivated a few plants from seeds. No, this is the last of the original lot."

"Hashish?"

He nodded. "A musician came around quite a bit courting Lillian last year." He took another deep drag and then exhaled. A cloud of smoke hung in the air around us. I lit a Lucky Strike in self-defense.

"The herb eases my pain, but I save it for this place," he said as he sipped from his teacup. "How goes the investigation?"

"Alright. I do need a better sense of that debutante ball, what happened behind the scenes."

He thought on that one. "A number of people acted strangely. Of course, the whole pageant has evolved into—" he waved his hand dismissively, "what it needs to be, I suppose."

"Who acted strange?"

"Well, Lillian appeared to be drugged. Violet was more than her usual bundle of nerves. Their father, Joseph—" He paused to make sure I remembered who Joseph Arwald was.

The first time I'd met him, just three days ago, Old Man Arwald had treated me like his servant and threatened my family's livelihood. "He's hard to forget."

Dr. De Noailles nodded. "He's always impatient, like he'd rather be somewhere else. The entire lodge board seemed on edge. Maybe someone forgot the donation to the policeman's association, and they expected a raid." He laughed and wheezed.

"What about Violet's husband, Mr. Humphrey?"

"Hmm." He drank more tea and ground out the hash stub in the saucer. "Nothing unusual there. Taylor sat with me a long while and discussed his plans for a dig at Cahokia." He got up, using both canes, but fairly smoothly. "I need some exercise. Show you my treasures."

We toured his herbs, growing all around the side yard. "Now that one is *Levisticum officianale*. Lovage. Goes in a love works."

I peered at the mass of greenery and said, "Which one?"

He pointed with his cane to a huge plant in one of the few sunny spots. "I've given the matter a great deal of thought, and I think you and Lillian are a remarkable match."

"Excuse me?"

The doctor shouted in my ear, "My granddaughter. I think you should marry her."

That was about the last thing I expected him to say. "I hardly know her."

He dismissed my protest with a hand wave. "I recognize the people this family needs." He hobbled down the path to a shady mudhole under a tree. "That one is *Symphytum officinale*. Comfrey. The root is protective, and we'll be drying those leaves." He bent to pick comfrey leaves and stuff them in his pockets. He jammed a few in my pocket as well. "The leaves bring money."

"Thank you," I said as I held his elbow, fearing he'd fall with all the bending and stooping. "Lillian's engaged. They've set a date, I hear."

"Eh?" he pointed at another mass of green, broad-leaved and covered in white flowers, basking in the sunlight along the coach house wall. "*Nicotiana rustica*," he said. "Tobacco."

"Quite thrifty of you." I moved around so he could see my face since he was pretending not to be able to hear. "Lillian's been engaged to Kyffin Bernard for over a year."

"Bernard. Nothing against him. But not right for her." He took up the march again. "He's not valued for who he is." He gave me a sharp, reproachful glance as if the fake marriage were somehow my fault.

"I couldn't agree more. But this is what the two of them want to do."

"No, they've been manipulated and don't see an escape. They're doing the easiest thing and hope it works out." He paused and faced me. "It's not the child, is it?"

"Sir, with respect, this conversation is pointless."

"But I need you in the family." Dr. De Noailles's pout put me in mind of Lillian. "After I'm gone, my granddaughter must assist Esther to carry on the traditions. Lillian will need a proper helpmate."

"Violet's your granddaughter, too. And married to a helpful sort of person, I guess."

Anger flashed in his eyes, but his voice sounded sad as he said, "Taylor's turned out to be such a disappointment."

I wouldn't touch that with a ten-foot pole. Or maybe I would. "He seems to dote on Violet." Sort of.

The old man waved his hand. "Of course, of course. He's fine as a husband, I expect. Don't know or care. He loves the ancient realms." He poked at my chest with an extended index finger. "Yet he thinks our heritage is a tool, a means to an end. The ancestors and spirits don't love him back. Not like you."

"I don't know what you mean. And Lillian doesn't want to marry me." *And I didn't want to marry her.*

"Nonsense. She fancies you." He slapped me on the back with a lot more force than I expected and lead me toward a path into the woods. "Now, this is remarkable, what I'll show you next."

"More plants?"

"No, no—a surprise. You'll appreciate it."

Chapter Twelve

Encumbered Assets

Dr. De Noailles dropped the subject of my nuptials, but I felt like it was the end of a scrimmage rather than the match. We crossed the wide lawn, taking in the view of the river far below. The doctor leaned on a cane and gripped my arm with the other hand as we picked our way along a deer trail that followed a trickling stream. Water dripped from a rock face's mossy ledge into a small pool, the source of the stream we'd followed. Obscured by bright red and yellow undergrowth, a low cave lurked under the rocks.

The doctor took a leather pouch from his pocket and glanced at me. "Tobacco," he said. "An offering to the water spirits." He sprinkled a pinch on the pool and spoke a few words I couldn't make out.

"Let's go in," he said, turning to the cave mouth proper. Although some rough wooden steps led up to the cave, it looked impossible for him to mount them.

"Sir, you'll not be climbing about in a cave?"

He made an irritated noise at me then said, "You go up first, and then you can lend me a hand. Nip in there and light the lantern. To your left."

The old man had given me his other cane to carry for him, so I used it to thrash the leaf-rot-covered ground to flush out snakes. I poked my head in the foyer. A source of dim light was ahead, but I still couldn't see much. I felt rather than saw the lantern hanging from a chain on the wall and lit it and then returned to the entrance to haul Dr. De Noailles up the rocks and stairs. Once at the cave mouth he didn't even need to duck, just turn sideways a bit to access the large, open cave room. I followed and hoped I'd be quick enough to catch him when he fell.

"I am here," Dr. De Noailles called out. "I've brought this young man, called Sean Joye. A traveler from far across the waters."

High above us, sunlight filtered through a crack in the rocks. A fire pit was in evidence in the center of the space, large stones surrounding it.

"Build us a little fire here, will you?"

A few bits of firewood were at the ready there. I gathered some kindling near the cave entrance. The tinder consisted of the last piece of blank tablet paper Matthew gave me that morning. As the fire licked the kindling, he again produced his tobacco pouch and what appeared to be a dried-up bird wing. He fed our little blaze a handful of tobacco, filling the space with smoke that he directed at the two of us with his feathers.

"Spirits and ancestors, we come to visit you today. I offer tobacco in your honor. We come to learn from you. This young man is particularly ignorant and in need of your teaching. Thank you for allowing this visit today."

I tried to be suitably solemn and not cough at the holy smoke hanging in my throat. It weren't the first time I'd been blessed with smoke—incensing the altar boys was part of every high mass. Of course, this smoke wasn't frankincense, but rather a fine, sweet tobacco, nothing at all like the Prince Albert I generally bought.

The doctor left off blessing me, perched on one of the fire pit stones, and let the smoke find its way out through the crack in the ceiling.

I took a stone seat and looked around, my eyes now more adjusted to the cave's twilight. Remarkable paintings covered the walls. Some were animals, others were human shapes and symbols. I didn't know their meaning, but they tickled my memories, like a tune, familiar yet forgotten. "Did you make these?" I asked.

"No, no. They're a thousand years old. From the time of the mound builders, I'd say."

I looked closer at the lower figures. They weren't just painted but also carved in the rock. A lively squiggle, obviously a snake, caught my eye. I felt it call me to look at it. To touch it. My hand reached out, but I stopped myself. No good would come of that. Water dripped from above, and I could hear running water somewhere deeper in the cave. Tiny bats, hidden among icicle-like stone formations, clung to the eaves of the place and chirped and stirred in the waning light of the afternoon. I felt stuck in time. Or between time.

"And what is this place, exactly?"

"A ritual site," Dr. De Noailles said. "We've always called it Vision Cave. An ancient version of the Osage House of Mysteries. This room—the meeting room—teaches the nature of the cosmos as clearly as the decorative elements of a medieval cathedral."

He lectured on the artwork in a voice low and hypnotic, occasionally waving his cane for emphasis. "See the three registers of images? Upper, middle, lower," he spoke as he pointed with his cane. "There. The Middle World. That's us. Humans, plants, and animals. Our role is to keep balance among the worlds. What a piss-poor job we've made of it, too. At one time the lodge—" He was so irritated, he had no words. He regrouped and began again.

"What we do here affects the Above and Beneath Worlds. Every day is a new assault, a man-made assault, on the balance."

I could pick out more and more details in the space. I noticed a narrow opening in the rear of the cave. "What's that?"

"Leads to several chambers for burial and another for initiation and spirit quests. I haven't been in there in years. Very difficult to access." Dr. De Noailles shook his head. "I was last in there to bless my son's vision quest before he left for France in 1917."

"Violet and Lillian never mentioned an uncle."

"He's dead now," he said as he pointed the cane at the ceiling. "What do you think that is?"

I saw figures with wings. "Angels? Heaven?"

He snorted, "You Catholics. No, to put it simply, that's Above World. Home of the Thunderers. Powerful spirits who rule the air. What do you think they make of those aero planes and dirigibles? Or the dirt pumped out of factory chimneys day and night?"

In my youth, I was an eager-to-please student. "They don't like it?" I hazarded.

"Well, yes, obviously. And?"

I wracked my brain and stared into the cheery little fire I'd made. A log teetered on a smaller one that was burning away to nothing, then fell and rolled away from the heap. He poked it back into place with his cane.

"Balance," I said. "Upsets the balance."

"Exactly. We're not doing our job, so the Thunderers must step in with tornados, lightning storms, fires, wars, and the like."

Pleased with myself, I pointed to other figures and said, "And this one? Wings, too, but looks more like a snake."

"An Underwater Spirit, possibly She'-ki himself, represented with wings—the ability to travel between worlds," the doctor said. "The most powerful, in many ways."

"Tornados are pretty powerful. Took the top off your city house, if I recall."

"Birth and death. Water and earth," he exclaimed, whacking the ground with his cane for emphasis. "Much more formidable than a wind storm. She'-ki rules there, chief of all the Underwater Spirits."

"And sends the Underwater Spirits to correct the balance with—" Some sort of disaster, I reasoned. "What?"

"What do you think?" Dr. De Noailles's eyes twinkled in the firelight.

"Floods?"

He nodded. "Earthquakes. Locust swarms. Disease."

We sat in silence for a moment. Outside the cave, out in the Middle World, cicadas screeched their evening song. He poked at a crevice between the stones around the fire circle with his cane and said, "There's a box in there. Fetch it out."

I must've looked as reluctant as I felt.

"I just checked for snakes," he sighed. "It's safe."

I picked up a stick and poked about a bit myself, then used it to retrieve a heavy metal box and hand it to him.

He struggled for a moment to open the rusty lid. "Here," he said. "Our prize artifacts."

Dr. De Noailles displayed a carved stone figure made into a pipe. It depicted a woman with a basket of corn or something on her back. Next, he handed me a small disk—a prehistoric coin, perhaps—decorated with a long-nosed figure wearing dangly earrings. I'd swear the earrings had faces on them. The box held a half dozen things like that. "These are over a thousand years old."

"Mound people stuff?" I wondered if he had some point to this history lesson.

"Yes. Rescued from looters," he said as he picked up a fringed leather roll. "This isn't as old, but more precious. Left with my grandfather for safekeeping when the Missouri Osage were expelled by the government."

"What is it?" As I spoke, I noticed the disk felt warm in my hands. I glanced down and thought the earrings in the image winked at me. Obviously, a trick of the light. "And why your grandfather?"

Dr. De Noailles thought on that a minute. "He was a hard man, but he respected the old ways." He stroked the leather. "This is a medicine bundle. He taught me that it holds items sacred to She'-ki. The elders—'the little old men' as they're called—decided the bundle needed to stay near the great river confluence here. In the old days, my grandfather and a few trusted friends would open it with great ceremony once a year or so, to honor She'-ki and the Underwater Spirits."

"Part of the balancing job?"

"Exactly," he said, appearing pleased I wasn't entirely stupid. Then his face darkened, "Through the years, that group—their descendants—became the 'Piasa Lodge.'"

"Is that what's troubling you?"

At last, the time had come for the doctor to spit it out.

"Artifacts have gone missing lately."

I thought of the mess that was his home. "Someone didn't mislay them?"

"I may be old, but I know the relics. They're the most valuable things in my house. It could all burn down, for all I care, but those things—"

"So, you hid the special items here?"

Dr. De Noailles gripped my hand. "If something happens to me, someone needs to know where these relics are. Especially the medicine bundle. Misuse will harm my descendants."

"Ain't you worried I'll come back and steal them?"

He smiled and shook his head, whispering, "They're well-guarded."

*   *   *

The doctor and I made our way back to the house. He was exhausted and adjourned for a nap, while Miss Esther said goodbye to me, adding, "Remember. Mind your heart."

In the foyer, Lillian waited to walk me to the car. She linked her arm in mine as we strolled across the lawn piled high with fallen leaves. "So, what's on Grandfather's mind?"

"The usual elderly gent concerns. Marry off the grandkids. People stealing his treasures."

"What?" she said. "Stealing?"

"Yeah, things are missing. Probably mislaid them."

"Of course," Lillian said as she wound her arms around my neck and pulled me close to her, pressing her body into mine against the car door. "You're so smart."

I heard voices from up at the house. Matthew and Miss Esther. "Bank's closed, doll," I said, extricating myself. "Here comes my passenger."

She pouted, pretty and not very convincing. "Well, call me. Actually, you'll have to call the gas station down at the bottom of the hill. They'll send a boy up on a bike to tell me I have a call."

"Grand system."

She shrugged and said, "Grandfather's house. Grandfather's rules."

Matthew climbed into the passenger seat, lugging an enormous covered basket.

"Whadda ya got there?" I said as we drove away.

"Oh, sandwiches, apples, cake. Miss Esther thought I might get hungry on the way back," he said as he dug deeper. "Some jars of jelly and honey for my mom and auntie. Black walnuts, already husked and shelled." He opened the bag and sniffed. "Mmm, roasted. Those would be for my uncle, I expect."

"Miss Esther seems to have taken a shine to you."

"I guess. She had a boy, killed in the war," he yawned, curled up in the seat, and leaned his head against the door. "Women like to fuss over someone," he said, from all the wisdom of his years. He then promptly fell asleep.

I stopped for petrol and thought things over.

Could Miss Esther and Dr. De Noailles be talking about the same son, a son they'd had together? Maybe the photo I saw in the shack. *Was the candle magic*—that's what I now know to call it— *aimed to protect him or just keep the memory alive?* I needed to ask Lillian and Violet about their uncle.

I was bone tired as the Model T rattled across the railroad tracks into Alton. It'd been a long day and I hadn't answered any- one's questions. Everyone in the family seemed to be on edge. *What would make high-society people so jumpy?* I went through the list: Out-of-wedlock child. Hasty marriage of convenience. Missing artifacts. *What else?*

I shook Matthew to wake him and asked, "Hey, kid, you mind one more stop?"

*   *   *

The sun set as me and Matthew drove into Edwardsville. The townsfolk had rolled up the sidewalks for the night and gone home to their dinner. The courthouse was locked up tight as a drum. Lights were on in the jail, of course, and the sheriff's office. I parked the car in the adjacent cornfield and left Matthew sweating behind the wheel with the engine running, as I slipped over to the sheriff's office where we'd worked earlier in the day.

I couldn't believe my luck. The window in the storage room was still open. I raised it a tad more and climbed through it. Groping my way to the desk, I found the files still there, right where I'd left them. But as I tiptoed back to the window, I bumped into a metal wastebasket I hadn't seen. I froze for a moment but heard no running steps. Relieved, I started back to the window, but just then the door banged opened. The light switch clicked on as a deputy entered.

"What the hell—" He struggled to free his gun from a hip holster.

I dove out the open window, hit the ground rolling, and jumped up before the deputy could make it to the window. As I ran, he shot randomly into the dark, the bullet ricocheting off some trashcans to the hiss and caterwaul of a cat. I crashed through the corn shucks and beelined to the car. As I jumped up on the running board, I shouted, "Go—Go—Go—" and pounded the Model T's side. Matthew didn't need to be told twice. He hopped on the gear selector, then the fuel, and we plowed through the corn rows out into the night. I opened the door and tumbled in, still hugging the files.

Somehow, we cleared the town without anyone from the sheriff's department catching up with us. We changed drivers at the crossroad, laughing like the crazy fools we were. Nothing like a bit of divilment to work up an appetite. "Break out the picnic," I said.

"Yes, sir," he said as he unwrapped a sandwich and handed me half. "You do stuff like this all the time?"

"Not usually," I replied as I took a bite. I pointed to the file. "There's an electric torch in the glove box. Read some to me while we travel."

He opened the folder. "We got—" he said as he rustled the pages, taking a quick inventory, "let's see, Madison County witness statements, missing person report filed by Mrs. Humphrey, a bunch of pictures—" He turned one over. "These are marked 'SLPD.' Carbon copies of something—a lot of onion skins here." He showed me the sheaf of thin paper. "These are the St. Louis Police records."

"Now we're getting somewhere. Start at the beginning." I munched on my ham sandwich while he talked.

The gist was Violet called the Sheriff's office from the petrol station and made the first report. Reading between the lines, she'd been crisp and controlled, but in a barely restrained panic.

The sheriff talked to everyone in the house, from Dr. De Noailles to the servants and property caretakers. Everyone but Miss Esther, who was listed as a resident of the house, but not home for any visits by the sheriff or St. Louis police detectives. It was clear the sheriff thought Humphrey and Lillian were being evasive. Dr. De Noailles was his blustery, condescending self, but the worry showed in his statement. And he outright refused to answer questions about Miss Esther's whereabouts. Joseph Arwald arrived on Saturday, the day after the child went missing, to lay down the law.

"Now, this is interesting," said Matthew. "There was a ransom drop. We didn't see that mentioned in the newspapers."

"Nothing in the autopsy report was in the news, either," I said. No wonder those reporters repeated the same thing over and over and printed blurry, stolen pictures.

As we drove west, we pieced the story together. At noon on Sunday, September 23, the cook at the Arwalds' home found a misspelled ransom note tacked to the back door. It said to bring $50,000 to an alley behind a greengrocer in the old Kerry Patch neighborhood at midnight on Tuesday. Leave the money in a box of apples that would be waiting there. *Mr. A. a loan. No cops. Babe in gud care.*

Arwald provided the money. He hired Continental Op agents to stake out the location. Around two o'clock in the morning, a produce truck arrived. Two men unloaded sacks of potatoes and onions, and then took the box of apples. The private security men followed them to a truck farm in nearby Florissant. The private detectives tipped the local law, which dealt with the men. No child was there.

Matthew and I got home well past dark. I paid him ten dollars for the day's work—a lot, I know, but he'd earned it. "Did Miss Esther ever say what happened to her son?" I asked.

"The war happened," he said as he put the money in his pocket and put on an apron to start on the pile of dishes in the sink. "He went missing in action in the Argonne Forest. What's sad is she didn't find out for sure that he was dead until just last fall."

Chapter Thirteen

Fringe Benefits

The dinner rush was well underway when Matthew and I got back to the Belfast Bar from Alton. Aiming to help him with the sinkful of dishes that awaited, I hung up my coat and hat to discover my shoulder holster empty. I realized the familiar weight of a gun under my right arm had been missing for most of the day, which gave me a turn until I remembered I'd put it in the glove box before we went into the café in Venice. I resolved to nip out and get it as soon as the dish pile was less formidable.

Padraig, Eliza, and Maud were all working the bar. The boys, Gerald and Patrick, watched over their baby brother, Francis, who toddled among the barflies. All three of them were in the way of a darts match, but the players didn't seem to mind none.

When the dishes were under control, I seized the moment to have the flat to myself for a rare bit of relaxation. The hubbub downstairs was reduced to a soothing background noise by the closed door, and I'd barely shed my shoes and loosened my braces when Violet showed up at the flat's outer entrance. The brave woman had climbed the wooden stairs that clung to the pub's backside to reach me.

"God. What a day," she said as I opened the door. Her black wool suit was too hot for the weather but tailored to show off every curve. A purple cloche hat with a bit of net across her forehead warmed her cool blue eyes. "I've brought your final payment." I could hear her chauffeured Rolls idling at the curb.

I'd seen this moment coming. Working for Violet had been my excuse to snoop around for Lillian. With the baby found and the abortionist story dropped, I knew I'd be sacked. Yet I was stuck on how to respond.

Violet breezed past me into Padraig's small parlor, dislodged a wicked-looking hat pin from her hair, and tossed her hat on a crate covered by a bit of chintz. You wouldn't know it wasn't a fine sideboard unless you peeked underneath. Lavender gloves followed. She circled the room, as if there were some choice as to where to sit, and then all but collapsed on the settee. She opened her bag. "A celebration is in order. Have you a couple of glasses?"

"I might."

She produced a flask as I looked around in the one wall cupboard. "Have you tried the Green Fairy—absinthe?" Violet said. "Usually poured over a sugar cube."

"No, I haven't." That sounded quite dangerous. Not the sugar. The faerie. "I could get sugar from the kitchen downstairs," I suggested, bringing her a jelly jar and a coffee mug.

"Never mind," she said as she poured shots of the green liquid into my fine crystal stemware and lifted the jar in a toast. "Pan, Artemis, Dionysus. Come to our aid."

I thought it was an odd sort of toast, not knowing Violet's hobbies as I do now. "Amen," I replied as I sipped the liquor. It was very fancy, potent, and tasted of licorice and peril. I toasted her in return, "Sláinte."

"Today, you—" Violet held out the jar for a refill. "What? Searched our house in Alton?"

"A social visit. Your sister invited me," I said as I poured from the flask. "I know you don't need me no more."

"And the visit to the sheriff's office?" she huffed. "Are you unclear as to the terms of your employment?"

"I know, I know. But Lillian has questions, too. She can't see the big picture, and none of you want to talk."

She looked at my barely touched mug and then glared at me. "Do you usually let a lady drink alone?"

Well, no, I didn't. I drained the cup and poured a refill. "Tell me what's going on."

"I'm sorry we brought you into this," she said as she sipped the liquor. "The situation seems to be similar to when Lillian shirked her duties at the debutante ball. But all is well. The child is found. Yet you—" Violet poked me in the chest with her index finger, "—continue to buzz around our business."

I gulped my drink, aware of how wonderful she smelled. Violet wasn't wearing her usual Shalimar. Tonight, her scent washed me with the pure, clean peace I used to feel after communion.

With difficulty I focused on my real job, to help Lillian fill in blanks in her memory and to defend her against her family, against this very lovely lady seething on my settee. "The little one is found. But is all well?"

She looked up. "It is, at least for the baby."

"This must be hard for you."

She stared at the crucifix on the wall over the door. "Whatever do you mean?" she said from a faraway place.

"I mean, losing a child, as you did—"

Violet's head whipped around and her eyes froze me solid as she hissed, "I won't talk about it."

I felt like a first-class heel. "Of course. Sorry." I shifted to give her a little more space and drank some more of her God-awful hooch. "Who do you think is the father?"

I could swear she let out a gasp, and then her eyes narrowed. "You don't know him. This is entirely a family matter."

"I get it. Butt out."

"Don't think so much," she said, dropping the lady-of-the-manner attitude and smiling a teasing sort of half-grin, an older, glamorous version of Lillian for half a second. "You're not that smart."

"Aye, I'm not," I said as I set down the mug and took her hands in mine. "And for that, I can't take your money."

Silence built between us as we fell into each other's eyes. At last, Violet looked away, her glance flicking to our hands intertwined on her lap. Her nails began to trace crazy triangles across my palms. Our knees touched and I felt cold and hot at the same time. She was weaving a spell and tying it up tight. Violet leaned in close, her candy-scented breath caressing my face, and whispered, "Watch over me, always. Come to my aid when I call."

I was lost in her eyes, like the very first time I looked into them. I found that if I leaned in too close and tried to escape, that I'd only be caught again by the beads of sweat on her forehead and the damp, blonde hair frizzed around her ears and neck. Somewhere time stopped. I tried to crawl back to reality by focusing on her words. Had she said, "Come to her aid?"

"You can always count on me," I managed to spit out. "That goes without saying."

I watched Violet's mouth move. "I don't exactly know how you do it, but people see in you what they like best." Her red lipstick was faded and a bit smeared.

"Which people?"

"Lillian's always ready for a petting party, and you do oblige." Lips, tongue, and teeth listed my iniquities.

"You know this because—?"

"Quite obvious." She dismissed my lustfulness with a toss of her head, then ticked off the next deadly sin. "My grandfather thinks he's recruited another soul for the family Piasa cult. And Taylor—"

The roar from the pub was suddenly louder for a moment, and then a door slammed. The spell in the air between us broke in shards of fae laughter rattling around in my head.

Violet looked toward the door and dropped my hands, "What was that?"

"Old building." Honestly, I wasn't sure. "'Twill be falling in on us one fine day."

She wobbled to her feet and circled the room to gather her belongings. Then she removed a check from her bag and placed it on the crate-table.

"But I didn't find the baby," I said. "That's what you wanted all along."

Under no obligation to be truthful with the help, Violet didn't deny lying to me. "You spent time on the task and I want things to be square. Just cash the check."

I stood and finished my drink. An impulse, strong and compelling, perhaps the generations of peasants in my blood, urged me to doff my cap and bow. I fought it.

"Are we square?" she asked as she picked up her hat. "You're done with us?"

"You don't owe me nothing." I walked over and looked at the check. Lots of zeros, there. Padraig would kill me if I refused it. "Thanks for coming by." I picked up her check, tore it into tiny bits, and threw it in the rubbish bin.

Violet sighed and put on her hat. "I'm not writing another."

I nodded. "I'm curious about something. How did you figure the baby was at the convent?"

"Oh, that," she said as she twisted the doorknob. "Well, you refused to work for us at first, so Father assigned Kyffin to the task. He easily located the child and, like the good friend he is, told me."

Violet then opened the door and walked out into the night.

*   *   *

Kyffin's betrayal of Lillian, and by extension, myself, hit me like a fist in the breadbasket. If I'd trusted anybody in this whole mess, it was him. I threw myself down the back stairs to the Model T. I had to find him, but as I cranked the engine, I realized I had no clear idea what I was going to do when I did.

If I'd learned anything in General Collin's squad during our Troubles, it was to put aside thoughts of revenge before going on a job. This visit must be an impressive lesson. Violet had bossed Kyffin around his entire life, and he had to break that pattern now.

Proceeding north on Tamm, I'd be at Kyffin's place in a few minutes and needed a plan. Surprise would be my only ally. He had me on reach, height, and that boxing medal from the 1920 Olympics. I'd get in one good punch. Maybe.

He lived on the third floor of a swank building right across from Forest Park. The only lights I saw were in his place on the third floor. Tenants were still out and about for the evening, it seemed, and I found a parking space in front for a change. My Webley was still in the glovebox. A stroke of bad luck, that. I slipped it in my trouser pocket for the moment.

"'Evening," said the doorman. He'd seen me park and held open the hefty wood-and-glass door. If he was surprised that I was out and about without a hat and coat, he didn't show it.

I ran up the steps and grabbed the door out of his hands. "Rest yourself, Jonesy. Mr. Bernard in?" If Kyffin wasn't home, I'd start the round of clubs and speaks he liked.

Jonesy had been gassed in the Great War and took a full minute to recover his breath enough to talk. "Just came in, sir. With a loaded briefcase. Shall I call up?"

"No, don't bother. That will give him time to think of an excuse not to go out."

"Works too hard," Jonesy gasped, "since Mr. Blake moved out." He looked worried. "Rent might be. . . problem now."

I doubted that very much. And it was news to me that Evan was out of the picture. He hadn't said a word when I talked to him yesterday. I tried to look in the know with a nonchalant, "Maybe."

"Need anything else?" he said as he looked at his watch. "My shift's over."

"Naw," I said. "I'll be fine. Go on home."

"Good evening, then."

I tipped Jonesy, crossed the marble lobby, and took the first set of steps at a sauntering pace, but as soon as I was out of his sight ran up the next two flights. I took a couple of deep breaths as I walked down the hall to Kyffin's flat and tried to think of what to say. Eventually, I gave up and rang the doorbell.

At first, I heard nothing and was about to decide Kyffin had gone out. Then I heard his steps—crisp, firm, in charge—approaching. The knob rattled and the door swung open. He was still dressed for the office, although his tie and collar were off. His right hand held a glass of amber liquid. A radio somewhere was tuned to a baseball game. The Senators were at bat.

Delight spread across Kyffin's face, then surprise. Then, a real surprise, as I delivered a quick right uppercut followed by a left across the jaw. My strategy was based on the theory that such a pretty jawline had to be glass. Had to.

It wasn't. He dropped his drink and jabbed once, twice, three times to my solar plexus before pinning my arms to my side. He was trying to not hurt me and hadn't done a very good job. "What the hell's the matter with you?" he said.

I needed to puke. I wriggled out of his grasp and threw a wild blow that somehow connected with his nose, which promptly started bleeding. "Violet told me."

"Batter swings. It's—a foul tip," said the radio announcer. The crowd murmured.

Kyffin wiped his nose on the back of his hand and assumed a classic boxing stance, fists guarding his face, knees flexed, and mobile. He bounced a bit, back and forth on the balls of his feet. Taking me serious now. Maybe. "Told you what?"

He'd studied boxing in college. So what. I'd been schooled in the Belfast streets. Of course, that mostly consisted of throwing bits of brick at the packs of Prod kids who were throwing bits of brick at us.

I punched at his midsection as I smashed his instep with my right foot. Inches away from my face, he smelled like blood and sweat and whiskey. I made an effort to remember what I was so mad about and managed say, "Lillian hid her baby and you ratted her out."

The voice of the radio in the parlor interjected, "The windup. The pitch. It looks low and outside. Called strike two." The crowd booed.

"Let me explain," he yelled as he landed a wicked cross cut to my right ear. He wasn't holding back now. All I could hear was the ocean's roar—the North Sea at Giant's Causeway, I think—and fell to my knees, swaying. I grabbed his legs, which brought him to the floor. His fall smashed a small table and scattered cigarettes, mail, and business cards across the foyer.

I pinned him to the floor, at least for a moment. The room lurched and darkened. I made the effort to form words. Or at least try. Things went black while I dreamed I fell into a warm bath that smelled like Kyffin.

I suppose knocking me unconscious gave him a chance to flip himself free and kneel on my chest. Anyway, I came to a moment later, his warm breath in my face, as he said, "Yes, but—I didn't know."

At least I could hear again. I pretended to give up and closed my eyes. I did not feel well at all. I sensed him relax a bit and took that moment to twist away, leap up, and slam myself down on his back. I bit randomly and caught his ear lobe. The blood's metallic tang mixed on my lips with my sweat.

With an, "oomph," of expelled air, he collapsed to the floor.

"Bases loaded. Clean-up batter on deck," the radio announcer informed us.

"We agreed—" I started to say, but he recovered and bucked me off his back. I clattered across the foyer, slid into the parlor, and upset a plant stand. A fern crashed to the polished hardwood floor. Kyffin started to struggle to his feet but slipped over broken flower pot bits.

Flailing on the floor, my hand brushed back across the lead crystal whiskey tumbler he'd dropped. I picked it up, staggered to my feet, and swung it at the back of his head. Of course, I missed and tripped over him. We both fell to our backs on the Persian carpet. My Webley poked me, but I was too tired to move. We lay there a moment and panted as the fern fronds tickled our faces. Our shoulders touched. He rubbed his jaw and mumbled, "That sort of hurt."

"You're just trying to make me feel better," I said as I stared at the ceiling and wished for a smoke, a drink, *something, anything,* to distract myself from what I was feeling.

"No, really. It'll bruise, I think." Kyffin's hand touched mine. Our fingers locked.

Our breaths slowed, synched, and deepened.

"Batter swings and connects. It's fair. The centerfielder runs back. Back—Back—"

"Oh, what the hell," I murmured and kissed him full on the mouth. He kissed me back, and I was done for.

*   *   *

I kind of lost the thread of why I thought Kyffin had betrayed Lillian. I thought we'd talk about it over a dinner of whatever was in his larder. Which wasn't much. Walking about in my pants for the second time that day, I cobbled together a passable Welsh rarebit from a fine English cheddar that had seen better days, beer, and stale bread.

Kyffin sat at the dinette in a quilted dressing gown and pressed the steak meant for his dinner to his jaw while he pretended to read the evening news. The paper rattled with his need to talk—write an agenda, discuss our feelings, maybe make some charts and tables. Definitely draw up a contract or at least a short letter of intent. But he had the good sense not to press me just yet. I truly didn't know what to think about me and him, so I thought of nothing at all. We ate and discussed the baseball. I was, frankly, embarrassed I'd mistrusted him. I needed to apologize and didn't know how. So, I pretended to understand the upcoming World Series. After we ate, Kyffin produced leftover birthday cake and flat champagne from the icebox. "You're certainly full of surprises."

"Yeah." I couldn't very well deny that.

"All these months. I had no idea—well, maybe a little. Which I wrote off to wishful thinking."

"OK," I grunted and looked at the wine he'd pour in my water glass. Better not. Booze had gotten me in enough trouble for the night.

He collected the plates, and then rinsed and stacked them in the sink for some servant who would probably appear in the morning. "You're not going to talk to me?"

I took a deep breath and said, "I'm sorry I hit you. I'm more sorry I didn't trust you." I ate a small bite of cake and dropped my fork. Too sweet. "Violet said you helped her locate Lillian's baby."

He sat down. "I'm afraid I made an honest mistake," he said, "which I've taken steps to rectify."

"Go on."

"On Sunday, I dropped you at Arwald's and went to my office." Kyffin's lucky coin appeared out of nowhere, and he flipped and caught it. "After a few hours, Violet called. She begged me to find the 'abortionist,' since you wouldn't." His lazy smile teased me. "See, it's all your fault."

"We promised each other we'd protect Lillian."

"Yes, we did." Kyffin flushed, looked away, and then back at me. "I truly believed helping Violet would protect Lillian. She's hardly more than a child and shows no more sense than a child would, either," he said as he leaned back in his chair. "I inquired at the cab companies without any luck, and then I thought I'd start at the other end, in England." He tossed the coin and caught it again, perfectly. "I cabled Humphrey's family estate, where she stayed for the summer."

I'd not thought of that. "Smart."

He shrugged. "Is all this necessary right now? What about us and what just happened? Wh—"

"Just tell me fecking how you found the convent."

Kyffin looked more pained than at any point in our fight. "OK, if that's the way it is," he said, measuring each word before dispensing it, drop by drop. "Next, I found a porter who'd worked last Friday. I also talked to Lillian's best friend, sworn to secrecy, but—"

"I've met Nancy. Sweet girl."

"She enjoyed talking to you, I imagine." His voice had a bitter edge. "You flirt with everybody, don't you?" He got up to fetch a coffee canister from the pantry.

I didn't want to think about how very true that dig was and tried to make myself useful, looking through all the cabinets for cups.

"There, over the sink," he said, pointing to the only one I hadn't opened. "Anyway, Violet called, about eleven on Sunday night. I told her what I'd learned: Lillian arrived, very pregnant indeed, in St. Louis on Friday morning by train. She'd visited Nancy in hopes of cash. She had a place to stay but Nancy didn't know, or wouldn't say, where this refuge was." Kyffin looked at me, doubt in his eyes. "Violet didn't mention any change in Lillian's condition when she called."

"She hadn't lied to you yet. Lillian woke up just after midnight on Sunday, while I was there."

"Of course you were." He slammed the percolator works back in the coffee pot and set it on the hob. "I got a wire from England on Monday morning. Lillian left September fourteenth, and they were happy to see her gone."

"Not a good houseguest? And don't you need to put water in there, too?"

He grabbed the pot off the flame and struggled with the lid and the basket. "Decidedly not. She'd disappeared to the Continent for weeks at a time all summer."

I took the coffee pot out of Kyffin's shaking hands and held them a moment. We stood very close. Blond stubble glazed his bruised jaw and a shiner had begun to bloom around his right eye. I caught a whiff of wine and my sweat. "How'd you find the convent?" I whispered.

"Goddamit, Sean. Don't use me. You're in love with Lillian, aren't you?"

Driving home from Alton, I'd thought long and hard on Miss Esther's advice and my feelings about Lillian. "That's shite," I replied and kissed him long, hard, and thoroughly. "*You're* the one set to marry her."

He smiled. A little. "I'm already a jealous fool."

We managed the percolator and a cooling of tempers. Over hot, black coffee he finished his story.

"The cabbie who'd picked her up at Nancy's got back to me Tuesday morning and told me he'd taken her to Mount St. Michael's. I had an interesting visit to the convent."

"I'm sure." I was out of cigarettes. He kept a carton atop the icebox, and I helped myself.

"The chief nun—"

"Mother Superior," I said over my shoulder.

"Yes, that's it," he said as he sipped coffee. "Light one for me, too. Mother Superior Mary Gabriel couldn't have been kinder."

"I always feel like she's about to whack me with a ruler." I dealt with the smokes for the two of us.

He seemed to enjoy that thought. "Maybe you just need to seduce her, too."

"Not funny."

"Anyway, it was obvious Lillian had stayed at the convent, the nuns helped her with the birth, and the child was most likely still on the premises."

"So, why'd Lillian leave?"

"I don't exactly know," he said as he took a long drag and exhaled, watching the red-embered tip burn.

I let the silence build.

Eventually, Kyffin spoke again, his voice very low, "As soon as I left Mother Mary Gabriel, I called Violet and told her the baby was probably at the convent. Violet didn't say anything about Lillian's recovery." He looked pained, knowing his best friend had used him.

I've had my fill of traitors. Sold out to the British Army by my wife, I sat in Crumlin Road Gaol for months awaiting the King's pleasure for my hanging. Death didn't bother me nearly as much as the betrayal. Even now, just thinking on Norah made my chest feel empty and smothered, like she'd taken my lungs along with my trust.

I got up and held him, knowing all the while nothing I could do would ever fix his pain. Kyffin pulled away and looked up at me. "I can't believe Violet would intentionally deceive me."

I kept my mouth shut for once. *He'll wise up in his own time.*

He leaned back in his chair and shrugged. "Yet I became concerned that maybe Violet shouldn't know about the convent, after all. I discovered that Lillian had recovered and been discharged from the hospital. When I offered to intervene with Violet on Lillian's behalf, she was confident the nuns wouldn't willingly turn over the baby to anyone but her."

"And sometime in all this, you set a wedding date?"

"It goes without saying, doesn't it? She's had a child out of wedlock. Her father and I insisted Lillian rectify the situation immediately."

I had to laugh.

"What's so funny?"

Surely, he knew Lillian better than that. "Don't mind me. Go on."

"About then Dr. De Noailles asked me to audit the Piasa Lodge records. He had some longstanding concerns," Kyffin said as he ground out his smoke and finished his coffee. "Then suddenly Lillian had to have that baby in her arms, immediately. She was most insistent I drive her."

"But you tapped me to drive."

"Well, yes. Anyone could drive her to the convent. She could've driven herself, for that matter. I was the only one available with the training to make something out of a financial ledger."

"She didn't like your plan much."

Kyffin collected our cups and saucers and said, "She'd better accustom herself to my plans. She'll be my wife in a few days."

Did the poor chump have any idea what he was getting himself into? "Find anything out for the doctor?"

He rinsed and stacked the cups with the other dishes. "It's not appropriate to talk out of turn about mere suspicions. I've a meeting in a little while to ask for an explanation."

A late-night meeting about crooked books? "I'll come with you."

"No. It's best for me to clear things up," he replied, heading for the bedroom. "Privately."

I followed and found my trousers on the floor. "Take a real gun, at least," I said handing him my Webley, which by some miracle was still in my pocket.

"Ah, the Mark VI. Bit of a pain to reload, don't you think?" Kyffin handed it back. "I have a derringer."

I pushed the revolver back into his hand. "When you shoot people with it, they stop coming at you. Then you don't need to reload."

"Fine," he said as he selected a suit from the closet and fetched a fresh shirt from a chest of drawers. "I'll be back by two. You'll be here?"

"If you like," I said, putting on my trousers.

"Maybe you'll have even more surprises."

I shrugged. "Could be." I had no earthly idea. Honestly, I felt a bit trapped. Kyffin seemed to need quite a lot from me. I feared I'd just destroyed a good friendship on a lustful whim.

I watched him dress for the most important meeting of his life and leave the flat. I paced and thought about following him, then told myself that was stupid. The man had survived the bloody Red Baron himself, for Christ's sake. *Von Richthofen hadn't kill Kyffin and not for lack of trying. Surely he could handle some St. Louis businessman.*

I wandered the flat and distracted myself with the crazy paintings Kyffin bought in Europe right after the war. They were about shapes, colors, and lines, looking like nothing in particular and everything in the world, all at the same time.

Around one o'clock I tried to sleep. His bed was soft compared to my usual cot at Padraig's, but I tossed, turned, and looked at the alarm clock's glowing dial every fifteen minutes. I eventually fell asleep, I guess, because I remember waking up. I'll never forget it. The room was freezing. Kyffin shook my shoulder, whispering, "Sean, Sean. Wake up." His warm breath smelled like cigars. I wrapped tighter in the blankets I'd kicked around all night. "Jesus-mary-and-joseph, man. Go brush your teeth."

"Now," his voice hissed right in my ear. "Get out of here. Right now."

I opened my eyes and turned toward the voice. No one was there. Gray early morning light filtered through the Venetian blinds. Birdsong from the park greeted the day. The room was so cold I could see my breath. I could feel Kyffin in the room, but he wasn't to be seen, anywhere. I peeped out the blinds and rubbed frost off the window as a couple of cops piled out of a car and rushed up the steps. I grabbed my clothes and shoes and hopped out the window onto the fire escape to dress. I could hear the cops pound up the stairs. I made for my car, the engine roaring to life on the first crank. A bull looked out the window and spotted the Model T. They all look alike, right? But I couldn't help feeling, as I drove away, that things were getting very bad very quickly.

Chapter Fourteen

Balance Sheet

I drove back to Padraig's bar in a fog, both in my heart and through the low, dirty clouds that had invaded the streets from the river overnight. Something felt very wrong, but I didn't know what. So many wrong things had happened in the past few hours. Mostly I worried over Kyffin. At first, I could barely breathe around the knot of dread in my chest. Then that foul beast, optimism, crept in. People are delayed at appointments all the time. And cops roust everyone, sooner or later. That warning—smacked of the fae it did—but was most likely just a dream.

The city was barely awake. Crossing Padraig's postage stamp of a backyard, I upset a couple of chickens escaped from the coop. They clucked their alarm and scattered as I made for the kitchen door to slip into the pub. If I was lucky, I'd avoid Padraig and Eliza, sneak into bed, and they'd never know I was out all night. For some reason, that always bothered them a lot.

As fate would have it, I had no luck at all that morning. Padraig awaited me in the kitchen, beads—our father's, I think—between his fingers and appeared to be praying the rosary. This was unheard of. The rosary part. He was often up early.

"Isn't it a fine day?" I greeted. I opened the icebox, took out a chunk of ice to wrap in a dishcloth, and held it over my eye. He'd opened the windows wide. Damp, garbage-scented air crept in from the alley.

"Feels like rain, to me," he said as he opened his eyes and looked up from his devotions. "Ain't I been sitting here all night?"

"You shouldn't worry over me."

"But I do. You're my baby brother."

I poured myself some coffee.

"And what happened to you?" Padraig pointed to my eye. "Hope you gave as good as you got."

"I'd say I did. You should see the other guy."

He didn't laugh. "And now I've got to throw you out in the street."

This didn't sound good, but he told me to move now and again. He always changed his mind. "I'll be finding my own place as soon as things at work calm down a bit," I said.

"Now. Pack up and get out. And don't speak to the children."

He might as well have slugged me in my tender jaw. "I'll speak to whoever I damn well please," I shouted and slammed down the cup, then marched toward the door to the public room.

Padraig leaped from his seat and barred my way, his arms crossed. "You're a man grown, of course. I understand needing a good fuck now and again," he said and half-smiled. "A house full of kids and bills to pay will beat it out of you soon enough."

He hadn't sworn at me in five minutes. I suspected he was actually mad. Padraig is fifteen years older than me, but if you think that means he's been a second father, you'd be wrong. When it came to "family life," he'd left sorting me—and I required a good bit of sorting—to our Da and oldest brother, Seamus. Even my Ma made a brief appearance at a critical time to put her oar in.

And how could he already know whatever it was that just happened with Kyffin?

"You can't be bringing your floozies here," Padraig yelled, the color rising in his face. "I've young children to think of and a respectable woman for my wife." He sighed and shook his head. "I've looked the other way too long: Gangsters. Dirty cops. Dirtier politicians. But I can't have sins of the flesh under my roof."

"Ah." He'd had no problem taking the dirty money I'd earned from gangsters, cops, and politicians. And I couldn't imagine what "sins of the flesh" he meant. "But—"

"But nothing. Maud walked in on you and that trollop. Fancy society lady, my arse. She'll do you a ton of good, I'll wager."

I felt rotten, though I had to wonder what had brought Maud up to the flat at just the wrong moment. "I'll talk to the girl," I said as I made to move around him. "We weren't—"

He grabbed my shoulders and looked down at me. Da's beads pressed into my arm. "The child saw what she saw."

I twisted out of his grasp. "Let me explain to her."

"No, you won't," he said, shoving me in the chest.

Caught off guard, I stumbled a bit against the sink.

"Her parents will explain." He pushed me again, but I'd braced for it this time. "Her priest will explain, and you'll get the hell out and not talk to her again."

I stepped closer and shoved a bit myself, pitching my voice low, "Bloody sin under *your* bloody roof? I'm paying for this roof and have been for the past year."

He blanched and stepped back.

"How ya going to keep your roof over their heads, without me?" I regretted my words the moment they left my mouth.

"We'll manage," he said, no conviction at all in his voice. "The Lord will provide."

I needed to let this blow over, then fix it. I focused again on my Maudie. "I want to apologize to Maud."

Padraig thought that one over then said, "Perhaps I'll allow it." His anger was gone, and warning was all I saw in his eyes. "But you don't want to face her today, believe me. Let her cool off a bit."

I realized he was right. "I guess I'll get a room at the YMCA."

"Go pack before Eliza tears into ya."

*   *   *

I gathered my belongings quickly enough, careful to not wake the boys. Maud and Eliza weren't around. I drove the Judge's model T to a carpark near the train station and left it there. The cops could find it easily enough if they looked.

I couldn't carry a suitcase around all day, so I went over to the Railroad YMCA, just across Twenty-First Street from the train station. They didn't have a vacancy, but the clerk thought a room or two would open up by the afternoon. I paid in advance to hold the potential bed. He was also willing to rent me a locker, so I stashed my suitcase and walked to the rumor mill. By which I mean, courthouse. I needed to know what the police raid at Kyffin's was all about.

A lot of cops buzzed around Memorial Plaza, which didn't strike me as unusual, the courthouse being practically next to police headquarters. I struggled through a crowd congregated between the huge pillars guarding the courthouse entrance to see a group of broom-and-mop-ladened black men huddled in the hallway that led to phone booths, bathrooms, and stairwells. Their eyes were fixed on a bull a few paces away, grilling one of their number. I picked out Mrs. Mac among a knot of people in the foyer.

"Good day, Mrs. Mac," I said and tipped my hat. "What's going on?"

"Ack, well. You." She looked me up and down. "Ain't seen you in a month of Sundays. You pretty much left me in the lurch." She pulled her shawl tighter and confided, "As best I can tell, the haunts are all upset about something or other."

"I thought that stopped. And you weren't happy with my services, anyway."

"You're a fool, but I'd give you another chance. And they've been oh so bad again."

I looked around the dark, cavernous lobby. No ghosts. A couple of beat officers allowed obvious cop types on the lift to the upper floors and made everyone else take one of the others, which only went as far as the tenth floor. "I don't care what the ghosts are doing. Why are the cops here?"

"You should care about the haunts. They're up to no good."

I sighed. In for a penny, in for a pound, I took the bait and asked, "When did it start again?"

"Well, it's not like they ever stopped, but nothing was thrown or moved all summer. I'd just see them wandering around, kinda sad and gloomy-like," she said as she demonstrated a sad and gloomy ghost shuffle. It was terrifying.

"And now?"

Mrs. Mac waved her arms. "Today they're running around, throwing things. Slamming doors."

"The cops ain't here for that."

"No, that poor man got attacked."

A chill went up my spine. "An attack?"

"Well, don't ya know? Murder. Bloody murder. Well, almost. The poor bloke got his brains bashed in. Still breathing, though."

The premonition that had sparred with me since my early morning dream of Kyffin punched me hard in the stomach. "Who?"

"That nice young Mr. Bernard. They was wheeling him out when I got to work this morning."

I swallowed over the lump in my throat and croaked out, "Kyffin Bernard?"

"That's what I said, didn't I? How many Mr. Bernards come to court?"

"You saw him?" I had a crazy thought. "Can you see him now?" *If I followed her into the haunted fen she insisted I visit, could I see him?*

She sighed at my theological ignorance and explained, "He ain't dead yet, as far as I know. And stands to reason I won't see him when he passes. He'll fly off to heaven, I'm sure. Such a nice young man. Always tipped me and had fat envelopes for all of us every Boxing Day. Did you know him?"

"Yeah," I said. I wanted details but didn't want to hear them. "What are the haunts doing now?"

Mrs. Mac pointed across the lobby and whispered, "The queen's there." She hid her face in my shirt front as if she were crying, produced a flask from her pocket, and took a quick nip. "With that man."

I looked and didn't see anything. I took a deep breath, cleared out thoughts of Kyffin as best I could. I reached into that clear, focused spot one needs before a job—a "hit" as the American gangsters say. I looked toward the man like he was my mark for the day. The footsteps and voices echoing through the foyer around me fell silent. Gray mist wrapped the man. When I looked at the mist kinda cross-eyed, a form appeared, increasingly clear—the Mississippian priestess who haunted the place. As the man stood in a trance, she held his head between her hands and peered into his eyes. Then she moved one hand to his chest and held it over his heart. At last, she released him and was gone. The man looked confused, shook his head, and headed toward the lifts.

"What do you think she wants?" Mrs. Mac said.

I had an idea. "Maybe we should ask her."

Mrs. Mac looked up at me and grimaced. I guess that was meant to be a smile. "Tonight?"

I shrugged. "No time like the present."

"I'll meet you at nine o'clock."

I agreed and headed toward the lift, hoping to learn what the hell had happened to my friend.

*   *   *

The cop on duty stopped me and said, "Upper floors are closed, buddy. Appeals court cancelled."

"I need to see the detective in charge."

"No way. This here's a crime scene."

I was expecting that. "It's for the Judge," I said.

"Got my orders," he said as he slapped his night stick in his palm. "You can take the other lifts to the Judge's office."

I saw no point in arguing and took one of the other lifts to the tenth floor and then ran up the stairs to twelve. The fancy foyer and promenade where they'd held the Piasa Lodge Ball last winter occupied most of the twelfth floor. A quick peek from the stairwell door showed nothing going on, although a building security guard stood watch, just in case.

I headed up another couple of flights to the library on the thirteenth floor. From the deserted judges' lounge, I could hear people milling around the reference desk and the pop of camera flashes. As best I could tell, the focus of their attention was the reading room, a bright and airy space on the opposite side of the library from the lounge.

I again mounted the stairs to the mezzanine, which housed offices, lots of books, and empty shelves for future books. The balcony overlooking the reading room would be my best perch to scope out the scene. But I exited the mezzanine stairwell straight into the arms of yet another cop.

"You goddamn reporters are gonna just have to wait for a statement," he said. "Go back over to headquarters."

"I'm not a reporter," I said as I showed him my court identification. "I work for the Judge."

A middle-aged black man in a sharp suit, vest, and tie overheard us and came over. "This is my scene. The judges were told to stay home." He turned to shout down at a uniformed cop near an open staircase, which connected the mezzanine with the reading room. "Don't touch anything. We're going to dust for fingerprints."

"The Judge needs to know the progress," I said. "What happened?"

"Where do I know you from?" He moved back down the hall toward the soon-to-be fingerprinted crime scene to make sure the cop took him seriously. "Don't touch that rock," he said to the men standing around in the reading room. "Probably the weapon."

As I followed him, the detective turned back to me and said, "You're the Judge's driver or something."

"Or something." I knew this cop very well. He was a local celebrity of sorts. Had solved two or three high-profile cases this year alone, including an important bank embezzlement case in the spring. That, along with being the first black man to become detective sergeant, made him about as famous as a cop had any call to be. Detective Sergeant George Brewer. And he knew me because he'd nicked me last year. I hoped he wouldn't remember.

"We just heard the victim was Bernard," I said. "The Judge wants me to gather the facts, off the record."

He acted like he was considering my request, then said, "The Judge can call me at headquarters."

"You want to play that card?" I warned.

He looked me over again, finally focused. *This wasn't going well.* "Thing is," Brewer said, "I don't see the Judge caring one way or the other. Maybe it's you that cares." He flipped open his notebook, "Name?"

"He's Sean Joye," said the uniform, who'd tagged along behind us. "He showed me his court card."

Recognition shone in Brewer's eyes. *He'd made me, alright.* "Address?"

"I'm house hunting."

"Vagrant." He wrote that down. "Quite a shiner you got there. Where were you last night?"

"Around. It's a bit of a blur."

At that point, another uniformed cop called to him with questions about the fingerprint process. I got a quick look at his open notepad. *Kyffin Bernard. Aberdeen Bldg, #4 Knghwy. Bryan Cave Law. Stairs. Head wound. Fell vs pushed?*

He turned back to me, wrote a few more lines, and then closed the book and put it in his pocket. "Scram," Brewer told me.

"The Judge likes to be in the loop. You know that." It was a stupid cover story, but I'd best stick with it.

"I'll send a report over to him as soon as I write it."

I nodded. This was getting me nowhere, other than on a list of people to roust. Whoever Kyffin met with last night either tried to kill him or sent him to the law library to be killed. Brewer wasn't going to get an answer from the courthouse cleaning crew. I thought about leveling with the detective, but whoever attacked Kyffin probably owned the police department. During the whole conversation with Brewer, I'd avoided looking over the balcony rail at the reading room, but I did so then. I owed it to Kyffin. It looked to be the floor of a slaughterhouse. The room darkened and swayed.

"You look kind of sick," Brewer said. "First time at a crime scene? Besides your own, I mean."

If I looked anywhere near as bad as I felt, he'd be calling me a doctor. The cop at my elbow sniggered, "Head wounds do bleed a lot."

He was right. Kyffin had, indeed, bled all over the place. I've seen more blood, but nothing worse. Ever.

"I need some air, is all." I stumbled, just a bit, and lurched into Brewer. He caught me, clearly amused, and said, "Steady on. You young toughs are all alike."

I was in no state to argue and let the cop escort me back to the stairwell and send me on my way. I took the stairs at a run, pushed through the lobby, and out the Eleventh Street entrance. I sucked in a deep breath of cool stinking air, as I walked around the corner to the loading dock entrance for a bit of privacy.

I opened Brewer's notepad. *Found by watchman on rounds. 4 a.m. Law library reading room. Stairs. Blunt force trauma to head.* Underlined, in block letters, *Large, rounded stone at scene.*

I read on. *Appt book: 11 p.m.— "J". No address.*

J could mean almost anything: "Jury." "Judge." Hell, it could stand for "Joye." That didn't look good, but there you are.

I dropped the notepad in a rubbish bin and walked away. I knew another J.

Chapter Fifteen

Liquidation

I had no time to waste and hailed a cab at Chestnut and Twelfth. While I was in the courthouse the fog had turned into sooty smog, and the cab's lamps glowed in the mist. The car nosed into rush hour traffic. I looked at my watch. *How could it only be eight o'clock in the morning?* As I took a deep breath, I noticed my hands were shaking. The bloody scene in the library hung in my brain, making it hard to think straight. But I felt something was off.

"Where to?" the cabbie asked.

Good question. My first thought was the closest hospital. To sit by Kyffin all day and night, guarding against the follow-up attack that was sure to come. "J" had wanted Kyffin dead and was probably in a panic that he'd survived. But maybe "J" didn't know that yet. Perhaps I had a little time. And, it occurred to me, the thought unbidden and unwelcome, that perhaps Éire really had followed me to America, and I could still bargain with her for help.

"Hey, buddy. You awake?"

"Sorry," I mumbled and gave him an address. I sank back in the seat. No. Éire's price would be too high, and a magical bargain would be Kyffin's ruin as well as my own.

The driver tried to make cabbie-type conversation, his voice a faint and annoying drone from the front seat. I stared out the window. We weren't going much of anywhere, in the line of Model Ts clogging Chestnut Street.

I'd never been so angry and with so little outlet for it in my entire life. And that's covering quite a lot—Da's murder. Norah's betrayal. Michael Collins' assassination. Eight hundred years of struggle against the British. But anger had no place in what I needed to do now. Nor revenge. It was time for strategy. I needed to calm myself, think logically, and figure out who'd tried to kill Kyffin. Then I could shoot the effing bastard in the head when he least expected it.

Kyffin had been nosing around for the Arwalds, same as me. My guess was he'd found something and talked about it to the wrong person.

I handed the hack a dollar and told him to keep the change. I'd get there faster on foot.

*   *   *

I beat the cab to the Wainwright Building and sped to Arwald's penthouse office. The din of the place slapped me as I got off the lift. It felt like weeks since I'd been here, kidding with Kyffin across the empty room, but it was just last Sunday morning.

Twenty or so gents shouted into phones or called across the room to other gents and a few ladies writing numbers on big chalkboards. Rattling stock tickers spit ribbons of paper on the floor. The workers paid me no mind, but Arwald's gatekeeper was another story. The secretary leaped up from behind her desk with a one-minute-there-young-man look on her face as I flung open Arwald's door.

He glanced up from a newspaper spread across his desk. "Joye? What are you doing here?" He lumbered out of his chair. "Violet paid you off last night," he smirked. "Not enough, eh?"

"It was plenty. Did you meet Kyffin last night here or at the courts building?"

As I expected, Arwald poker-faced the question. He killed time choosing and lighting a cigar. He dropped the band on the desk and took a puff, then said, "What makes you think I met Bernard last night?"

"You're not denying it."

"I neither confirm nor deny. I don't see what concern it would be to you. You've finished your work for us and been paid."

"It became my concern about four o'clock this morning when Kyffin was found nearly dead."

Arwald's hands gripped the desk edge. "Good God. What?"

I'll give him credit—his act was convincing. "Your name was in his appointment book. So, if you attacked him here, there'd be blood traces—" I looked at the floor, "and transport over to the courts building would be tricky."

"How dare you insinuate—" Arwald moved around the desk and up in my face, about my height but somehow looming over me. His breath reeked of cigar smoke. Whatever brand it was seemed familiar. I took a stab in the dark. Money irregularities were always a safe bet.

"Kyffin knew something was off with the Piasa Lodge books," I said, "and threatened to expose you."

"You should leave," he said.

"I can leave, but eventually the police will trace his whereabout last night and be by to see you. Maybe you're not so interesting now. Future father-in-law. All nice and cozy. What they need is a motive. When they find out Kyffin audited the lodge records—"

"I'll give you a little advice, Joye. Drop it. This matter doesn't concern you."

I wanted to beat the smug look off his face but opted for an even more reckless approach. "I know what he found out, about the lodge." I had no idea what Kyffin had found out about the lodge. "I don't think you'd appreciate it in the press."

Arwald was an old guy, but solid. Old footballer. Maybe rugby. And he was angry. He barreled into me and pinned me against the desk, yelling, "Drop it. Keep your mouth shut." He thrust the lit cigar at my face to emphasize each clipped phrase. "Stay away from me and my family." Then he backed off a bit and laughed. "You think I don't know about you?"

At this point in the intimidation game, showing an impressive weapon might be indicated. But I didn't have a gun with me. I'd given my Webley to Kyffin and my much more reliable Luger was locked in a suitcase at the YMCA. Trying to con Old Arwald, I moved my left hand under my right coat lapel, where the shoulder holster would normally be. He grabbed my hand and pressed the flesh of the palm with the cigar tip. *Well, that hurt like hell.* "What the fuck," I yelled as I pushed back my coat to show that I was unarmed as the door burst open and two company bulls plowed into the office.

"He attacked me," Arwald said.

"Fecking shite—He attacked me."

The men were professionals but wanted to show off for their boss and roughed me up a bit more than necessary. "Should we call the cops?" the taller one asked Arwald between gut punches. "You filing charges?"

He considered it, watching his man work me over, then said, "Not at this time. I can do so later, if necessary. You two are witnesses."

"Right, boss. Whatever you say." The bulls stopped hitting me and dragged me out of the office. "You gonna come along quiet?"

"Yeah, yeah. I know my way out."

"We're gonna walk along with you. Just to keep you company."

They chatted about the baseball teams with the lift operator on the way down, occasionally trying to include me in the conversation to show there were no hard feelings.

Out on the sidewalk, the taller one said, "You got a rep for being smart, so, don't disappoint me. Remember whatever he told you to do. Or not do. Get it?"

"Got it."

Chapter Sixteen

Double=Entry Bookkeeping

I walked east on Chestnut as I wrapped a handkerchief around my burned palm, like that would do it some good. The mist gave way to a spitting sort of drizzle and I ducked into a bright-lit diner for a coffee, smoke, and think. The morning rush was over and the place quiet, wrapped in the aroma of bacon and tobacco.

I had to stop reacting to every breeze that blew and make a plan. Kyffin had poked around the train station, talked to cabbies, and cabled Humphrey's people in Oxford. He confronted someone about the Piasa Lodge records. Unfortunately, in addition to not telling me who he planned to meet, he hadn't told me where he'd gone to review the books. Dr. De Noailles would know, but he was in Alton and didn't have a phone.

I looked at the cigar band I swiped from Arwald's desk. Same brand as the Judge. No wonder it smelled familiar. And I remembered the warning dream early this morning, that felt like Kyffin and smelled like cigar smoke. The band was evidence against Arwald. But I needed to rule out the Judge, although I very much doubted he'd spent Wednesday night smoking cigars with Kyffin.

I stepped into the phone booth at the end of the counter, folded the door behind me, and dropped a nickel. "I need to talk to the Judge, please," I said into the mouthpiece once I was connected. I was told to wait as much clicking and rustling went on. After a short wait, I heard a voice. "Pauline Dolan here."

"It's Sean. Can I come over to see the Judge?"

There was a long pause on her end. "I see. Well, I may not meet my deadline this month."

"Can he talk, ma'am?"

"No, not at all. Something's come up. I'm sorry."

"You're not alone?"

"That's right," Mrs. Judge laughed. "I'll have to *cop* a plea, I suppose. But my problems are your problems."

"The bulls are with you and the Judge right now."

"Exactly."

I knew the police would finger me for the person who was at Kyffin's place early this morning sooner or later. I guess it was to be sooner. "I need to know who the officers of the Piasa Lodge are. Secretary or treasurer, maybe. Whoever has the records."

"Well, I appreciate it. Your understanding of my situation is remarkable. I need to make a trip to the reference desk at the library to finish the article. And, *well*, that's just not in the *cards* today."

"Ah, good idea. Thanks. And I didn't do it, whatever it is they think I did."

"I know. Again, thank you. I'll finish by the weekend. Good-bye."

Bless her, she'd not only warned me off from the Judge's house but also told me the name of the lodge official to chat up.

I wasn't far from the main library, where Matthew and I had read old newspapers yesterday morning. I asked for an address on someone named "Wellcard" or "Cardwell" connected to the Piasa

Lodge, and it took the reference librarian but a minute to locate the information I needed.

But first, the hospital. I didn't know how I'd manage to guard Kyffin and investigate the attack at the same time, but I'd put off seeing him as long as I could stand.

*   *   *

As to which hospital, Barnes was as good a guess as any and turned out to be right. I didn't even have to ask the information clerk if Kyffin was there. A gaggle of newspaper reporters and photographers harassed a plain-clothes cop in the rotunda lobby. He was a big guy in a top coat and gray fedora, not quite broad as he was tall, but getting there. His tight collar gave his red face an even rosier tone. The press all shouted questions, but one voice, dripping with a Queens accent, brayed above them all. "Officer. Officer. Jerome Oliver here. Any arrest yet?"

The cop seemed to have about had his fill of them all, particularly Jerome Oliver. "You new in town?" he asked the reporter. "It's Detective Milo Draper. Get it right."

Many a man would've crawled under a rock if a bull spoke to him like that, but Oliver blabbed on, "Any suspects?"

A silent Draper gave him a look that would remove paint, and the other reporters jostled Oliver back toward the rear of the crowd.

Draper climbed onto a low-slung wooden chair, which creaked under his weight. *This could get interesting.* He shielded his eyes from the popping camera flashes with one hand and said, "Gentlemen. I'll now read a statement." He raked his gaze over the pack, caught my eye, and scowled. I didn't know him and wondered what that was about. Meanwhile, the reporters had all quieted down like schoolboys under the care of a particularly strict nun.

"Earlier today, Mr. Kyffin Bernard, Esquire, attorney-at-law, resident of St. Louis, was found in the Civil Courts Building seriously injured and unconscious. He is under doctors' care at this hospital. Surgery is going on right now. His family is aware and at the bedside. Investigation of accident versus criminal assault is underway. Any information the public can provide would be appreciated. That is all," he said as he gave us one last reproving stare and then climbed down from his perch. A cordon of uniforms pushed the reporters toward the exit, entangling me as well.

"Not so fast. I'm not a reporter," I told the officer who had me by the lapels.

"A gawker, eh? Be gone with ye," he said, giving me a not-so-gentle push.

Before I knew it, I found myself out the door, stumbling down the hospital's granite stairs.

Jerome Oliver caught me by the elbow and said, "Easy there, buddy. New on the cops beat? They always pull this bullshit." His voice dropped, "We'll have to go in through the loading dock."

"Thanks," I said and straightened my coat. "No, I'm not a reporter. I was just trying to visit someone in the hospital."

He looked me up and down. "Say, you're the Judge's man, aren't you?"

"I thought you were new in town."

"Naw. I been here since the fair." With a moment's thought, he caught my drift. "Oh, that back there? Sometimes you gotta rattle them a bit to get a straight answer. Detective Milo Draper." He rolled his eyes. "Cops get on my nerves."

Truer words never spoke. I tipped my hat and said, "Gotta go visit my friend." I wasn't about to take Draper's word for it that Kyffin was alive and in surgery.

"Well, see you around." He turned to go, then stopped to ask, "What's the Judge's interest in all this?"

"Who says he's interested? I'm just visiting." And I sure wasn't buying that Kyffin accidentally fell down a flight of stairs and dropped a big rock, whatever Draper might say.

Oliver made a note and without looking up said, "And I didn't get your name."

"No, you didn't," I replied as I opened the door and went back into the hospital lobby.

The cop who'd rousted me was still there. "Move it along, boyo."

"Like I told you, I'm not a reporter. I have a friend here."

He rocked back and forth on his heels and gently fondled the billy club in his hand. "Your friend will have to do without your visit today. Orders."

"Why?"

The flatfoot shrugged and said, "Couldn't we be spending some time together at headquarters, finding out why?"

"Don't be bothering yourself, then." I matched him, brogue for brogue. "Sure I'll be on my way."

The front door's not the only way into a place. And Kyffin seemed to be well guarded for the moment. At least from the press.

*   *   *

An introduction to Mr. Cardwell, the Piasa Lodge treasurer, would've helped, but I couldn't think how to pull that off quickly, so I decided to just wing it and took the Delmar Streetcar out toward University City. I walked a few blocks to a treelined development of swank houses. Cardwell's was a fake Elizabethan model on Yale Avenue.

A maid let me in without demanding much in the way of explanation for my visit, took my hat, and stationed me on a low, red velvet chaise lounge. A blue-eyed cat, light brown with a black face and ears, came by and meowed a greeting. As I leaned over to rub its head, another pounced out of nowhere on the seat next to me, demanding attention, too. About then the master of the house appeared.

"Vanth. Aita. Give the man some room, for heaven's sake." He was an older gent, but spry, and practically leaped forward to extend his hand. "I don't believe we've had the pleasure. I'm Jason Cardwell." His smoking jacket blended almost perfectly with the fuzzy gold-and-black wallpaper. I had to mind his fluffy white hair just to keep track of him.

I dislodged a cat from my lap and stood. We shook hands. "Sorry to barge in like this. I'm—" *How much sharing was necessary?* "Lawrence Jones."

Vanth, or maybe Aita, meowed skeptically.

"Dr. De Noailles asked me to check on a few things in the lodge archives for him. He's writing a history."

"Ah, Mr. Bernard missed something? That's hard to believe. So studious. So thorough."

Would Kyffin ever be studious or thorough again? As if we'd conjured him, I began to feel Kyffin in the room with us.

At the cinema, magic is a jolt of electricity, or some poor fool falls into a trance, but that's not what happened to me. All I felt was a ripple, from someplace far away yet nearby, right to me. Wisps of the Veil, dabbing at my face again.

I looked at Cardwell. His expression was expectant, eager, and mostly harmless. If he felt the same presence, he didn't show it. On the other hand, the cats, ears and tails erect, stared at a space about two feet to my left. Kyffin had thrown me a tether and I grabbed it.

"Follow-up questions," I explained to my host.

"Of course. There always are. I'm a historian myself of Etruscan art. Lucky Dr. De Noailles—a wealth of bright, young research assistants." He smiled what he obviously thought was a disarming smile. "This way to the study. I haven't even put the records away yet." He took my arm and guided me through a parlor crammed with carved ebony furniture and objects of art. Every flat surface displayed some sort of jar, bottle, or urn of the Greco-Roman variety.

"Quite a collection you have here. I'm afraid I'll break something valuable."

"What's the point of owning nice things if you can't enjoy them?" Cardwell launched into a tour of the collection and I inwardly cursed myself for acting interested.

When he took a breath, I interrupted, "Maybe I could take a raincheck on the tour. Dr. De Noailles is in a bit of a rush."

"Of course. Your interest would be indigenous North American artifacts. Several good things are in the office. They belong to the lodge."

"Mr. Bernard looked at those things?"

"Some. He was mostly at the books." We passed through a dark passage to the rear of the house. "Boring," he whispered in my ear. "I'm treasurer only because no one else will do it."

Cardwell opened a door to reveal a dim, stuffy office, a little light from the overcast day seeping in around drawn shades. "Right here," he said and pointed to a rolltop desk. Scribbled notes were tacked all over the wall next to the desk, and papers jammed the cubbies and drawers along its front. The desk was open—had to be, what with the pile of dark green ledger books. Several bankers' boxes were stacked on the floor nearby.

"I'll ring for some tea," he offered as he turned on a desk lamp.

"Don't go to any trouble."

"None at all, I assure you. I'll just sit here, quiet as a mouse, and drink tea. In case you have any questions." He settled in a chair near a cold fireplace and one of his cats jumped in his lap. "Hello there, Vanth," he said as he tickled it under the chin. "Tell me about yourself, Mr. Jones. I assume you're one of Taylor Humphrey's new men. Where did you study? Trinity College?"

"Yeah, that's right." I knew where Trinity College was in Dublin. Nice pub right across the way. I wasn't aware Humphrey had new men, but I could play along. "But I should get to work."

"Well, all the ledgers and minutes are there. And the archive boxes. Mr. Bernard spent the better part of Tuesday evening with them. Wouldn't even break for dinner."

Well aware of Cardwell's eyes on me, I wished I had some idea of what I was looking for, conscious of how much better Kyffin could do a task like this. I had my doubts he'd survive the day.

I opened the first book, an accounting ledger. I counted eight different bank account numbers, and all seemed to be active. Sums were added and subtracted, back and forth, around and about, all the various accounts. In truth, I couldn't make heads nor tails of it.

I tugged on that mental connection to Kyffin I'd felt earlier. If the Good People have taken you, mate, if you've any power at all to help, I could use it, I thought.

I imagined Kyffin pale and motionless in a hospital bed, but a more lively presence seemed to be right there—anxious, angry, eager to share a clue.

A cat leaped to the desktop and meowed.

"Do you know, Aita?" I whispered.

It sat on the page, obstructing everything but a disbursement classified as an investment. I moved the cat and noticed quite a lot of similar entries across all the accounts. My head began to hurt and I rubbed my eyes.

Giving up for the moment, I turned to the next book. It was the thickest, labeled *Membership,* and I didn't need no roaming spirit or Siamese cat to explain it, in light of Cardwell's remark about Humphrey's new men.

The first pages explained the membership rules, and there were a lot. Next, the early members and their bonafides: Family heritage, property, and sponsorship. It continued in that vein for generations of slow accrual, barely replacing dead members. But for the past two years, lots of new members had joined, their sponsorship and family heritage sections sketchy or even blank.

Someone had packed the membership, and Cardwell, pretending to doze over *Plutarch's Lives*, had to know something was off.

I found a long ruler in the jammed desk drawer, placed it along the last page's inner margin, and ripped it out at the binding as I coughed. I shoved the page in my pocket.

"Just curious." I turned to Cardwell. "Has your membership requirements changed recently?"

He roused with a start. "Why, ah, not officially. The board grants exceptions from time to time."

"The board is the most important members? Like you, for instance?"

He laughed, "Not at all." He wagged a finger at me and teased, "Flattery will get you far, though."

He listed off a half dozen familiar names. No surprises there, being as they're plastered on buildings all over the town. The only ones that seemed connected to this case were Dr. De Noailles and Lillian's father, Joseph Arwald.

I nodded, closed the book, and opened the volume labeled *Curator's Catalogue.*

"Take a break, Mr. Jones," Cardwell said, crossing the room to put his hand on my shoulder. "Let me show you some interesting historical research."

I'd not felt a breath of air the hour or so I'd spent in the room, but at that moment a breeze ruffled the pages of the open book, at first stirring, then flipping them, one by one faster and faster, stopping at last with a page labeled: *Artifacts*. Me and Aita stared at it.

Cardwell looked at the page over my shoulder and said, "You're interested in our collection, of course. It is quite special. But if you read Armstrong, who proves without a doubt that what we call the Mound Builders were actually the lost tribe of Israel—"

"Uh-huh." A list of items as well as labeled drawings and photographs were pasted into the ledger: *Ax, Hair ornament(?), Bowl,* and the like. For some, a place name I recognized was noted, like Cahokia or St. Louis.

He took the ledger and handed me another book, *The Piasa, or, the Devil Among the Indians*. "We have Old Testament evidence, and Armstrong explains the ancient land bridges."

I ignored his distracting tall tale, and peered at the glass cases, much like at Dr. De Noailles's house, in the dark corners of the room.

"Are the things listed in this ledger in your cases over there?"

"Mr. Bernard started to take an inventory." Cardwell looked embarrassed. "Members are supposed to check them out, but it's an honor system."

"People can be careless."

"Exactly." He seemed relieved I didn't scold him. I had a feeling Kyffin hadn't been so nice. He's got pretty high standards for people doing their jobs correctly.

Cardwell showed me where things had been signed out. Some were signed back in, but others were still out and about. "And these—" he gestured to the case, "are gone. And not signed out." He'd crumpled into his chair. "I'm mortified," he said into his hands. "How could I let this happen?"

I sat beside him and patted his shoulder. "It looks to me like this is entirely too much work for one person to deal with," I said, the soul of sympathy.

He raised his eyes, eager to agree with me. "It is, it is." He clutched my arm.

"And you have your own research to do, right?"

"I do."

"So, here's a thought. Maybe I should finish the inventory. Contact these jokers who borrowed stuff months ago. Look," I said, pointing at a dozen or more entries. "Taylor Humphrey's had these pieces for over a year."

"You'd have time to do that?"

"Well, it only seems right."

Together we finished the inventory of the artifacts in his house, and he sent me off with his original curator's catalogue. I scooped up the other two ledgers as well on my way out.

Chapter Seventeen

Variable Costs

I expected to be nicked at any moment, ladened with heavy ledger books full of evidence I didn't understand. And I needed to talk to Humphrey about borrowed artifacts and his, "new men," before that happened. I took a cab to the Arwald mansion, although I could ill afford it, and had the hack driver make a brief detour to Matthew's home in the Ville neighborhood. He charged me double.

Matthew's family lived with an uncle and aunt in a tidy brick bungalow on Goode Avenue. Not a leaf from a large shade tree dared litter the small manicured lawn, and red and yellow flowers spilled out of green window boxes.

The cabbie glanced around, uneasy, his engine idling, as I ran up to the door and rang the bell.

Matthew answered, a biscuit in his mouth and a mug of milk in his hand. "Mr. Sean," he mumbled. "What're you doing here?"

"Sorry to drop in like this. I'm in a jam."

"Why ain't I surprised?" He swallowed, then said, "Lord, my manners. My auntie would skin me." Matthew opened the door wider. "Come in, come in."

"Thanks, but no," I replied as I glanced back over my shoulder at the cab. It was still there, at least. "Meter running." I hefted the books in my arms. "Got a job for you, if you want it."

The kid's eyes sparkled behind his wire-rimmed glasses. "Of course." He put down his snack.

I explained I needed him to look in the ledgers for missing money and then hold onto the books.

"I can start right now," he said as he hugged the ledgers to his chest. "And remember about putting in a good word with Maud."

I guess he didn't know I was in Maud's doghouse. "Be happy to," I said.

*   *   *

I had my doubts Humphrey would even see me after our little dust-up at the convent, but sure enough, within a few minutes of the butler announcing me, he limped into the foyer.

"Joye," he exclaimed and extended his hand. "Dia duit, á Seán. Good to see you, old man. Violet went over to Alton to be with her family." He guided me toward the stairs. "Let's talk in my study. I assume you heard about Bernard," he said as we climbed. "Or was there something else?"

I let him show me into a nice-sized room crammed with books. Embers glowed in a big fireplace. Precious little need for a fire now; by noon the temperature'd climbed to seventy-five degrees. Just not right for the second day of October. I took a seat. "Yeah, I know. I walked into the crime scene investigation this morning. But I do have a few questions for you."

Humphrey looked alarmed for a moment, then went to the sideboard and poured drinks. "I know it's a little early for the cocktail hour, but I think brandy is in order. Especially in order," he said as he handed me one.

"Thanks," I said and pretended to take a sip and sat the snifter on a table next to my chair. *Where to start?* "Kyffin told me Violet had him tracing Lillian's whereabouts. Well, we all know now that meant looking for the baby. Did he find anything in the rounds of it that might have threatened someone?"

While he thought about that, I thought about what Sister Mary Gabriel had said: She'd followed a trail of evil all over Europe and into the United States, and it ended with Taylor Humphrey. I trusted her opinion, be it a woman's intuition or a soldier's gut instinct. This tidy man hemming and hawing before me may or may not be a killer, but women weren't safe around him. That I knew.

"I don't want to be rude," Humphrey said. "But—how to say this? I thought Violet had settled our account with you. The police are investigating the attack on Bernard. And believe me, the full force of the De Noailles-Arwald family position bears down on the commissioner at this moment. Bernard was one of us, and this crime will not go unsolved." He sipped his brandy and smiled. "I expect an arrest at any time."

I shrugged. "I'm not easy to offend. And yes, your *wife*—" I returned his smile, "settled up just fine. I'm completely satisfied. She was most generous."

Humphrey polished off his brandy and hopped up to refill the glass. "Good, good," he said without looking at me. "I'm glad. So, your interest in this crime is—" He returned to his seat and again met my eyes, "Idle curiosity? Or a more personal affront?"

I pretended to drink some more, trying to read him, and said at last, "Well, I'm a curious person. As are you."

He inclined his head, a subtle but not-at-all humble bow, and admitted, "I *am* a scholar. One must be curious, as well as intellectually rigorous." Humphrey leaned forward. "Correlation does not prove causality. Investigating—"

"You all lied to me," I said.

"I'll grant you we weren't entirely forthcoming. Need to know and whatnot."

I swirled the brandy around in the snifter. "Uh-huh."

He held up a hand, the Oxford don cautioning a mouthy scholar, and continued the lecture, "Investigating a missing newborn in the days before an attack doesn't mean said attack had anything to do with that investigation."

"True, but—"

"He's a lawyer," Humphrey said. "Dealt with who knows what sort of unsavory elements."

Kyffin made his pocket money suing rich people on behalf of other rich people. So, yeah, unsavory elements, but probably not what Humphrey meant.

He cocked his head to one side and smiled again. "Bernard's not a true man, despite appearances. Unnatural attachment with that roommate. At the very least." Humphrey showed me some teeth. "Don't you think? You two seemed to be so very close."

I'll admit to being a bit rattled. I pretended I was there to shoot him in the head, which made me feel a little more in charge. "I'm not close to nobody."

He raised an eyebrow and then observed, "A perverted relationship is always a blackmail vulnerability. For anyone." He held up his brandy snifter and looked me dead in the eyes to toast, "Sláinte." He knocked it back and set the glass on the table. "Especially a person of Bernard's position in the community."

I made no move to return the toast as I studied Humphrey's face. "He was investigating the Piasa Lodge."

He didn't bat an eye as he said, "I wonder why he'd do that?"

I let the silence build while I got out my pipe and tobacco and fiddled with smoking for a while.

He finally spoke, "Well, if there were irregularities—" Humphrey walked over to the desk and took a cigarette from a silver box. "Financial, for example." He lit the cigarette and took a deep drag. "I wouldn't know, of course, but you might bring it up with Violet's father."

"Joseph Arwald."

"Yes. He's more on the business side of things. I frankly couldn't even tell you who the treasurer is. Now, Dr. De Noailles," he continued as he blew out a cloud of smoke. "He's the oldest living member. Remembers, a bit too nostalgically, perhaps, when the lodge was more a spiritual home than a civic organization." Humphrey sat again and flicked ash into a silver tray on the table. "He might consider normal operations for a modern businessman's club to be 'irregular.' Or, conversely, he might push behind the scenes for mystic rituals that others find dangerous, even criminal. He's addicted to illegal drugs. Did you know that?"

I smoked my pipe and let him talk. Things Dr. De Noailles had said about grounding and centering came to me. And what I already knew about focus. My mind searched for that tether to Kyffin and tugged at it. *Still there.* I felt—no—I could see Humphrey's rising panic. And his secret, a door he slammed and locked behind him, to keep me from getting too close.

"There appear to be some lodge artifacts missing," I said.

I could hear Humphrey exhale.

As cool as you please, he moved his chair closer to me. "Let me speak frankly. I may have seriously misjudged you over the past few months, in which case you can attribute my words to 'the eccentric professor,' leave here, and get on with your life."

"Frank speech would be welcome," I said, then blew smoke at him.

Humphrey grimaced and snubbed out his cigarette. "Magick is real in the world."

I'd heard this one before. "You've mentioned that."

"Yes," leaning forward he said, "and you never rise to my bait."

I shrugged.

He touched my knee. "I keep trying different flies."

"Sometimes the fish just ain't hungry," I set the pipe down, "or the weather's too cold or hot. Sunshine's not right."

"So, conditions change." Humphrey's words gushed out, "My studies go far beyond the mysticism that Dr. De Noailles and his consort practice, useful in its way, but mere spirituality. No, I study the scientific application of untapped physical principles. Natural philosophy." He paused to catch his breath then said, "Is the fish still pondering the lure?"

The fish thought it was pure shite, but I played along, wondering where the hook was buried. "How could it not?"

"Good, good. People like us have a calling." Humphrey scooted his chair even closer to mine. "A vocation, as you Roman Catholics say. One fine day the Other Realm plucks us out of the water. No need for lures, bait, and hooks."

"A net?"

"Perhaps," he smiled. "I was eight years old, just of an age to slip off and explore beyond the manor's grounds on my own. Our village is built within an ancient henge. In renaissance times they took down some of the stones to build houses." He shook his head. "Sound familiar? Man hasn't learned much." His eyes were a mite weepy. "It was just at dusk, Midsummer's Eve. I was supposed to be asleep, but who could rest? I made my way to the henge. The night was full of fireflies and the eastern sky full of stars."

The room darkened. The gloaming was upon us and here we sat, jawing like a couple of old women. "And you saw ghostly druids?" I teased. "Perhaps a faerie troop?"

"I expected better of you," Humphrey said, but went back to his story. "I *saw* nothing but felt the Veil open. For the rest of my life, I've searched for the way back. I've studied the hermetic writings—" he stood, walked over to the window, and looked out, "and conducted magical research all over the world with the most learned of mages." He leaned his forehead against the glass and gripped the drapery. "Mostly, I've only achieved small success with minor cantrips." He released the fabric and, squaring his shoulders, said, "But of late, I've made real progress and had a few impressive effects. I'm hopeful, but the energy sources aren't sufficient to work my will. I need direct access to the raw, wild Magick of the Other Realm."

When Humphrey turned back to face me, he'd harnessed every ounce of command in his personality. I faced, not a sentimental scholar, but rather Taylor Humphrey, Esquire, of Avebury Park, a tenured professor at Merton College, Oxford, and captain, the Queen's Own Oxfordshire Hussars. His voice boomed, "Face your call and accept it."

Swells with notions have lorded it over me for years. I just let his shite wash by, not resisting or submitting. He was merely there. As was I. Time ticked on. "You can't assume all the Irish have the Sight," I finally observed as I tapped the ash from the pipe.

"I assume nothing. I can tell."

As far as I knew, he was right: All magic did come from Faerie, and I didn't care to talk of it. For most of my life, I physically *couldn't* talk of it. The Good Folks had seen to that with a geas—a spell. "Maybe I can't remember," I said as I tried to look innocent. "The Good People mess with your memories, you know."

"Do they now?" Humphrey ran over to his desk, all scholar again. He opened a notebook and wrote something down. "We must work together," he said, more to the page than me.

I walked around the desk to stand behind him and grip his shoulder, his tweed jacket rough against my hand. He twitched like a frightened rabbit and kept his eyes downcast. I took the Mont Blanc out of his hand, holding his soft, sweaty palm for a long moment. I finally released him and laid the pen aside. Humphrey breathed a little hiccup as I leaned over his shoulder to read the notebook, my breath disturbing a few hairs at his temple that had escaped pomade. He didn't resist as I thumbed through his book, reading his most intimate thoughts. He seemed to have lost all power of movement and could only watch.

It was a sort of magical research diary. Some entries were copied from books, many in Latin and referenced, of course. Others were his ideas or descriptions of some ritual he tried and how it went. Nothing about being in London as Mother Mary Gabriel had mentioned. But there could be other notebooks. Since I had Humphrey's attention, I pulled the list of names out of my pocket and laid it before him on the desk.

"Know any of these blokes?" I whispered in his ear.

He sucked in his breath.

The door clicked open, breaking the moment. "Taylor, I'm back," Violet said.

We both looked up.

She pulled off her gloves. "Oh, hello, Mr. Joye." If finding us in a clinch surprised her, she didn't show it.

I folded the ledger page away in my pocket, and Humphrey grabbed my arm as he stumbled to his feet. He walked over to his wife to kiss her cheek. "How did dear Lillian take the news?"

"In shock, I'd say. Grandfather is beside himself. Marched up to his cave—" Violet paused and explained to me, "He has an actual cave. 'Vision Cave,' he calls it." Then turning back to Humphrey to finish her thought, "and wouldn't come out." She looked at me. "Will you stay for tea?"

"Or do you have to run along?" Humphrey handed me my pipe, took my arm, and walked me out of the room. "I enjoyed our conversation. We should talk more. Perhaps at my club."

"Ah, sure, anytime," I said. *If you haven't got me thrown in jail.* I'd had the upper hand for a minute, but he'd held out two possibilities for my future, both firmly within his control.

Chapter Eighteen

⎯⎯∞⎯⎯

Bad Debt

I walked down Washington Terrace from the Arwald mansion toward Union as the sun set behind me. The connection I'd had with Kyffin for most of the day was gone and I felt alone. I could see the hospital in the distance. Surely by now, the docs had patched him up. Or he'd died. I needed to know which one. With that cheery thought, I looked forward to a quick bath and shave, maybe some clean clothes, before sneaking into the hospital.

I took a streetcar to the Railroad YMCA, dragged myself up the stairs and past the bright-tiled locomotive emblems that lined the entrance, and across the terrazzo floor. Two or three men, ready for dinner, sat in a far corner of the quiet lobby. One read the sports page to the others.

I'll admit I looked a little rough around the edges, but it wasn't the fecking Chase Hotel. Yet the young fella behind the dark walnut registration desk only had to take one look at me before yelling behind him into an office, "He's here."

A small, bedeviled chap, tuffs of gray hair sticking up at odd angles and a drop of sweat rolling down his forehead, peeked out of the office. He slipped into his jacket as he shut the door behind him. "Can I help you?" he said as his eyes glanced off mine, then shifted away.

"I paid for a room earlier today." I jerked my thumb at the clerk. "He thought you'd have something by evening."

The man—his badge declared him, "Nevil Yancy, Assistant Manager"—shuffled some papers and made a show of looking through a registration book. His collar was starched stiff and dug into his neck with every turn of his head. He'd cut his own throat by the end of this conversation. "Ah, Mr. Joye. I'm sorry. That room is no longer available."

"I paid in advance for it," I said, leaning over the counter, "Mr. Yancy."

"Well, mix-ups happen." He opened a cash box and counted out a couple of dollar bills. "Here. A refund."

I didn't move to take the money. Both of them shifted their weight uneasily and glanced at each other. Back at me. The floor. The ceiling. The railway workers put down their paper, the front desk suddenly more interesting than the upcoming World Series. "So," I finally pocketed the cash, "out of curiosity, did they threaten you? Or just bribe you?"

The clerk blushed, and Yancy sputtered a protest.

"A specific person worries you?" I said, at the tail end of my patience. "Joseph Arwald, say?"

"There simply isn't a room for you."

Somewhere beyond the lobby, forks and plates clicked as the dinner table was set. A whiff of beef and potatoes drifted through the room, and I realized I hadn't eaten since breakfast.

"Look," I made no effort to lower my voice. "A man was attacked and might die. A woman and her baby are in danger." The case's tangled threads loosened a bit in some unused corner of my mind.

"Another child was kidnapped and murdered. And someone's shutting me down, good and proper, in every way he can think of." I slid the two dollars back across the desk and said, "Why don't you have a room for me all of a sudden?"

Yancy and the clerk looked at each other and around the lobby. "Boys," Yancy said to our audience. "Go see if the housekeeper needs help with setting the tables."

"What?" They protested in unison.

Yancy was a little guy, but he had an air about him. He glared like a walking boss, and they jumped up right quick. Then he motioned me back behind the counter to his office. "If you'll come with me. I took the liberty to retrieve your luggage. It's back here." He closed the office door behind us. He didn't offer me a chair. I guess I wasn't supposed to stay long.

Fine by me. "Make it snappy."

"I got a phone call," Yancy said. "I didn't know the voice, but I could tell he was on the board by the things he knew and the way he talked about the association."

He kept his eyes focused on the desk blotter as he spoke. "He said you were a known sexual invert, and the board would be scandalized to learn I was renting to such people."

That was ridiculous. I'd been married, for Christ's sake. "You generally believe everything strangers on the phone tell you?"

"The truth isn't important." Yancy looked up and said, "Someone on the board, or close to the board, doesn't want you here. He could give any reason or no reason at all. The fact that we're the Young Men's Christian Association makes us sensitive to scandal of this sort."

I sorted through all the doors I'd rattled in the course of the day. Behind one of them was someone who'd leaned on the YMCA. But how'd he even known I'd tried to get a room here?

"You've made a powerful enemy, I'd say." Yancy handed over my suitcase. "Try the soup kitchen at Carr and Second Street."

"Thanks. I'll get by." I showed myself out.

*   *   *

I walked across the street to Union Station and stowed my belongings in a locker. At the luncheonette in the terminal, I considered my next move: The blue-plate special was fifty cents and came with pie and coffee. I went with that. While I waited for my food, I looked through an evening paper someone had abandoned on the counter. Kyffin was still alive, in "serious condition," and under constant guard. So they claimed. The police pleaded for witnesses to come forward.

I resolved to break into the hospital as soon as I'd shoveled in a meal. I only half—not even half—trusted the cops to stop the second attack I knew would come. While I ate supper, I read about a nasty automobile accident on Kingshighway right in front of Barnes Hospital. Guy named Phillip Gray had survived, barely, a head-on with a delivery van. A voice rang out over the din of the busy railway station, "Hey, Shamus. I gotta beef with you."

Seamus is my oldest brother, still fighting the good fight back in Belfast, so I automatically looked up from my chicken pot pie. A man slid onto the stool next to me as he waved off the waitress. "I'm talking to you, Mr. Detective."

I'd forgotten that bit of Yank slang: Shamus means detective. The East Coast bray belonged to the reporter I'd met at the hospital earlier. "Mr. Oliver, isn't it?" I folded up the paper. "You following me around?"

He pointed at my eye and asked, "Who'd you tick off?"

A muffled voice, impossible to understand, squawked over a loudspeaker in the terminal.

"No one," I said.

Oliver looked puzzled and pointed out at the terminal and then his ear. I leaned in closer and shouted, "Walked into a door." He smelled like a writer. That is to say, like whiskey.

"I don't know what your game is—" the boarding announcement ended just as Oliver shouted, "but the Arwald story is mine." Several travelers at the lunch counter looked over at him. I whacked him in the arm. "What story?" I whispered. "And weren't you covering *the hospital* this morning?" He smiled and touched the side of his nose. "Gotcha. Maybe you're not so dumb, after all." He took a notebook and pencil out of his pocket. "Just don't ball it for me. This one's going to get me a staff job back in New York."

"Fair enough. I'd never take bread out of a man's mouth. Just how am I balling it for you?"

"Nosing around. Getting people's backs up. Maybe you don't know who you're dealing with."

The terminal's hubbub suddenly washed over the lunch counter. I could barely hear myself think. "Maybe I don't," I shouted.

Oliver's eyes lit on my bread plate. I pushed it over to him, and he fell on the food, making a butter sandwich out of all the pats in the dish. "You're OK, brother. Trade information?"

I didn't have much information, so I had no problem trading nothing for something. "You first," I said as I passed him the jelly pot from the rack.

In a moment of relative quiet, he asked, "How long you been in our little burg?" He incorporated the jam into his dinner.

"Little over a year."

Shielding his mouth with one hand, Oliver said, "I would've thought the Judge explained things to you."

"Maybe he has."

"You're not showing that much sense." He ate a few bites in silence, and then looked around. We were alone at the lunch counter. "We call them the 'Big Cinch.' The folks that *really* run things," he said between mouthfuls. "The money men, the leaders, the movers and shakers that own everything from the electric company to the streetcars to the bridges. And more. Much more."

"I've heard the expression," I said, draining my coffee cup and watching a new horde of travelers pour into the luncheonette.

"So, you were around last winter." He'd finished his butter sandwich and gazed at the half a slice of pie I'd left on my plate.

I handed it over. "Yeah," I said, looking around for the waitress with the check. With every seat at the counter now occupied, she was scrambling to take orders.

"Then you musta seen those big parades the Big Cinch puts on, to show us lowlifes who's really in control. All the Big Cinch clubs have one. The Piasa Lodge, for instance."

I started to get his drift. "Owned lock, stock, and barrel by Joseph Arwald."

He snorted. "They're the worst," he said. "Chief Ouatoga comes from Cahokia Mounds, blesses the city, and tells us to obey our betters."

"Why would an honest working man care about an old Mississippian?" I nodded to the waitress who held up a coffee pot with a questioning look on her face.

"Don't be a dolt. He's one of the old boys, all dressed up. It's a show. But the money they spend on the spectacle. Parades with lighted floats, pageants, tableaux, and big dances." Oliver seemed to drift off into an old memory of something quite pleasant. "Like at the Fair," he murmured. "You should've seen the Fair."

"So I hear. Constantly. I was four years old and a world away." I lit one of Kyffin's cigarettes and offered the pack to Oliver. He took two. I whispered, "But what does a parade have to do with the 'Arwald story'? Or Kyffin Bernard?"

"Say, I've been shooting my mouth off plenty—what've you got?"

"Winter, hmm," I mumbled, trying to look knowledgeable.

"Yeah, Shamus, 'winter.' Something happen?"

"Lillian Arwald had a row with her father, right before the deb ball. Moved out for a brief while."

Oliver looked excited by this bit of news. "Oh, boy. That's hot. Thanks." He scribbled in his notepad, then hopped up to leave. "See ya around."

"Wait a minute," I said, grabbing his sleeve. "What's that got to do with Kyffin being attacked?"

"He was her sweetie, wasn't he? Probably mouthed off to the wrong person, not thinking it could get rough." Oliver leaned over to speak in my ear over the din. "But all those swells got their thugs at the ready," he said just before he ran off.

I sat for a bit. *Why did that old news—Lillian's fight with her father—mean so much to Oliver?* I didn't know, but it was time to focus on how to find Kyffin in the giant maze that was Barnes Hospital. I couldn't exactly ask at the front desk, with the cops lounging in the lobby, ready to roust me on sight. I scanned the auto accident story in the paper again, left sixty cents on the counter, and made a quick phone call. "Mr. Gray's ward, please," I said to the hospital operator, flattening my vowels to the best St. Louis accent I could muster.

"That would be the fifth floor, Trauma Surgery. One moment, please. I'll connect you." I hung up and strolled to the streetcar stop to catch a ride back to the Central West End.

*   *   *

I used the emergency room route into the hospital again, found a likely stairwell, and ended up in a back hall on the fifth floor. As I passed a door marked *House Officer on Call,* I followed a hunch and peeked inside. The room was dark and full of snoring. I could make out a narrow bed with a sleeping figure—a doctor, I guess—catching a few winks while he could. I borrowed his white coat from the wall hook and stowed my hat and jacket in the stairwell.

The doctor's coat pockets yielded a pair of thick, tortoise-shell glasses, a physician's handbook, and one of those things for listening to hearts. I hung it around my neck like doctors do, read the section in the book about brain injuries, and put on the glasses. I made my way to the trauma surgery unit, for "a consultation," a term I'd just learned from the handbook.

With the glasses on, walking a straight line without bumping into anything took most of my attention. The lobby was laid out much like the one on the maternity ward where we'd waited for Lillian. The cop guarding Kyffin was sound asleep in a chair near the lift. Exactly what I expected. A few worried-looking people sat in the chairs and pretended to read magazines, and I wondered which were Kyffin's folks. The visiting hours were posted on the wall. A glance at my watch told me I needed to hurry up. Someone might try to visit Kyffin soon.

There was no way to get into the ward without the matron seeing me, so I staggered toward her desk. She stood as I approached and said, "Good evening, doctor." Her face was a blur and her voice disapproving.

"Ah, yes," I muttered. "Neurology consultation on—" I pulled a piece of paper out of the coat pocket and pretended to review it. It was a grocery list. "Bernard."

"Oh, the head trauma." She looked at a clipboard on her desk. "Bed Seven, Dr.—?"

I said the first thing that popped into my head. "Ward. I'm Dr. Bernard Ward."

"Dr. Ward. This way," she said as she ushered me into an open room with rows of beds lining two walls. A large window framed a dark, cloudy sky, but lights from Kingshighway—moving cars, traffic signals, and light standards—chased each other across the room.

A nurse, tall and in charge, descended on me. My head started to hurt from looking through the spectacles, and I felt a bit queasy.

"Dr. Ward is here for a neuro consult," said my matron-guard, as she turned to me. "Doctor, meet the head nurse, Miss Gaines."

Miss Gaines sniffed. Even with the spectacles, I could tell she looked skeptical and then hostile, a watchdog about to bare her fangs.

I heard a growl form in her throat and knew I was done for, but then another nurse at a nearby bedside said, "Oh, Mr. Gray." She began to minister to her patient with efficient moves. I didn't get what she was doing, but things seemed bad for Gray. "Miss Gaines, he's cyanotic," the nurse said.

"Matron, alert the cardiac team," said Miss Gaines as she rushed to Gray. The matron pointed down the row to a bed by the window as she dashed away to get help and called out to me, "Dr. Ward, that's Seven."

*   *   *

I had precious little time to see Kyffin, so I pushed down my dread and hurried over to Bed Seven. I pulled the curtains closed and took off the fecking glasses.

He'd had visitors, that much was obvious. A vase of lilies stood on a bedside table along with several get-well cards.

I'd pictured Kyffin a hundred times throughout the day, and most of those images were pretty bloody. It was a bit of a relief to see him for real. "Did ya ever see such a clean corpse?" I asked myself, echoing one of my granny's favorite observations at a wake. The strong connection I'd felt with him on and off all day was gone. *Did that mean he was already dead?*

A wire contraption kept his neck straight and gauze wrapped his shaved head. He was quite pale, which made the bruises on his face, chest, and shoulders look even worse. To me, he looked pretty dead, but his chest moved, just barely, up and down under the white sheets.

I traced Kyffin's jawline with the back of my hand, ruffing the blond stubble. He didn't stir.

"Hey, buddy. You need a shave."

Nothing.

I got closer and spoke right into his ear. "Open your eyes."

He didn't.

I jostled him. "Quit playing around."

No reaction.

Kyffin had smelled of a death-wish—heady, exciting, seductive— the entire time I'd known him. And here we were. God damn him.

I stood over his bed and swore, calling him every name in the book and making up a few more. City lights through the window played across the drawn curtain, and then I noticed a child's drawing tacked to the wall. A little girl waving at an airplane in the sky.

Jesus. "I didn't mean any of that." I took his hand, knowing his injury was my fault. I'd let him go alone to confront somebody about a crime, even though I knew better, that my fear for him was not the normal worry over a mate out on a tricky job. Whatever the hell lay on the other side of the Veil had once again rapped on my door and demanded I let it in.

"I'll do better," I told him. "I'll fix things and keep you safe."

I'm not sure how long I stood there, holding Kyffin's hand. He didn't move a muscle, but somehow, I felt him with me again. Peace washed over me as if I'd just received the blessed Body and Blood.

I needed something, anything of his, just to keep that connection alive. I opened a drawer of the bedside table: reading glasses, the Ronson, his lucky franc coin. Maybe not so lucky. I slipped it into my pocket and whispered, "I'll give this back when you get well."

I put on the doctor's glasses again and stumbled for the door. A crowd of nurses and doctors had a cart of medicine and wicked-looking tools at Gray's bedside and seemed intent to try them all. In my professional opinion, the man was dead. But I left them to it and hurried away.

I returned the borrowed coat to the still-sleeping doctor, retrieved my gear, and found a pay phone near the cafeteria. I dialed the hospital operator. "Fifth-floor trauma," I said, in the gruffest voice I could manage.

"Connecting you."

In a few moments, I heard the click of the ward's phone's pick-up. Before the matron even got out a greeting, I cut in, "This is Detective Draper. Wake up that idiot flatfoot by the lift. Tell him when I say guard an injured witness, I mean 'at the bedside.' Got it?"

"Yes, sir. I'll tell him right away." Her voice dropped, "I think he was feeling a mite squeamish, you know. Some people are like that around blood and such."

"Well, he's in the wrong line of work," I thundered, really getting into the role. "He can be walking a beat by morning."

"Of course. I'm sure he'll get used to the hospital. I'm off to get him right now."

"See that you do." I hung up and checked my watch. I needed to hurry to the Civil Courts Building if I was to meet Mrs. Mac by nine o'clock.

∽∘∞∘∽

Chapter Nineteen

Amortization

Iarrived fifteen minutes early to meet Mrs. Mac at the courts building loading dock. The night was overcast but warm, and the flops and speaks across the street lively, the parties spilling out onto the street. From the shadows, I was in a perfect position to see a short, dark-clad figure pause at the service entrance door, glance about, and lean over the lock. In less than a minute he slipped inside. Mrs. Mac arrived on the stroke of nine. "You understand what to do?"

"Actually," I said, "I still don't know what you expect of me with your haunts."

"They ain't mine. And I expect you to not drive them to attack us again, for one thing. You're a charmer—do whatever it is you do to politely tell them to be on their way."

"I'm not," I sighed. "I've no inside dope on the fae. And you've the Sight, yourself."

Mrs. Mac wrapped her shawl tighter. "'Tis different."

"I don't see how."

"That's because you're a great lummox." She squared her shoulders and marched toward the door, shouting, "Let's be at it."

As I followed I said, "I just saw someone break in. You didn't recruit anyone else, did you?"

"Not I. Sure it weren't the night watchman?"

"I don't think so."

She shrugged. "Can't be helped. You might have to clock him, whoever he is. Can you do *that* quietly?"

"Yes, ma'am."

She kept look out while I picked the lock. We'd agreed to start in the library. The priestess haunted that level the last time we tried this fools' errand, after the Piasa Lodge Ball.

Mrs. Mac and me got off the freight elevator on the thirteenth floor just as a dark figure stepped out of the stairwell into the hallway. The person looked right and then left, saw us, and ducked back down the stairwell. I grabbed at the figure, and we both fell hard, tumbling down the stairs to the twelfth-floor mezzanine landing. He carried a canvas sling case that clattered to the floor. Mrs. Mac stood at the top of the stairs and hissed, "Quiet, ya idiot."

My quarry, a small person, was quite easy to flip over and knee in the small of the back but wasn't giving up without a fight. He struggled, making a play for what I had to assume was a pocketed weapon.

"Easy, fella. Whadda ya got here?" A pat-down revealed salt, a bottle of holy water, and a paper scrap. The case concealed a shotgun and a good supply of ammo.

"Young man," a woman's Cork-accented voice said, "Unhand me, this instant."

I'd unhanded her, jumped up, and held out my palms for a paddling before I even realized it. "Mother Mary Gabriel?"

She didn't hit me, but rather grabbed my hands and hoisted herself to her feet. "Thank you."

She was dressed in a nun's black and gray but wore trousers. It was the most amazing thing I'd ever seen in my life.

"What are you doing here?" we both said.

Mother Mary Gabriel gave me that look. "You first." It's a wonder the cops don't have a squad of school sisters on the interrogation team.

"Ah, helping out my friend up there," I indicated Mrs. Mac, on the landing above us. "Mother Mary Gabriel, please meet Mrs. Charity MacSweeney."

"How do," called Mrs. Mac.

"Mrs. Mac, this is Mother Mary Gabriel," I said. "She runs Mount St. Michael's Convent."

"Lovely to meet you," said the nun, as she returned her belongings to the various pockets of her remarkable trousers and slung the gun over her shoulder. Turning to me, she said, "But what are you two doing here?"

"This might sound strange, but Mrs. Mac sees spirits in the courts building."

"You see them, too," Mrs. Mac corrected me.

"Yes, well, I have. Crazy, I know," I said. "And they're more active since the assault last night—"

"Oh, even before that," she further corrected.

The sister started up the stairs to Mrs. Mac in a right hurry.

"Yes, well. She asked me to—"

To Mrs. Mac, Mother Mary Gabriel said, "Investigate?" She inclined her head at me. "What does this one know about spiritual investigations? You need to consult a professional regarding such things."

"Aye, and where would I be finding such a professional? The Church of Rome, you'll say, I'm sure."

"Well, in a way. Not that you'd get far with the hierarchy. Me, on the other hand—"

And so they chatted away, thick as thieves, while I climbed the stairs to join them. "Sorry to interrupt, sister. But what're you doing here?"

"I found this evidence," she said as she showed us the scrap of paper she'd brought with her, a drawing of a room, with little numbers and squiggles in the margins.

"Also, I've located an undocumented floor in this building—the eleventh. Not on any directory, and the lifts don't go there. It must be where Taylor Humphrey's cult meets."

I scratched my head.

"A private lift goes to eleven," said Mrs. Mac. "But it ain't no cult. Just a fancy gentleman's club."

Sister snorted. "The door to the eleventh-floor landing was"—she waved the paper in our faces—"locked. Magically locked."

"Aye, you'd be needing a key," Mrs. Mac said. "But the members mostly take the lift."

"Wait a minute," I said. "There's a men's club in this here building?"

"'Tis an open secret," said Mrs. Mac. "Ya didn't get your invitation in the post?"

"It's the meeting place of an evil cult," Sister said. "I can tell by the design of the room."

"Yes, yes," Mrs. Mac interrupted. "'Tis the Piasa Lodge meeting place. A den of sin, I'll be bound." She turned her back on me and said to Mother Mary Gabriel, "So, you say with your papist witchcraft you can rid my life of haunts?"

"My dear woman, my faith is the very opposite of witchcraft. In the name of our Lord, I can compel spirits to depart this realm and go on to their place in the afterlife."

"These spirits seem to be ancient Mississippians," I interrupted. "Would they pay any mind to a Christian exorcism?"

Mother Mary Gabriel had to think on that one. "Did you figure that out yourself? But—" She wavered, an expert suddenly out of her depth, before saying, "I'll consult some Jesuit colleagues and come back prepared to exorcise the building in the most appropriate way."

I tapped the paper in her hand. "What's this 'evidence' mean?"

"It shows the room was built to magical specifications. I copied this from the blueprints."

"And how'd you get those blueprints?"

"Hard work, young man. Hours of research and study." She turned to leave. "Try it sometime."

The nun's story was moving way too fast for me. "So did you find any more evidence in this 'evil cult' magical room?"

"Well, no. I couldn't actually get in. The wards barred me from the eleventh floor," she replied as she shifted her weight from foot to foot.

I nodded, "So you'll be needing a key."

"Have you had a brain injury, perhaps?" Enuciating each word, she said, "Magical locks are something else I need to research so I can counteract the spells." She patted my hand, the tender gesture taking me by surprise. "Concentrate on finding out Taylor Humphrey's interest in Lillian's baby." Mother Mary Gabriel shoved me toward the exit and vanished into the stairwell shadows, her voice trailed back out of the darkness, "Leave this cursed place to experts."

That sounded good to me, but I now had an idea where Lillian might have been right before Mrs. Mac and me found her the night of the debutante ball. We took the stairs down two levels, the old lady complaining about her knees the entire time. So much for stealth.

As we approached the eleventh-floor stairwell door, I said, "There could be spells on this place. Curses or something. Be ready to defend yourself."

Mrs. Mac muttered, "Papists," under her breath and defended herself with a stiff belt from her flask.

As for me, I squeezed Kyffin's lucky coin, still in my pocket, and found that safe spot inside me.

*   *   *

The stairwell door lock looked simple enough, but I felt reluctant to touch it. Suddenly unmotivated, opening the door seemed a waste of time. I'd turned away when Mrs. Mac pushed me back to it. "That nun done told ya the lock was cursed. Hex it right back." So mostly to shut her up, I picked the lock and swung the door open on well-oiled hinges.

Mrs. Mac and me were in a back hallway. Voices, music, and light filtered down short, intersecting passages. The place occupied, a search was out of the question. *Maybe Mrs. Mac could pretend to be a cleaning lady, but what was I supposed to do?*

She grabbed my arm and pulled me into a utility room. "Uniforms and such in here." A mechanic's greasy coveralls hung on a peg. I put them on over my clothes and found an impressive wrench on a shelf. She grabbed a mop and bucket.

We crept down the hall, around the corner, and spotted a reception desk across from the lift. The doors opened, and a couple of fat cats got off to be greeted by a maître d' at the desk. We scurried back through the service hall and around the other way, which led to a casino area. A half dozen or so gents played cards or dice, swilled brandy, and clutched cigars, their glances sliding right over us. "The help," don't you know. We advanced through the smoke haze past a bar. I didn't see any exits, only back the way we'd come in.

Finally, someone noticed us: The bouncer, his monkey suit straining against the heft of his biceps. As he barreled down on me, I shifted the wrench in my hand and wondered how much physical security they had up here. Mrs. Mac grabbed my arm and shouted, "'Tis this way. Overflowing 'tis." She pulled me toward a hallway that led into the far side of the club.

The bouncer looked alarmed as he whispered in a thick Cockney accent, "Keep your voice down." He glanced around at the members, then whispered, "No one tells me anything. Fix it, mac. And make it snappy."

"Sure thing," I twanged in my best Missourah accent.

We made it snappy, all right, and hurried down the hall past a couple of closed doors, around the corner, and down another hall. At last, we came to the large room Sister had pointed out on her diagram. The magical ward on this room was even stronger than the one protecting the eleventh-floor entrance. I wanted to give it up. But I touched the coin in my pocket and found my tether to Kyffin again. I had the flimsy lock open in no time.

Hot air enwrapped us as I pushed open the door. The room was pitch black, dark as a cave. Mrs. Mac hit the light switch, revealing a sacristy sort of place: a wooden cupboard on the far wall, a high table in the center of the room, and robes hung on pegs. Gold-leafed round medallions decorated with the Piasa image covered the ceiling. "I'm going to check that cabinet," I said, my voice bouncing around the room, echoing off the ceiling.

"Well, step lively then. 'Tis a foul, evil place."

Mrs. Mac was right. The room was dirty with energy and charged with power. I felt all the deadly sins tempt me, one by one. But mostly—greed. My desires were as real as the oak-paneled walls' faint incense aroma. *How dare they rob the poor, just because they could?* Arwald, Humphrey, and the like—the Big Cinch. I'd show them. Somehow. Someday.

"Don't just stare at the wall like the great lummox ya are," Mrs. Mac said.

I whirled on her, my fist gripping the wrench.

"Ya going to search the room or not?"

She was right. I'd meant to check the cabinets. Might be something of value in there. My temper defused a bit. At first glance, it looked like a sacristy cupboard: books, a chalice, paten, and a folded altar cloth. Even the salt cellar didn't seem entirely out of place. But I'd no idea what the mirror, dagger, and chalk were for and didn't care. The chalice might be worth something at a pawn shop. Maybe the books were rare.

Just as I picked up the chalice—it was quite nice—Mrs. Mac whispered, "What's that noise?"

I paused. She cracked open the door to peek out just as the bouncer and an even bigger guy, a real bruiser, burst into the room. The bouncer marched toward me while his partner threw the old lady to the floor.

With some regret, I dropped the chalice and hefted the wrench with both hands, ready to fight and to lose. Mrs. Mac scrambled to her feet, I was relieved to see, just as the bouncer loomed within my reach. "Run," I called out to her as I landed a kick to his groin and swung at his face with my wrench.

I succeeded in making him mad, and he punched me with an uppercut. I saw stars for a second, then his buddy joined in with a left-right to the breadbasket. I fell, my dead weight on the bruiser at least, the both of us tumbling to the floor. I'd dropped the wrench in the rounds of it and rolled away, shielding my vital organs. I heard a thud and looked up to see that Mrs. Mac had struck the bruiser with the wrench as he struggled to his feet. "Take that, you numpty scrote," she crowed.

Her target was more surprised than injured. The bouncer said, "Here, here. None of that now, missus." More of a gent than the other fella, I guess, he pinned her arms behind her and marched her toward the door.

Grabbing my best chance to even the odds, I got to my knees, grabbed the dagger from the cabinet, and crawled over to the bruiser staggering to his feet. At that moment the energy in the room shifted. Like ozone in a lightning storm, clean, clear air swirled through the chamber. Books, candles, and everything else in the cupboard flew around the room, the robes fluttering along after them. At least I didn't crave the chalice anymore.

Drumming filled the room, and I saw the priestess. She hovered near the bouncer, his head between her hands. She peered into his eyes for a moment before her touch sent him into a screaming heebie jeebie fit. He released Mrs. Mac and ran out of the place.

The room filled with mist and fear as the priestess then pointed at me and my man. The bruiser shouted, "No, no. Get back." But he weren't worried about me and the dagger. He was talking at her. The priestess closed her fist and withdrew her arm, which seemed to release him. He scuttled across the floor and scrambled out the door.

I slid across the room to Mrs. Mac. She hadn't moved a muscle since the bouncer released her. "Let's go," I said, pushing her toward the door.

She snapped out of it, only to hit me on the arm. "What've you done now, eejit?"

"Never mind. Just go."

For once she did as I said, and I made to follow her out the door. But the priestess weren't done with me. Our eyes met, and terror twisted through my gut. But something else was deep in me, that anchor I'd set up before I even came into this place, and I grabbed it.

"Come on, then," I said, beckoning her forward, "and get on with it." She looked wary, but in the blink of an eye, she was on me, her hands on my chest and forehead. I about shite myself at her touch, so cold, in the grave so very long.

I felt her rummaging around in my head and heart, looking for something. I don't know how long I stood rooted to the spot, my mind numb. Finally, I found the strength to form words. I doubted I needed to talk out loud for her to understand me, but speaking my thoughts seemed to give them more weight. "You don't like what's going on here. Neither do I."

The priestess paid me no mind.

"I'm thinking this place was your faerie fort, and my people have made a right mess of it. Am I right?"

The drums quieted, and the flying objects all dropped to the floor. The room darkened, and I was alone.

Chapter Twenty

Line of Credit

Escaping the gentlemen's club was quite easy, as everyone in the place was terrorized by haunts while we dashed through the club to the service lift and away. I imagine any fella who didn't have a heart attack on the spot soon called it a night. Mrs. Mac waved off my offer to see her home and toddled to the bus stop.

I sat on the courthouse steps, smoked a cigarette, and thought. What I thought about was Dr. De Noailles's big old house in Lafayette Square, a perfect place to squat unless he'd left a servant to watch over the place. But I got the idea there was little money to spare in that household. Annie was the only servant I'd ever actually seen and moved with the family backed and forth between Alton and St. Louis. It was worth a try, anyway.

I was still pretty sore at Lillian. She was using Kyffin to keep her father's money tap on, without a hint of affection for him or appreciation of what he offered her. But she and her little girl were in trouble, and I'd promised both her and Kyffin that I'd help them. If I had to help her, then she had to support the investigation. With food, bathwater, and possibly a big soft bed.

I took the 21:48 bus to Union Station, collected my suitcase, and then hopped a streetcar to Lafayette Square. The park across the street from Dr. De Noailles's house was dark and empty.

No one answered the doorbell at the front or my knock on the rear door. The lock was ridiculously easy to open, and I was in the kitchen in under a minute. The place felt deserted. The Franklin stove in the servants' area was stone cold. I stoked and lit it, then put on water for tea. While it heated, I walked through the house, just to be sure I was alone. The washroom had its own water heater, so I stoked and lit that one, too, making free with Dr. De Noailles's coal.

Lillian's suite was much like I left it Monday afternoon, but the big steamer trunk was gone. To Alton, I imagined. Clothes lay strewn across the bed, shoes littered the floor, and scarves and belts hung off the lamps. Books were piled on the cozy window seat. Most seemed to be archeology, like *Mississippian Mound Death Cult*. Lillian was way more studious than she let on.

This mess of a case was littered with a lot of books. I had to laugh at myself, calling my nosing around "a case." Maybe I *did* think I was a shamus. But something felt off. Something about books—maybe the Piasa Lodge ledgers I'd left with Matthew. I sat on the floor and opened some of Lillian's archeology books. The Lodge records' pictures and words came back to me, and I compared them with the illustrations. Some of the artifacts in the ledgers sounded like the sort of things she'd been reading about, but I still didn't know what I was looking for.

I took a deep breath, closed my eyes, and cleared my mind. I tried hard not to try. As I opened my eyes, they lit on a folded card under the bed. It was Miss Lillian Arwald's Piasa Lodge Debutante Ball dance card, each dance of the evening promised to a prominent gent. I didn't know many of the people. Except for Kyffin, of course. And Humphrey. Then my eyes lit on another name I knew very well. His Honor, Judge James Dolan.

*   *   *

I pocketed the dance card for further consideration and washed up. Dr. De Noailles hadn't left any fresh food, but the pantry held some tinned soup and the like. I about inhaled a can of sardines before stretching out on the settee in the parlor. It seemed I'd only just closed my eyes when I heard running water. I bolted upright. Someone was in the washroom, filling the bathtub.

I pulled on my trousers, crept down the hall, and listened at the door. With a squeak of the handle, the water stopped flowing, and then I heard a splash or two. And crying. Someone was crying in the bathtub.

I could gather my things and sneak out. Whoever it was would be none the wiser. But the crying got louder, a real banshee of a wail.

I stood there a good while and finally tapped the door. "I don't mean to startle you. It's Sean Joye, a friend of Dr. De Noailles. Are you alright?"

The weeping paused. "Copper?" Lillian's voice was small and sad through the closed door. "Why are you in my house?"

"Long story. You don't sound so good."

"I'm not," she sniffled.

"Do you want to talk?"

I heard splashing and then she called out, "Come in and hand me a robe."

I opened the door. Lillian had steamed up the room pretty good and stood dripping in the tub. Plenty of warm, pink skin peeked out from behind clusters of strategically placed soap bubbles.

"God, it's cold. Close the door," she said.

I did, and then grabbed a red wrap-type dress off the floor and offered it to her.

She blanched. "Not that."

I had to agree. A chill had passed over me as soon as I touched it.

I stowed the dress away and helped her into a dingy chenille robe and out of the tub. Lillian headed to the window seat in her bedroom, dumping the books on the floor to lounge on the cushions. She peered through the blinds at the dark street below as I sat down beside her.

Her lips were pale, and her eyes red and swollen. Lillian is a small person but generally fills the room. Now, she folded in on herself and curled up against my shoulder. She began to weep again. "Oh, Copper. He's dead. He's dead. I—"

Her words were a punch in the gut. I pulled her away from me to look at her face. "Kyffin was fine a few hours ago. What did you hear at the hospital?"

Lillian shook her head and swallowed hard then said, "I just meant, I'm worried."

I wrapped her in my arms and kissed the top of her head. "We're all worried, doll. But no cause to bury the man before we need to."

"You're on my side, aren't you?"

"You know I am." She felt like a lump of ice in my arms. "You're so cold. You getting sick?" I made her get in bed under a pile of quilts and tucked a hot-water bottle in with her.

"Thanks," Lillian said. "Maybe I *am* sick."

"Well, get some rest," I said as I turned out the bedside lamp and stood to leave her.

"No." Her hand shot out from under the covers to grab my hand. "Leave the light on."

I couldn't figure what was going on with her, but I was glad of her concern for Kyffin. "You know, I've been kinda sore at you since yesterday."

She looked surprised and asked, "What'd I do?"

"You sounded like a gold digger. Kyffin's lack of a fortune and all."

Lillian smiled. "You shouldn't take anything I say seriously, Copper."

"Life's a gag. I get it."

"Sean." All I could see were her eyes, peeking above the covers. "I don't want to be alone. Stay with me?"

"Sure thing, doll."

She closed her eyes and curled up in a ball. I stretched out next to her on top of the quilts and stared at the ceiling, thinking.

The next thing I knew hazy gray daylight filtered in through the blinds. Wind whipped around the eaves, rattling the windows. Lillian was gone. The quilts were smooth as if she'd never slept there. The books were stacked back on the window seat.

I was on my own again.

Chapter Twenty-One

Collateral Damage

It was time to face the music about the Judge's car being a material witness, as it were, to a crime, so I ate the last of the doctor's tinned sardines and got on a streetcar headed to the courts building.

Our Indian summer was gone. Dark clouds hung over the city and the brisk wind grew colder by the minute. I'd forgotten my fedora in the Piasa Lodge maintenance room, so I'd lifted a flat tweed cap from the coat rack in Dr. De Noailles's servant's quarters. On a whim, I got off the streetcar at Chouteau and switched lines to Dogtown. I needed to talk to Maud. She'd had over a day to cool off, so maybe it'd be safe to show my face. I climbed the hill up Tamm and fought a northerly headwind to the Belfast Bar. I wished I'd stolen an overcoat from De Noailles's house, too. The bar was locked up tight—the front door chained and padlocked with a *Closed By Police Order* sign stuck to the glass. A couple of windows, really pretty stained glass Padraig had salvaged from a church being torn down, were boarded over. I ran around the building to the back stairs and smack dab into Matthew, who carried my load of green ledgers in his arms. "Where is everybody?" I asked.

"Maud, Miss Eliza, and the kids are staying with her church people. The cops took Mr. Padraig off, but I heard they let him out again last night. He's drinking at the barbershop down the street."

I remembered Joseph Arwald's threats against Padraig's place. He'd pay for this. "Thanks, kid." I took the books out of his arms. "Find anything?" The goods on that Arwald bastard were right there, in my hands. Just a matter of understanding what I had.

"Well, sort of," Matthew said as he stared at the ground. "I did look at them some. My aunt helped me, too."

"And?"

He took the financial book out of my arms and opened it. He used the back steps as a table, fighting the wind to show me the pages. "See here. This isn't reasonable. A whole lot of money is going for investment fees. A whole lot," he explained as he flipped a few more pages. "And here, this too," Matthew continued. "These folks have no cash. It's almost all tied up in investments. They borrow for day-to-day expenses, and the interest rate they pay—let's just say it's high."

"This is great." I didn't understand what it meant, but Kyffin would've. It was most likely what got his brains bashed in.

"But Mr. Sean." Matthew looked at the ground and gulped. "I was bringing the books back 'cause my uncle said I can't—"

Uh-oh, I thought. "Your uncle forbade you to work with me."

He looked up, relief in his eyes. "He said it ain't safe."

"You told him about the sheriff?"

He studied the grapevines about to pull down the alley fence. "No. Something else he heard. He said—" Matthew plucked a grape and ate it. "These are ripe. Somebody should pick them."

"They belong to Vito, the barber. What did your uncle say?"

"Just—he'd heard something. That maybe a young fella's not—safe—you know, alone with you."

How could Arwald possibly know to lean on the kid's uncle? Then I realized I took Matthew to the Alton house, told them his real name, and between Miss Esther and Lillian, they'd probably wormed his entire life story out of him.

That gombeen Arwald—a grasping, ill-willed, sorry excuse for a human being, was behind my troubles. I was done with any drop of Christian charity I might ever have owed the man. I looked up at the clouds. "I set the crows' curse upon you, Joseph Arwald." I wasn't sure where the words came from, but they sprang to my lips like I hexed people every day. My voice was low. Soothing, even, as I intoned, "May your enterprises lie in ruin, and you not see the morning." The blustery day went calm. "May you die reviled, alone, and without a priest, all your many sins heavy on your heart." Rain began to patter on the grape leaves. "May twelve demons drag you to hell to serve as the devil's cat's breakfast."

Matthew's eyes widened and he stepped away.

His movement brought me back to the moment. "You don't think I'd ever—"

"No, of course not," he said, although his eyes held some doubt.

"Well, thanks again for your help."

"I'm sorry," Matthew muttered as he raced off to catch his bus, struggling with an umbrella as he ran.

*　　*　　*

I lugged the volumes to Vito's barbershop, a tiny building across from the railroad tracks. It was completely unlike my brother to visit Vito except for a haircut, although he was friendly enough with the barber. Padraig was among the many in the neighborhood with small grape arbors on his property, cultivated and harvested by Vito to make enough wine for his own family.

When I entered, Vito looked up from a customer, his face a sketch of worry. "Ah," he smiled. "You here for Mr. Padraig, yes?" he said as he ushered me out of the small shop area into an even smaller flat and opened the cellar door. "And when you gonna get your haircut, Mr. Sean? Been over a week."

"Don't I know it." I creaked down the steep, narrow stairs to the basement. The floor was packed earth and the walls thick quarry stone. Frayed electric wires snaked across the ceiling between a couple of bright fixtures. The place was dark as Hades but for those pools of light. One hung like a spotlight over my brother's slumped figure. He sat at a wooden table with a brown jug at his elbow.

Padraig looked up at the sound of my tread on the stairs. "Sean, me boy. Sit down," he grinned, "have a drink with me."

"Let's get you home."

"That's the trouble, ain't it? Home is under police—" He screwed up his face, searching for a word. Not finding it, he started again. "Police—" Padraig gave up, threw back the contents of his glass, and tried a new tactic. "Revenuers closed it. Locked it. We're kicked out in the street."

"You don't serve alcohol," I said as I fetched a chair from the corner.

"And so 'tis odd that—" he poured another glass of wine, "they managed to find quite a bit."

The chair's rush seat was frayed, so I sort of perched on its edge and hoped for the best. "Must have brought it with them."

"Ya think so?" Padraig held up his glass in a toast. "Sláinte, little brother. You're all the cops wanted to talk about. Not my 'speak-easy' at all."

I felt sick. "When did all this happen?"

He thought that one over, then said, "Yesterday afternoon."

After I confronted Joseph Arwald about the attack on Kyffin. The chair's seat unraveled a bit more, and I hopped up. "It's my fault."

"Aye, you're right there. I don't know how or why, but you're up to your neck in it."

"I'm sorry but," I grabbed his arm, "let's find Eliza. And I'll fix things. I'll talk to the Judge."

"Ah, yes, your precious high-and-mighty judge." Padraig shook me off, threw the wine down his throat, and slammed the tumbler on the table. "I'll take care of my own family without your help, thank you very much." He tottered to his feet, saying, "Right now."

I tried to steady him, but he shrugged me off. With great and wounded dignity, he wobbled up the stairs. The door had him stymied for a minute, but he got it open and marched with care into the barbershop, where Vito was just settling up with his haircut customer.

"Vito, my friend," Padraig said. "You're a prince. I'll return the hospitality if I ever have a business again."

"It's nothing. Let me make you something to eat before you go," Vito said as he guided Padraig back into the kitchenette of his flat. "The missus bought nice salsiccia. I'll make eggs. Some coffee. Sound good?"

Vito seemed to have things in hand, and Padraig preferred his company to mine, in any case. The barber agreed to hold onto my ledger books for a while. I gave him a dollar and a "bless you" as I left.

I resumed my route to the courts building. Not only did I need to get the Judge to forgive me for getting him involved in a high-profile crime but also to part with a Federal government favor to get Padraig back in business. This Arwald shite was going to cost me plenty.

*   *   *

I found the Judge in his office, pacing in front of the window and in no mood for anything.

"Where the fuck have you been for the past three days? And where's my car?" the Judge asked as he strode around the desk to better strangle me. "No, wait," he held up one hand. "I know. Police impound. Evidence in an attempted murder case."

"I can explain," I said, backing away. I bumped his desk and reached back instinctively to protect the old stone ax he kept there, but my hand just touched smooth mahogany. "Say, where's your rock?"

"I gave the stone ax to that limey, Taylor Humphrey. But don't change the subject. My car?"

"Well, I drove the car to visit my friend."

"Who managed to get himself attacked in my building."

"I imagine Kyffin did that just to inconvenience you. Anyway, the cops went to his flat, as cops do, and I guess they saw me leave in the car," I shrugged. "I hear you had a visit at your house yesterday."

"Yes, I did. To learn from the police a car registered to me is connected to a violent crime—" he halted his march around the room and lit a cigar to calm himself. "A man killed in my workplace—"

"He's dead then?" I held my breath for his answer.

He waved his hand. "Might as well be."

I let out the air in a flood of probably misguided relief. "I can see how that would be upsetting. I'm sorry." I seemed to say that a lot lately.

He took a chair. "I've nothing against Kyffin Bernard. Fine young attorney. Always on time, prepared, and knows his stuff. But the police asked if I was in his apartment Wednesday night. It looks suspicious." He looked at me, suspicious.

"It might look odd for you to be there."

He leaned forward. "The commissioner's throwing his weight around, sending men to ask me for an alibi. I wouldn't be surprised if he runs for mayor against me next year."

"Being at the flat while Kyffin was getting beaned in the head here is a good one."

The Judge's voice was cold as he said, "Whatever you were doing there all night, the police will make it look bad." He tapped cigar ash in a large ashtray. "There's been rumors about Bernard and that roommate of his. Little jokes no one believes." He puffed and blew smoke at the ceiling. "He's a war hero, for Christ's sake."

"You're right. He *is* a war hero. And a good friend," I said as I pulled up a chair across from the Judge and sat. "I didn't attack him."

"I didn't say you did. But did you—?" he looked away. "You know. Unnatural things."

I considered and rejected a lot of explanations, excuses, and lies. *Was last night so different than the hurly-burly of a rough match or a good fight? A difference more in degree than in kind.* Through the Judge's window, I could see the plaza in front of the courthouse. Under lowering clouds, the wind picked up quite lively, snapping the flags right smart.

"Jesus. I'll take that as a yes," the Judge's voice dropped. "I'm running for mayor." He looked me in the eyes. "Son, I can't have this in my office." Shaking his head, he said, "I had you pegged as a bit of a ladies' man."

I lit a cigarette, most likely the last I'd ever have with the Judge, while I tried to find the words to defend myself. There weren't any.

"Well, you'd better stick with the ladies. At least act like it," he said as he put a hand on my shoulder. "I'm gonna have to fire you.

And you need to go on your way, immediately. Maybe try life out in California or somewhere. But go now. *Right now.*"

I'd been expecting the Judge to fire or even deport me ever since the bulls saw me leave Kyffin's place. But I suppose I didn't want to see the Judge's disapproving face, so I'd stayed away as long as I could. Though he'd sort of blackmailed me into working for him in the first place, I'd gotten used to him. I liked my work. I liked the Judge. I snuffed out the cigarette and said, "Thanks for all you done for me. And good luck with the mayor's race." We shook on it. "Oh, and if you could see your way clear to helping my brother out with a bit of revenuer trouble, we'd all be in your debt."

The Judge nodded. "I'll look into it. No promises."

As I put on the cap I'd stolen from Dr. De Noailles, I asked, "Don't suppose you remember dancing with Lillian Arwald at the Piasa Lodge Ball last winter?"

"What?" He looked surprised. "Why, no, I didn't." Puffing thoughtfully on the cigar, he said, "She stood me up. Nowhere to be found when my dance came around."

I left the Judge's office to find the secretary gone out and Mrs. MacSweeney attacking an ornamental plant with her feather duster. It was a good guess she'd listened to us through the keyhole.

"Oh, you startled me, boy. I was so thinking about this poor shrubbery, stuck in this dark corner."

"Want me to move it closer to the window?"

"Ack, no. I guess His Honor knows where he wants his furnishings to be," she said as she pushed her cart toward the outer door.

I held it open for her. "Were you able to catch all that?"

"Whatever do you mean?" She said, then guided the cart through the doorway and out into the hall toward the large open foyer by the lift bank.

"What we were talking about in there."

"Well, I—" pushing past the lifts toward the courtroom on the opposite end of the floor from the Judge's office, she hissed, "Sounds liked you're sacked."

"Yes, I am. It's been a rough day or two. Lost my lodgings, job, and ride." And best friend.

"Ah, well. Life's a sore fight for half a loaf." As Mrs. Mac trudged her cart across the terrazzo, she called back over her shoulder, "If you be needing a place to stay, I've got an attic room I sometimes let out."

I was touched. "Thanks. I'll keep that in mind."

"Not free. I've expenses. You'll have to get another job."

"I understand."

*   *   *

I had a hunch the cops were about to arrest me, right then and there. Maybe from the way the Judge told me to go to California. I took the stairs to the first floor and caught a glimpse of Detective Milo "Get-It-Right" Draper parked in the lobby. A couple of flatfoots approached him, and then the three of them headed toward the lifts.

I continued down the stairs to the basement, exited from the loading dock, and walked around the building to Market Street. I was bloody well sick of constantly looking over my shoulder for cops. My bad luck held, and as I crossed Market at Twelfth an unusually observant cop loitering about Memorial Plaza spotted me.

I pretended I didn't hear him call for me to stop, melding into the mid-morning courthouse crowd. As I slithered through the throng of lawyers, litigants, and defendants, I glanced over my shoulder. I'd picked up a long tail of flatfoots, shoving folks aside and shouting out for someone to, "stop that man." No one made a move to help, more interested in getting to court on time than assisting the police. A frustrated patrolman drew his weapon and fired it in the air, shouting, "Make way!"

That got everyone's attention and the crowd parted.

A streetcar was barreling up Twelfth Street about twenty feet away from me, looking a lot like my last play. I dashed in front of it, the streetcar missing my backside by inches as it rolled to a stop.

I'd evaded the cops for the moment but was now stuck in the middle of the street as a line of cars crept south. Each driver honked in turn as he passed. The cops should've had me right then and there, but the people pouring off the streetcar hemmed them in. The southbound traffic finally halted, and I ran.

Some cops chased me toward City Hall, others fanning out into the streets to the west. At Walnut I crossed back to the eastside of Twelfth Street and ran up the steps of a tall, skinny layer-cake-of-a-building, flung open the door, and climbed yet more steps. I halted at the front desk. A uniformed cop looked up from a pile of papers.

"Top of the morning, my good sir," I wheezed.

"Yeah."

"My name is Michael Sean George Joye, 1317 Tamm Avenue. Ain't your fine constables aiming to serve me an arrest warrant, now?"

His expression changed not a whit. He inclined his head at a wooden bench across from his desk, and murmured, "Wait there."

And so I cooled my heels as the officer pulled a folder out of a filing cabinet and lay it on the desk. He opened it and examined the first sheet. Satisfied it wasn't me, he put it face down next to the folder. He licked his thumb, flipped up the edge of the next sheet, and picked it up. This one had a photo, so he looked over at me, back at the picture, and back at me. He sighed and put the paper face down on top of the first. This routine went on for some time. I couldn't imagine where Draper and his men had got to. But it did give me some time to think.

~∞∞~

Chapter Twenty-Two

In the Red

In a way it was a relief, to get it over with. And I wasn't actually nicked. The bulls just wanted to talk. For now. We sat in the basement of police headquarters and talked the rest of the morning and all afternoon, evening, and night. Me and Draper. Sometimes Brewer, the detective sergeant from the crime scene, was there. They both seemed pleased the Judge had fired me and fixed on what I was doing at Kyffin's place Wednesday night. The conversation was pretty much the same, over and over. Draper would say, "So you and Bernard had a lovers' spat—the evidence is all over your face. Then you broke into his place to get something. What was it?"

I was more interested in who was behind this play. So, while I had the bulls at my disposal, I focused on that line of questioning. I'd shrug and needle Draper in some way, like, "Don't you get tired of the swells telling you how to do your job? Blokes ain't done a day's work in their lives—"

Then he'd punch me in the kidney. Again. Along with a good bit of swearing and name-calling. He was a creative man, I'll give him that. Every so often Brewer would pretend to restrain him.

Draper would curse and slam the door as he left, and Brewer would give me a cigarette or a cup of coffee. He'd shake his head and say something like, "I just don't know how long I can control him." Or "Better tell him what he wants to know."

It was pathetic. And to think this routine usually worked.

The first few hours, I didn't have a whole lot to say, which seemed to irritate them. Draper sounded both fascinated and disgusted with the notion that something unnatural had happened between me and Kyffin, an idea put in his head by whoever threatened the YMCA—presumably Old Man Arwald. *Was this line supposed to scare me? Or maybe incite the cops to more violence?*

All they had on me was the Judge's car leaving Kyffin's street about six the morning he was attacked. And that I'd been in a fight. As I pointed out, neither was a crime, but all that was the cops' problem, not mine. My read was that the police had been ordered to roust me. Draper resented it and took it out on me, as cops do. On the other hand, he was pretty free with information. That could be his little way of saying, "up yours," to the Big Cinch. But something changed around midday, right at dinner time. Not my dinner—Draper's, which he took great pleasure in eating in front of me. Brewer came in, gave me the evil eye, and motioned for Draper to follow him.

They came back an hour later to talk about Joseph Arwald. How long I'd known him, when I last saw him, stuff like that. What I was doing last night. But more important than the change in questions, their attitude had changed. With a little focus—pain is an excellent focus—I could see the wariness and hostility that clung to them, a thick, dark film of disgust.

As evening approached, a cop brought in a file folder. Draper looked through the papers, then looked at me. "How'd a motherfuckingcunt bog-trotter like you ever get a concealed carry license?" he sputtered as he closed the folder. "Don't tell me. The Judge. Some bullshit court job."

"Yeah, I'm—was—a bailiff or something."

"Well, I guess you lost that job, eh?" said Brewer. "So, you don't have that license anymore." They passed significant glances back and forth for a while.

"Where's your gun?" said Draper.

"What gun?" I couldn't imagine what they were driving at. Kyffin hadn't been shot.

"People 'round town know you carry a Webley Mark VI," said Brewer. "Top-breaker like that is kinda distinctive in these parts."

"Let me think." I was weighing various lies when Draper punched me in the jaw. I'd lose some teeth over this interview. For the first eight hours or so, Draper'd been careful not to leave marks that would show, but his impatience and fatigue were getting the better of him. Yes, indeed, I had him right where I wanted him.

I spit blood on his floor, then inquired, "What was your question again?"

And so it went. Around midnight—I saw a clock when Brewer walked me to the jacks for the first time since I got there—I thought I'd cracked the case wide open. Brewer readjusted my manacles from the back to the front as he said, "I'd be pretty sore at the Judge, if I was you, brother. He's left you in the lurch."

I concentrated on seeing straight and the complicated task of pissing with manacles on. There's a knack to it, and frankly, I was out of practice.

"Bernard was attacked with a big rock," he whispered. "Some kind of Indian artifact. Been sitting on the Judge's desk for months."

Pissing was a blessed relief. Pissing blood, a bit distressing.

"Is that so?" The Judge had just told me he gave the artifact to Humphrey. Of course, that's what he'd say if he'd beaned a lawyer with it. But I couldn't picture the Judge attacking anyone. If he wanted a lawyer whacked up the side of the head, he'd have told me to do it.

"Think about it," Brewer said as we walked back to the interrogation room. "You don't owe him anything."

"I will."

What I thought about was another stone ax, the one the priestess-ghost threw at me the night of the Piasa party. And I knew, from our little dust-up in the lodge's secret meeting room, that the courthouse haunts were all stirred up again. With that cheery thought, I returned to my chair, ready to resume my questioning of Draper. But he wasn't there, and Brewer left me alone for a while. Another trick aimed to break the prisoner with boredom, I guess. I'd managed to fall asleep when I heard the door open and close and a chair drag across the floor. A match scraped the cement wall and I smelled tobacco smoke. I inhaled deeply without opening my eyes. I knew it was Draper, and he'd decided to confess, at last.

"OK, son. I've got to decide whether to charge you with murder or not."

My heart dropped into my stomach. I opened my eyes. "Kyffin's dead, then?"

"No, Bernard's alive, as far as I know." Draper took a long drag on the cigarette and looked at me. Really stared, ready to judge my reaction to his words. "Joseph Arwald was shot with your gun."

"What?"

"Old Man Arwald. Dead," he said as he leaned back in the chair. "So stop playing around. Give me some straight answers for a change."

If I told him the truth, that I'd given the Webley to Kyffin, that placed me in the flat, right where they wanted me to be for some unclear reason. *And why should he believe me?* "I don't know nothing about it."

"I was afraid that's what you'd say."

We began again. "Where were you last night?" Draper asked.

Last night I'd broke into a hospital, impersonated a doctor, and then burgled the Civil Courts Building. Mrs. Mac was with me for some of that, so—alibi, right? Later, I was cuddled up with Miss Lillian Arwald on her bed. I didn't see how I could share any of that with the police, at least without consulting Mrs. Mac and Lillian. "Oh, around and about."

"You hated Arwald. You threatened him yesterday morning. I've a roomful of witnesses."

Arwald being shot had to be connected to Kyffin's attack. At least one of my clients—Violet, Lillian, Mother Mary Gabriel, or Mrs. Mac—surely knew something. I needed to know how she wanted me to play it.

I didn't let Draper beat a confession out of me, but it was hard. By three o'clock in the morning, I was really tired. I knew the drill. Sign the little paper they had at the ready, and they'd let me sleep. Possibly have a bite of breakfast and some medical attention.

But I've been through this before when I was just a kid and it was the British Army not a midwestern flatfoot on the job. I'd rather not get the crap kicked out of me, but it's a thing that happens now and again.

I'd dozed off, and a dream of a woman's laughter woke me, with the sure conviction I had to get out of the police station. It was about six o'clock, I guess. The sky had lightened, but not much, and rain pelted the tiny, high windows of the basement interrogation room. Draper had left me with a sleepy uniform cop.

"You should have found the Webley and Kyffin's own derringer on him."

The cop startled, "What? Did you say something?"

I repeated myself. My only hope of getting out of there was to give them something. Maybe they'd think they could follow me, and I'd lead them to some evidence. "Kyffin told me he had a late-night meeting. Sounded fishy to me. He carries a derringer, but I thought more firepower would make a better impression if it came down to hard cases."

The cop left and came back with Brewer, which was a lucky break—the last person I wanted to talk to was Draper.

Brewer was clean, sharp, and pressed, sipping a cuppa joe and ready for the new day. "So, you're saying whoever bashed Bernard took the weapon and shot Arwald?" he asked.

"No, I'm not. Anyone he met after talking to me could've lifted it. Or anyone who came across him, lying there on the floor in a bad way. The building guard. The beat cops. Hell, *you* could have it for all I know. That's what I'm saying."

He thought about that one. "We only have your word you lent the gun to Bernard."

"But don't it make more sense than your story? Yeah, I was in the flat. The doorman saw me go in around ten o'clock. And I waited for Kyffin to bring my gun back. A weapon like that ain't cheap."

"Why didn't you say all this in the first place? And why'd you run?"

"I didn't like Draper's attitude. And who says I ran? I turned myself in."

They cut me loose around eight in the morning, with not much more than a "don't leave town." I gave the desk sergeant the Belfast Bar's address as my residence, and he handed me a large envelope filled with my shoelaces, braces, and the contents of my pockets. I was a free man again, at least for the moment.

Draper and Brewer wanted to solve the case. I think we all agreed the attack on Kyffin and Arwald's murder were connected somehow. Spending the better part of a day and night working me

over didn't move things along much. Maybe they fed me information to get a little help. And I did the same.

*   *   *

Thunderstorms rumbled across the city as I walked to the corner
of Market and Twelfth to catch a southbound streetcar. I wanted a
cigarette but felt too tired to light it.

I guess I did have a pretty good motive. For the Arwald murder,
anyway. And for all the cops knew, the means. It was my gun, after
all. As for the opportunity, they were pretty vague about the time
frame I needed to account for.

I figured they'd released me with the view to catch me red-
handed later, and sure enough, I spotted a flatfoot about half a
block away, trying to look inconspicuous in the drizzle. We were
the only people out on the street. After ten minutes or so, I got
tired of waiting in the cold rain. I jogged over to him. "I don't know
what's wrong with the streetcars, but I'm gonna take a cab. I live
over the Belfast Bar on Tamm. You know the place?"

He nodded.

"OK. Good day to you," I said, then tipped my wet cap and
flagged down a taxi.

The cab driver told me the long-simmering streetcar strike had
started that morning. Cab fares were double. So, I spent the last
of my money getting to Lafayette Square. I had the driver take a
round-about route. My man from police headquarters had flagged
down a handy patrol car, but we shook him in the warren of streets
around Soulard Market. I didn't see anyone else.

It seemed years ago but was only three days since I'd torn up
Violet's hundred-dollar check. A lot had changed since then, and
I had to laugh at my pride. Someone had it in for me—the raid
at the Belfast, the cold shoulder at the YMCA, and the Judge's

backstabbing. Not to mention the beating from the police. And my prime suspect was dead. Hell, maybe I did somehow kill Joseph Arwald.

I let myself in Dr. De Noailles's back door. I ate some peaches straight out of the tin, stripped off my wet, filthy clothes, and then washed up and shaved in cold water. All the while, I tried to think, tired as I was. The headache that usually goes with such a thrashing had set in, so I kept it simple. *What had I learned from the bulls?*

Sometime Thursday night, Joseph Arwald was shot and killed with my gun, the gun I'd lent Kyffin on Wednesday night.

Kyffin was in a coma at the hospital. Good alibi.

Who else would have access to that gun? That one made my head hurt.

I opened my suitcase full of dirty clothes. I did have one pair of clean pants, and my best suit was still bagged on its hanger from the cleaners. I ransacked Dr. De Noailles's chifforobe to come up with a shirt. It was tailored to his twisted body and bunched up over my right shoulder.

Anyone Kyffin met that night could've ended up with the Webley. The person that attacked him, the person he planned to meet, or someone else along the way. Or whoever found him. Or walked past him without helping. Or the cops at the scene. Well, that narrowed it down.

I was proud of myself for following a train of thought to the end. As a reward, I went to the parlor and fixed myself a laudanum cocktail like I'd made Dr. De Noailles the first time we met last winter. I stretched out on the settee, gulped it down, and thought some more. I needed to see Lillian, Violet, and Mother Mary Gabriel before I talked to the police again, a reckoning that would come sooner or later.

The brandy and opium kicked in quick. Nothing hurt. I felt safe, warm, and comfortable. It would all turn out just fine. I listened to the restful patter of rain on the roof and slipped into sleep.

*   *   *

I heard Kyffin's voice somewhere in the distance and tried to follow it. The place was pitch black but smelled like dirt. I knew I was deep underground, the weight of the earth bearing down on me. He seemed to be reading someone the riot act. I'd never heard such anger from him. I reached out in the dark for something to guide me. My fingers touched a smooth, irregular surface. Suddenly I had an electric torch in my hand and switched it on. A wall of bones greeted me—skulls, ribs, and thigh bones piled and packed along the passage.

I felt guilty, responsible for them all. Here and there among the bones was a trinket, bowl, or statue, old and fragile. The bone pile shifted and started to swallow up the artifacts, and I felt compelled to save them before they were gone forever, but I had to find Kyffin. I heard a blow and cry of pain. I ran, not getting any closer to the end of the corridor, until I tripped over a body and fell in a heap.

"Sean, wake up," said Kyffin's voice in my ear. I felt his hand on my shoulder and turned to see him, whole and healthy, his usual self.

Relief flooded me as I said, "I dreamed you got beat up pretty bad."

Kyffin laughed and took off his hat. His head was bashed in and blood streamed down his face.

"Copper. Come on, wake up." Now it was Lillian's voice, and she was crying.

Confused and groggy, I sat up on the settee. The rain clouds had lifted while I slept, and the late afternoon sun poured through a colored-glass window and spread red, blue, and green light all over the faded parlor carpet. "What?"

"The baby. She's gone. He's got her, I know it. Everyone's trying to blame Esther, but I know it was Taylor."

I heard Lillian's words but couldn't follow their meaning. About all that registered was a dame weeping on my shoulder. I handed her a pocket square—I had no clean handkerchiefs—and told her to blow her nose.

"The baby's started being colicky. I was up most of the night. When she finally slept, grandfather made me take a nap."

"When was this?" My mouth felt like cotton wool. I needed water. I shuffled to the tap in the kitchen, Lillian trailing after me.

"Yesterday. Grandfather made me take laudanum."

"I guess you were upset about your Da."

She nodded. "But—" she hiccupped tears again, "he knew laudanum would knock me out." Lillian's voice dropped to a whisper, "I think he's—" she hiccupped, "in with Taylor."

I drained the glass of water, then filled it again. "Maybe. Drink this, all at once."

She gulped down the water.

"What did you say about Miss Esther?"

She paused, waiting to see if the hiccups were gone, then said, "We can't find her. So the sheriff says Esther took the baby."

Something didn't make sense. I was dying from a hangover, or maybe brain damaged, and I just couldn't figure out what was off.

"But *I* know *Taylor* has my baby," Lillian said. "Make him give her back."

"How do you know?"

"I just do. Please believe me."

Hadn't Mother Mary Gabriel warned me about Humphrey doing this very thing? "Of course I believe you. What do you have on him?"

"He practices black magic." Lillian clouded up again. "Real evil stuff."

"Like what?"

She looked away. I could barely hear her whisper, "Manipulating people and hurting them from a distance. Sexual energy to power spells."

"Did Mother Mary Gabriel tell you all this?"

She shook her head.

"You've seen him do these things?"

"Well, he says things. He's mentioned sacrifices. And once—" Lillian spun around to face me, tears streaming down her face. "Oh, it's so hazy and confusing. I think he—" she grabbed my arm, "did things to me. Things I don't want to remember." She about dragged me out the door. "You'll have to trust me."

"Whoa. I'd feel better facing him with trousers and shoes. And I'll get my gun."

Lillian looked a little surprised and hiccupped again. "Yes, of course, you'd have more than one." She filled the cup and drank more water. "Hurry and get ready. I'll bring the car around to the front."

Chapter Twenty-Three

Bankruptcy

It was a good thing Lillian had driven her grandfather's old Cadillac limo over from Alton. No streetcars ran because of the strike. The motormen had walked off the job at the appointed hour and left the streetcars on the tracks. At four o'clock in the afternoon, managers were still clearing the cars back to the depot. Picketers aimed to prevent them and crowds hassled the picketers. Sympathy strikes by other unions and groups were springing up all over town.

The streets were packed with cars and people. Lillian zigzagged down a new street at every bottleneck, ranting about Humphrey— his dark past, devil worship, sexual perversions. On and on.

I was sobering up. "Does Humphrey have any particular aim in all this sin?" I thought to ask.

"Money." She looked at me, waving both hands around. "Treasure."

"Jesus-mary-and-joseph, woman," I shouted, pointing out the windscreen. "People in the fecking road."

Lillian slammed the brakes, which inspired honking horns down the line behind us. "Oh, thanks."

"Do you want me to drive?"

"No, no. It calms me. But everyone is so slow," she said as she leaned on the horn.

"There's a street protest going on."

She seemed to notice the picket signs for the first time. "Swell."

"So, did you just now remember all this about Humphrey, or just now see fit to tell me?"

"A bit of both, I guess."

"And he thinks he can get money from magic?"

She nodded then said, "Gold, silver, gems, stuff like that."

"Ah."

The man was certifiable. I knew not one story in which a human kept use of a fae treasure horde. It generally turned to dust in the sunlight or cursed the man and his family for generations. We had to get that child out of his hands immediately.

The traffic and protesters thinned as we moved north of Forest Park, and we made better time, although it took over two hours to get from Lafayette Square to the Arwald house on Washington Terrace. She could've walked it in less time, although I'm not sure I would've made it there any faster. I was still pretty shook from my time with the cops.

The Washington Terrace attendant hurried to close the gate behind us. The doors and windows of Old Arwald's mansion were decked out in black bunting, ready for his funeral. The butler greeted Lillian warmly, me not so much, but offered to hold my cap. She brushed past him and walked through the house, shouting for her family. "But no one is at home, Miss Lillian," the butler said. "I believe Mr. and Mrs. Humphrey went to discuss the funeral service with the bishop. At least that's what the schedule book states." She took the grand staircase two at a time. "Bullshit," she shouted, her voice echoing around the foyer. "Violet. I'm sorry. Please, help me!" Me and the butler followed her throughout the house, bottom to top. I believed she was worried, but something else was going on. Something she wasn't telling me. Lillian finally gave up, refused tea, and we left, sitting silently in the car as the sun set. At last, she spoke. "They're at the Civil Courts Building already."

"Where?"

"His cult's meeting place."

I started the car. "And you know this how?"

"I—" her hands in her lap, Lillian twisted my last clean pocket square over and over. "I overheard them talking."

"Humphrey and Violet?"

"Yes," she said. "They want to control the Piasa, somehow. To get her treasure."

"They think—" I searched my memory of talks with Dr. De Noailles, "that's possible?"

"Taylor does. And he can be pretty convincing."

The last time I talked with Humphrey, he'd invited me to join his magical research. "And they need a baby for this—spell?"

"Yes, like in the one story."

"With the chief's child as bait? And the poison-arrow ambush?" I asked as I dug through her handbag, fished out her smokes, and lit cigarettes for both of us. "Doesn't your grandfather say that one's bull? A white man's fairytale?"

"Taylor believes it," she said as she accepted the smoke and smiled faintly. "And he's an Oxford don, don't you know."

"Well, pip-fecking-pip. Let's go," I replied as I nosed the old Caddie through the gate and across the Union Avenue traffic to Delmar. We headed downtown, and before very long slowed to a creep. Thousands marched by torchlight ahead of us down Washington Avenue.

*   *   *

We crawled along until we came to a standstill amid the hat factories around Washington and Twelfth, about half a mile from the Civil Courts Building. All the businesses were dark, although the gas lamps along the streets shone along with the torches the marchers carried.

We abandoned the car and hoofed it, struggling through the crowd. The air was thick with tension, just about ready to boil. It wasn't a safe place to be, and I aimed to get Lillian out of it as soon as possible. Part of the traffic hold-up was a man giving a speech in the middle of Twelfth Street, right in front of City Hall. Some folks shouted him down and other folks threatened the hecklers. As we readied to cross Twelfth Street, a squad of cops poured out of police headquarters, waving billy clubs with enthusiasm. About then someone threw a punch, and all hell broke loose.

Me and Lillian wove and dodged our way through the crowd. We clung together, ducked, and sidestepped most of it, and managed to get across the street in one piece. In Memorial Plaza, practically on the courthouse steps, a couple of bruisers and a cop had a black picketer down on the ground, beating him to a bloody pulp.

As we hurried by, I shouted, "Officer, the mob's looting the Jack Daniel's warehouse. Better step lively."

"What's this then?" the flatfoot said, then took off down the street, tweeting his whistle.

The thugs lost interest in their man right quick. "Come on," one said to his mates, "free whiskey."

The picketer had the good sense to scramble away. To home, I hoped, and to fight another day.

We ran across the plaza toward the courthouse. A wall of flatfoots protected the main entrance, so we made our way to the service door near the loading dock. People milled around Chestnut, but most were on their way to the action at City Hall and didn't pay any attention to us. Once in the courts building's dark and silent service corridor, I could smell smoke. I hoped it was from outside, but the air tingled with a sense of something wrong, and I shivered.

"This way," Lilian said.

I drew the Luger I'd brought and released the safety. As I passed the doorway to the break room, I felt compelled to open it. When I hit the light switch, nothing happened. The building's power was out. I'd brought an electric torch from the car, its light picking out security guards gagged and bound to chairs in a corner. They stared ahead, blank and still, their pupils wide open even as I shined the bright light at them.

"Drugged," I whispered to Lillian.

"Or under a spell," she said.

I shook the old coot who gave me the evil eye every time I came into the building. "Wake up, granddad," I whispered in his good ear. "Come on. Get to work."

He blinked.

Lillian shouted at the other two, "It's Lillian Arwald. Help us."

I hushed her but heard steps approach down the hall. I trained my light and weapon at the door. Lillian stumbled into me just as the door opened, and I caught her as a bright electric torch caught us.

"'Tis Miss Arwald, eh?" said a Cockney voice, young and bright.

How did these thugs know her? I blinked in the light, then looked away and hoped my vision would return in time to see who to shoot.

"Yes, it's me." Lillian strolled toward them. "Stop shining lights in our eyes."

"Right-o, miss," a different Cockney voice said. An older bloke.

"Please attend to these men," she said, pointing at the guards in the corner.

"We've orders, miss," said the older man.

"Well, you've got new orders," Lillian said.

"Right-o," the young one said as he sauntered into the room and made for the guards.

Yes, indeed. I had a bad feeling. I recognized the older bloke as the bouncer I'd run into last time I'd been creeping around the courts building. He waved us out into the hallway, a revolver in his hand, and pointed at my Luger. "I'll take care of that."

I wasn't ready for this fight, truly. He was the taller of the pair, although they were both tall, broad-shouldered, stevedore types. Nonetheless, no way was I giving up my gun. "The hell you will, buddy."

Lillian walked right up to him, the top of her head about clearing his mid-chest. *God, that man was big.* "It's fine," she said. "I'll vouch for him." She must know them through the lodge I reasoned.

The ox looked unconvinced.

"Oh my, the air is close in here," Lillian moaned, fanning herself with my pocket square so vigorously it flung out of her hand into the room behind her. "Could you get that? I feel so woozy."

When the thug bent down, she whopped him up the side of the head with her electric torch and pushed him over with a well-planted foot. She slammed the door shut, shouting, "Help me hold the door."

I grabbed the handle and resisted as our man tried to turn it, but it wasn't much of a long-term solution.

A key ring Lillian must have lifted from a tied-up guard appeared in her hands, and she locked the door. "Run," she yelled as she sprinted down the dark hall.

Lillian didn't have to tell me twice. We put as much distance between us and the thugs as we could. With the power out, we had to hoof it up the stairs. For the first few flights, I asked her about the men, how they knew her, what the hell was going on. She was vague, noncommittal, and much faster than me, but always urging me forward, "Hurry. You've got to stop Taylor."

I did my best, but by the fifth flight my legs were jelly and I couldn't speak. About that time, I heard a door slam and voices below me in the stairwell, which put a spring in my step. I caught up with Lillian on the seventh floor. "Let's switch stairwells," I said.

We ran down the back hall to the opposite end of the building and resumed our climb, dragging ourselves up the stairs with the help of banisters and each other.

At the eleventh floor, where I'd found the ritual room disguised as a gentlemen's club, the stairwell door was frozen. A familiar chill ran up my back and grabbed me around the heart. I opened it and stepped into the hall. Lillian, continuing the climb, protested, "No, this way."

The walls, doors, and windows of the eleventh floor were frost-caked. Icicles dangled from the ceiling. The floor was a glossy, frozen sheet. Before me appeared the Mississippian priestess, radiating hate.

I'd never felt so small and scorned, and that's saying a lot.

The door behind me opened. Lillian said, "Sean, where are—" Then she gasped and started to cry. "I feel so—I'm so—"

"And ain't the haunt messing with you, now?" I said. "Getting in your head and all."

The ghost priestess raised her hand and brandished a feathered staff. *Was it possible to be even colder?* I was stiff with ice and fear. This was it. She'd come to carry me off to her faerie mound, deep in the earth, never to see the light of day again.

My mind was so numb it was easy to focus. There we were, the priestess and me, in my dream from earlier in the day—a deep underground barrow of a boneyard. Her treasures were there, too. Now she was a flesh-and-blood woman. I expected a thrashing, but she reached out and touched my head with one hand and my heart with the other.

Her hands burned like the dickens and made me feel sick and ashamed of myself. Ready to eat a bullet and put an end to it all. But angry, too. I didn't need some haunt to tell me what a wretch I am—I'm well aware.

As turnabout is fair play, I touched her face. The pain was worse, if that's possible. I could smell my hand's burning flesh, and see it blacken and drip off my bones. But if she was reading me, I was reading her: She'd walked this place since the day my stupid people dug up her grave mound, disturbed her bones, and stole her treasures. And a worse defilement of her land loomed. I was close to seeing it, when Lillian screamed, a shock that pulled me back into the frozen room.

Three ghosts menaced Lillian, who'd collapsed to the floor, crying and clutching her handbag.

"Get hold of yourself," I said. "Think of your baby."

She looked at me, blank at first, but my words seemed to soak in at last. "Yes." She stood and said, "Whoever's there. Let me pass."

"Can't you see them?"

She shook her head.

"They're the mound builders."

Lillian gave a little cry, whimpering, "Sorry. So sorry." She dug in her bag and pulled out a small leather pouch. "See what I have."

Dr. De Noailles had shown me this object—the She'-ki medicine bundle, entrusted to his family by the evicted Osage.

Lillian couldn't see the confused look on the haunts, but I could. The priestess caught wise first, made a bow to the bundle, and motioned her troops to drop back.

I pulled Lillian out the door, and she dragged me toward the icy steps. "This way," she said, "come on."

We slid and scrambled up three more flights of stairs right quick, me panting questions at her all the while. I had no idea where she was leading me and she just urged me to climb the stairs faster.

*   *   *

Lillian and me landed in an attic I had no idea existed, above the library mezzanine. It was a barn of a place, cold, dark, and damp from all the rain earlier in the day. Banks of lift machinery—the building had ten, plus freight lifts—crowded the room and scented the air with industry: oil, grease, and hot metal. Far above us I could sense rather than see the stepped pyramid that capped the building and supported the two griffins that decorated the roof.

"We hiding up here, or what?" I said.

She hemmed and hawed around.

"Got something to tell me?"

Lillian bit her lip. "I—uh—there's another chamber. That one you were headed to downstairs, in the Piasa club, that's nothing. Taylor has another space, for the real magic."

I counted to ten under my breath. Losing my temper wouldn't help, satisfying as it might be. "Could you be troubling yourself to tell me where it is?"

"It's in one of the griffins on the roof." She pointed up, to a series of catwalks, connected by flights of ladders affixed to the walls, leading to the apex of the pyramid.

"How the hell—"

"There's a trapdoor up there. It's perfectly safe."

The bloody roof. "Let's go, then."

We climbed more quickly than I expected, and in a few minutes, I popped up through a hatch in the ceiling into a dark, dusty-smelling space. I shone my torchlight around a good-sized if misshapened room. Griffin shaped, I guess you'd call it. "No one here."

"The chamber's in the other griffin. We have to go outside to get to it." She picked out a small door with her light. I was pretty disoriented, but it seemed to be on the backside of the aluminum beast.

I fought a fierce headwind to crack open the hatch and we stumbled out onto a platform between the two griffins' backsides. I gasped in the cold and Lillian huddled against me. Across from us, in the second griffin's backside, was a door, the twin of the one we'd just exited.

Moonlight, trashcan fires, and the city's rage bounced off the rooftop ornaments. Far below—beyond the ten pyramid steps, the library, the Piasa Lodge's gentlemen's club, and the twelve floors of courtrooms—shouts and sirens raged on, along with the occasional gunshot.

My vision was well accustomed to the dark by then. Two men crouched on the pyramid steps, one to the north, the other to the south, peering over the building's edge, the riot more interesting than guard duty.

Lillian spotted them, too, and hissed, "Shoot them."

I didn't see much cause for that, at least right then. I traded the gun for a garrote in my coat pocket and, clinging to the shadows, dragged off one bloke and throttled him out cold while his mate gawked at the fires below.

I aimed to silence the second guard likewise, only to find Lillian already approaching him from behind. I expected her to bean him with the electric torch she had at the ready, but he must have heard her steps. He turned around and tipped his hat. Then he escorted her to the door in the back of the griffin.

Lillian had answered none of my questions since we'd entered the building. I had a sensation of something very wrong.

But, in for a penny, I switched back to the Luger and snuck up on Lillian's guard. I poked him in the back with the weapon, growling, "Let her go."

The thug raised his hands. "Hey, friend, you got me all wrong."

Lillian looked at me over her shoulder, her face the picture of a worried mother. "Sorry," she said as she tapped the little door. The handle turned and the portal swung open.

The trap snapped.

Humphrey lounged in the doorway, backlit by the room's flickering candles. Heat and the smoke of burning sage wrapped around us. I could see Violet beyond him. She cuddled the baby and fed her a bottle. "Excellent. You've brought him along, just in time." Humphrey smiled at Lillian. "I knew you'd see reason." Over his shoulder, he called to Violet, "Didn't I just say that, darling?"

Chapter Twenty-Four

Margin Call

When I tried to catch Lillian's eye, she turned away.

"Welcome in, welcome in," Humphrey said as he took Lillian's hand and waved us forward with a fancy knife.

I didn't see any advantage to cutting up at this point, so I followed Lillian into the smoky room. The rooftop guard resumed his post, I guess, but the two guards who'd chased us up from the basement appeared in the doorway. "Boss will take care of this for you, mate," said the older bloke as he relieved me of the Luger and handed it to Humphrey, who tucked it in his pocket.

The room was small and strange, being the inside of a griffin statue and all. A large circle and odd symbols were daubed on the floor and images like at Dr. De Noailles's cave decorated the walls and floor. A couple of men—more of the stevedore-type Humphrey seemed to favor—stood off to the side, drumming on leathers stretched over wooden frames. "Quite a set-up you've got here," I stalled.

Humphrey's intent hung in the air, as thick and stifling as the smoke: Impress the Good People with his power over the "Piasa." And in the rounds of it, steal a treasure from one of this continent's faerie familiars. He'd mastered the lore, and, of course, made some white-man improvements.

He laughed and said, "I do my best." He waved the dagger around. "Decor isn't important. It's the energy we need. That's where you come in."

Back to that. "Don't bother the Good People. It never ends well."

"Ah," he replied as he turned to Lillian, who was watching her baby in her sister's arms. "I take it Joye's not here willingly?"

"He'd never agree to help."

"Perhaps. Yet he knows he has powers, and the possibilities intrigue him, as much as he denies it." The professor in him started the day's lecture. "Magick is all about vital life-force energy."

I'd never felt so backed against a wall. Lillian was always a loose cannon, but I thought I could depend on her to do the best for her child. Yet, here she was, in cahoots with her sworn enemy for some sort of magic spell. A spell that involved me.

"And a very few people—you, for instance—are gifted with a connection." Humphrey's eyes pleaded from behind his cool, educated mask. He'd yammered at me about ritual magic for months and outright invited me to join him the other day. Now, the offer was a threat. Killing him, as Lillian and even Mother Mary Gabriel urged me to do before he spilled the beans could be a mistake.

Lillian snuggled against me, cranking up her best seductive grift, to say, "Sean, please, help us with this." She ran her fingers up my chest, and then kissed me thoroughly, her hand slipping under my coat to my shoulder rig, where she slid an object into the holster.

The younger guard smirked, "Not the time nor the place, miss."

Sometimes honesty is best. Not often, but sometimes. "I'll take a pass," I said, "This set-up stinks to high heaven," sweat trickling down my face. I lit a cigarette and took a deep drag. Tried a smoke ring, which I can sometimes manage. Finally, I said, "The infant sacrifice part, possibly."

"Well, that's disappointing, but not entirely unexpected," Humphrey said as he nodded to the thug at my elbow, who ground out my smoke and frog-marched me over to the painted circle.

"I've a theory," Humphrey explained, his breath cooling my cheek as he held the knife to my throat, "that the sacrifice of a true natural adept like yourself would unleash vast powers. Channeling such energy into a spell might be tricky, but not impossible."

The fancy, stage-prop-looking blade turned out to be sharp enough. I could feel the blood dribble down my neck.

"Don't be ridiculous, Taylor," Violet said. I hadn't noticed that she'd joined us at the circle. "You based your ritual on the Piasa legend. The chief's child as bait." She kissed the baby in her arms on the forehead. "This child. Your child."

"She's right," Lillian chimed in. "We don't need a death to call the Piasa. And the binding magic will be right this time."

"This time?" Violet said, turning on her sister.

Humphrey stopped cutting on me to listen to them. "This blood might be enough. And other strong forces are available." He pointed his knife at Violet and then Lillian. "These two, for instance," he said to me. "The hatred. You can see it, can't you?"

Indeed, I could. A black mist of rivalry and resentment wrapped the two sisters, poisoning the air.

"My darling," Humphrey said to Violet. "Lillian wants to destroy your world again. Remember your dear mother? What a happy little girl you were, until this interloper came along, driving your mother insane? And remember how Lillian betrayed us? How you worried when she ran off with the child that she'd promised you?"

Protectiveness surged through me. He shouldn't taunt Violet with those dark days. I'd knock his block off, that's what I'd do. "Leave her alone," I yelled, struggling against the man who held me.

"Always such a gentleman," Humphrey said. "But she's my wife. I'll say whatever I like."

I couldn't tell if Violet paid him any mind. She squeezed the small bundle, and the child wiggled in her arms. She spoke to her sister, "Answer me. What did you mean by 'this time'?"

Lillian darted at Violet, but Humphrey caught her, murmuring in her ear, "Violet's always been the favorite. You? Rejected. Unwanted. A charity case for your crazy grandfather."

The darkness entangling the sisters bubbled, stank, and whirled into the deepening shadows. He shoved Lillian at the other guard and strode to the center of the room. With raised arms, Humphrey made some complicated motions with the bloody knife, while he shouted strange words. They weren't English. Or Latin or Gaeilge, either. Sparks cracked around the ceiling, and the skyscraper shuddered as booms echoed through the building from the street below.

Lillian whispered into my ear, "He's going to call the Piasa."

Humphrey fixed his gaze on Violet and inclined his head toward the ritual circle.

*   *   *

But instead, Violet stepped away from the circle and shuffled toward a small table in a dark corner of the room. On it sat a pitcher and basin. As she filled the basin with water she began to speak in a loud, theatrical voice, "As you promised us, Great One, even though the little ones pass into the realms of spirits, they shall, by clinging to you and using your strength, recover consciousness."

Humphrey stood there, dumbfounded for a moment while the drummers kept up their steady beat. A racket from the outside settled into a rhythm, pounding in time with the drummers.

Outside, the street riot seemed about to break into the courts building.

Humphrey suddenly shouted, "No. You'll ruin everything." Humphrey commanded his troops as he barreled toward her, "Get her, you men. Stop her."

Then something *really* strange happened. Violet caught my eye and said, "Protect me," as she gave a little nod toward Humphrey. My brain had room for one thing: I had to stop Humphrey.

I broke free of my guard, slugged him on general principle, and then tackled Humphrey. With great satisfaction, I strong-armed him and held his own pretty knife to his throat. Another, more reasonable, part of my mind chimed in, informing me Violet had bewitched me somewhere along the line. My job was to save the baby, not stand by while her aunt drowned her. But I still trusted Violet to know best.

Humphrey wrenched himself out of my grasp as Violet intoned, "I beg you, chief of the dark realms, of birth and death, of water and earth, of night and winter, and all that sleeps and crawls and swims. Command the Underwater Spirit to wipe away the mud from the mouth and eyes of my child, Antoine Humphrey, and bring him to the day, to the light, to the air. To me."

The drummers had leaped to Humphrey's defense, and the room was still, but for the pounding on the building from far below. The courthouse gave a little shake.

Violet hovered the sleeping baby over the basin of water. She bit her lower lip. "Take this—" she closed her eyes as she let out a deep breath, "precious life in exchange."

"No," Lillian screamed. "You goddamnfuckingcunt." She struggled free of her guard and charged at her sister. "I'll kill you," she spat.

At that moment shrieks echoed through the metal chamber. All the guards covered their ears. Wind clattered around the roof-top and flung open the hatch. A gale burst into the room, snuffing candles and swirling robes, blankets, and books in a cyclone of white ice crystals.

The men fought the wind as they tried to escape, shielding their bodies and crying out in pain.

I don't think they could see the dozen or so Mississippian spirits who pummeled them with stone hatchets and blocked their path to the door. The priestess gestured, and a group detached to attack Humphrey. He sank to his knees under the blows.

Lillian was already on Violet, who had pressed the baby to her chest. Lillian tried to peel the child away from her sister as the priestess shrieked in Violet's face, rage and hatred slapping her over and over again. Violet looked around for help and reached out to command me, but whatever spell she'd used was broke by the ghost invasion. I looked for a way to pluck the child out of the mess swirling around her.

Humphrey was down, but not out. He smiled up at me, a crazy smile. Although he couldn't see the haunts, Humphrey seemed to feed off their energy.

"Old Ones, heed me and aid my purposes," he intoned as he squeezed his knife out of my hand and waved it in my face. Humphrey spoke in a loud, sing-song voice, like a priest at mass. And the words were Latin. I knew that much. I strained my memory to parse his command, but I didn't need to understand the words. I could feel his message in every muscle of my body.

"Help me," he said, aloud, but also in my mind, as he hurried toward Violet.

Get the hell out of my head, I thought. Every crime he'd been accused of loomed large—murder, rape, lording his filthy privilege over my country. Stealing my language and heritage. I knew he was guilty of all. I hadn't truly hated him until then. Yet still, he compelled me to follow him toward the battling sisters.

"Get Lillian," he said.

I tried not to, I really did. Humphrey's hooks in my mind sent sharp jabs of pain through my head. I pulled Lillian off Violet while he slugged his wife and pulled the baby out of her arms. The child stirred and protested for a moment. Lillian clawed and twisted in my arms, shouting, "Copper, what's the matter with you?" Humphrey'd magicked me, good and proper, that's what.

"Let me go," she hissed, jamming her heel into my instep.

I throttled Lillian in a chokehold. Almost blind from the pain in my head, I was about to crush her windpipe. I had to escape Humphrey's control, right then, or I'd kill her. I searched my mind for a safe place, a place he hadn't found yet. I focused on the riot outside.

Thump.

Thump.

Thump on the courthouse doors.

I heard a loud boom from outside and a bell rang. I was in a different place and at a different time. Frankincense and lilies filled the darkness. Lights blazed, destroying the night. I struggled to hold the Easter candle aloft, heavy in my eight-year-old hands. In my parish church back home in Belfast, the Hallelujah embraced me, and then the priest's words and the people's response. As soon as the rite began, the candles' smoke twisted around me—choking black smoke. The voice I heard spoke Latin, true, but the familiar voice of my pastor had changed. Now I heard Humphrey's clipped British accent and the words, not holy at all, commanded me to help him in his abominations. I dropped the candle and the altar burst into flames. I ran, panting, home.

Home was the old Belfast Bar on Falls Road. Before the fire. Before Da was murdered by the police. The room was bright in the gaslights, crowded, and smelled like honest sweat and beer. A low buzz of conversation with frequent laughter and snatches of song filled the air. Da stood behind the bar, his face lighting up as I burst in the front door.

"And ain't you barging in the front door like the constabulary?" he joked.

"I ain't no bloody policeman," I said, my twelve-year-old self serious, conceited, and having no sense of humor at all.

"But aren't you now?" said another voice. A British voice. Humphrey. "Haven't you abandoned it all? Your ideals? Your country? Your father? Forgot that he was murdered because you weren't home that night? Even when they got the wrong Michael Joye?"

Again, I ran. Through the kitchen and out the back door, anywhere to get away from his voice.

"Here," I heard Miss Esther whisper. "In here, boy."

I found myself in her shack in the Alton woods.

"Have some tea," she said, leaning over me with a steaming cup of her elderberry brew, her golden eyes kind. "This place is safe."

I felt calm in the deep pool of her gaze. Calm enough to relax, to reach out and root myself. As sure as the sacraments, I was connected, through the thirteen-story skyscraper, its foundations, all the way down to its footings, to the earth beneath us.

I released Lillian and she launched herself at Humphrey, who pulled my Luger out of his pocket and pointed it at her. She stopped and looked back at me for help.

The baby slept on Humphrey's other arm. The ghosts tugged at him, but he swatted them away with the gun as he dumped the child into the center of the circle painted on the floor.

*   *   *

"Hold it right there," a voice behind me boomed over the din of the riot, the ghosts, and the baby's wailing. Mother Mary Gabriel leveled her shotgun at Humphrey.

He looked amused, then not so amused when she pumped the lever and dropped a shell in the chamber. "Goodness, madam. Please. There has been a terrible misunderstanding."

Now that I had a bit of my wits about me again, I remembered Lillian had slipped me what I hoped was a gun. Where she'd got it, I hadn't a clue, but now would be a good time to use it. Yet my left hand dangled at my side, refusing to move to the holster.

"I understand perfectly," Mother Mary Gabriel replied, entirely fixed on her quarry, oblivious to me, ghosts, and society dames. "You deny the deaths of Anna Medvedikova and her child Martin in London? The disappearance of an infant from the foundling home in Marseilles?"

"What?" said Lillian. She made a play for the baby, but Humphrey motioned her back with the Luger.

"Of course I deny it," he said, wearing his most innocent smile.

"Gretchen Müller and her baby Marta in Essen?"

"Those names mean nothing to me," he said as he approached the nun while I stood there like an eejit and struggled against the dredges of whatever he'd done to me.

Mother Mary Gabriel swallowed and her steady grip on the shotgun wavered. "Do you deny seducing a young girl in Cork in 1897?" her voice broke. "Mary O'Shaughnessy? Bargaining your child by her to demons?"

"No—yes. I—" he paused. "I—I—don't know what you're talking about."

I felt his power waning. *Who the hell was this Irish victim?* Mother Mary Gabriel never mentioned a girl from Cork. Although, she herself was once a girl from Cork.

"I've ample proof," the nun said.

Humphrey recovered his poise and trained the Luger at her. "Then call the police."

"Oh, you'd like that." Mother Mary Gabriel stepped closer. "You and your kind here own the police."

With a dismissive gesture at the baby on the floor, he said, "With this insignificant life, I'll ensorcell a being of unimagined wealth and save Monk's Mound."

"Get away from the child," said Mother Mary Gabriel. "And put down your gun."

He laughed. "Just a tiny bit more blood energy is required, I think." He produced a fancy knife in his left hand. "An elegant tool, wouldn't you say?" The ghost priestess, who'd been menacing Violet all the while, poured across the room to tie Humphrey in icy bonds that slowed him a little.

I'd pulled myself together enough to make a play. I hoped. I drew the gun Lillian had slipped me, a familiar derringer. Kyffin's. I didn't have time to think on that. "You'll do what Sister says if you know what's good for you."

"Hmm?" Humphrey's knife hovered over the baby's throat. "So you've a gun, too. And perhaps you've broken my spell. Or perhaps at the last second, you'll not be able to pull the trigger."

"Ready to risk it?"

"But really, a derringer?" he smirked. "From way over there?" He limped toward me, well away from the child at least. "Is this better?" He stretched out his arms, a knife in one hand, a gun in the other, and said, "Do I make a better target?" He started up the Latin incantations again as he incised the air with the knife and pointed it at me, Lillian, and the nun.

I felt his hooks again but grabbed at the strong connection that anchored me to the earth. I could see Mother Mary Gabriel understood a lot more of his Latin than I did. The anger coloring her face drained to a white dread. She crossed herself and mouthed a prayer, reaching for her own solid rock.

Humphrey kept up his attack, wave on wave of dark intention. It was about all I could do to not fall before him. A glassy-eyed Lillian shuffled to the corner and picked up a drum. Finally, I managed to will myself to shoot, but the bullet missed him by a mile and ricocheted around the metal room in a most alarming way. At least that broke Humphrey's concentration and I felt him release us. At that range with a shotgun, Mother Mary Gabriel was bound to hit him. She'd declared him guilty and sentenced him to death long ago. But I thought I knew why she hesitated. She may have hunted and destroyed monsters for years, but for all her big talk, this was a living man. And maybe a man she'd once loved. A monster, but a human with a soul. She didn't want his death on her conscience. Hell, *I* didn't want his death on her conscience.

Humphrey saw the doubt on her face and grabbed at the shotgun's muzzle.

I fired.

The derringer's last bullet knocked him down. He looked surprised and dropped my Luger as he crumpled to the floor.

My army training kicked in. I picked up the gun and shot Taylor Humphrey in the head.

Violet screamed, and the baby let out a loud wail as the building rocked again.

*   *   *

Metal on metal shrieked above us. The rooftop griffin ripped apart, wrapped in the claws of a beast. A human-like, bearded face poked in at us from a long, scaled neck, its branching antlers barely clearing the space. Golden eyes fired with anger searched the room and focused on Violet. As the beast paused and turned to tear off a bit more metal with sharp claws, I could see massive, leathery wings and a scaly, twisting body.

How many times had I seen this image over the past year, doing everything from riding on floats to selling farm equipment? Years of tall tales, slander, and fabrication may have transformed her appearance into the lie called "Piasa," but this weren't no bedtime story. A flesh-and-blood Underwater Spirit menaced us all.

Had the Underwater Spirit answered Humphrey's summons or Violet's prayers? Maybe she'd heard, but more likely, I thought at the time, anyway, that she'd come to reclaim a bit of stolen culture.

We froze, all but for the wailing child.

Violet scrambled under the little table. The Underwater Spirit had a clear shot at her, slashing with talons as she cowered. I fired the Luger and hit her square, the bullet doing no more harm than a pebble. But it drew the spirit's attention away from Violet. She swatted me with a claw and I flew across the room and bounced off the metal wall. Blood filled my vision and the knock on the head did me no good. I was seeing stars as the Underwater Spirit scooped the crying child up in a massive paw. The baby hushed.

"Nooooo," Lillian yelled and ran across the room. The Underwater Spirit watched her for a second, and then returned her attention to the baby, cradling the tike in her talons and cooing like a mourning dove. Her low, throaty song shook the chamber. She looked around at us humans, bowed to the ghost priestess, and flapped out through the busted griffin into the night, Lillian's baby clutched in her paws.

Chapter Twenty-Five

Repossession

The three women and I were alone in the ritual room. The guards had all run off and the ghosts had dispersed, for the moment at least. Stunned, we stared up at the hole where the Underwater Spirit used to be. Somehow Violet, in her little cell of pain and delusion just minutes before, got over the shock first. Without a word, she bolted for the door. Lillian grabbed my sleeve and pulled me along after her, saying, "The Piasa would go to her lair. Let's follow her."

"No. I'll go," said Mother Mary Gabriel. "Taylor Humphrey summoned a demon." Her jaw clenched. "You two would risk your immortal souls in such a battle."

"She's not a demon," I said. "She's a spirit." I had no ready explanation for the solid form we'd just encountered. Puzzling that one out would require a two-pipe think. "And pretty angry with humans at the moment. I'll not be putting a nun in harm's way." Humphrey's body lay crumpled on the floor where I'd shot him. "Stay here and think of something to tell the police."

She started to argue with me, but I interrupted, "Sister, we don't have time for this."

I could see the wheels in her brain turning as a scheme formed. "Well, be cautious." She put down her shotgun, dug through her pockets, and handed me a crucifix. "Go with my blessing." She rested her hands on my head for a moment, then Lillian's. "The Lord will protect his warriors."

"Yeah, if you say so." She had her theology a bit off, but I wasn't going to be the one to tell her.

"Go, go," said Mother Mary Gabriel. "I'll take care of things here."

I wasn't sure if a nun's idea of taking care of a dead body was the same as mine, but I had no choice.

Lillian yelled from the doorway, "Hurry the hell up, Copper."

"And we're going where now?" I followed her to the access hatch in the other griffin.

"Her lair. You know, like in the story. There's a passage through Grandfather's cave."

Well, that was news to me. Even the ever-chatty Dr. De Noailles had left out crucial information.

"You seem to know a lot about the Underwater Spirit," I said as we climbed down the first attic ladder. The building shook occasionally, likely from the pounding on the front doors.

"We'll need grandfather's help. She's powerful, capricious, and dangerous. Not necessarily our friend."

That I could believe. The Good People are never your friend. Baby stealing—a classic move of theirs. The best you can do is not make an enemy. But I wasn't going to allow them another child. Not this time.

As we sped down thirteen flights of stairs, I prayed the mob hadn't attacked the back of the building. At the lobby level, tear gas was seeping around the doors from the full-on riot in progress outside. We'd never make it back to her car in one piece. Hell, for all I knew that car had been destroyed by now.

I dragged her out the deserted service entrance and away from the riot. We happened upon an unattended patrol car, blessed no doubt by guardian angels, that started up on the first crank. Hopping in, we took off toward the Eads Bridge. I turned on the siren and the traffic pulled over, giving us a wide berth. Lillian heaved a sigh as we left the tumult behind us. She buried her face in her hands. "I've so fucked things up," she murmured to herself.

"What haven't you told me?" I shouted over the siren's wail. "Talk."

"It won't help," she sighed and lit a cigarette. "But why not? It's a long drive."

She had a lot to answer for, but my first concern was yours truly. "What did Humphrey mean— 'You brought him along'?"

Lillian offered me a drag off her smoke.

I took and kept it. "You've been working with him the whole time, haven't you?"

We approached the bridge, siren still blaring. East St. Louis city cop cars and barricades blocked the Illinois side, their red lights flashing in the dark. A car ahead of me stopped, made a U-turn, and headed back to Missouri.

She lit another cigarette and said, "Let me explain."

"Spit it out, doll."

The cops didn't seem inclined to move out of the road. I sped up, and Lillian gripped the dashboard. "Back last winter, I had to get away from Taylor and Violet."

This story always seemed to circle back to that debutante ball.

She didn't say anything else, just stared out the window at the flashing lights ahead.

Me and my screaming siren barreled on toward the roadblock. At the last possible moment, the police dragged their barricades out of the road and scattered. I caught a few surprised looks as we rolled past them. I tipped my cap. A small triumph, but tonight I'd take what I could get. I made my way toward the main road to Alton and turned off the siren.

Lillian let out a little moan. "She's going to drown my baby."

"Who?" A few raindrops fell, and I turned on the windscreen wipers. "Violet?"

She shook her head. "The Piasa." She blew her nose on the shreds of my pocket square. "In a lot of the old stories from tribes up and down the river—" she sobbed, "the Underwater Spirits steal children and drown them in the floodwaters. They're found later, eyes, nose, and mouth caked with mud."

I'd about had it with the waterworks and said, "How'd you know Humphrey's plans? Really?"

She slid across the bench seat and hid her face on my shoulder. I was pretty sure it was dislocated, and her snuggling just made it hurt worse. But pain is a focus, and I could take a step back and be a bit more objective.

"Lillian?"

"I'm so ashamed."

I found that hard to believe, although she smelled pretty scared. "You'll feel better if you tell it," I said, trying to sound comforting.

She sat up straight and scooted away, saying, "I know because I worked out the ritual with him."

"For treasure?"

"Look at my life, Copper. I'm stuck here. A stupid position in society and no money to finance it. I need to get away and live well when I do."

I still had questions for Lillian. Lots of them. "You made me think Humphrey raped you. Didn't that weigh on my mind just now, when I killed him?"

"Hold up there, Copper. I never said that."

And all this time I took her for being too embarrassed to speak directly. I slammed the brakes, grabbed her by the shoulders, and shouted right in her face, "Well, doll, you got me. But that's pretty low. People who are hurt have enough trouble getting folks to believe them."

"I needed your help," Lillian said. "Don't be so mean. *You* made me be the Piasa Queen."

Even the rain scolded me as it pelted the car roof. Lillian always knew just what to say to me. "Were any of your tales about Humphrey true?" I asked.

"Oh, they're all true," she said as she traced the path of a raindrop snaking its way down the window. "But he never made me do anything. You know what I mean. He didn't force me."

I calmed my voice and pitched it nice and sympathetic to say, "The night of the party, you were wandering around the building, drugged."

"Well, it was a drag. I took something for my nerves."

"So, it was all an innocent night of upper-class fun?"

She shrugged.

I smashed the fuel pedal, jerking the car back onto the dark country road, and let the silence build as we drove. Most people can't stand quiet for long. At last, Lillian spoke, her voice low and matter-of-fact, no teasing or flirting in it. A Lillian I'd not met before. "The idea was to recreate the Piasa legend, as Russell described it. The chief's—that would be Taylor's—own child as bait. We'd capture the Piasa magically, and the child would be unharmed. For various astrological reasons, the night of the debutante ball was ideal for the conception."

I didn't know what to say. Of all the lines I'd ever heard to get someone in the sack, this one took the biscuit. "And—?"

She said nothing as we rattled through Alton, locked down tight at the midnight hour. Just north of town, the bluffs towered over railroad tracks along the river.

"Well, as it got closer to the appointed night, I had second thoughts. So, I went to the convent."

Her troubles really are all on me, I thought as I drove past the railyard. Bleachers were set up and a large tarp covered a portion of the bluff's rock face. A sign informed us of upcoming festivities— *Site of the Piasa Bird Rock Painting. Dedication, Sunday, Oct 5, 1924.* Tomorrow.

"Pull over," Lillian said. "Maybe she came here."

I obeyed, although I thought we would have already noticed a material spirit as big as an ox creeping about. As I rolled to a stop she leaped from the car, calling out into the dark. I couldn't make out all the words, but the message was clear, "Spare my child." All the while the slow rain soaked her to the bone.

Granted, I'd persuaded her to go to the ball and thus back into Humphrey's bed. On the other hand, Lillian was one of the biggest liars I've ever met. Or maybe she would've changed her mind again and gone home all on her own. I wasn't sure what, if anything, I owed her. But I wasn't about to sit back and let any sort of supernatural being steal away a human child without a fight. And, liar that she was, I was still positive I could trust her to back me up in a fight for her baby.

*   *   *

Lillian didn't wait too long for a reply from the Underwater Spirit before she gave up and returned to the car. The spitting drizzle stopped as we bounced up the gravel switchbacks to the De Noailles house on the bluff crest. The clouds cleared, and the moon lit the road to the house, picking out the crystals among the white limestone drive.

"I'm going to get Grandfather," Lillian said as she hopped out of the car before I'd come to a full stop. She pointed at the dark woods in the distance. "Leave me the car and take that path to the cave."

"Yeah, I've been there." But not in the dark.

A little coupe was parked in a flowerbed, the driver's door hanging open. "Violet's car," Lillian said. "Be careful."

Every torn muscle in my body tight from the long drive, I crawled out of the police car like an old man and hobbled into the woods, praying I wouldn't get lost. With surprisingly little difficulty, I located the cave entrance behind a dark mass of shrubbery. After stumbling up the steps to its mouth, I slid through the narrow entrance and paused at rustling and electric torchlight ahead.

"Who's there?" a female voice said. "Tony, is that you? Come to mommy, baby."

Another presence *was* with me and Violet in that cave, and it wasn't a dead little boy. The Underwater Spirit smelled like the cave itself, but deeper, older, and simply more of it—as if you took all the deep, sleeping places of the earth and squished them together for a million years. And I felt power. Not the petty lording it over each other we humans think makes for a big shot. No, grand old birth and death. Beginnings and endings. Alpha and omega.

My mind, or soul, maybe, touched the spirit.

"Go." The sound of rushing water rumbled in my head. "Go now, and I won't drown you just yet," said a voice both strange and familiar, its words closed and guarded. She hid something. Something tender.

Light played across my face and blinded me. "Get back and leave me alone," said Violet. "I've—I've got a—gun."

I doubted that very much but stuck up my hands. "Easy, now," I said. "No call for gunplay." Blinking, I could make out a resin torch in her hand. Violet moved it around, casting light and shadow along the chamber's edges, while she called out, "You've been paid. Now, please, my boy." As she searched, she lit more of the torches embedded in the walls. "One year old. Long curly hair. He—he hadn't even had his first haircut yet."

The cave's images—animals, people, symbols—paraded in the moving light. In the deepest corner of the chamber, the torchlight fell on the Underwater Spirit painting and the narrow opening in the rock face beneath it. The light glinted off something metallic in the shadows.

At the courts building, we'd seen the dragon-like "Piasa," a popular image about town. But now the Underwater Spirit looked just like her cave painting. Big as an ox, she dwarfed the rocks she tried to hide behind. Her body, covered in copper-green scales, snaked among the stones. Golden studs ornamented her ears and her golden eyes shone in the torchlight. Her face was a cat's, and her antlers meant business. She snarled, brandishing rows of dagger-sharp teeth.

Just beyond her, the infant slept in a nest of dry leaves, rabbit fur, and smooth pebbles. Violet pointed to the baby and said, "You have her. And Taylor is dead. This is balance, yes?" She scrambled over the rocks. "Take me to my child, please."

The Underwater Spirit seemed to understand Violet's words but re-positioned herself between us and the baby. The shrubs at the cave mouth rustled behind us and she roared, grabbed the infant in her paws, and moved away. I turned to see Lillian guiding her grandfather into the cave. He gasped for breath and clung to her.

"Please give her back," Lillian shouted at the Underwater Spirit. "I don't want your treasure anymore. I just want my baby. I never thought—" She settled the old man at his fire pit seat. "I didn't know—"

The spirit's eyes gleamed in the dark.

"She's all I want," Lillian said.

Chapter Twenty-Six

The Bottom Line

"My dear," Dr. De Noailles said to the Underwater Spirit. "What's all this?"

The spirit's ears perked up at his voice and she started to nestle the child back in the bed of fur and leaves. But then Lillian stepped toward her baby and the Underwater Spirit clutched the infant all the tighter in her paws.

"I hate that there's no other way to bring Tony back," Violet said to her grandfather, and then pointed at Lillian. "But she—"

"Me?" Lillian glared at her sister. "When Taylor asked me to have his baby for you to adopt, *you* intended to murder her!"

"It's your fault Tony's gone," Violet yelled as she pushed Lillian to the ground and raised her hand to slap her, but Lillian was no slouch at self-defense. Struggling away from the line of fire, she flipped Violet onto her back and rolled on top of her.

"Girls," Dr. De Noailles wheezed, "stop it. This instant." He treated a coughing fit with a slug off his brandy flask.

I dove in to separate the combatants. "This spirit stole your child," I said as Violet slapped at Lillian, grazing my right ear. "Your family." I tried to hold them apart, but they clawed and cursed at each other, anyway. All the while the Underwater Spirit cradled the baby, crooning in response to the little one's whimpers.

"She's a better parent than any of my spawn, I'll be bound," the doctor said as he hit Violet and Lillian each smartly on the back with his cane. "Tell me what you've been up to."

Lillian rushed to tattle first, "Taylor said we could use ritual magic to control the Piasa and her treasure. He wrote a spell based on one of the old John Russell stories."

The old man turned red, about ready to have a fit. "The fairytale fabricated by that newspaperman?"

"Taylor disagreed," Violet said. "That it was a fabrication, I mean."

Lillian nodded and reached out to her sister. "But we can do this without him."

The gesture looked peaceful enough, so I stepped back.

"We know the spell," Lillian said. "The summoning was the hard part, right?"

Violet took Lillian's hands. "Tony?" She turned to face the Underwater Spirit.

Lillian nodded. "We can make her give us both the children." She began a chant, her voice hesitant and cracking. She stumbled over some words, but the song grew stronger as Violet joined her. My Latin was pretty much limited to mass responses, but I got the general idea. "Obey us," they sang. "Give us what we want. On pains of many nasty things."

Dr. De Noailles hit at them again with his cane, shouting, "Stop that. You'll hurt her." His granddaughters just stepped away, closer to the Underwater Spirit, who crouched against the cave wall, uneasy and growling. The babe tucked under one front leg, she raked at them with an extended claw but was too far away to do any damage. The ground shook for a second, and rocks crashed to the cave floor.

I couldn't see a play for me to get the child away from the Underwater Spirit right then. As Lillian and Violet sang, the spirit changed from a copper-plated-horned-feline-snake of a creature to the demon-dragon, "Piasa," who'd made off with the infant in the first place.

The sisters dropped hands long enough to draw a circle, fancy symbols along its edge, on the cave floor with charred sticks from the fire pit.

Dr. De Noailles saw their bet and raised it, chanting his own Osage song, sketching a fish on the rock wall with charcoal, and tapping a slow beat with his cane on the cave floor. His voice echoed around and around the chamber and almost drowned out his granddaughters' words.

While the doctor, Violet, and Lillian wrangled musically, the Underwater Spirit retreated farther back into the cave and escaped through the crack in the wall. I ducked down the passage after her, soon losing what little light filtered through the crack behind me. The ritual duel between magic and faith filled the cave, and I followed the Underwater Spirit as best I could. Just when I thought she'd lost me in the many twisting side passages, a glimpse of scales shone in my electric torchlight, and I hurried to catch up.

The damp soaked my clothes, making the cold air feel all the colder. Bats and insects rustled and chirped. And always the sound of water. Running, dripping water. I scratched the wall with the butt of the torch to mark side tunnels but worried I wouldn't notice the marks on my way back. In short, I was scared of getting lost. Of dying doing something stupid. Following the Underwater Spirit down this passage was particularly stupid. There was water enough to survive, and I suppose I could catch crickets and the like to eat. The cold would be what got me, long before I was hungry or thirsty.

No real path before me, I just climbed over, squeezed through, and knocked my head on rocks. I had to move slowly, and she left me far behind. Sound traveled through the cave in odd ways. Sometimes I thought I could hear the little one, making soft, happy baby sounds, and I took some comfort in that, her coos reminding me of my little sister, Brigid.

Granny McGuinn always pegged me as having the Sight, which didn't sit well with Ma. Mostly to distract myself from imagining my slow death in the dark and cold, I thought about every uncanny experience of my life, and there were a lot of them. But the worst of them all was the night the fae stole Brigid. Not quite two years old, I watched, helpless, as a faerie lift her from her crib, replacing her with a glamoured bundle of sticks.

As a toddler, I collected words like a magpie, looking for the right ones to describe what I'd seen. But the faerie's geas—a spell to prevent me from speaking on it, big vocabulary or not—held fast my tongue, on the topic of faeries at any rate, for years. When I finally did manage to make my priest understand something was wrong, the fae tricked him into falling off the church roof. He'd promised to help me, and they killed him. After that, I ignored the Good People so as to not endanger anyone else. But maybe it was time to face the world beyond the Veil.

Moving through the cave at a better pace, I avoided hazards by sense rather than sight. The Underwater Spirit was far ahead, yet her heartbeat rumbled like a waterfall through my chest. My intentions reached out to her. I could see her golden eyes glowing in the darkness.

The spirit reached into my mind and showed me our river valley: Barren hills, riddled with mines. Rivers churned and fouled by steamboats. Streams choked with factories' poisons. Her underwater realm seemed beyond repair, and harmony was lost forever. "The people of the Middle World have forsaken the balance," she said.

"We don't know how to do it right no more." Because the Osage, the Illini, the Shawnee, and so many other tribes were killed outright or herded off to tiny plots of land to die. But, while I like justice as well as the next man, I couldn't let her carry off another child in the name of righting wrongs. "The baby is innocent of all this."

"Thus, fitting payment."

"She's a person—we love her," I screamed, as powerless as a two-year-old. I found myself alone in the dark. "Come back," my voice echoed around me. I ran forward, jammed my foot into a crevice, and tripped. I tumbled down and saw stars for a second, and then noticed my motionless body, lying on the passage floor. "Looking kinda dead there, mate," I said, nudging myself with a spectral toe.

"Come." The Underwater Spirit's golden eyes beckoned me forward.

I followed her into an image of the past—a place warm with people and sweat, the air thick with the smoke of fires and burning herbs. The smell of roasted meats and fried bread made me as hungry as if I'd fasted the entire Easter cycle, even in my ghost form.

Drums pounded, and gourds rattled in time to rhythmic chants that shook the chamber. I felt very young and in over my head, and then woke myself with coughing, ammonia burning my nose.

"Good," Dr. De Noailles said as he helped me sit up, flashed a light in one eye, then the other, and then handed me his hip flask. "Drink this."

Brandy. Probably laced with laudanum. Maybe it would get me on my feet, though, and out of this cave. "You shouldn't be here," I said. "Not safe."

He shone his torchlight on my ankle. "That foot is wedged in there tight."

"How did you even—" I left off my question to scream like a little girl as he started to wiggle my foot out of the shoe.

"Sprained. Maybe broken," he said, tearing strips off my shirt-tail. "Drink more brandy."

I obeyed.

"It's swelling," he said as he jammed my foot back into the shoe he'd freed from the rocks. That hurt even worse, but I was ready for him this time and merely sworn.

He splinted my leg and then helped me to my feet, holding my arm as we hobbled along. At least he knew these passages.

"Where are the granddaughters?" I asked.

"They started arguing again." His torchlight played off a wide passage leading off to the right.

"The Underwater Spirit won't hurt the child, will she?"

"She loves that baby," he said, shaking his head. "And she loved my grandson. She watches over us all, in the way that seems right to her."

Gray light from a small cave mouth filtered into the passage ahead of us. Perched at the entrance was the Underwater Spirit, cradling the child in her paws and looking out over the river below.

As we approached, the cave floor heaved, and I fell to my knees. Dr. De Noailles stumbled and plopped down on a large rock, wheezing. Rockslides crashed onto the railway tracks along the river, the noise bouncing back up the cliff walls. Startled crows fled their treetop roosts, filling the air with pounding wings and angry caws. The Underwater Spirit shifted the baby into her talons and flapped her leathery wings, poised on the cliff edge.

I had one more shot at this job, and my Luger wasn't the weapon for it. Clearing my mind of thoughts and feelings, I let go of regrets and fears. The brandy and laudanum possibly helped with that.

The Underwater Spirit seemed to love the baby. Maybe I could turn that against her.

I reached out to touch her, not with my hands, but with my will.

But what I touched wasn't the Underwater Spirit. Instead, the green grass of Lapinduff Mountain's drumlin hills tickled my hands. I was back in County Cavan, the site of the sorriest debacle of my quite sorry military career. A real place it seemed, yet a fae glamour as well. The faerie Éire had tempted me in Cavan. And here we were again.

"Well met, master traveler," Éire said. "Far doeth thou journey."

The place seemed so real. The countryside, the sheep's distant bleat, the lingering smell of last night's peat fire. Tipped off by my wife, Norah, the British had captured my unit at Lapinduff in May of 1921. I managed to get out alive, only to face the gallows, convicted of treason. "Your lot aiming to steal this baby, too, are you?" I said.

She only smiled in that irritatingly condescending way the fae have.

I was pleased to find that I also had a Luger in this mind-space. I pointed it straight at her. "I won't let you."

She laughed. "I do trow, ye be a bit thick. Comely, true enough, yet thick."

"Alright, you fecking know-it-all. Help me save the child from the spirit."

"Verily, thy hand, do stretch it forth thine fate to grasp. Its master can ye be if thou willest it."

"You make no bloody sense." Fog crept up the hills, swirling around our feet.

"Thou doeth fret for one child? What of the good folk of thine realm—weak, robbed, and the prey of nobles turned brigand? People thou vowest to protect, yet thou usest not the weapon close by, one fit for thine hand alone."

"If you mean magic or something uncanny like that, I can't do it." Clouds had gathered, a few drops of rain pattered on the ground. "And you're most likely a demon from Hell, sent to tempt me. There'll be a price, I'll be bound."

Éire looked shocked. Shocked and dismayed I'd think such a thing. "I do vouchsafe thou shalt be mine *master*. Aye, and teach thee, I shalt, to weave thy will into the tapestry of this sorry orb. As mine consort taught thine mother and grandmother before thee."

While the folks round and about Carrickfergus consulted my Granny McGuinn about troublesome butter witches and the ill effects from the evil eye, I knew her to be a good Christian woman who made her Easter duty and died shriven. And my sot of a mother? If what Éire said was true, magic didn't agree with her any more than drink did. But I'll admit the faerie's words shook me. "You lying bitch," was all I could manage to spit out before the vision of her was gone, as were the rainy green hills and dawn mist.

Nothing but Éire's laughter lingered in my ears as I continued to stumble through another fae space, not real, yet solid, and so bright the very air glowed.

Again, I stood on the cave's threshold and again I saw the Underwater Spirit's shared vision of her feasting people. And she was in their midst, breathing in the food's aroma, the music's rhythm, and the dancers' energy. She grew larger and more beautiful by the second. Scales bright, fur glossy, and antlers thick, strong, and sharp. Her golden eyes, deep pools of colors, reflected shades of brown, green, and violet in the firelight. From across the room, she stared at me. Finally, I recognized her.

The Underwater Spirit was Miss Esther. I didn't understand how or why but couldn't deny it.

*   *   *

Energy swirled around me—light and heat and emotion, all intent on honor for the underwater realm and its guardians. Miss Esther was both the human woman I'd come to know and the spirit gracing me in that moment. Thinking of her as some sort of New World Good People was as irreverent as calling the Blessed Mother fae.

We faced each other, the images of the past dancing around us.

"And ain't we humans royally fucked it up?" I said. "Pardon my French, ma'am. But people are lost and drifting. But this little one, her death won't even begin to fix it. You know that."

"She will live on. In my realm."

A thought struck me, and I tried it on for size, saying, "The little boy—you tried to fix things before."

"My avatar's child was lost in a faraway land. He couldn't get home."

"So, Violet's son—"

The Underwater Spirit lowered her head. "A child of the Middle World offered to come to me and abide in our Beneath-World kingdom. A child who loves me well and has no fear."

"The doctor loves you, too. Worked for the balance, as best he could, all his life. He'd want his family to go on."

"This child isn't safe in their corrupt and tainted hands."

"You got that right. But I promise I'll do everything in my power to protect her. She deserves a chance at life. She could do great things."

The Underwater Spirit looked at the baby, who stared up at her. I swear they were talking over the whole sorry business with their eyes and thoughts. Finally, she nodded and beckoned me forward.

On an impulse, I reached out to touch her furry cat-muzzle and stroke her bejeweled ears. I guess a touch in the spirit world breaks the spell, or trance, or whatever it was.

I found myself in the here-and-now, facing the real-world Underwater Spirit. Dr. Noailles, slumped on the stone seat he'd grabbed in the earth tremor, looked to be in a bad way. She handed me the bundle, the little mite protesting to leave her, then she prowled around the cave. She sniffed, snorted, and nudged at the old man, who reached up one hand to stroke her maul.

Gathering Dr. De Noailles up in her claws, she flew out the cave as the first morning rays painted the gray trees red, yellow, and orange. I watched her join the red-tailed hawks to soar on the thermals high above the river.

The cave floor bucked and swayed as new cracks opened in the walls around us. The bluff trembled, rattling loose boulders to splash in the river below. A thick haze of white limestone dust filled the air. I pressed the baby against my chest as I coughed and choked, and almost missed the look on the doctor's face as the Underwater Spirit swooped and banked near the cave mouth. He shouted something at me, but the wind snatched his words away.

At that moment a flock of bats poured into their roost, chittering and darting this way and that. I crouched as they flew over me, deep into the cave, only to be met by screaming women. I looked up to see Violet and Lillian on the ground, covering their heads with their arms. The bats disappeared down the passage, and Lillian ran to the ledge. "Grandfather," she cried out to him. But he didn't hear. The Underwater Spirit banked around the prominence and dove sharply at the river.

We heard a splash, and all the birds in the trees took squawking flight.

*   *   *

We had a lot of lying—I mean explaining—to do. But money helps.

By some miracle, the passage back to the main chamber hadn't entirely caved in during the earthquake. The women and I shifted a bit of rubble and, passing the child back and forth, helped each other climb through the cave. None of us had a word to say. We dragged ourselves to the house and collapsed on the lawn.

"We should search for him," I said after a few minutes. Lillian and Violet looked at me like I was crazy, but I felt the little one agreed with me. "The cops' first question will be, 'Where have you searched?' We need to have actually searched."

Lillian stayed home with her baby, while me and Violet drove both cars to the river, the last place we'd seen the doctor. That much was true, at least. Parking at the Alton railyard, we walked through the shrubs along the river like we might find some trace of their grandfather. I still had the old man's flask and made quite free with it.

"Look, a man's shoe," Violet said as she fished a waterlogged spectator brogue out of the water. "He was wearing these, right?"

I nodded.

"We'll show it to the sheriff," she said as she poked among the driftwood, dead fish, and river debris for more things to lie about. I cleaned the cop car out really well and ditched it, hoping for the best. Since I'd murdered Humphrey with the Luger, it seemed a good time to chuck it in the river.

On the way back to the house, Violet stopped at the petrol station to call my old friend, Sheriff Charlie. Me, Lillian, and Violet worked out a story while we waited for him. It was simple. Grandfather had wandered off. *Old men and toddlers do that, right?* He'd talked about fishing, so when we didn't find him in the woods near the house, we searched the river. Found the shoe. *Miss Esther?* She'd gone off to Oklahoma days ago to offer moral support to their relatives on the Osage tribal lands.

The sheriff took his sweet time coming up to the house. We hadn't last parted on good terms, so I left the Arwald sisters to talk to him while I ransacked the house for survival supplies.

I found Dr. De Noailles's medical cabinet, restocked on pain killers, and wrapped my swollen ankle right tight with bandages. As I fixed coffee and toast in the kitchen, I could overhear the sheriff with Lillian and Violet.

Sheriff Charlie was short-tempered but trying to hold it together for the citizens as he said, "I don't mind telling you ladies we've got our hands full. Got to assess the earthquake damage on top of keeping the St. Louis riot from spreading over to here."

"I doubt there's much risk of that," said Lillian.

He sighed in that way people do to keep from throttling someone. "Folks are jumpy. You might be too young to remember the race riot on our side of the river a few years back."

Violet answered him, her voice dripping with the upper-class sarcasm she was so good at. "Of course, you must *appear* to care for the common good. It's just one missing old man. A leading citizen. He turned this house into a hospital during the Spanish flu epidemic. A few years back."

The sheriff's tone stood up and saluted right quick. "Yes, ma'am. I'll notify the boatmen downstream to drag the river."

"Thank you, sheriff," said Violet. "It means a lot to us."

"Now, I'm going to have to list him as 'missing, presumed drowned' and schedule a coroner's inquest."

One of them pretended to faint or something and the other clucked around and made the sheriff fetch brandy from the tea trolley. He beat a hasty retreat as soon as he could after that.

I hobbled in with coffee and some blankets I'd found, handing each a cup and a wrap. They were both pale, disheveled, and had dark rings under their eyes. Lillian began to shake. She gulped the hot coffee and huddled under the blanket, but kept an eye on her sister, ready to attack again as soon as she had the strength.

Violet accepted the cup but made no move to drink it. She made no moves at all. A half-smile played across her face, and her eyes were glassy. I arranged a blanket across her shoulders while she stared straight ahead, whether out the window, at something in the room, or a vision only she could see, I'd no idea.

The baby slept in her cradle, none the worse for wear, as far as I could tell. I drank my coffee while I watched each woman sort out the night.

No more than ten minutes went by before Lillian threw off her blanket, slammed down the cup, and marched over to her sister to shout, "You were going to drown my baby." She grabbed a handful of hair, and I was on my feet. "A baby you claimed you wanted to adopt." She jerked Violet's head back to look her in the face. Violet's full cup of coffee clunked on the rug, a dark pool soaking into the Persian carpet.

I hobbled over to untangled the two. "Now, now. Plenty of crime to go around here." Violet's expression hadn't changed a whit. I held Lillian by the wrists as she raged at her sister. She was a pretty talented swearer and knew a few I'd never heard. Violet didn't even blink.

At last, Lillian collapsed on my chest in tears, sobbing, "What's wrong with her?"

"Looks shell-shocked. Violet needs to go to the hospital."

"No publicity," Lillian said, an Arwald to the end.

I called the family attorney from the petrol station. The conversation was awkward, and the arrangements took most of the morning, but by noon Violet was hustled off to a private sanitarium out in the sticks somewhere, and Lillian and the baby were on their way home in a chauffeur-driven limousine.

I was surprised I hadn't been nicked for killing Humphrey yet, but the cops had been pretty busy. I used what little time I had left to clean up anything in Vision Cave that might look suspicious and then hitched a ride to the Piasa Bluff painting in Alton, set to be dedicated that afternoon. It seemed an appropriate place to meet my fate.

Chapter Twenty-Seven

Bad Debt

Kyffin laughed, a rich, satisfying roar that was good to hear again. He wiped his eyes, then laughed some more. "Gran—granny punish—" he eventually said, "you?"

I puffed on my pipe and nodded. "Aye that." The mantel clock chimed four. I was behind my time. "I didn't walk quite right for nigh to a week," I said as I tapped the ash out into the ashtray at my elbow.

"I bet," he said and smiled his glorious smile.

He'd lost at least a stone in the hospital. From a distance, I might mistake him for the slim twenty-two-year-old flying ace whose photo glared at me from the mantel. But Kyffin's face was tired and lined, and at his temples, gray hairs mingled with the blond.

"I should be going," I said as I stood up and put the still-warm pipe in my pocket. An ancient basset hound, snoozing by the fireplace, opened his eyes and roused himself. Kyffin grasped the arms of his chair and started to push as he planted his feet square in front of him. "Don't get up." I hurried across the room to his side. "I can see myself out."

"Want to," he said, steadying himself against a table as he grasped his cane in his left hand. "Good for me. Yes?"

"Yes," I said, taking his right elbow.

At the first step, his knees gave out, and he sunk back into the chair. He bit his lip, frustration lining his face. "Fuck."

The dog padded across the room and rested his head on Kyffin's knee.

"You'll get it soon," I said. "You're stronger than yesterday."

"I am?" He pondered that a moment, then extended his right hand. "Thanks. Kind. Kind of you. Come. Any. Anytime. Enjoyed meeting. You."

We shook hands. "And I enjoyed meeting you," I said as I turned to go.

"Don't forget."

I turned back. "What?"

He patted the dog on the head and said, "Your dog. Don't. Forget your dog."

I sighed, "He's your dog."

Kyffin looked surprised but nodded and rubbed the dog's muzzle. "Good dog."

I built up the fire before I left and held the photograph for a moment before slipping it into my pocket. His mother met me in the hall with my coat and hat. "What do you think? Any improvement?"

"Honestly?" I shook my head.

"You're a good friend, to come every day," she said.

"All I can do." I shrugged into the coat and put on my hat. "I wish he remembered you, at least."

She looked a little teary. "Doctor says, 'Don't give up.' It's early yet."

I tipped my hat and went out the door into the late October chill.

"Don't give up," she said, as she closed the door behind me.

*　　*　　*

All Hallow's Eve. The turn of the year. A good time to mend fences and wrap up business. I had use of a car for a change and stopped by my brother's bar on my way to visit Lillian in Alton. I hoped Padraig, Eliza, and most of all Maud had forgiven me by now. A month had passed since Padraig put me out. I was renting an attic room from Mrs. Mac. The arrangement worked well enough. If I ever got lonely, I went downstairs, and she fussed and scolded, which made me feel right at home.

I came in the pub's front door like a customer. The warm, at-home smells of brew, smoke, and chowder, the dinner special on this chilly night, hit me like a physical blow. *God, I'd missed them.*

Padraig was behind the bar serving drinks. "Special tonight is fucking fish chowder," he said to the cold wind I'd let in, without looking up. "Comes with bread and a Bevo or coffee."

The crowd was good for so early on a Friday evening. A buzz of conversation filled the air along with the gray smoke haze. Chest puffed out with self-importance, my oldest nephew, Patrick, handed out bread baskets to diners in the booths along the back wall, while his mother served chowder bowls from a tray. Nine-year-old Gerald and baby Francis, grown into a toddler in knee-pants in the month I'd been gone, admired the effect of a lit candle in the jack-o'-lantern they'd just carved. Maud sat with them, supervising without lifting her eyes from the book in front of her.

The scene hurt my heart.

At last, Padraig looked up.

I held my breath and hoped he'd at least give me a chance to say my piece, but ready for a quick exit.

"Well, see what the fucking black cat dragged in," he said.

The whole room stared at me. Regulars I knew well. Friends, I'd thought, until recently. The room was silent. Ah, well. It was worth a try. I opened the door to leave again.

But Patrick would have none of that. He yelled, "Uncle Sean," and ran across the room to climb all over me, joined by Francis latched onto my leg. "Where've you been?" They pulled me to the floor where we lay in a laughing heap. Gerald sidled over, clearly not knowing what to do about all the ruckus.

Maud ran to us, scolding the boys, "Patrick. Francis." She pulled them away and helped me up. "Let the man breathe, will ya?"

I turned to Gerald and offered a handshake. He glanced at his father, then took my hand. "Yes," he said. "What became of you?"

"Ain't I here now?"

Patrick dragged me to an empty booth, filling the air with a steady stream of chatter. The other boys and Maud followed. I looked over at their parents. Eliza, stone-faced, started toward us, but Padraig caught her eye and shook his head. She descended on him instead, pulling him into the kitchen.

"Maudie," I said. "I came here to say sorry." I hadn't thought it through much farther than that.

She'd grown up in just a few weeks, almost as tall as me and slender as a rail. Gone were the pigtails, her hair pinned up in a grown-lady twist. She smiled, then her face sobered, the spitting image of her mother. "And?"

I'd no idea what she wanted from me. She'd mistaken what was going on with me and Violet in the flat, but I had a feeling I'd never convince her of that. I took her hand and shut down my thoughts. Shadows gathered, time gave a little hiccup, and her life, from the birth I'd witnessed to this moment passed in an instant. Her hurt flowed over me, and I saw, at least dimly, my part in it all. She'd loved me, loyally, truly, better than anyone, and I'd been too thick to even notice.

I started with the hurt and felt along from there, slowly finding the words, "You're not that much younger than me, really, and I've treated you like a child. You're my friend—a better ear than any father-confessor—and I've preferred to spend time with strangers. Backstabbing women, to boot."

Maud's expression was that of a particularly strict teacher. My work was not up to snuff, but maybe she'd pass me, anyway, if I did extra assignments. With a firm nod of her head, she said, "Suppose that will do." She pushed Francis and Gerald over along the booth and took a seat, "I trust you've learned your lesson."

"Yes, ma'am," I said as I shed my coat and hat. "How're you getting along with your job?" Mrs. Judge had offered her a paid position, which, for Padraig, was a whole different story than sending her off to school. He accepted the offer right quick, from what I heard.

She lowered her voice, "Hardly a job at all. A little dusting. Sometimes I help the cook in the morning. Peel a few turnips or the like."

"See much of your friend, young Matthew?"

"A bit. He up and quit washing dishes to work in the Judge's office after school."

I knew that, having used my last marker with the Judge to get the job offer extended to the kid. "I thought maybe he'd be around the Judge's house."

"Brought papers over in the evening once, I think," Maud said. "Mostly Mrs. Judge has me studying, so I don't know who's in or out of the house."

I could picture it well. "What do you study?"

"American history, grammar and spelling, sums and ciphering."

"That's a lot."

"Française. J'étudie Française."

"That's enough fucking frog talk," Padraig said, sounding rough, but his eyes shone with admiration for his clever girl. He patted her head, almost affectionate. "Go help your mother now." He eyed his sons. "Clean up the fucking pumpkin guts." They hopped out of the booth and made for the carving table. "And best put your lantern out before the phantom carriage comes to carry ya all off." He sat across from me and asked, "How ya been, baby brother?"

"Middling fair. You all look well."

He nodded. "Aye. Maud's a housemaid now. Pays a fucking lot more than I thought it would. And the boys are more help now that—"

"They have to be."

"Just so."

I could feel Eliza's eyes burning a hole in me. Padraig felt it, too. He turned around and called to her across the room, "Fuck it, woman. I'll talk to my brother if I fucking want to."

She huffed back to the kitchen, leaving Maud to serve from behind the bar.

"Look," he said. "I don't mind ya coming around now and then. We're family, after all."

"I thank you, Padraig. That's all I want."

"But no fancy women." His voice dropped, "Or fucking nancies." He turned a disturbing shade of red as he whispered, "Can't abide the things I've heard about ya."

Ah, here it comes, I thought. "Understood. And there's no one I'd care to bring round, anyway."

"Good," he said, his voice low. "Back when ya was married— you had no troubles—with, you know—your marital duty—"

A more miserable man I'd never seen. So, I had to tweak him just a bit more. "Norah was nothing but trouble," I said. "You know that."

He glowered and hissed, "Not what I meant at all."

"Just pulling your leg. No, no family life problems."

"Aye, well, there. So, it can't be true. What they say."

"So, you have work, Sean." It was Eliza, bringing us a couple of Bevo. "As a peeper, I hear. "

"Eliza, nice to see you. I'd swear you're interested in my doings." She snorted.

"I've a bit of work finding things, figuring stuff out, and the like."

As it happened, a slow but steady stream of folks asked me for help with discrete inquiries of various sorts. Not a lot, just enough. I was mostly paid in favors. Like the use of a car, for instance. The Judge's fingerprints were all over the whole enterprise. So, yes, I'd become some sort of copper, thank you very much. But the Judge weren't sending the people that wanted to talk about ghosts. Or pixie infestations. Or hexes. I laid that on Mrs. Mac's door, and she didn't deny it.

"As far as I'm concerned, when you get an honest job—" Eliza's voice dropped to a whisper, "and leave off the sodomy, you'd be welcome here."

"Well, ain't it grand that it's my fucking place, not yours. I'll let in whoever the hell I want," Padraig growled. "I'll serve old Nick himself if I want."

She crossed herself and scuttled back to the bar.

"I don't want to be causing trouble between you two," I said, standing to go.

"She'll come 'round. Give her time," he advised as he walked me to the door. Patrick left off the pumpkin clean-up to give me a sticky hug.

Maud waved from behind the bar. I wasn't entirely out of her doghouse, I guess.

"And Eliza's right, you know," Padraig said. "Drop all this nonsense. Make a good confession, find a real job, and marry a sensible woman."

I opened the door and said, "If only it was that easy."

*   *   *

I shivered in the cold wind as I knocked on the door of the Alton house. Lillian opened it right away, the baby in her arms.

"Good evening, Miss Susan," I said to the child. The baby found me quite funny and smiled. She had her father's smile.

"Copper," Lillian shrieked as she gave me a half-hug. "I didn't expect you tonight. Dinner is tomorrow. Professor LaFlesche just got here from Nebraska this afternoon."

She had found correspondence between the elderly scholar and her grandfather and written him for advice about some of the artifacts. He was both an anthropologist and member of the Omaha Nation, so presumably would know the right thing to do with them. He'd offered to take the She'-ki medicine bundle to the Osage tribal territory in Oklahoma.

Lillian's parlor was bright, the drapes were drawn snug against the cold, and dance tunes played on the phonograph. Her steamer trunk sat in the foyer, and half-packed suitcases lay open on the dining room table.

"You going to Oklahoma, too?"

"Ah, no. Taking a little trip to Florida. Get away from all this—unpleasantness."

"And how's Violet?"

I hadn't seen her since Joseph Arwald's funeral, which also included memorials for Taylor Humphrey, who was to be buried back in England at his beloved standing stones, and Dr. De Noailles, whose body was never found. Yes, indeed, I did attend the service. I'm shameless. And how did I not get arrested for Humphrey's killing? His death was laid to "a person or persons unknown," during the riot. Mother Mary Gabriel has pull I'd not dreamed of. Archdiocesan pull, at the very least, possibly higher.

"My sister isn't well."

"I hoped she'd be a bit improved."

I'd guided Violet through the funeral and burial. About all she did was walk and sit. She said not a word to me or anyone else.

"I shouldn't have made her leave the sanitarium for the funeral, I guess. But people would talk if she didn't attend." The baby had nodded off against Lillian's shoulder.

She let me hold the child for a moment, and then I laid her in her cradle near the warm fireplace. "So, you finally named her after your mother."

"Yes, Susan," Lillian said. "That was silly of me, I guess, to wait so long. I couldn't think of the future. But now—" she plopped down on a chaise lounge, "things are brighter."

"Coming back for the trials?"

A janitor from the Civil Courts Building sat in gaol, charged with the attack on Kyffin Bernard. His cousin, a night watchman from the Wainwright, was charged with Joseph Arwald's murder. The tale was that the janitor mugged Kyffin, stealing and selling the guns. My Webley was used by the Wainwright night watchman to murder Arwald. Kyffin's derringer found its way to the streetcar riot, where Humphrey had the misfortune to be in the wrong place at the wrong time.

Lillian asked for a drink and I brought it to her.

"Why would I do that? Not like I'm a witness or anything."

I shrugged. "Just wondering. Your fiancé and father being the victims and all."

She looked worried. "Do you think people will expect me to testify?"

I took off my hat and tossed it on an easy chair. "Oh, before I forget," I said as I fished around in my coat pocket and handed her a piece of paper.

She looked at it, then looked at me. "What's this?"

"The name you've been pretending to not remember. Your old boyfriend. Your grandfather quite liked him. Or at least the hashish he shared. Plays drums for a jazz band."

"I know *who* it is. Why are you giving me this? And what does 'Southern Hotel, Ste. Genevieve,' mean?"

"That's where he'll be this New Year's Eve," I said. I slipped out of my topcoat, and it joined the hat. "He might like to know about his daughter."

She gave up the clueless act and said, "You're probably right. But I don't want to get married. Or share her."

"Up to you."

The rumor, whether she'd cooked it up or just let people make natural assumptions, was that Kyffin was little Susan's father, his unfortunate "robbery" delaying the shotgun wedding. Gossip buzzed for a few days, but the story had already faded from the public eye.

I checked my watch and pulled up a chair right close to her. "Is there anything you want to tell me about the night Kyffin was attacked?"

"What do you mean?" she said as she looked down at her hands in her lap and then over at the child, who was staring at her own fist in rapt amazement. Lillian started to get up.

I eased her back on the chaise lounge. "What I mean is, I know you tried to kill him, and then shot your father."

The color drained from her face.

"Just tell me what happened. It has something to do with all those artifacts you stole and sold."

Tears began to run down Lillian's cheeks, as she said, "What a horrible thing to say. I thought we were friends. More than friends."

"I guarantee you'll feel better if you tell someone the truth."

"I was here, in Alton when Kyffin—fell—that janitor robbed him. You know that."

"Your grandfather's Cadillac was seen at the Civil Courts building Wednesday night, and Miss Esther told me she heard you come in close to dawn Thursday morning." I'd made all that up. But she didn't know that.

"So what?" she pouted. "That doesn't mean I drove the car. And Esther is gone. She can't say one way or the other if I was home."

"You knew I'd lost my Webley. I lent it to Kyffin on Wednesday night. No one but me and him knew that."

She drained her liquor glass then said, "You're confusing me, Sean."

"When we were going to the Courts Building to stop the ritual, I said, 'I'll get a gun,' and you looked surprised and said, 'Yes, of course, you'd have more than one.' What did that mean?"

She opened and closed her mouth a few times. For once, no lies.

"Kyffin felt safe with you—who wouldn't? I guess he was walking down the stairs ahead of you, for you to be able to clobber him as you did."

She hid her face in her hands and sobbed as if I'd broken her heart.

"The guns fell out of his pocket when he fell down the stairs. Or maybe you found them when you searched him, looking for his notes. He knew the archivist's records showed missing artifacts. He knew you'd made side trips from England all summer. Maybe he didn't suspect you yet, but it just was a matter of time."

Since tears hadn't worked, Lillian left off the waterworks as easily as she'd started them, smirking, "If the police had any proof, they'd have arrested me before now."

"They have their blind spots. Rich, pretty, young females being a big one."

Lillian snorted and lit a cigarette. "Be that as it may, I'm in the clear."

I took the smoke out of her hand. "Anyway, you picked up Kyffin's derringer and my Webley in the rounds of it. You shot your father with my gun and gave me the derringer to kill Humphrey."

She stood and stretched. "Proof?"

"You were at your grandfather's house, with me, right after your father was murdered, not Alton. I saved that bloody dress. It's in a safe place. Also, your prints off the water glass from your house can be matched to fingerprints off the Webley."

I didn't have any physical evidence on her. But she didn't know that.

Lillian gasped, "You'd tell the police? You hate cops."

That was true. "What I can't figure is why you shot your father."

She bit her lip and wrung her hands, eyes pleading. "Please, Sean, after everything we've meant to each other. We could go away. Far away. I control my family fortune now."

That fortune was in tatters, but maybe no one had told her yet. It wasn't a hundred percent clear how Old Arwald was blowing through money so fast, but the shady business in the Piasa Lodge ledgers led straight back to him.

"Don't think so, doll. Why slug Kyffin? You could've talked him into anything."

"Not anything," she said. "Not anything. If he tied me to Taylor and the ritual—" She walked over to the phonograph.

I tried to look in the know. "You were ready to back out of that scheme. Kyffin could've helped you."

"But the first time—If he knew what really happened to Violet's little Tony. That would be it. I—I—was too ashamed." She set the needle on the record and Debussy filled the room.

The night the Underwater Spirit interrupted Humphrey's ritual to rescue little Susan was a bit of a blur, but I did recall Violet becoming convinced that her child's death was Lillian's fault. "You saying you and Humphrey tried that hooey before?"

Lillian nodded. "It didn't work. Nothing at all happened. But later in the day, Tony disappeared from his bedroom. You know the rest. The Piasa drowned him because we offered him up."

What a mess. Those "kidnappers" sitting on death row at Menard Penitentiary would never get off. "The Piasa stole the baby" was no defense at all.

"So, who did Kyffin see that Wednesday night? You?"

"No. Father had finally agreed to talk to me alone—I simply had to have more money. He pressed me to get married right away. If I did, 'I'd want for nothing.' I took that as a good sign and planned to sleep over. When I came downstairs to say goodnight, I overhead Kyffin and father." Lillian's voice grew cold, bitter, a tone I'd never heard from her. "Kyffin confronted father about missing artifacts from the Lodge collection. He had other concerns as well, a whole list of irregularities. Father blamed it all on Taylor, who he called to set up a meeting for Kyffin, immediately."

She crossed the room and picked up the sleeping baby. "Anyway, I rushed over to Taylor's office in the courts building. I warned him what Kyffin intended, and he sent me down the hall to hide. But, of course, I overheard the two of them. Taylor was—"

The child stirred in her arms and whimpered.

"—horrid." Lillian paced and patted her child's back. "Kyffin seemed to suspect Taylor of stealing artifacts. But Taylor insinuated things about me, encouraging Kyffin to dig further. They talked about me like I was a stupid little girl." Her face glowed with the insult. Her energy—I'd been training myself to take note of such things—crackled like electric sparks and smelled of burnt rubber. The room felt darker. "They had to protect me from myself."

She gripped the child tighter, and Susan began to cry. Lillian turned to me, accusing, "Like you all do. Men." Her voice could've removed varnish. "Anyway, I didn't even realize I'd picked up the stone ax while I was in Taylor's office. I followed Kyffin to the steps." She swaddled the child and lay her in the cradle with a dummy in her mouth. "So smart, but he didn't hear me. I was right behind him as he started down the stairs."

Lillian crept away from the cradle, and the child calmed. "I think I said his name. Anyway, he turned and said—he said—"

"What?" Knowing Kyffin, I could well imagine. "As his wife, you'd better learn to love, honor, and obey? Rules are rules? Whatever you'd been up to, it stops right now?"

"You know him pretty well, don't you? He made me so fucking angry, I—I—lashed out. I didn't hit him that hard, really, but the stone ax was in the bag. I ran to him after he fell, and the bag's latch came undone. I scooped up my things from the floor but missed the stone ax. I didn't mean—"

"But took the time to pick up both of the guns." I'd had just about enough. I pulled aside the drapes and looked out the French doors.

"Copper, you understand, right? It was an accident."

I watched the barge lights on the river far below.

"Sorry, doll. You set me up to take the rap for your father's murder."

"I didn't mean—I had to have some money to leave town. I just wanted to scare Father," she said. "*You* told me the Webley would scare people." She smiled, and, I swear to God—batted her eyes. "Remember the day we met? I certainly do."

Damn it. She was doing it again. "Someone is gone," I said. "Someone important to me."

"More important than I am?"

"Actually, yeah." I got out a cigarette, dropped the packet to the floor, and bent to pick it up.

She struck at me with something heavy, while I ducked, caught her wrists, and twisted them just enough for her to drop the silver candlestick.

"Let's not do this," I said to her as I pinned her arms to her sides. "You get all that, sheriff?"

A voice from the kitchen called out, "Sure did."

Quivering, Lillian spit the accusation, "You're in love with him, aren't you?"

The front door opened and closed. Two sets of steps clicked across the stone floor. Lillian's electric anger scorched my hands. "Goodbye, doll." I didn't turn around. "You located Mrs. Judge, Draper?"

"Yeah. And you were right. Didn't have to be asked twice."

"She's here for the baby, I suppose?" Lillian said.

Mrs. Judge stepped over to the cradle. "You don't want her in the foundling system while all this gets sorted."

"She's all I care about," Lillian said as Draper approached.

"Lillian Arwald, I have a warrant here for your arrest. You gonna cut up or come along quiet?"

She thought that one over. She eyed the exits and the sheriff blocking the back door. Maybe she considered the cold, the dark, and the child.

"You're smarter than that," I said.

She ignored me, telling Mrs. Judge, "She has diapers and things in the nursery." And to the sleeping baby, "I'll get you tomorrow."

"Come along," said Draper. "Where's your coat?"

"My lawyer—" Lillian started to say.

"He's waiting at police headquarters."

Epilogue

I'd found a page of Humphrey's journal that seemed to be just what I needed. The books I'd grabbed from his ritual room were a tough slough, but slough through them I did. His fancy journal was a lot more to the point. The later pages were devoted to his Mississippian spirit necromancy and "Piasa" summoning. Which had gone horribly wrong, so maybe I should take that as a warning he didn't really know what he was doing. Another red flag I really should have noticed—none of the spells he actually pulled off felt like fae magic. He'd tapped another power source, altogether.

But I was desperate. Not quite desperate enough to sell my soul to the fae, for I had no doubt that was the catch behind Éire's offer of magical help. Yet, if the universe concealed a Big Cinch for me—a way to pull the hidden strings and do some good in the world—I was determined to give it a go. And maybe that overeducated fool, Humphrey, was on to something.

The earlier entries were copied from books. He seemed to have started the journal—it's called a grimoire, I've learned—as a university student. Each page had lots of references and footnotes and comments.

I'd spent hours every day in my attic room at Mrs. Mac's house, pouring over the pages until my eyes burned. His notes were a confusing mix of Egyptian, Roman, and Greek gods, angelic words of power, and algebra equations. I strained to parse the meaning of his words and to recall my church Latin until my head hurt.

Speaking of which, I was on shaky spiritual ground. If something sounds like idolatry and looks like idolatry, it probably *is* idolatry. I seemed to have found a commandment I hadn't broken yet and was right on it to rectify the situation.

Yet I plowed ahead with my plan. I'd bathed, shaved, and put on clean clothes after coming back from Lillian's. Now I opened my window and looked outside. November first. All Saint's Day. As best I could tell from his astrology notes, the hour was ripe for my intention. Clear, cold air flowed into the room along with the moonlight. The waxing moon, a day or so from its fullness, lit the desk where I'd laid out the things I needed, altar-like. The light spilled across the chalk circle I'd made on the floor.

The most important item was Kyffin's lucky franc coin. I'd left it on my sunny windowsill, covered in salt, for a week. That was supposed to clean it. Next, I had the fancy dagger Humphrey had held to my throat as well as some church incense, provided by Mother Mary Gabriel with hardly any awkward questions. The photo of Kyffin, of course; I'd just borrowed it from his mother's house. A votive candle I'd nicked from the church's St. Jude's chapel was a little flourish of my own. If anything was an impossible cause, this was.

I looked at the moon again, lit the candle and the incense, and purified myself and the circle. I took a deep breath, grounded myself deep into the earth while reaching my mind up and out to the moon and stars and whatever lay beyond. I picked up the dagger and pointed it at the sloped attic ceiling. Already I felt dirty with the guilt of this obviously pagan ritual. But, in for a penny, I touched the dagger hilt to my forehead, heart, groin, and shoulders, then brought the dagger, still upright, to my chest, where I clasped my hands together. The tether I'd felt to Kyffin when he was in a coma was long gone. But I had my memories and I brought each forward. It hurt to dig so deep and relive every bit of craic we'd had together. Every laugh, every touch, every kiss.

"Iesus Nazarenus Rex Iadaeorum," I intoned, doubting all the while Our Lord wanted anything at all to do with this crock of shite. Yet He hadn't heeded any of my other prayers over the past month. I couldn't help but wonder if there was someone else I could talk to.

The next part invoked some bloke called Hermes Trismegistus as well as Osiris and Isis, Egyptian gods of resurrection, protection, and magic. Why'd they care to lend a hand, I'd no idea.

"Mnemosyne, I beg your aid." A Greek goddess, but in charge of memory. *Did she enjoy consorting with Egyptians? Seemed a bit dodgy.*

With a bit of a stage-magician flourish I didn't know I had in me, I pointed the dagger at the coin.

"Memento mei, memento mei, memento mei," I intoned to the coin. By this token, remember me. I compel you.

Remember me.

Afterword

This tale is a work of alternative historical fantasy fiction, rooted in real history, yet entirely fabricated. It takes place in a reality very different from our own. Historical details may vary from the "real" timeline for narratively interesting reasons. For example, the St. Louis Civil Courts Building was not completed until 1929, and a Mississippian mound wasn't destroyed in its construction. (As far as I know. A tenement area was cleared, so maybe before that . . .)

Two actual historical documents appear in this story. The men in the hospital waiting room read a newspaper story about the new Piasa painting. That story by F. A. Behymer appeared in the September 24, 1924, *St. Louis Post-Dispatch*. Sean and Matthew read a modified version of the often-repeated Russell Piasa Legend in an ad for plows. That ad appears in the 1910 Hapgood Plow Co. Catalogue No. 11—*Legend of the Piasa Bird After Which We Names Our Celebrated Double Lift Sulky and Gang*. This catalog and its charming engraving of two Piasas pulling a plow ridden by Mr. Hapgood is held by the Missouri History Museum Library and Research Center, St. Louis, MO.

Pronunciation Guide

Aoibheall: A (long "a") veel (like "veal")

De Noailles: Duh noi-ya (Like "noise" and then a long "a")

Fáilte isteach: Fall-sha ish-shook

Dia duit: De-ah gwit

á Seán: ah Shawn

Gaeilge: Gale-gah

Sláinte: Slawn-sha (but with a bit of "ch" gliding with the "sh")

Frongoch: Frown-gock (hard, guttural ck, rhymes with "glock")

Kyffin: Kef-in (Long "e" as in "key." Sounds a lot like Kevin, but with an f sound in the middle gliding with a bit of v.)

Padraig: Pad-ray-g ("g" as in "gold")

Craic: Crack

Acknowledgments

Many people have lent a hand to this book over the years, but I'd especially like to thank my husband and family for their emotional support, Charlie Franco and Montag Press Collective for your faith in the story and help with the gritty details of publishing, and everyone who provided input on one of the dozens of manuscript versions. The Corner Coffeehouse Group was there in early days as well as the Word Sisters. Carol Kruchowski is always a trusted beta reader. Thanks to Renato Pinto for the remarkable cover art—what you see is the image I've carried in my mind for years.

Professional help ranged from the factual—Patrick Allie, former Military and Arms Curator, Missouri History Museum; Carol Diaz-Granados, Research Associate, Washington University in St. Louis and James R. Duncan, former director, Missouri State Museum, on the Mississippian cosmos; Dr. Andrea Hunter, Tribal Historic Preservation Officer, Osage Nation; Michael Kahn, who took the time to answer truly random questions about the St. Louis Civil Courts Building (and describes the iconic courthouse roof in his excellent novel, *The Mourning Sexton*) to the technical— Meghan Pinson of My Two Cents Editing and her helpful gang of beta and sensitivity readers.

A silly amount of research went into this work of speculative fiction, so special thanks to the staffs of the following institutions: Missouri History Museum Library and Research Center (hi, Kelly, Randy, and Emily), Alton Museum of History and Art, Mobile Medical Museum, Mobile Carnival Museum, Lafayettesquare.org, and Cahokia Mounds Interpretive Center.

Even with all these fine folks' help, the final choices for the book came down to me. This is a work of speculative fiction for a general audience; sometimes facts get in the way of story. And sometimes writers just get things wrong. All errors in fact or judgment are my own.

"We respectfully acknowledge that we are on the traditional, ancestral lands of the Osage Nation. The process of knowing and acknowledging the land we stand on is a way of honoring and expressing gratitude for the ancestral Osage people who were on this land before us." (Osage Lands Acknowledgement, osageculture.com)

"The Osage Nation is currently engaged in the protection and preservation of one of our ancestral mounds, Sugarloaf Mound in south St. Louis. The Nation accepts donations to help support our effort to preserve one of the last remaining mounds in the St. Louis area by specifying Sugarloaf Mound support when donating to the Osage Nation Foundation. The Osage Nation respectfully request that you honor our land. Thank you." (Osageculture.com)

A portion of the royalties from the sale of *The Big Cinch* will benefit the Sugarloaf Mound preservation project.

About the Author

Speculative Fiction with a Historical Twist! Kathy L. Brown lives and writes in St. Louis, Missouri, USA. Her hometown and its history inspire much of her fiction. When she's not thinking about how haunted everything is, she enjoys hiking, crafts, and cooking for her family. *The Big Cinch* is her first published novel. Additional Sean Joye investigations include a novella, *The Resurrectionist,* and a novelette, *Water of Life.* Her blog and other musings live at kathylbrown.com.

Photo by Jon Aikin.

Praise for *The Big Cinch*

Think of *The Big Cinch* as the spooky love child of Dashiell Hammett's *The Maltese Falcon* and Stephen King's *The Shining*. Hammett gave us Sam Spade, a cynical investigator in the treacherous world of the 1920s San Francisco. Kathy L. Brown's cynical investigator is Sean Joye, an ex-IRA soldier in the treacherous world of the 1920s St. Louis. But her detective has to deal with ghosts as well. Enjoy this clever melding of a noir mystery and dark fantasy!

— Michael A. Kahn,
trial lawyer and award-winning author
of *the Rachel Gold mystery series*

What a marvel Brown has created in Sean Joye, an IRA soldier-turned-River City-henchman with the uncanny ability to endear himself to just about anyone—man or woman, rich or poor, criminal or saintly, earthly or immaterial. There's nary a dull moment in his puckish, streetwise, surprisingly enlightened company.

— Christopher Clancy,
author of *We Take Care of Our Own*

Sean Joye is a charmer guaranteed to seduce the reader of Kathy L. Brown's *The Big Cinch*. He is determined to find the truth, no matter how many hearts and laws he has to break along the way. He takes the reader into the very heart of Prohibition Era St. Louis, exposing scandals while riling spirits. You will love traveling along with this flirtatious sleuth as he pieces together all of the clues, proving that the bad boys really are more fun.

— Charis Emanon,
author of *51 Ways To End Your World*

The fae-touched IRA veteran-turned-St. Louis investigator Sean Joye returns with a vengeance in *The Big Cinch*, a daunting adventure that sees the St. Louis of old come to vivid life in Kathy L. Brown's capable hands. Sean's search for the missing baby girl of a wealthy St. Louis debutante leads him into an increasingly dangerous web of supernatural intrigue that touches on not only local history but the restrictive social mores of the early 20th century. A fascinating tale!

— Daniel Waugh,
author of *Gangs of St. Louis*

With unencumbered prose and the sure-footed pace of a gumshoe hot on the case, Kathy L. Brown manages to blend a whiskey-dripping pair of fantastical worlds in her grainy new novel, *The Big Cinch*.

Cinch follows Sean Joye, veteran of both the Irish Rebellion of the early 20th Century and the American criminal underbelly, as he stalks the quite literally haunted streets of post-Great War St. Louis, a whole damn city built on top of an Ancient Indian Burial Ground. Joye's a Private Dick in the classic sense, but driven by a sensibility appropriate to the modern age. He's also peculiarly sensitive to the things most of us can't see, whether it's the ulterior motives of damsel feigning distress or the howling ghost of a vengeful Mississippian princess.

Part *Chinatown*, part *Carnival Row*, and teeming with insight into real and imagined worlds seldom seen, *The Big Cinch* delivers a pulpy dive entirely unique unto itself.

— Paul d. Miller,
author of *Albrecht Drue, ghostpuncher.* and
Albrecht Drue, Paranormal Dick.

Old money. A missing child. Forbidden Love. Murder. The sights and sounds of 1920s St. Louis shines in this paranormal whodunit by Kathy L. Brown. Crisp writing and snappy dialogue are reminiscent of Cohen brothers' "Miller's Crossing" as Brown skillfully brings to life complex characters that leap off the pages. A late-night page turner, you won't be able to put this supernatural mystery down until the heart-stopping end.

— Stephen Paul Sayers,
author of *A Taker of Morrows*

This highly entertaining novel is set in prohibition-era St. Louis. The story is populated by a bevvvy of film-noir types—corrupt officials, corrupted society swells, a tough Irishman, Sean Joye, with a heart of (a bit tarnished) gold, poor little rich girls and even a roughneck Mother Superior. Sean soon finds himself up to his neck in shady wheelings and dealings, but not only on the purely mundane level. He is also involved with the more esoteric and mystical actors that come to the fore in the unfolding drama. Here this book really delighted me, mixing as it does so neatly that somewhat grim sort of 1920's Cagney scenario with a fine eye for descriptive detail and a touch of humor. But this tale is not all dames and derringers. There is also some insight into the culture, myths, and legends of the region's Native American inhabitants. And here lies the intersection in time in Ms. Brown's novel. What Sean discovers is how ancient belief is being perverted to no good ends—but the ancient powers are not mere passive bystanders to be used with impunity. Can powers from before the dawn play the decisive role in this tangled mesh of 20th Century duplicities?

— Peter Keaveny,
author of *The Reeking Hegs*

www.ingramcontent.com/pod-product-compliance
Lightning Source LLC
Chambersburg PA
CBHW020930260626
47169CB00006B/1658